A Dazzle

a novel
by Alexandra Kendall

CRANTHORPE
—MILLNER—

A CIP catalogue record for this title is available from the British Library.

First published (2020)

ISBN 978-1-912964-22-2 (Paperback)

www.cranthorpemillner.com

Cranthorpe Millner Publishers

About the Author

Alexandra (Sandy) Kendall trained as a fine artist. After leaving art school, she continued to paint and also write, though she never tried to get anything published. After her third son was born, she took up a position as head of art in a prep school where she remained for 28 years. On her retirement, she was able to devote more time to her own art, and also to fulfil her long-term ambition to write fiction. "A Dazzle of Poplars" is her first novel.

www.sandystudio.co.uk

I am extremely grateful to my family, friends and acquaintances who have taken the time to help me make this book a reality. I would like to say a huge thank you to Eleanor and Jane, who gave their time freely to proofread the various iterations the novel has gone through as it evolved, giving me invaluable advice along the way. To Andy for his expert authorly advice, to Louisa who advised me on police procedures, to the various members of my family for reading it in its rougher versions and giving me their very helpful feedback, and finally to my husband Nigel, who has also read it at least twice at various stages and eliminated many glaring typos while always giving me tremendous encouragement. Big hugs to you all!

For some time I have been trying to find the right word for the shimmering glancing twinkling movement of the poplar leaves in the sun and wind. This afternoon I saw the word written on the poplar leaves. It was 'dazzle'. The dazzle of the poplars.

Reverend Robert Francis Kilvert

Night had almost fallen, and deep pools of shadow under the willows crept outwards to engulf the riverbank and the fields behind the towpath. The river, swollen by the recent rain, reflected the dying light in the sky as it surged past, bearing fallen willow leaves swiftly along.

A young woman stood gazing down into the water, clutching her shawl tightly around her shoulders against the chill of the autumn evening. She stepped out from the shadow of the willow. Slowly, she untied her bonnet and dropped it onto the grass. Her hair caught the breeze and blew out round her pale face. Slipping the shawl from her shoulders, she discarded it next to her bonnet. She stepped to the very edge of the riverbank, until the toes of her boots overhung the short drop to the water. Slowly, deliberately, she stepped out into nothingness. The splash of her slight body hitting the water was lost in the low roar of the wind in the trees and the rushing of the river. As the water closed over her head, her hair, like waterweed, spread out for an instant on the surface, before a powerful undercurrent sucked her down into the black depths of the river as it raced on into the darkness.

Chapter I

As she turned the old green Mini into the unmade, potholed lane, Kate caught her breath when she saw the poplars towering against the late afternoon sky, each leaf quivering in the brisk October breeze. They seemed like an endorsement of the idea that was growing in her mind.

The solicitor had informed her that the house was on the right-hand side, some way down the lane, and it was not long before she saw the solitary little cottage, huddled among the stand of poplars, behind an overgrown hedge. The fact that it was surrounded by such a magnificent cluster of the trees that she loved so much added to her excitement. When she stopped the car and opened the door, the sound of the brisk breeze in the treetops flooded over her like a waterfall, like the sound of the sea at high tide. It was like a homecoming.

*

The letter had arrived on the morning of the opening of Jake's exhibition. She had not had time to look at it till evening, after the exhausting culmination of weeks of hard slog. It had been a hugely successful first day, extremely well attended thanks to her PR efforts, with a number of works already sold. Jake had been on a high all day, especially after David Straker himself had put in an appearance and proceeded to buy three pieces, including the *Pods* installation, which had taken up much of the studio space.

Looking round at the milling crowd as she handed out glasses of wine, Kate felt gratified that all the emails and invitations she had sent out had attracted so many punters. The show had gone a long way to establish Jake as being up there with the new generation of young, cutting-edge British artists.

She had not really expected Jake to acknowledge her efforts in his introductory speech, even though she had put her own work on hold for the weeks leading up to the opening. Straker had agreed to sponsor Jake after admitting to having been "blown away" by Jake's degree show. He had lost no time in making available to Jake funds provided by the foundation he had recently set up, whose raison d'être was to help promising art school graduates. But it had been Kate who had found the premises - a disused warehouse in the East End, which Jake could use as a studio-cum-exhibition area. It was she who had organised carpenters and decorators to partition off areas, creating spaces within the space; people to transport the pieces from the run-down garage he had been working in, technicians to help install the work, the printing of catalogues, and a hundred other things that Jake could not possibly bother his handsome, curly-haired head about while working round the clock to get his new installation finished in time for the show.

No, she had not expected effusive thanks, but some small acknowledgement in his speech at the opening would not have come amiss. Feeling suddenly bone-weary and somewhat redundant, she had left early, not bothering to tell Jake, who was surrounded by a crowd of wine-swigging women -wine that she had bought, chilled and set out.

She let herself into their flat, throwing her jacket over a chair and kicking off her shoes with relief. The letter was still on the battered cane chair near the front door where she had dumped it after scooping it up with the junk mail and bills from the doormat that morning.

Opening the letter, she found to her surprise it was from a firm of solicitors, Lambton, Stoke & Peel.

Sinking into the sagging armchair near the window, she read it, first with some mystification, then with a growing sense of excitement.

> *Dear Miss Atkins,*
>
> *As you will know, your great aunt, Miss Amelia Hopkirk passed away recently, and I would like to express my condolences. This letter is to inform you that Lambton, Stoke & Peel are acting as her executors. I am pleased also to inform you that she has named you as the sole beneficiary of her will. Her estate comprises her house and*

4

a sum of money. I hope that after tax and other liabilities have been dealt with, your great aunt's house, Lavender Cottage, and approximately £20,000 will pass to you. I believe you met her on only a few occasions, but she formed a high opinion of you and wished to help you in your career as an artist.

It may be that you will want to retain the property, but should you wish to sell, we will be happy to undertake the conveyancing if you would like us to do so.

The letter went on to say that should she want to view the cottage, once probate had been granted, she should contact a Mrs Babbidge who lived up the lane from the cottage and had a key, as she had been keeping an eye on the place since the old lady died.

Kate leant back in the chair. It was hard to believe that she was the owner of a cottage, and one with a name that seemed too romantic to be true, not to mention the twenty thousand pounds which, though not exactly a fortune, was twenty thousand pounds more than she had at the moment. She sat gazing out of the window, trying to take it in. Why had her great aunt made her the sole beneficiary of her will? Possibly there were no other relations to leave her estate to, but as the letter said, she had only met Amelia Hopkirk a few times, the last time when she was nineteen, at her own mother's funeral. She remembered an elegant, rather beautiful woman, already in her eighties, who had shown great interest in her art. She had been surprisingly *au fait* with the contemporary art scene, and still went to art exhibitions in London and elsewhere.

Kate watched a red bus making its way down the street below. Would she keep the cottage? How could she when she had her life in London with Jake? The Putney flat they shared was also where she did her painting, in one corner of the large, shabby sitting room; painting which had been sadly neglected for the past few weeks, even though she too had a deadline - to complete enough work for her joint show with fellow art school graduates, Grace, Bea and Mimi. The show was scheduled for the following April and she had a lot to do before then.

She had been unable to focus on her own work, with all the

5

arrangements to be made for Jake's show. What little she had done during those weeks, she knew did not cut the mustard. One evening she had taken a tub of white emulsion and wiped out the lot. Jake had simply shrugged and said only, "It *was* pretty crap, wasn't it?"

Ah yes, Jake. Jake with his Greek god looks, his extraordinary talent, his single-minded intensity when working on a piece, his moody silences, during which she felt she may as well not be there, for all the notice he took of her. And now, at the culmination of all the frantic preparations for his show, her sense of anti-climax forced her to realise that she played a very small part in his life.

When she had been in her first year at art school, he had been in his final one. She had been immensely flattered when he sought her out and eventually decreed that they should move in together.

She had been passionately in love with him then, subsuming her own needs to his requirements - tolerating, though with anguish, his flings with other women, his unexplained absences from the flat, his drug taking, which, though low level, was abhorrent to her.

Sitting there at the window, looking out at the rainy evening and the river sliding past beyond the trees on the other side of the road, she became aware of a feeling of resentment towards Jake. Resentment mixed with a growing determination to reconnect with her own calling as an artist. She looked across at the stack of blank canvases in her painting corner. She needed to get away, to be inside her own head, to develop all the ideas seething in her mind.

*

Kate shut the car door and walked to the little gate, its paint peeling and half off its hinges, and gazed, enraptured, at the tiny cottage. Built in the late 1500s, it had been partially renovated in Victorian times, but retained much of its Tudor character. The tiny, diamond-paned windows reflected the light from the evening sky and the warm pink brick of the walls was echoed by the mossy and overgrown brick path that led to the front door.

For a moment, Kate stood very still, taking it all in. The sound of the poplars swaying overhead was like the breaking and hissing out of waves over shingle on the seashore. She shut her eyes. The sound enveloped her and seemed to rinse away all the hurt and disillusionment of the past months. She breathed in the smell of the long grass, still beaded with moisture from the recent rain. When she opened her eyes, the last rays of the setting sun behind her pierced the tattered remains of the rain clouds and turned the windowpanes to winking facets of gold.

Seized with impatience to go and look inside the cottage, she locked the car and started walking down the lane to the far end, where she had been told Mrs Babbidge lived. To her right, the line of poplars followed the lane, curving round from the back of the cottage and edging a field of rough pastureland. At first, there were no other houses visible in the lane, but then, as she rounded a bend, a large and exquisite Elizabethan house came into view, half-timbered, built of mellow old pink brick, similar to those of Lavender cottage. It was set a little back from the lane on the left-hand side, with a sign on the garden gate which read *Woodcote House*. Perhaps Lavender Cottage had been one of the worker's cottages from the original estate, since the big house seemed to be from the same period.

As she drew level with Woodcote House, a light was switched on in one of the downstairs rooms, and Kate glimpsed a girl of about six, with long, pale gold hair, coming into the room to sit down at a baby grand piano in the corner, her back to the window. The wind had dropped for a moment, and in the sudden silence, Kate heard the tinkle of piano music drifting out into the evening air. As she walked on, a white cottage came into view on the right-hand side, picked out by the raking light of the sinking sun. The lane seemed to peter out about there so, assuming that this must be Mrs Babbidge's cottage, Kate opened the white-painted gate and walked up the immaculate little garden to the front door.

Mrs Babbidge, brisk and plump, greeted Kate with a warm smile that made her feel instantly at ease. She insisted Kate came in for a cup of tea and to meet her husband Bill, who came to the kitchen door at her call. As round and friendly as his wife, he shook Kate's hand vigorously, then pottered off, saying he would leave them to chat. Sitting in the bright little

7

kitchen, Kate asked Mrs Babbidge how well she had known her great aunt, Amelia Hopkirk.

"I knew old Miss Hopkirk very well," Lily Babbidge said over her shoulder, pouring hot water from the kettle into a shiny, brown teapot. "I used to get her bits and pieces of shopping and prescriptions, that sort of thing." She gave the teapot a swirl. "Got a bit forgetful towards the end, but she was a marvellous woman in her day. Drove ambulances in The Blitz you know."

"She never married, did she?"

"She was engaged to be married. Her fiancé was badly wounded during the war, in France I believe. He was shipped home but died not long after. He was the love of her life. Never looked at another man again." Mrs Babbidge's pale blue eyes moistened slightly, then she patted Kate's hand. "Well, that was a long time ago." She poured tea into rose-patterned cups and handed one to Kate.

Lily Babbidge kept up a comfortable stream of chatter as Kate sipped her tea and munched on a freshly made rock cake, while the evening light began to fade outside the kitchen window. Finishing her tea and impatient to see inside the cottage, she rose to go.

"Thank you so much for the tea Mrs Babbidge. Just what I needed."

"Here's the key, dear. Do you want me to come with you? It's getting dark and you may find it a little spooky - a bit chilly, too; there's no central heating. The electric is still connected though."

"No, I'll be fine thanks. I'll bring the key back when I've finished."

A blue twilight enveloped the lane, the puddles in the potholes reflecting the sky, as Kate made her way back to the cottage. Drawing level with the big house, she could still just hear the piano music over the sound of the strengthening wind. Something made her look up, and she was startled to see the face of a woman, pale against the darkened room behind her, looking down from one of the upper windows. In the fading light, framed in dark hair, the face was beautiful but somehow remote. Kate's gaze was distracted by a movement from the lit sitting room below, as a man came into the room and walked over to where the child was

8

playing the piano. Kate caught a glimpse of his face before he turned towards the child, and, as he did so, she felt a strange sensation deep within her, almost like a shifting of gears. It was gone in an instant, but it shook her a little. She glanced up at the upper window again; the woman had gone.

Kate shivered. A gust of wind swept round the side of the house and she quickened her pace, soon reaching the gate of the cottage, hanging lopsidedly on its one remaining hinge. Walking up the overgrown path to the front door, she caught a distinct scent of lavender, even though the flowers on the lavender bushes bordering the path had finished flowering, their tall shrivelled flower spikes rustling among the seed-heads of grasses with which they were entangled. It was curious, but Kate was too excited to wonder about it. She put the key in the lock of the peeling front door and pushed it open. It was almost dark inside and feeling for the light switch, she flicked it on and gazed around.

The door opened onto a step which led down into the sitting room which, though smelling a little musty, was neat and dusted - no doubt due to the efforts of Mrs Babbidge. Kate was entranced by the oak beams across the ceiling and by the inglenook fireplace, which took up most of one wall, complete with a set of cast iron fire dogs. A sofa and armchair, a bit worn but comfortable-looking, faced the fireplace, together with a low coffee table. Opposite the fireplace a small dining table and four wooden chairs stood by the deep-silled window, on which was grouped a collection of jugs of different shapes and sizes. A bureau and a bookcase on the end wall and some rugs scattered about on the wooden floor, including a large one by the fire, were the only other furniture in the room, apart from a few pictures hanging on the walls. Kate looked at them with interest. There were three good watercolour landscapes, and two oils, both interiors of firelit kitchens inhabited by a couple in Victorian dress. But there was one little picture hanging near the front door, which seemed to be a faded Victorian Valentine card. Briefly, Kate wondered who it had been sent to and why it was hanging on the wall in a dark corner. On the same wall was a doorway, covered with a green curtain, behind which a steep flight of stairs led to the upper floor.

9

Another door led to a small kitchen, with a ceramic sink, an antediluvian cooker, a washing machine, a dresser and a cupboard, all of which, apart from the washing machine, had probably been there since the fifties. Looking in the cupboards and the dresser, Kate saw that all of her great aunt's crockery, cutlery, cooking utensils, and other kitchen paraphernalia were still there, tidily stacked. A phrase her grandmother used to say came into her mind: "A place for everything, and everything in its place." A door with glass panes in the top half led out from the kitchen to the darkened back garden. Kate cupped her hand round her eyes, with her face against the glass panel of the door, but could see nothing outside except the tops of the trees swaying against the sky. She went back through the sitting room and, finding the light switch for the stairs behind the curtain at the bottom of the stairwell, made her way up the wooden steps, her footsteps sounding hollow on the uncarpeted treads. There were two doors facing each other at the top. She opened the one on the right and was immediately aware of the sound of the poplars just outside, their wind-tossed lower branches only a few feet from the window.

A double bed with a brass bedstead, its mattress covered with a patchwork quilt, a bedside table, a dressing table and a wardrobe nearly filled the room, and a partitioned off section revealed a small bathroom at the far end. Opening the heavy oak door of the wardrobe, which creaked protestingly, Kate discovered that her great aunt's clothes were still hanging there, and the drawer at the bottom was filled with neatly folded woollens and other clothes. A faded pink Chinese rug covered the middle of the floor, and in a corner sat a two-bar electric heater.

When Kate opened the door of the other bedroom and flicked the switch, there was a loud pop as the light bulb blew. The room was sparsely furnished, as far as she could see in the light filtering in from the other room, with only a chest of drawers, a small table and a wooden chair. She walked over to the window and looked out into the darkness. The fields on the other side of the lane were shadowy behind the hedge, and ragged clouds, dimly seen, scudded across the sky. She suddenly had the feeling that she was being watched and, at the same moment, smelt the strong heady scent of lavender again. She swung round, her eyes

10

searching the shadows, but the room was empty. She shivered involuntarily and told herself with a rueful smile that her imagination was running away with her. A dark rectangle on the opposite wall turned out to be the door of a built-in cupboard, stained black.

Back downstairs, she was surprised to see how late it was, and went around shutting doors and turning out the lights before letting herself out and locking the door after her. She stood for a moment in the dark, tangled garden. Yes, this was what she needed. This was where she would be able to think straight. Be her own person again.

She decided to drive rather than walk down the lane to return the key to Mrs Babbidge and, as she passed the big house, she felt her eyes drawn to the windows again: but now there was no-one to be seen and the room with the piano was in darkness.

*

It was late when Kate got back to the flat that night, finding Jake stretched out on the sofa fast asleep with an empty bottle of wine on the floor next to him. Still in her coat, she stood looking down at him, noting the two days' growth of blond stubble on his chin, the curve of his lips, the way his hair curled over his ears. His T-shirt was covered in plaster dust and paint and his jeans had gaping holes in the knees. His hands, with their long sensitive fingers, were stained with paint and sported several half-healed cuts and scrapes. God, how she had loved this man... and he had loved her back, in his way. But now she felt that something had changed. There was a certain distancing, as though she were looking at him through a pane of glass; from the other side of a kind of disillusionment. It was a feeling that seemed to be inexplicably connected with a windy lane and a man walking into a room.

As Kate turned to take off her coat, Jake stirred and opened his eyes.

"Hey, babe, you're back! I saw your note on the table. What's the old girl's house like?" His words were a little slurred, his eyes slightly unfocused. Kate noticed the remains of a joint in the ashtray next to the wine bottle.

11

"It's absolutely sweet. Really old and tiny."

"How much do you think you'll get for it?"

She threw her coat over the back of a chair.

"I'm not selling it."

"What! Not selling? What on earth are you going to do with it then?"

"I'm going to live in it."

Jake sat up, knocking over the empty bottle as he swung his legs to the floor.

"Live in it? Are you mad? What about your work? What about me? What about your show? You'll drop off the radar, Kate. You don't mean you're going to live there permanently?"

"That's the general idea, yes. I'll be able to work better there. There are always people coming and going here, and the weeks before your show were a complete washout for me work-wise. I need to get masses done before April."

"But what about us? You and me?"

Kate looked at him levelly. "Lately there doesn't seem to have been much of an 'us', does there?"

"But Kate, you know how busy I've been, with the show and all the hoo-ha that entailed. And now the commissions are coming in, I've got a lot on."

"Were you working all last night then? I happen to know you were round at the Honourable Lucinda Moreton's Belgravia flat!"

"How the hell did you know that?"

"I have friends in high places."

"I bet it was Paul. How is it that gay men always know what's going on anywhere?"

"Never mind how I know."

"Look, she was talking about me doing a piece for her parents' country house. It was a bit of PR, that's all."

"All night?"

"Oh, give it a rest, can't you? She doesn't mean anything. You know how I feel about you, Kate."

He came across to her and cupped her face in his hands, pushing a

12

wiggly strand of deep auburn hair off her forehead.

"You're my beautiful Pre-Raphaelite muse. You can't leave."

Kate felt herself falling again under the influence of his potent physical presence and beauty. She let him kiss her and take her to bed.

But the decision she had made standing in the garden of the cottage on a windy October evening, remained firm.

*

"Turn right, just along here somewhere. Yes, there! Tuckers Lane." Kate pointed towards the half-hidden turning off the B road they were on and Paul eased the transit van into the narrow lane, the overhanging branches of trees brushing the roof. Watery sunlight cast streaks of shadow across the lane as they bumped slowly along the rutted track, the stacks of canvases and other paraphernalia bouncing about somewhat alarmingly in the back. As they rounded the bend and the poplars came into view, Kate saw that their leaves had turned yellower in the weeks since she had first seen them. Their flickering gold made her catch her breath again.

"There are the poplars I told you about," she said, pointing. "Aren't they wonderful?"

"Yeah, they're pretty amazing. And is that the cottage?"

"Yes, here we are. What do you think?"

"Nice. You could turn into a witch and live here with a black cat and a toad or two."

Kate gave him a friendly push and when Paul drew up outside the gate, she opened the van door. Again, the poplars' sea-sound enveloped her.

"Listen," she said as Paul got out of the van. They both stood still for a minute, looking up at the treetops.

Then Paul said briskly. "Very peaceful, but we've a lot to do. You said the solicitors have sent you the keys? Open up then."

On this bright, late October afternoon, the cottage looked cheerful and welcoming as they let themselves in, though it did show up the fact

13

that the walls were sorely in need of a lick of paint, and the kitchen in particular was in dire need of renovation.

"Where are you going to do your painting?" Paul asked, back in the sitting room after they had made a quick tour of the cottage.

"It'll have to be in here," Kate answered. "I thought at first the second bedroom, but it's a bit small and it'll be difficult to get the bigger canvases round the bend in the stairs. Anyway, there's no central heating, and I'll have to keep warm by lighting a fire. Hope the chimney isn't blocked or anything."

"Well, how about in this corner?" Paul indicated the corner on the front wall. "There's room for the easel if we push the table along a bit."

The next two hours were taken up with bringing stuff in from the van and putting it in approximately the right places. Kate had bought a new mattress for the bed, so they dragged the old one down the narrow stairs and stashed it in the now empty van, so that Paul could take it to the dump.

"Wonder if the old lady died in that bed," Paul muttered as they manhandled the mattress down the path.

Kate had decided that the second bedroom would be the place she would do her illustrating work, with which she had been keeping body and soul together since she had left art school. She had sold a few paintings, but was not yet commanding very high prices and the illustrating work was a lifesaver. Among the few pieces of furniture she had accumulated and had kept in the Putney flat, was a desk from her childhood home in Dorset. She had claimed it when her father had remarried and moved to Yorkshire. This they dragged with great difficulty up the stairs and installed in the second bedroom. The room also became a repository for anything they did not know what to do with - suitcases, books, some smaller canvases and her portfolios. They brought the table which had been in the room down to the sitting room, for Kate to use to put her painting things on.

"What we need now is tea!" Paul said when they were back downstairs. "Did you bring any?" He went into the kitchen and started rummaging in one of the cardboard boxes they had dumped there.

Kate had not wanted to denude the Putney flat of cooking utensils, even though she had bought many of them, so she had left them there, resolving to use her great aunt's things.

"Ah ha! Teabags!" exclaimed Paul. "Bet you haven't got any milk though."

"And that's where you're wrong," smirked Kate, locating the milk carton in another box.

They sat companionably on the sagging sofa, sipping tea and eating digestive biscuits as the afternoon turned into evening and the shadows started to gather in the little sitting room. Suddenly, the enormity of what she was doing came home to Kate. She was physically, if not quite emotionally, walking out on the person with whom she had once been completely besotted. She would be on her own, with no-one to answer to, and it scared her.

Paul sensed her change of mood and glanced at her. "You alright, Kate?"

Kate let out a sigh: "Yeah, I'll be fine. It's just, I did love him you know, and I think I'm sort of grieving for... for... something that's dying."

"But you haven't actually split with Jake, have you?"

"I haven't said to him, 'It's over' or anything. But we're bound to drift apart. Well, we've been drifting for a while now. At least, he's been doing most of the drifting - into the willing arms of the likes of the Honourable Lucinda. Thanks for the tip, by the way. I needed to know."

"I agonised over whether to tell you. He was all over her in the pub, the night you were at Mimi's, and she just stood gazing adoringly at him the whole evening. Then I saw them leave together."

"Well, it isn't the first time." She put her hand over his and gave it a squeeze. "What would I do without you Paul? You're always there for me. And thanks for today. I'd have had to hire a van and I don't know how I'd have got that desk and the mattress up the stairs."

Paul put his arm round her shoulders.

"You've been a good friend to me too, and it's largely due to those

15

amazing photos I took of you that I have such an impressive portfolio. If ever I were to turn straight, it would be because of you!"

Kate laughed, her mood lightening. "Yes, and pigs might fly! Anyway, we'd better be heading back. It's getting late."

"You're not getting the Mini and driving back down tonight, are you?"

"God, no! Too knackered. Anyway, I told Jake we'd have a last night together. If he remembers! I'll come back down tomorrow with the last bits and pieces in the Mini."

As they locked the front door of the cottage and walked down towards the gate, a gleaming, green Land Rover Discovery was crunching along the unmade lane towards them. Paul's transit was partially blocking the lane and the Discovery had to go onto the opposite grass verge to get by. As it drew level, Kate recognised the man at the wheel - the same man who had come into the room as she had walked past the big house down the lane on her first visit. Again she felt a slight shock, almost of recognition, again gone in an instant. He stopped the car by the cottage gate and lowered the driver's window.

"Hi there! You must be the new owner of Lavender Cottage. Mrs B. told me all about you." He extended his hand through the open window. "Tim Crawford. I live just up the lane." He gave a nod in the direction of Woodcote House. Kate nearly said, "I know" but stopped herself, and stepped forward to shake his proffered hand, the contact somehow making her a little flustered.

"Hi! I'm Kate Atkins." She glanced at the transit. "Sorry for blocking the lane."

"No problem at all. Plenty of room."

Kate turned to introduce Paul. "This is my friend Paul Logan. He's been helping me bring some stuff down from London."

"Hello Paul, nice to meet you." Tim turned back to Kate, as she stood there looking like some sort of changeling in the evening light, with her wild auburn hair blowing round her face. "Are you moving in today?" he asked her.

"Not quite, I've got to go back to London to pick up my car - can't face driving down again tonight. I'll come down tomorrow. But first I must pop along to tell Mrs Babbidge I've sort of moved in."

"Mrs B? Well, actually, she'll be at my house now. I'll tell her if you like. She's my sort of housekeeper-cum-childminder. Lovely woman, been a tower of strength to me ever since... since my wife died." His voice gave a slight tremor as he spoke the last words, but he recovered immediately and put the car into gear. "I'll tell Mrs B. you've been moving in, shall I?"

"Yes, thanks. Well, bye for now. Probably see you around."

"Yes, probably. Bye."

The car purred off and disappeared round the bend in the lane.

Kate turned to look back at the cottage. Just three windows faced out onto the lane - the kitchen window, a little one on the front wall of the sitting room, which was partially covered in ivy, and the window of the smaller bedroom. The upper window, as it had done on that first day, back in September, was reflecting the evening sky and the clouds sliding past, which gave the impression of movement behind the small panes. Paul put a hand on her shoulder, startling her slightly.

"Better get going, Kate," he said softly.

*

That evening, when Kate got back, she was gratified to find that Jake had not only remembered that it was her last night, but had got in a pizza and a bottle of wine for them. He seemed subdued and was uncharacteristically quiet. Looking at him across the table, at his familiar, beautiful face, she almost regretted her decision. She looked round the big, untidy room with its tall windows overlooking the river, at the now empty corner where her easel used to stand, with just a few working drawings still stuck to the wall.

Jake saw her look. "Change your mind? Don't go, Kate! Stay with me. I'll be good."

"Look, let's just say I'm taking time out to work. I need to be on my

17

own for a bit. I need to be inside my head, to focus. I've masses to do for the show and I've not been able to work effectively here."

He grunted and said grudgingly; "Well, I suppose I can understand that. But you can't damn well stop me from coming down to see you and you'll come up often, won't you?"

"Of course. I'll always be popping up, to see exhibitions, sort out arrangements for the show with Mimi and co."

"And to see me. Just let me know you're coming - so I'll be here."

"Or someone else isn't!"

He put on an outraged face. Kate laughed and came around the table to stand behind his chair and put her arms round his neck. Taking her hands, he pulled her onto his lap.

"I'll miss you, babe," he murmured, his lips on her throat.

Later, in bed, when Jake had gone to sleep, Kate lay staring up at the ceiling. One thought kept coming back into her mind. Tim had said his wife was dead, so whose was the lovely pale face she had seen, looking down at her from the upstairs window of his house on that first evening?

Chapter II

The next morning, Jake's mood had changed. He was irritable and quite brusque, leaving for his studio before she had finished packing up the rest of her clothes and other bits and pieces she hadn't taken the day before. On his way out, he paused just long enough to give her a quick, almost cursory hug, and with the casual remark, "I'll come down sometime. Leave instructions on how to get there" flung over his shoulder, he was gone. Kate went to the window and looking down, saw him emerge from the front door of the flats, his rucksack slung over one shoulder. She watched his blond head disappear down the road. He was already talking on his mobile.

Her packing finished, she sat down at the table by the window to write out the address and instructions on how to get to the cottage. Leaving the note on the table she walked to the door. But before opening it, she stopped and walked back to the window. She stood looking down the road along which Jake had disappeared earlier. Then with a slight shake of her head, she picked up the piece of paper on which she had written the address, tore it in half and stuffed it into her pocket. Then she went out and clicked the door shut behind her.

The day had started overcast and gloomy and by the time Kate reached the cottage, the rain had set in and was coming down in sheets. She parked as close to the overgrown garden hedge as she could, so as not to block the lane, and got drenched lugging her bags into the cottage.

She immediately noticed that a large basket of logs and a cardboard box of kindling were standing on the hearth, which had definitely not been there the day before. A piece of paper protruded from among the logs. She pulled it out and read the note,

Kate,

Mrs B, ever thoughtful, was saying that you'll be needing a "bit of a fire" tonight, as the evenings are getting a bit chilly, so I took the liberty of borrowing her (your) key to let myself in with these logs - we have a shed full! Didn't want to leave them outside in case they got wet. Hope you don't mind.

Tim.

P.S. Matches and newspaper on the mantlepiece.

Mind? She was ridiculously touched and grateful. She was already feeling rather alone and vulnerable, and now she felt her eyes welling with tears at the thoughtful act. Driving down as the rain started, she had cursed inwardly that any wood in the garden or surrounding countryside would be soaked, putting paid to her vision of a cosy fire that evening. Now she lost no time in grabbing some of the newspaper, scrunching it up, putting the twigs on top, and finally adding a couple of the logs.

But before she lit the fire, she thought she ought to go and thank her benefactor. It being a Saturday, there was a good chance he might be at home. She slung on her coat, pulled up the hood, and let herself out into the rain again. Poplar leaves, sodden with rain, plopped down from the trees above and littered the long grass in the garden. Trying to avoid the puddles, she made her way up the lane. As she rounded the bend, she saw a red Volvo drawn up on the verge next to the big house. The house itself was set quite close to the lane, behind a low wall made of old brick, with most of the garden at the back. There was a garage and turning area at the far side of the house, on which was parked Tim Crawford's green Discovery. Crowding in on the other side of the garage was a thicket of trees. The wrought-iron gate squeaked as she opened it and clanged shut as she walked down the path.

The knocker on the front door was in the shape of a lion's head, with a ring in its mouth. She knocked, and immediately a cacophony of barking came from inside. Shortly after, the door was opened by a young boy of about ten or eleven, holding on to the collar of a yellow Labrador, who

20

carried on barking madly until the boy said sharply, "Shush, Binky! Sit, boy." The dog stopped barking and obediently sat down. Kate put out her hand to stroke his head. She saw the beginnings of a wag at the end of the dog's tail.

The boy grinned. "I think he likes you. Scratch behind his ears, and he'll be your friend for ever."

Kate held out her hand. "I'm Kate Atkins, your new neighbour - from the cottage down the lane."

He shook her hand and gave another friendly grin. He was thin and wiry, with a sprinkling of freckles on his nose and unruly brown hair that stuck up at the back.

"I'm Freddie Crawford. How do you do?" he said with quaint formality. "Did you see the logs? I helped Dad take them to your house."

"Yes, I did. That's why I popped in - to say thanks."

He stood back. "Come in. You look a bit wet."

Kate stepped just inside the front porch. "Well, I won't stop. I'll drip all over the carpet."

The boy called over his shoulder. "Dad! Here a moment. It's the lady from the cottage."

He let go of Binky's collar, and Kate bent down to scratch behind the dog's ears. Binky put one paw up on her knee and his tail thumped the floor.

She looked up when Tim came out of a room to the right. *The room with the piano,* Kate thought.

"Hello again," he said, putting his hand on the boy's shoulder. He wore an old grey sweater and baggy, corduroy trousers. His brown hair was the same colour as his son's and almost as tousled. His eyes were very blue. He gave her a friendly smile. "Don't stand there at the door, come in."

"No, I won't stop. I just wanted to say thank you so much for the logs and the kindling. It was so thoughtful."

"Well, as I said, it was Mrs B's idea - she always knows the right thing to do."

A woman's voice called from the drawing room. "Are you ready to

21

go, Freddie? Duncan says you have to be there by two."

The owner of the voice came out of the door from which Tim had emerged. She was an elegant and very attractive blonde, exquisitely made up, dressed in designer jeans, a cream cashmere sweater and fleece-lined suede gilet. She put a be-ringed hand possessively on Tim's arm, and looked enquiringly from Kate to Tim.

"Ah, Elaine, this is Kate er - sorry, I've forgotten your surname."

"Atkins," Kate said, suddenly feeling very shabby before this vision of perfection.

"Kate, this is Elaine Grainger. She's been a life-saver with the school run and things," Tim said, as Elaine extended a languid, manicured hand, which Kate shook with her damp, snaggle-nailed one.

Elaine's eyes flicked over the bedraggled figure in front of her, taking in the wet strands of hair escaping from the hood of her duffle coat, the muddy trainers: but taking in too, with a tiny twinge of fear, the large, green eyes, the heart-shaped face, the full, soft mouth.

"Elaine is picking up Freddie to take him and her son Duncan to some laser quest party or other," Tim said, as a boy of about Freddie's age came out of a room at the far end of the hall. He had a round face and blond hair, which flopped into his eyes. And then the hall seemed to fill up with people as a girl - *the piano player,* thought Kate - came running down the stairs, stopping on the bottom step, and at the same time Mrs Babbidge came bustling out of the kitchen in her coat with a plastic rain-hat on her head and an umbrella in her hand.

"I've washed up, Tim," she said, "and left supper in the fridge." Her eyes lit up as she caught sight of Kate, standing damply on the doormat. "Oh! Hello, dear. Goodness, you look soaked. Have you managed to light a fire yet? Did you take the logs over, Tim?"

"Yes, we did," Freddie cut in. "Kate came to say thank you."

"And thank you too, for thinking of it, Mrs B," Kate interposed with a smile.

"Is there anything else you need, Kate dear?" Mrs Babbidge asked, squeezing past Tim, Elaine, the dog and Freddie.

"No, I'm fine thanks."

22

"Well, just ask if you do need anything, won't you. If I'm not at home, I'll probably be here. Bye all," she called as she scurried off down the path, putting up her umbrella as she went.

The little girl ducked under her father's arm and smiled at Kate.

Kate smiled back. "Hello, I'm Kate."

"And my name is Amy," the girl said. "You look a bit like a fairy-witch."

"Amy!" admonished her father. "You mustn't say things like that, it's rude."

"It's not rude. Fairy-witches are good. *And* pretty."

Kate laughed. "Well, I wish I had a magic wand to sort out all my stuff. I better go and make a start on it. Thanks again for the logs."

She gave the dog a last pat, smiled at the children and turned to go.

"Shout if you need anything," Tim called out, as she reached the gate.

"We'd probably hear you if you did actually shout from your house," Freddie added, grinning.

There would come a time when Kate would remember those words.

As she walked back down the lane, she heard the red Volvo start up and, after turning around, it came bouncing down the lane rather fast. Freddie in the back seat gave her a wave and, as she waved back, the back tyre of the car splashed into a puddle, sending a spray of muddy water onto her already damp jeans. Looking up at the car in annoyance, she saw Freddie's embarrassed face looking out of the rear window as the car disappeared down the track.

Feeling thoroughly chilled and wet, Kate let herself into the cottage and immediately put a match to the fire she had laid earlier. The kindling and the logs were well dried and the fire leapt up immediately, filling the room with a warm glow. She made herself a cup of coffee and, dragging a clean pair of jeans out of a bag, changed out of her wet things.

Later, warm and dry again, she took some of the stuff she had brought that morning upstairs. Thinking of the blown light bulb in the second bedroom, she went back down to find the new one she had remembered to buy, among the boxes cluttering up the tiny kitchen. Back

23

upstairs, she dragged the chair to the middle of the room, and standing on it, changed the bulb. The room, gloomy in the rainy afternoon, sprang into light as she flicked the switch on, and Kate busied herself for a time, trying to tidy the boxes, canvases and other paraphernalia that she and Paul had stacked there the previous day. She opened the cupboard set into the wall, hoping to store some odds and ends in there. Inside was a clothes rail and a shelf near the bottom. Pushed under the shelf was an old tin trunk. Kate dragged it out and unfastening the catches, lifted the lid, fully expecting it to be empty.

It was not empty. What looked like an old sheet had been used to wrap up something. Kneeling on the floor in front of the chest and unfolding the sheet, Kate discovered that inside was an exquisitely made wedding dress of yellowing satin, with some beautiful lace at the neck and cuffs. Carefully unfolding it, Kate saw that it was made in the style fashionable in the 1940s. Wrapped up along with the dress was a long veil of silk net and nestling between the two was a folded handkerchief, embroidered with blue forget-me-nots. Tears pricked Kate's eyes as she knelt on the floor beside the trunk with the dress and veil in her lap. The dress must have been her great aunt's, bought in anticipation of her wedding. Kate thought of the happiness of the woman who had so looked forward to wearing the dress, on a wedding day that never came. Happiness which had turned to loss and tragedy when 'the love of her life' had been fatally wounded on some bloody battlefield. A tragedy that had resonated down the years, as the young woman drifted into middle age and on into extreme old age. Alone. Always alone.

At the bottom of the trunk was a leather writing case, in which was a bundle of letters tied with a blue ribbon. Undoing the ribbon, Kate slipped one of the letters from its envelope. The date at the top of the letter, written in faded brownish ink, was 16th May 1942. Kate saw the words *My dearest Amelia*, before turning the pages to the end of the letter, wanting to find out who they were from. As she had thought, the letter was from the man Amelia had been due to marry. It ended with the words *Your loving fiancé James*. She quickly refolded the flimsy paper, suddenly feeling like an intruder. It felt wrong to be reading someone else's love

24

letters. She retied the ribbon and as she replaced the bundle of letters in the writing case, she saw the corner of a photograph and pulled it out. It was of a laughing young woman in a flowery frock, her hand clasped in the crook of the arm of a tall, young man in the uniform of an army captain. Behind them was part of a house which looked very like the Crawford's house down the lane.

After she had refolded the wedding dress and veil and wrapped them in the sheet, Kate dragged the trunk back to the built-in cupboard at the corner of the room. It only just fitted in the space under the shelf. Shutting the cupboard door, she thought she caught a faint scent of lavender again.

That night Kate slept fitfully. The rain had continued to fall heavily, rattling against the bedroom window as the wind rose and gusted round the cottage, occasionally making a kind of sobbing sound in the chimney cavity on the inner wall. Having fallen into a deep sleep just before dawn, Kate woke to a bright and breezy morning. For a while she lay looking out of the window at the flickering gold of the poplar leaves, listening to their music. It was a day for a new beginning.

She spent the morning in a flurry of activity, unpacking the boxes in the kitchen, stowing her clothes in the bedroom, setting out her painting equipment. She discovered a cupboard under the eaves in the bathroom in which was a heavy, old, leather suitcase. Not knowing what else to do with them, she folded her great aunt's clothes from the wardrobe and packed them away in there. By lunchtime she was tired, hot and hungry, so cutting herself a hunk of bread, she topped it with a thick piece of cheese, and let herself out of the door in the kitchen to explore the little back garden, which was even more overgrown than the one at the front. The stand of poplars was just on the other side of the garden fence, in the corner of the adjoining field, and they continued in a curving line round the field behind the cottage and back to meet the lane again. Sunlight filtered through the leaves hissing high overhead, casting shifting shadows over the long grass of the overgrown patch of lawn. She noticed a lean-to wood store, roofed but open at the side, against the outside kitchen wall, with a few logs still remaining at the bottom, half covered by a drift of dead leaves. Next to that was a concrete coal bunker, empty except for a few lumps of coal right at the back.

Beyond the lawn, a partially broken-down rose arch gave on to what must have once been a small vegetable patch. Kate was delighted to discover a garden shed, almost hidden by a young rowan tree, at the far end of the garden. Sliding back the cast iron bolt on the door with some difficulty, Kate pushed it open, dislodging thick festoons of cobwebs as she did so. Inside was an old lawnmower, a few garden tools and a broom leaning against the wall. Loops of string and wire hung from nails. There was a small window, curtained in cobwebs, under which was a shelf cluttered with rusty pots of household paint. To her surprise, the shed was quite dry, although very dusty and spider-infested, and she resolved to clean it out and use it as a workshop to make up the stretchers for her canvases. She had the ones she had painted over, which she could store here, but she would need more.

"No time like the present," Kate murmured to herself. She went back into the house, bundled her hair into a scarf, and went back to the shed. Using the broom she had found and sneezing copiously, she spent the rest of the afternoon brushing cobwebs from the walls and ceiling, sweeping the floor and generally causing great consternation to the resident spider population. By the time she had finished, the evening was drawing in. Pulling the door shut, she went back into the house, resolving to lose no time in having a bath. She had switched on the immersion heater the night before, so she was confident there would be plenty of hot water. But before she could go up, she heard voices outside the front door and immediately heard a knock. Going to the door, she unlocked it and lifted the latch.

Tim, standing on the doorstep of the cottage beside his two children, looked quizzically at the scruffy little figure before him. Her face was grimy with dust, especially round her nose. Her hair was tied back under a green scarf, which had a strand of dusty cobweb hanging from it, and she was dressed in an outsize checked shirt and old jeans. Kate pushed a stray strand of hair from her face with a grubby hand. "Oh, hi! Have you been knocking long?" she said. "I was clearing out the shed at the back."

26

"No, we've just arrived. We wanted to ask - do fairy-witches like chicken casserole? Mrs B. has made us an enormous amount and we wondered if you would like to come to Sunday supper, seeing as you've just moved in and are probably in need of sustenance."

Kate hesitated slightly. She had been looking forward to a hot bath and snuggling up by the fire with her sketch book, to work through some ideas.

The little girl, standing beside her father, put her hand on Kate's arm. "Oh please come! There's apple pie as well; I helped Mrs B. make it. We put pastry leaves on top as decorations."

Kate smiled: "In that case, I'd love to come. I just must have a bath first. I'm covered in spider's webs and things."

"You didn't *kill* the spiders did you?" the boy, Freddie, asked anxiously. "I could have captured them and taken them to my spider sanctuary."

"I hope I didn't. I just sort of brushed the webs off the walls and the spiders scuttled away. There was one really enormous one. I shooed him out of the door."

"Good," Freddie said, relieved. "I'm glad you didn't kill them. They're part of the food chain."

"Freddie is very keen on food chains, especially his place in them! He eats like a horse," Tim said, giving Freddie a playful poke in the stomach. "Well, we'll let you have your bath and we'll see you about seven then," he added. Calling for the dog which was nosing round the garden, he gave a wave and they tramped off out of the gate and disappeared down the lane.

When Kate, now clean and changed, knocked on the door of Woodcote, she was greeted with the same flurry of barking from Binky and the door was again opened by Freddie, who showed her into the drawing room. Tim was standing by the fire with a drink in his hand and came towards her welcomingly. "Hello again. What would you like to drink? There's some cold white wine or maybe a G&T?"

"Wine would be lovely, thanks."

"I'll just get it. Do sit down."

Kate sat down on a chair by the fire. Freddie had disappeared and she was alone in the room. She glanced around. The room had a cosy feel, with two comfortable sofas and a deep armchair drawn in a semi-circle round the fire. The baby grand piano, which Kate had seen Amy playing on that first evening, stood in one corner and the windows, which looked out onto the lane, were in recesses with cushioned window seats. On the broad, stone mantelpiece were some photographs and Kate got up to look at them. Her gaze was immediately drawn to the largest one. She picked it up. It was of a beautiful young woman with dark hair cut in a sleek bob. Kate gave a small gasp. She could have sworn it was the same face that she had seen looking down at her from the upstairs window when she had come to see the cottage the first time. Who was it? But Kate already knew the answer. Though the hair colour was different, the features, the shape of the face and the smile were identical to those of Amy. But how could that be? If Amy's mother was dead...

Tim came back into the room, making her jump slightly.

"My wife, Claire," he said quietly, seeing the photo in her hands. "She was killed in a car crash nearly two years ago. She was a concert pianist, on her way to perform in Liverpool. She skidded off the road. They said it was black ice."

"Oh, I'm so sorry. How absolutely terrible. How on earth did... are...you coping?" She stopped.

"It's alright, we talk about her all the time." He handed her a glass of wine. "Yes, it's been pretty hard. Amy was only four and was very bewildered and lost, but Freddie was the one I was really worried about. He's only recently begun to really laugh and start to enjoy life again. He's changed though. He's always thinking something's going to happen to me. He gets quite anxious."

The door opened and both the children came into the room. In the ensuing flurry of conversation, Kate had no time to think about the shiver that had run down her spine when she had seen the photograph on the mantelpiece.

Freddie was clutching two books which he thumped down on the coffee table. Kate read the titles. *The Royal Entomological Society Book of British Insects* and a less weighty tome, *Spiders of Britain and Northern Europe.* Freddie opened the one on spiders and spent the next ten minutes pointing out a variety of the creatures of all shapes and sizes, while Amy sat on the other side of her on the sofa, making faces and "ugh" sounds. Then he started on the book on insects, enthusing about the beauties of stag beetles, damselflies and the Eyed Hawkmoth.

Tim came to Kate's rescue by asking her about herself. She gave him a brief resumé of her situation, and about how she was hoping to get a lot of painting done for the joint exhibition in the spring. She, however, made no mention of Jake.

"I like painting too!" Amy exclaimed, jumping up from the hearth rug and grabbing Kate's hand. "We've put my pictures up in the kitchen. Come and see."

"We may as well have supper now anyway," Tim said, throwing another log on the fire. "We'll eat in the kitchen, if you don't mind."

"I'd much prefer it," Kate said, picking up her glass and allowing herself to be dragged into the large quarry-tiled kitchen by Amy's determined little hand.

Having admired the array of brightly coloured paintings of flowers, butterflies, rainbows and fairies which adorned the kitchen wall at the far end, Kate helped Freddie to set out plates while Tim took the casserole out of the oven. Soon they were all sitting round the large kitchen table, with Binky lying on the floor by Freddie's feet. Kate had not noticed how hungry she was after her day's exertions, but now she did justice to Mrs B's delicious and filling casserole. The conversation flowed easily. She got on well with the children, and found Tim very easy to talk to, discovering that he worked in the City, commuting up and back every day.

"Elaine kindly takes the children to school, since Freddie and Amy go to the same school as Duncan. She brings them back as well and Mrs B. is always here when they get back. There's usually a bit of juggling involved though - if one of the kids is ill or if there is after school judo for Freddie or something."

"Yes, and I *always* have to go to late class, because I come out before Freddie," Amy sighed resignedly.

29

"Yes, it's a long day for her," Tim said with a grimace. "When Claire's parents or my mother comes to stay, they can do the school run and life is a lot easier, but in between I don't know what we'd do without Mrs B. and Elaine. Also, a nice woman from the village comes in to clean and do the laundry three times a week"

"Does Elaine live nearby?" Kate asked, curious as to whether there was anything more to the arrangement than met the eye.

"Yes, just on the other side of the village. She moved here after her divorce over a year ago."

Tim started clearing away the supper things and Kate got up to help. When Tim went to the sink, Freddie said in a low voice to Kate, "I think Elaine likes Daddy. I think she wants to marry him."

Kate glanced at the boy. His face had a strange expression, half vulnerable, half defiant, that went to her heart. He turned away quickly and bent down to pat Binky.

When they had made good inroads into the apple pie, pastry leaves and all, Tim dispatched the children off to bed, going up to supervise operations while Kate stacked the dishwasher. When he came down again, Tim offered her coffee, but Kate shook her head. "No thanks, I better leave you in peace. Thank you so much for supper. I was starving!"

"You must come again. The kids have really taken to you."

"They are great kids," Kate said softly. "It's heartbreaking that they've lost their mother."

Tim stood at the door and watched as Kate walked to the gate and closed it behind her, turning to give him a wave before disappearing round the bend of the darkened lane. He went back inside and stood in front of the fire, looking at Claire's face smiling at him from the photograph on the mantelpiece. He stood there for a long time.

*

The good weather persisted for the next few days and standing at the window one morning a couple of days later sipping her coffee, Kate's heart was lifted by the sight of the gold leaves of the poplars, lit from

30

behind by the sun and shimmering against the intense blue of the sky. The individual square panes of the windows each framed a different, dancing section of leaves within the larger rectangle of the window as a whole.

On impulse, she rooted among her canvases to find one of the right dimensions and, quickly squeezing out paint onto her palette, she started to paint. Eager to catch the backlit effect before the sun moved round, as well as trying to capture the movement and shimmer of the leaves, she worked quickly, laying the paint on in swift, staccato brush strokes. By the time the sun had climbed higher and the leaves were lit more from the side, she had put in the backdrop of sky and trees and started on overlaying the grid work of the window. By evening, hardly having had a break, she had virtually finished the painting, apart from a few touches of light on the leaves and twigs. These she did the next morning, in the fleeting bursts of sunshine in between the cloudy intervals. She stepped back and surveyed the painting critically. She had never painted a work of this size so quickly before. The necessity of capturing the moment had made her work in a much freer style, and the chaos and movement of the leaves seemingly held in place by the formal rectangles of the windowpanes created an exciting tension within the picture plane.

By mid-afternoon, she felt that to fiddle around with the painting any more would dull its immediacy. Suddenly, she realised that she was ravenously hungry and that there was hardly any food in the house. She remembered that there was a village nearby which she had driven through on her way down. Putting her brushes in a jar of white spirit, she pulled on her coat and went out to the Mini - which started rather reluctantly - and went in search of a shop. She found a post office which doubled as a grocer's overlooking a small green, together with a pub, a village hall and a petrol station-cum-car servicing shop. Further round the green, past some cottages, she glimpsed a church spire rising above the trees.

The shop was tiny and cluttered, with a post office counter behind glass in one corner. Going round putting items into her basket, she heard the bell on the shop door jangle and heard the wailing of a child.

"Shush, Darren! Don't make such a noise! I'll get you some sweeties," a woman's voice chided softly.

31

"I want sweeties too," another child interjected.

"Well, let's just get something for tea, then we'll think about sweeties."

A woman came into the aisle where Kate was standing, dragging a small boy with one hand and holding a basket with the other. A slightly bigger girl lagged behind, sucking her thumb.

Kate smiled at the woman as she squeezed past her in the narrow aisle, noting her extreme thinness and rather careworn and distracted appearance. She also thought she could see the remains of a black eye. The woman smiled back, a smile which transformed her face.

Kate took her groceries to the checkout, which was staffed by a beautiful Indian girl and an older woman, presumably her mother. Leaving the shop, Kate drove in and filled up the Mini at the solitary petrol pump at the garage next door. Turning to go inside to pay, she nearly fell over a pair of scruffy boots protruding from under a jacked-up car on the forecourt.

"Whoops! Sorry!" she exclaimed, as the boots, followed by a pair of long thin legs and a body clad in very oily overalls, slid out from under the car, ending finally with a grinning face with a red bandana tied across the forehead, which failed to keep in place a shock of curly, black hair. The young man, who looked to be in his mid-twenties, yanked a grubby cloth from his back pocket and wiped his greasy hands on it, all the while eyeing Kate appreciatively with wicked brown eyes. He led the way inside and, taking her debit card, glanced at the name on it.

"Katherine A. Atkins," he muttered. "So, what do they call you? Katie?"

Kate laughed "Nearly. Just Kate."

"Aha! You wouldn't be the Kate that's come to live in old Miss Hopkirk's cottage, would you?"

"How on earth did you know that?" Kate cried, startled.

He tapped the side of his nose. "News travels fast in the village. Well, actually, my ma cleans for Tim, who lives up the lane from you, and Mrs B. who looks after his kids, is a good friend of hers. Mrs B.'s told mam all about the beautiful artist that's come to live here!" He winked

32

and gave a mock salute. "Mike the mechanic at your service. Any problems with the old Mini - just let me know."

"Well, now that you mention it, I have trouble starting it in damp weather. Maybe you could take a look at it sometime. As long as you don't charge a fortune."

"Be pleased to give her a once over - I do special deals for beautiful artists!"

He gave another wicked wink and Kate couldn't help laughing at his exaggerated leer.

"I could have a look at her next week if you like," Mike said a little more seriously. "I'll pick her up and bring her back."

"Great, which day would be best?"

Having arranged for the following Tuesday, Kate paid for the petrol and drove away from the garage. She hadn't gone far when she saw the thin figure of the woman she had seen in the shop struggling along the narrow pavement, pushing a buggy with one hand and holding on to the little girl with the other. Groceries were crammed into the basket attached to the back of the buggy.

The child was dragging her feet and wailing that she was tired when Kate stopped the car beside them.

She leaned over and opened the nearside door.

"Have you got far to go? Can I give you a lift anywhere?" she asked a little diffidently, not sure how the woman would react.

She was reassured by another warm smile. "Ooh! Thanks. Are you sure? Becky's ever so tired, poor mite, and Darren's got a nasty cough. But can you fit the pushchair in?"

"We'll manage," Kate said and got out of the car to help fold up the battered pushchair.

"I haven't got child seats, I'm afraid," Kate said. "I have a horrible feeling it's illegal to take children in cars without them."

"Oh dear!" the woman grimaced. "Well, it's only a short distance. Just this once."

She got in the back with the children, then Kate stowed the pushchair by the front passenger seat, fitting it in with some difficulty.

33

"Lucky it's not one of them modern space age buggies, we'd never get it in. I'm Annie by the way."

"And I'm Kate. I've just moved into the village."

They smiled at one another, Kate noticing that Annie was a lot younger than she had at first seemed to be. Having got the little girl strapped in at the back on a cushion, Annie sat the toddler on her lap, and directed Kate to a rundown-looking estate of houses just off the main road on the left. Two or three young lads leaning on bikes lounged on the corner of the road - rather optimistically called Paradise Close - that Annie directed Kate to turn into.

"It's number 4, just there," Annie said, pointing to a semi-detached house in a row of identical ones. Kate stopped the car, noticing that number 4 and the other half of the semi stood out from the other houses in the road in that their small front gardens looked better cared for and free of litter. Next door's was particularly pretty, its flower beds a riot of Michaelmas daisies. As Kate unloaded the pushchair from the car, a woman stood up from the bed she had been weeding and looked over the fence at them.

"Hello, Annie love. You're back quick." She glanced at Kate. "Got a lift I see." She gave Kate an approving nod.

Annie waved at the woman, then looked back at Kate. "This is Magda. She's ever such a good friend to me. Mags, this is Kate. She's just moved into the village."

Kate smiled, liking Magda immediately. She was a big-boned woman, who looked to be in her fifties, with a strong gypsyish face, her black hair scraped back in a ponytail. *An interesting face to paint*, Kate thought.

"Hang on, are you the artist lass called Kate who's inherited the cottage in Tuckers Lane?" Magda exclaimed, and laughed as Kate cried,

"Does everyone in this place know there's an artist called Kate living in old Miss Hopkirk's cottage?"

"Lily Babbidge told me about you and how those motherless kids she looks after have really taken to you. I go up to Tim's house to clean every week, but I only see the kids in the holidays."

"And you," Kate exclaimed in her turn, "must be the mother of Mike the mechanic, as he called himself. You have the same colouring. He told me his mother knows Mrs B."

It was Magda's turn to look surprised. "Oh, you've come across *him* have you? I bet he tried it on with you. He's a devil, that one," she said, her fond expression belying her acerbic words.

"Will you come in for a cup of tea?" Annie asked Kate in a slightly strained voice, casting a nervous glance towards the house. Magda caught the look, and said in a low voice; "It's alright, love, he's gone out. With that horrible friend of his - the one with the van."

Annie looked relieved and turned back to Kate. "You will come in won't you, for a quick cuppa?"

Kate felt it would be rude to say no, even though she was anxious to go home and get on with some work. Anyway, she liked Annie.

"I'd love to, thanks," she said, and taking Becky's hand, followed Annie into the narrow entrance passageway of the house, waving goodbye to Magda, who smiled back and bent down to continue with her weeding.

After stowing the pushchair in the cupboard under the stairs, Annie led Kate into the kitchen. Putting the toddler in his highchair and giving both him and Becky a drink of orange, she filled the kettle and switched it on. Kate sat at the little table, noticing that though the kitchen was in need of redecoration, it was spotlessly clean and tidy. While Annie put away the groceries and made the tea, they chatted about the children, the local school and the village in general, while the little boy Darren munched on a biscuit and Becky played on the floor with some toy saucepans and dried pasta. Kate could not help noticing that, as time went on, Annie became increasingly jumpy, glancing nervously towards the window whenever she heard a car.

Suddenly she froze as they heard a car stop and the door bang shut. Shortly afterwards, the front door opened, and a man's voice called loudly.

"Whose car's that outside?"

Annie half rose from her chair, her thin shoulders tense, as a man appeared at the doorway of the kitchen. He was big and burly, with close-cropped hair and a mass of tattoos on his arms. A striped T-shirt was stretched tightly over his large beer belly. He looked at Kate sitting at the table, her russet hair catching the light from the window.

"Who the hell are you?" he demanded, his eyes narrowing and darting from Kate to Annie and back again.

"This is Kate. She's just moved to the village." Annie glanced at Kate and gestured towards the man. "And this is Vince."

He made no move to shake hands, but turned to Annie. "So this is what you get up to when I'm out trying to earn some money. Sit around sipping tea like Lady Muck! Is me dinner ready? Reg's picking me up again at six." He turned and stomped up the stairs, ignoring the two children completely.

Kate drained her cup and got up. "I'll go now, Annie. I'm afraid I've made him cross by coming in."

"He's… it doesn't take much," she whispered. "It's not you – he…" Her voice tailed off hopelessly.

Kate squeezed her hand. "Thank you for the tea, Annie. Maybe you could come and have a cup with me sometime. Do you know where the cottage is?"

"Yes, I sometimes take the kids for a walk along there to get to the woods to see the bluebells in the spring. I used to see old Miss Hopkirk in her garden sometimes."

Kate said goodbye to the children and Annie accompanied her to the front door. Stepping outside, Kate looked back, but Annie had already closed the door, and Kate saw her face close up against the wavy Flemish glass panel set into the door. The distorting effect of the glass caused her face to fragment slightly. One eye was enlarged and separated from the rest of the face by a wave in the glass. Her mouth was slightly open, almost as if she was shouting silently. One of her hands was pressed against the glass. Kate lifted her hand in a wave and turned and walked to the gate. Getting into the car, she turned to look back at the house and caught a glimpse of the burly figure of Vince at the upstairs window, watching as she drove off.

The next morning, after putting the finishing touches to the painting

36

of the poplars seen through the window, Kate got out her sketchbook and, working at the table in the sitting room, started developing some ideas she had for the triptych she had been planning to paint before the poplars had side-tracked her. The shifting shadows cast by the October sunlight played across the paper she was working on, and Kate found herself incorporating the nuances of light and shade into her drawings, giving them an elusive, rather amorphous effect. Gradually, she found that her original idea for the work was changing, becoming overlaid by something new. She became so absorbed that she was surprised to see when she looked at her watch, that it was nearly two in the afternoon. Her stomach gave a protesting rumble.

She straightened her cramped shoulders and went to the kitchen, grabbed an apple and some cheese and looked through what she had done. Then, going again to the stack of canvases in the corner, she found the one she wanted - five foot by three foot, which she had made up in the Putney flat some weeks before. She no longer meant to use it for the painting she had made it for originally, but it was perfect for one of the panels of the triptych. She would have to get two more identical ones made up for the other two panels. For now though, feeling a rush of adrenaline, she felt she had to make a start. A kind of intense focus took hold of her as she scrabbled around among her paints and squeezed out the colours she wanted. Cerulean Blue, Burnt Sienna, Raw Umber, Indigo Blue, Burnt Umber, Emerald, Crimson, White, Yellow Ochre. She started blocking in areas of shadow and light. A face started emerging from the depths of shadow near the centre of the canvas. The face of a woman - fragmented, amorphous, distorted, but recognisably, Annie's face.

Towards midnight, a small scuffling noise near her feet brought her back out of the painting almost as though she was being physically dragged away. Looking down, she saw a mouse nosing around under the table. It stopped suddenly, sat up on its hind legs and regarded her with black, glittering eyes before scampering out of sight through a tiny hole in the skirting board. Kate suddenly realised she was exhausted. She had only stopped once since starting on the painting - to put the light on and get a coffee. Normally she preferred to work in daylight, but she had felt she must put down the bare bones of the confused but powerful mind picture of what she wanted to paint.

Sipping some instant soup, she stared at the painting. She had decided that it would be the central panel of the triptych. The face of the woman seemed to be close up against some transparent barrier which distorted her features. It could be glass or it could be water. But something was not right. She needed to get Annie to sit for her, and she needed to get hold of a sheet of Flemish glass.

*

Lily Babbidge opened the door of her cottage before Kate could ring the bell.

"Hello dear, I saw you coming from the kitchen window. How are you getting on? Anything you need?"

"Hello Mrs B. Yes, I've settled in nicely, and I've started to paint. But there's something I'd like to talk to you about if you have a minute."

"Yes, of course pet. Come in. Come and sit in the kitchen. I'm just making some scones for the children's tea up at the house. They always come in starving from school, especially Freddie."

Kate followed her into the kitchen where she sat cradling a mug of tea while Mrs Babbidge cut thick rounds of floury dough and put them on a baking tray.

"Mrs B," she started. "How well do you know Annie - er, I don't know her surname? She lives next to Magda, who I believe is a friend of yours."

"Oh, yes, that'll be Annie Coulter. I don't know her that well, but I do know she has a terrible time with that Vince. Magda says he's that violent towards her sometimes. I don't know why she stays with him. It's not as if they're married - they call it partners or something these days, don't they? I suppose she hasn't anywhere else to go. But I worry for those little mites of hers. Not that I think he's hit *them*. Just ignores them. Saves all his punches for poor Annie. How do you know her then? And you've met Mags?"

"Yes, yesterday. I saw Annie in the shop and later gave her a lift home. In the meantime, I also met Magda's son Mike, up at the garage. He's going to have a look at my old Mini next week." She took a sip of her tea. "The reason I wanted to talk about Annie is that I'd like her to sit for me, for a painting I'm doing, but I have a feeling that won't go down very well with the charming Vince."

Lily gathered up the offcuts of scone dough and rolled them out again to cut out some more with the scone cutter. "I think you're right there. In fact, I think he'd go ballistic," she said, peering over her half-moon glasses at Kate. "You wouldn't want the poor girl to get another bashing because of that, would you?"

Kate sighed. "I thought you'd say that. Maybe I could take some photos and work from those. I could take some if she came to my house when Vince was out somewhere. Does he work?"

Lily gave a derisive snort. "Work! He says he can't work because of a bad back, but it doesn't stop him going to the dog races and goodness knows where else with his dodgy-looking mates - so Magda tells me."

Bill Babbidge came into the kitchen through the back door. Seeing Kate, he gave her a big grin which made his cheeks bunch up like shiny red apples.

Kate smiled back. "Hello, Mr B. As you see, I'm getting in Mrs B's way when she's trying to cook."

"Not a bit." Lily opened the oven and slid the tray of scones in. "Kate was just asking about that poor girl Annie Coulter, you know, the one who lives next to Magda. She wants to paint her, but I said that Vince wouldn't take kindly to it."

"You can bet on that," Bill Babbidge said, his cheerful face becoming serious. "He's a nasty piece of work that one. I would steer clear of him if I were you."

"I intend to. But maybe if he's out…"

"I'll tell you what," Mrs B. said, wiping the flour from the work surface. "I could ask Magda to phone you when Vince goes out and you could pop over and have a word with Annie. Thing is though, Mags isn't always there. She works as a cleaner for various people in the village, including Tim. Anyway, we'll give it a try."

"Oh thanks, Mrs B. At least if I could get her to come over, I could get some photos. I mean, I'd pay her - oh, and that's another thing." She turned to Bill. "Is there a glass retailer anywhere around here? I need to buy a large sheet of Flemish glass." She smiled at Bill's puzzled look. "I need it for something I'm painting."

"Well, there's an industrial estate about six miles down the road. There's a glass place there." He looked at his wife. "That's where I got that replacement pane for the greenhouse when that branch fell on it last year."

"I also need some two-by-one section strips of wood. I need to make some stretchers. I've got a big roll of canvas, but no wood. Is there a wood merchant in the industrial estate?" She looked inquiringly at Bill. His eyes lit up, but before he could reply, Lily interjected: "Ah, now you've come to the right place, dear. Bill's a carpenter by trade. He's retired now of course, but he knows all about wood."

Bill nodded. "There isn't a wood merchant in the industrial estate, but I could ring up my mates at Brandon's where I used to get all my wood and get them to deliver some two-by-one to you." He paused as a thought occurred to him. "I could make up your stretchers for you if you like. Save you time."

"Oh Mr B. I couldn't possibly. I couldn't afford to pay you."

Bill looked affronted. "I wouldn't want paying, love. I like to keep my hand in, like."

"Yes, get him out from under my feet, give him something to do," Lily said with an affectionate chuckle. "Especially in the winter, when there's not much to do in the garden."

"You leave it to me, love. I'll sort out the wood. Let me know how much you want and then let me know when it arrives and I'll come over and make up the stretchers," Bill said, patting her arm.

"Mr B you *are* a pet," Kate said. gratefully. "I cleared out the shed in the back garden. You could use that as a workshop if there's enough room."

"Perfect," said Bill happily. "I know that shed from when I used to mow old Miss H's lawn. It's plenty big enough, as long as the stretchers aren't too enormous."

Having told Bill how much wood she needed and getting directions to the industrial estate, Kate thanked the Babbidges affectionately and let herself out into the bright morning. Walking back down the lane, she glanced towards Woodcote House as she passed. There was no-one at home and the house stood silent in the sunlight.

Going back into the cottage to get her purse, Kate glanced at the painting again. When she had come down this morning it had given her a slight shock. Incomplete though it was, the painting had a haunting quality to it which expressed the feeling she had experienced when painting it in the silence of the night. The canvas behind the blurred figure seemed to recede into an unfathomable chasm of shadow, the pale face hovering to the fore of the picture plane. But she could do no more until she had the photos of Annie, or Annie herself, behind the glass.

Chapter III

The low thump of music, followed by the banging of car doors made Kate glance up from putting the finishing touches to the illustration she was working on, sitting at her old desk in the smaller bedroom of the cottage. She had not heard anything from Magda, to whom she had given her mobile number via Lily Babbidge, and she had not dared bring the wrath of Vince down on Annie by contacting her directly, so she had been forced to be patient, putting aside the triptych panel to finish some illustrating work for a botanical text book, the deadline for which was approaching fast.

She had procured her sheet of Flemish glass from the glass merchant and it stood waiting beside the easel in the sitting room. The wood arrived the day after she ordered it, and Bill Babbidge had hurried over with alacrity to make up the other two stretchers for the triptych, as well as some others Kate needed. Kate would hear him whistling happily when she took out mugs of tea to the shed, grateful that the weather remained mild for late October. The canvases were beautifully made and stretched and he even insisted on priming them for her. The shed being nice and dry, Kate decided to store them there, to save cluttering up the small sitting room.

Kate stood up and peered down into the lane. She gave a cry of delight, only slightly tinged with exasperation, when she recognised Mimi's battered VW parked all askew on the grass verge behind Kate's Mini.

Immediately, there was a loud rapping on the door. Kate ran down the stairs and opened it to find not just Mimi but Bea and Grace too, standing on the doorstep, holding bottles of wine, pizzas and a large bag of crisps.

There was a great deal of squealing and hugging before Kate, laughing, dragged them into the house where they deposited their spoils on

42

the table.

Mimi, her hands on her narrow hips, confronted Kate. "We got fed up waiting for an invitation to your house-warming, so we decided we'd force one on you ourselves," she said sternly. "Old stick in the mud, burying yourself down here. It's a wonder you're not chewing on a straw."

Kate laughed again. "I'm only about forty miles from Central London you know. It's hardly Outer Mongolia. And I've been meaning to get in touch, but there's been so much to do. It's great to see you lot, though. I've really missed you." She gave them a group hug, then stepped back regarding them fondly. Mimi with her spiky magenta hair, rail-thin body clad in red and white striped tights under ripped micro shorts and a purple T-shirt over a skinny black sweater. Grace, curvy, pale and dreamy with long blonde hair half hiding her face, wearing a trailing skirt, dangly earrings and ropes of necklaces, and Bea, all Gothic black clothing, black hair escaping from a black scarf wound round her head and a silver ring in one nostril.

Grace looked round, entranced. "This cottage is so *sweet.*" She drifted over to the fireplace and peered up the chimney, then poked her head into the tiny kitchen. "Everything is so dinky."

"Yeah, it's cool," Bea said in her laconic way, throwing herself down on to the sagging armchair and, getting out her tobacco, started to make a roll up.

Mimi was standing in front of the half-finished painting on the easel. Kate glanced at her. Mimi's expression was unreadable. Then she said, "Kate, this is different. It's strange, it's… not like your usual stuff."

Kate had not wanted to discuss the painting; she was still working it out in her own mind. But now, being with her friends who understood the creative process, who were on her wavelength, she began tentatively to tell them about Annie and how she saw her trapped in a semi-invisible prison.

A loud knock on the front door interrupted her. "I'll get it," Mimi called over her shoulder, as she went to open the door.

"Well, hello," she purred in her hammed up *come-hither* voice. "And who might you be?"

43

Kate followed her to the door and saw Mike from the garage standing there, one shoulder leaning on the door jamb, regarding Mimi appreciatively.

Kate clapped a hand to her forehead. "Oh God, I totally forgot. It's Tuesday, isn't it? You were coming to pick up the Mini!"

Mike put on a look of mock indignation. "She forgot about me! I obviously made a big impression the other day!"

"I'll get the key," Kate said, laughing. She scrabbled about in the pockets of her coat hanging on the inside of the front door. "Here you are. How long will you keep it?"

"Oh, I'm sure I'll have her back by six," Mike said breezily.

At that, Mimi suddenly blurted out, "We're having a house-warming this evening, why don't you come and have a glass of wine later?" She glanced rather belatedly at Kate for confirmation.

"Yes, do." Kate didn't know whether to laugh at Mimi's audacity or to be embarrassed by it. She decided to go with the flow. "Mike, this is Mimi and…" she stood away from the door, pulling Mimi out of the way so that Mike could peer into the room, "this is Grace and Bea." Grace smiled shyly, while Bea waved her unlit cigarette at him.

"Blimey, there's three of 'em. I'll definitely be over," Mike exclaimed, winking at Kate.

"Oh, and bring a friend if you like," Mimi interjected. "Male. Balance it up a bit!"

"I'll see if Dave's around, he's always good for a laugh," replied Mike. He turned to Kate again.

"I'd better get going. I'll take the Mini and pick up my van when I bring her back."

"It's a him actually," Kate called to his retreating back. "His name's Trog."

Mike stuck his thumb in the air in acknowledgement, got into the car and, after one or two tries, got it started, made a multi-point turn in the lane and drove off.

"Cor! It was all I could do not to pinch his peachy little bum," Mimi

44

sighed, as she started to carry the pizzas into the kitchen.

"Mimi, you're outrageous," Grace said, peering out of the glass upper section of the door which opened on to the back garden from the kitchen. "Beautiful trees. Ooh, and horses in that field! I'm going to go and see them later, but first can we see upstairs? And can we stay the night? We've brought sleeping bags."

"Well, unless Mimi's not going to drink, and I don't see *that* happening, you'll have to," Kate said dryly. "Come on, I'll show you the upstairs, such as it is. It's not exactly Hampton Court Palace."

Bea dragged herself out of the armchair and clumped up the stairs after them in her biker boots. Kate had taken the other two into her bedroom, but Bea stopped at the top of the stairs and stood looking through the open door of the smaller bedroom. Slowly, she walked in. She went first to the window then turned and stood staring towards the cupboard set into the back wall.

"And this is the other..." As she came into the room, Kate's voice trailed off when she saw the black-clad figure of Bea, her heavily kohled eyes wide open, staring at the wall.

"What is it, Bea?" Kate went up and touched her arm. Bea started and looked at Kate, unseeing at first, then, her eyes focusing, she gave herself a little shake.

"It's...nothing. I just, I thought I heard - no, forget it."

"What? What did you hear?" Mimi said, looking from Bea to the back of the room.

Bea looked at her. "Someone crying - sobbing. Very quietly."

Kate shivered but said brightly; "It's the wind in the chimney. It often sounds like that. Come on, let's go down. I want to hear all about what's been happening. Has Geoff finalised the date for the show yet? Are you lot going to be ready by April? I'm not sure I am."

"Oh, I meant to tell you," Grace exclaimed. "Geoff called me and said the date's been put back to June. The property next door to his gallery came up for sale, and he decided to buy it and almost double his gallery space. There's going to be lots of refurbishment, so everything's got to be put back by at least two months. He asked me to tell the rest of

45

you." She shrugged. "Oh well, it gives us more time I suppose."

Before Bea followed the others back downstairs, she went to the cupboard and opened it. It was quite shallow and held only some clothes on hangers and an old tin trunk on the floor under a shelf. She shut the cupboard and went slowly back down to join her friends.

*

Tim eased the Discovery past the haphazardly parked VW in the lane, Kate's Mini, neatly drawn up on the grass verge, and a blue van with "Collins Autos" printed on the side. He recognised it as the van belonging to the garage in the village. Kate had visitors. And one of them must be that cheeky chap Mike. He briefly wondered why that annoyed him slightly. He stopped the car, partly out of curiosity and partly because he needed to ask Kate something. He heard the music as soon as he stepped out of the car, thumping out of the partly open front door. He rapped the knocker but, unable to get anyone to hear him, he pushed it open and stepped in.

There was a party of sorts going on inside. Kate was standing by the window, a glass of wine in her hand, talking to a tall, sandy-haired youth who looked vaguely familiar. A girl with flowing, hippyish clothes was swaying to the music, seemingly in a world of her own. On the sofa, a slightly intimidating-looking young woman dressed in black was drawing frantically in a sketch book, and a thin girl with extraordinarily coloured hair was dancing, draped over the lad from the garage.

Kate caught sight of Tim standing hesitantly in the doorway and waved at him. "Tim, come in, have a drink." She gestured with her glass towards the others. "This is Grace, that's Bea, and this crazy coot is Mimi. They suddenly turned up demanding that we have a house-warming party. Mike was doing my car, so they roped him and his friend in. You know Mike, I'm sure, and this is Dave. He occasionally works in the Jolly Farmer down the road."

Tim realised now where he had seen the other youth. Before he could protest, Mimi, having disentangled herself from Mike, thrust a tumbler of wine into Tim's hand, muttering to Kate as she turned away. "You didn't tell us about *him,* you crafty cow. He's delicious."

Kate poked her in the ribs, hissing, "Shut up, Mimi! If you dare say anything, I'll kill you."

Mimi rolled her eyes, grinned wickedly, and went back to the willing arms of Mike.

Kate turned back to Tim who was standing rather awkwardly, clutching the tumbler of wine.

"I'm sorry to gate-crash," Tim said. "I just wanted to ask you something."

"There's nothing to gate-crash. It's very impromptu - just my friends from art school, who I'm having a show with next year. What did you want to ask me?"

"I was wondering if you would feed Socrates for a couple of days."

"Socrates?"

"Amy's gerbil. It's half term next week and the kids will be at Claire's parents' from Monday to Wednesday. I'm taking a few days off to pick them up afterwards and take them to the West Country for a little holiday. Freddie's very keen to see the Eden Project. I would ask Mrs B. but I told her to take the time off, and she and Bill are going to Southend to stay with her sister. They'll be back on the Friday."

"Of course I'll feed Socrates, though I don't believe we were introduced when I came over for supper? What will he think?"

"Socrates, unlike his namesake, does not appear to think very much at all. As long as he gets his food and water, he's a happy bunny - well, gerbil. I was going to ask Elaine, but then I wondered if you would be so kind, since you're closer. Anyway, Elaine's a bit iffy about small animals."

"No problem, just leave me a key. Whereabouts in the house does Socrates live, and where is his food kept? Do I change the sawdust or whatever?"

"No, I'll change it before I go, and fill up the water tube. The food is in a tin box just next to the cage, which is in the muckabout room at the back. If you pop in at the weekend, we'll show you where he lives, and

47

formally introduce you."

"Okay, I expect this lot will have gone by then," Kate said, indicating her friends, who had been watching them covertly, while pretending to be otherwise occupied.

After Tim had gone, they sat around munching pizza and chatting, and Kate managed to have a quiet word with Mike about Annie.

"I expect your Mum hasn't been able to find an opportunity to see if Annie can get away for a short while. I'm really keen to get her here so that I can work on a painting of her and take some photos, but the last thing I want is for Vince to get wind of it."

Mike nodded, his mouth full of pizza. Swallowing, he took a gulp of the beer he had brought, saying he preferred it to wine. "Yeah, Mam mentioned it to me the other day. Vince has been hanging round the house a lot lately, during the day at least. I see him going out at night with Reg Perkins in Reg's van, and I hear them coming back about three in the morning. Bet they're up to no good."

"What, burglary or something?"

"Dunno. Wouldn't put it past them."

"Shouldn't you tell the police?"

"Not bloody likely. I'm having as little to do with Vince Dobbs as possible."

Kate felt a strange, cold shiver run up her spine. She could imagine the consequences of getting on the wrong side of Vince Dobbs.

"Look, I'll tell you what," Mike said. "I'll get Mam to tell Annie to walk round here if and when Vince is out during the day and hopefully you'll be at home. It's better than you fetching her; Vince is less likely to find out."

"OK, great, thanks Mike," Kate said gratefully. "It seems daft, all this subterfuge, but I don't want to cause trouble for Annie."

The "house-warming" wound up about eleven, Mike disentangling himself reluctantly from Mimi.

"Got to be at the garage by eight. Two cars to service. Oh, here's your bill, by the way," he said to Kate, pulling a crumpled invoice from his jeans pocket. "It's not too bad, just had to clean the spark plugs. I think you'll find it starts better now. Oh, and I'd better leave the van here and pick it up in the morning. I'm probably over the limit. Sorry Dave, you've got a longer walk home than me."

"No problemo. Good exercise," Dave said in his laid-back way. "Thanks for the party," he said to Kate, shrugging on his coat.

They all meandered outside to wave the lads off, watching them loping down the dark lane and disappearing into the night. Going back in behind the other girls through the lopsided gate, which Bill Babbidge had promised to fix for her, Kate stopped and lifted her face to the cool breeze, which hissed through the rapidly thinning leaves of the poplars. Looking the other way down the lane, she could see a faint light through the hedgerow bushes bordering the lane. A picture of Tim standing diffidently at the door of her cottage earlier that evening came into her mind, and a soft smile touched her lips.

Tim, leaving for the early train next morning, saw the van from the garage still parked outside the cottage, together with Mimi's VW and Kate's mini.

*

After Mike and Dave had left, the girls had talked long into the night, mainly discussing their coming show and the logistics involved. Kate promised to come up to Geoff's gallery in the near future, so that they could see what he was going to do with the new space which had become available. They all expressed a degree of panic, when they considered how much work they had to do before June. Then Mimi, sipping hot chocolate, turned to Kate:

"Since you're studiously avoiding asking about Jake, I'll fill you in anyway." She put her hand up to ward off Kate's protestations that she didn't want to know. "Yeah, yeah, sure, you're not interested. Well, I'll tell you anyway. He's still mooching about with that Lucinda, but he seems to treat her offhandedly, and she meekly takes it and lavishes gifts

49

on him all the time. She'd really like him to move in with her, but he won't. Says her place is too posh and chichi. And his place is probably too downmarket for her."

Kate laughed, surprised at how little this anecdote affected her. Jake seemed like a part of another life, another Kate.

Mimi, Grace and Bea left about eleven the next morning, Mimi expressing regret that she had still been asleep when Mike came to pick up his van. Kate had been a little sad to see them go. They, especially Mimi, with her mad social life, had highlighted the rather solitary existence she was leading now, even though the solitude was something she needed.

Kate settled down again to the illustrating work that had been interrupted the day before and, having finished by mid-afternoon, she drove to the post office to send it by registered post to the publishers.

Back at the cottage, not feeling in the right frame of mind to start painting, she pulled on her coat and headed off down the lane towards the woods at the far end, where the lane petered out into a footpath winding through the trees. The Crawford's house stood silent as she passed it. It was only four in the afternoon and the children were obviously not yet home from school. The Babbidge's cottage, too, seemed deserted, its windows winking in the afternoon sunlight.

It was still unseasonably mild for late October. The afternoon was quiet and dreamy, with hazy sunlight filtering through the oaks, their dry leaves making the faintest rustling in the occasional, slight breeze. Kate followed the path which meandered round to the left, skirted a field of stubble, then turned back into the wood again. Kate smelt wood smoke in the air and, seeing a blue haze through the trees off to the right, turned off the main path onto a barely discernible one which led out into an open grassy space.

She saw that the smoke was coming from the chimney of a tiny cottage, half hidden in a thicket of trees on the other side of the clearing. She stopped, enchanted to see that dotted about the clearing were what she at first took to be live animals, such was the skill with which they had been carved out of wood. She first noticed a roe deer and her fawn, the doe with her nose raised as if to sniff the air. Shortly after, Kate glimpsed a badger half-hidden in the blond grasses, then a big buck rabbit, an otter, a fox. As she stood motionless at the edge of the clearing, a tall thin man came out of the open door of the cottage. He sat down at a wooden table on which was a large, partly carved piece of wood. He looked up and whistled a strange note. A tawny shape detached itself from a nearby oak, flew down, and settled on a stump close to the table. An owl. Kate gasped in delight, a very slight sound, but the man looked up, startled. At first he didn't see her, standing in the dappled sunlight, her auburn hair, old green coat and brown trousers blending in with the sepia, burnt sienna and olive greens of her surroundings. When he did, he was startled anew: she looked like some sort of woodland being, with her hair lifting in the breeze, catching the light.

He stood up. "Come into the open, whether you are human or not!" he called in a deep baritone.

Kate came further out into the clearing a little hesitantly, not knowing quite what sort of a person this hermit-like man was. As she passed the roe deer carving, she instinctively put out her hand to stroke its back, a gesture that was not lost on Zachary.

"I thought you were one of them wood sprites at first. I've heard 'em, but never seem 'em. They call about the house of a winter's night," he intoned hollowly, but with a twinkle in his bright blue eyes. He had a short, grizzled beard and his long hair was tied back in a ponytail. He held out a large, brown, calloused hand to her. She held out her own and he shook it firmly. "Name's Zachary. Don't get many visitors in this neck of the woods."

"I'm Kate. I smelt the smoke and came to investigate. Sorry to intrude."

"You didn't intrude, you sort of appeared, like a vision, " Zachary said with a slow smile, eyes crinkling in a weather-beaten face. A silver ring glinted in his left ear.

Kate felt herself warming to him, all hesitancy forgotten. "Did you make all of these carvings?" she asked, her arm sweeping round the clearing, and her gaze coming to rest on the stump of wood on the table from which the shape of an owl was in the process of emerging.

51

"Well, I didn't so much make 'em as release 'em. I release 'em from the wood. The wood tells me which animal is inside."

"Like Michelangelo. It's the sort of thing he is supposed to have said about the block of marble he used for his *David*."

"I know what he means. This owl carving, he's the wooden equivalent of Bill here." He put out his arm and the owl flew up and perched on his sleeve. "It's a wonder he didn't take fright when you appeared. You must be a kindred spirit. He was a baby when I found him on the ground in the woods. Must have fallen out of the nest. He's tame, but wild at the same time."

"He's beautiful," Kate said softly, marvelling at the exquisite pattern of markings on the feathers, the huge dark eyes, the powerful talons. She walked over to the owl carving. Already the essential character of the creature was evident, in spite of its unfinished state.

"Do you sell your work?" Kate asked. "These sculptures are wonderful. They look alive."

"I sometimes take 'em to the local markets, but I don't get much of a price for 'em. Not the right sort of clientele."

"I'm sure you could get excellent prices in London."

"I'm not that bothered, I just do it for the love of it. I got dozens in that there shed."

"Oh! Can I see?"

"If you like." Zachary transferred the bird back on to the stump, then led Kate over to a dilapidated shed and flung open the door. There, on benches, shelves and all over the floor, were dozens of carvings of animals and birds - sinuous weasels and stoats, tiny voles, predatory kestrels, crouching pine martens ready to spring, a fox, turning his head, perhaps hearing the hunter's horn, crows with murderous beaks, a squirrel nibbling an acorn; all seemingly caught in mid motion, their polished eyes gleaming in the failing evening light. Kate gasped. She turned to Zachary, her eyes blazing. "You can't keep them hidden here! You must let people see them!" She picked up a fat toad, appreciating its satisfying squatness and the way the grain of the walnut wood described whorls of pattern on its back. "Let me talk to a gallery owner I know. Geoff *must* come down and see these!"

Zachary held up his hands in a stopping motion. "Whoa! Whoa! I don't know about that."

"Just let me talk to him and get him to come and see you. You don't have to decide anything yet."

Zachary shrugged his shoulders. "Well, I suppose that can't hurt. He'd probably say they weren't good enough for London folks."

"No way would he say that. I tell you these are fantastic! Did you teach yourself?"

"Well, me old dad was a bit of a woodsman, and he used to whittle little creatures out of twisty willow branches, and I kind of took it up meself. He only died five years ago, age of ninety-eight."

"Have you always lived here?" Kate asked, making her way outside again.

"Yep, man and boy. Scrape a living making these 'ere sculptures, and rustic garden furniture like them over there." He indicated an open-sided wood store to the right of the cottage, stacked with wood at the back, and containing some wooden mushrooms, garden chairs and stools, made with such skill and understanding of the nature of the wood grain and the incorporation of areas of rough bark into the designs, that Kate was delighted anew.

Zachary put out his hand and patted the half-carved owl on the table. "But it's me animal friends I prefer to work on."

"How do you transport them? You seem to be in the middle of nowhere."

"There's a lane out the front of the house. Goes out onto the main road. Got an old van. She's on 'er last legs mind you."

They chatted easily, Kate telling him something of herself and the work she had to do for her forthcoming exhibition.

As he listened to Kate, Zachary seemed gratified to have sensed that she had looked at his work with an artist's eye.

The evening was drawing in and the sun had gone down behind the trees, their branches dark against the afterglow in the sky. The shadows were gathering in the little clearing, making the animals dotted around seem even more alive, watching her. It occurred to Kate that she hardly knew this reclusive man and yet she felt completely safe in his company. Nevertheless, she felt she should be getting back.

"I suppose I'd better be going," she said, getting up from the wooden bench.

"Can I come and see *your* work sometime?" he asked, a little hesitantly.

"Of course. You can tell me if it's rubbish or not!"

"I know it won't be rubbish." He said it with a smile, but his tone was firm.

Kate walked back to the main path and when she eventually emerged back on to Tuckers Lane again, it was almost dark. The Babbidge's cottage looked cosy with the light shining from the kitchen window. She saw Bill standing at the sink at the window and heard the low murmur of the radio. Unseen out in the dark lane, Kate walked on, soon coming abreast of Woodcote House, from which lights were also shining at various windows. Involuntarily, she again glanced up at the upstairs window where she had seen the woman's face that first day. It was dark and blank.

Chapter IV

"Hi Geoff. It's Kate Atkins here."

"Kate! How's it going? Getting some work done in your country retreat? I saw Grace yesterday. She told me she'd seen you. Sorry about the show being postponed. It'll be worth it in the end, opens up more space, but it's taking an age. I've had to reschedule three shows before yours."

"Well, it can't be helped, and as you say, it'll give us more space. And more time. But I'm phoning about something else."

"Oh? What?"

"There's this amazing sculptor/carver guy I came across yesterday. Sort of a recluse, lives in the woods and carves animals from stumps and bits of wood he finds. They are truly amazing. Not in the pedestrian sense of pretty little animals, but in a living, breathing, red in tooth and claw sort of way. You really must come and see them. I'm sure they would sell like hot cakes at the gallery. Especially at Christmas time." Kate's words came out in a rush, her voice breathless with enthusiasm.

Geoff Banks chuckled. Kate had an appealing naivety and otherworldly side to her character, but there was also a sense that there was a steely core of independence under her apparent fragility. It seemed that she would give him no peace till he had looked at this strange recluse's carvings.

"Look, Kate. I'm up to my eyes at the moment. And the gallery's booked until October next year."

"Oh, but..."

"Hang on, hang on. I believe you when you say they're good. I trust your judgement." He paused. "I suppose I could put a few pieces in the foyer. But I'd like to see one or two examples first. How big are they? Look, I need to have a chat with the four of you about your exhibition. You need to sort out your spaces in the gallery. I could show you what we're doing about dividing up the internal space. It's quite radically different to what it was before. Could you come up sometime and bring a couple of small pieces of this carver guy's to show me?"

Kate was encouraged. "Yes, I'm sure Zachary would agree to that. There's a wonderful lizard and a water vole, for instance, that are small enough to bring."

They agreed that Kate would come up the following Monday and, after ringing off, Kate phoned Mimi to arrange to meet at Geoff's gallery, together with Grace and Bea.

Before Kate could ring off, Mimi asked; "How's your dishy city slicker?"

"He's not *my* city slicker," Kate protested. "I don't know, I haven't seen him since you lot were here. Oh, Lord! I'm supposed to go round and make the acquaintance of Socrates the gerbil. I'm supposed to be feeding it next week."

"Well, try not to kill him off. The gerbil, not the city slicker."

"I'll try not to." Kate wondered for a moment if Mimi had seen anything of Jake but decided against asking her. Mimi was bound to jump to the conclusion that she was pining for him, when nothing could be further from the truth. He seemed to be shut away in a different part of her life, at least for the time being.

As always, when Kate let herself out of the front door, the sound of the poplars swept over her, though they had a different sound now that the leaves were thinning. It was a higher, chillier sound. The leaves clustered more thickly on the outermost twigs and were still tinged with green, while the inner ones had thinned out and gleamed a pale gold. The weather had broken as well; a cold wind was blowing from the north west, bringing lowering, grey clouds speeding overhead. There was the odd spot of rain on the wind as Kate made her way up the lane and let herself through the garden gate of Woodcote House.

It was Lily Babbidge who opened the door, her face lighting up when she saw Kate.

"Hello, my dear. Come in. Ooh! It's chilly out there." She shut the door just as Amy appeared from a door at the end of the hall. Seeing Kate, she skipped delightedly up to her and grabbed her hand. "Come and see a necklace I'm making out of runner bean seeds. Freddie's doing the holes."

As Kate was dragged off to the family room at the back of the house, she called over her shoulder to Lily. "I've come to find out what to do for Socrates while everyone is away."

"Oh, good. I was a bit worried about that Elaine looking after him," Lily said quietly to Kate, following them into the big, messy room whose windows overlooked the large back garden. "He's in here where the necklace-making is going on. I'll leave it to the children to explain. I'm just getting lunch ready."

She bustled off, while Amy led Kate over to a table where Freddie was standing and on which was scattered a heap of runner bean seeds, shiny and plump. Freddie had an electric hand drill in his hand and was attempting to drill holes in the beans on a block of wood, with a fine drill bit. He smiled a greeting. "These are the seeds from the beans that got too big and tough. Mario, he's the gardener, said we could have what he doesn't need for next year." As he spoke, the bean he was trying to drill skittered away across the table. "They keep slipping, they're so smooth." Kate picked up a handful, appreciating the deep purple colour, streaked with black markings. "They're lovely, aren't they? A bit like polished stones. Why don't you make a little starter dent with a skewer or something, then the bit can grip it."

"Good idea. I'll go and look in Dad's toolbox for something." He jumped up, bumping into his father at the door. "Dad, have you got a pokey thing I can make a starter hole with?" he said, stopping and turning round halfway out of the door.

"Yes, you could use the bradawl. It's just a spike with a handle. In my toolbox in the garage." Freddie was already dashing off.

Tim smiled at Kate, his eyes crinkling at the corners. He looked pleased to see her. "Freddie always does things at breakneck speed," he said, stuffing his hands into the pockets of his shapeless cord trousers and leaning against the door frame.

Kate smiled back, their eyes meeting and holding the glance a fraction longer than either of them meant to.

"I … I've come to meet Socrates and find out what I have to do and when," Kate said quickly, dropping her eyes.

"Ah, yes. Yes, thanks. He's over here." Tim walked over to the corner where the gerbil was scuffling around in the sawdust, gnawing on a cardboard tube and shredding it to bits.

Amy appeared at Kate's elbow. "Do you want to hold him? He's quite tame."

Kate nodded and Amy opened the cage, picked up the little creature and handed him to Kate. She could feel his little feet treading the palm of her hand. She stroked the soft golden fur with the back of one finger, feeling the bones of his shoulders through the fur. "Which country do they come from?" she asked, just as Freddie came back into the room, carrying a bradawl.

"Mongolia. They also live in Africa and India," he said authoritatively. "The Mongolian ones live in desert areas. Look, he's got fur on the underside of his feet, to protect them from the hot sand."

Tim caught Kate's eye again and they both smiled at the mini lecture. "I think we have a budding David Attenborough here," Kate said admiringly, as she handed back Socrates to Amy to put away. "Where do you keep the food?"

"In this box," Amy answered, opening a biscuit tin beside the cage. It was full of a mixture of different seeds. "And you fill up the water in the tube if he needs it."

"We'll change the litter before we go," Freddie interpolated, "so you won't have to, but you can give him one of these cardboard tubes to play with and chew up now and again. He likes to make little burrows." He went back to the table and started to poke holes in the beans with the bradawl before drilling them.

Kate stayed for a while, helping Amy to thread beans onto the elastic thread. Tim sat at the table, leaning back in his chair, occasionally running his hand absent-mindedly through his hair and making it stand on end. He asked Kate how she had settled in.

"Oh, fine. It helped that the furniture was still all there. All I did was change the mattress on the bed." Kate found herself telling Tim about the old trunk she had found and its contents - the wedding dress, the veil, the bundle of letters. "I must ask Mrs B. if she knows anything about who my great aunt's fiancé was."

Mrs B, walking in at that moment with her coat on, heard Kate's remark and commented, "Well, you'd best talk to her friend, old Mrs Campbell. She lives in the village, near the church. She's in her nineties, but still bright as a button. She knew Miss Hopkirk very well."

"Thanks, Mrs B. I might well do that, if you think she won't mind."

"She won't. She's a dear old soul. Magda McLeary cleans for her. She's probably mentioned you to her already."

Soon after Mrs B. had hurried off to get Bill's lunch, Kate got up to leave. She said to Amy, "Don't worry about Socrates. I'll keep a good eye on him."

"Thank you, Kate." Amy looked up from her threading, then came over and gave her an impulsive kiss on the cheek.

Tim found himself envying that contact with Kate.

*

In the village shop that afternoon, Kate asked Mr Patel, the postmaster, if he knew which house belonged to Mrs Campbell.

"Oh, yes. In fact, we deliver her groceries every week. The house is called *The Beeches*, and it's next to the rectory, just past the church," Mr Patel informed her, looking at her over his spectacles. "She may be a bit slow answering the door; she's very old."

Kate put her shopping in the Mini and, leaving the car, walked across the green towards the church which she could see through the trees on the other side. Deciding to look inside the church, she went through the lych-gate and walked up the path between old, lichen-covered gravestones. She let herself in through the heavy, wooden door of the church and wandered around the quiet interior, which smelt faintly of the lilies

59

standing in vases near the altar. On her way out, she nearly bumped into the vicar who was coming in as she was leaving. He was a sprightly little man, with wispy, white hair surrounding a shiny, bald pate, and with a puckish, cheerful face. Kate put out her hand, introducing herself.

"Hello, I'm Kate Atkins."

The vicar shook her hand vigorously. "George Blackwell. Are you visiting?"

"No, actually. I've just come to live in a cottage I inherited from my great aunt Amelia Hopkins."

"Oh, how delightful. I knew Amelia very well. A stalwart of the church. An absolute stalwart. How nice that you've decided to live in Lavender Cottage!" He beamed at her, his wiry, white eyebrows waggling as he spoke.

"I'm just going to introduce myself to Mrs Campbell, who I believe knew my great aunt very well."

"Yes, yes indeed. They were great friends. Lydia Campbell's husband died many years ago, so they were both alone. Do you know where she lives? It's the next but one house on the left, *The Beeches*, just over there." He pointed further down the road that curved round the village green.

Kate thanked him and, waving goodbye, made her way to the gate he had indicated. The driveway was somewhat overgrown with weeds and shaded by overhanging beech trees. She spotted an ancient gardener slowly raking the vivid fallen beech leaves off the grass near the house. He did not seem to notice her. The house itself was almost completely covered in ivy, which was even starting to grow over some of the windows. Kate rang the bell and waited for several minutes. She was just about to ring again when she heard a rattling at the door, which opened a crack to reveal a bright eye peering at her. The door opened wider and a tiny old woman stood there, leaning on a stick and regarding her with intelligent grey eyes.

"Hello. Can I help you?" she enquired in a surprisingly strong voice.

"Hello, Mrs Campbell. I'm Kate Atkins," Kate said for the second time in ten minutes. "I'm Amelia Hopkirk's great niece. I'm living in her cottage that she left to me in her will."

"Oh, my dear, do come in. I was so fond of dear Amelia. Come through into the kitchen and we'll have a nice cup of tea."

"I don't want to put you to any trouble," Kate began, stepping over the threshold, but the old lady was already closing the front door and ushering her down the hall to the kitchen, a room frozen in the fifties, with an ancient cooker, a sink with a wooden draining board, a huge Welsh dresser with some beautiful old plates displayed in it, a well-worn kitchen table with sturdy oak chairs and a grandfather clock in the corner.

"Let me," Kate said, taking the kettle out of Lydia Campbell's hand and filling it at the sink. She spotted a box of matches near the hob and lit the gas under the kettle, then went to help Lydia take out cups and saucers from the dresser.

As they sat down at the table, Kate could not help contrasting her old life in London - the student flats with people coming and going, music playing, the smell of paint and smoke and alcohol, bodies draped everywhere, wearing a motley assortment of clothes - with sitting here in this quiet kitchen, the clock ticking sonorously in the shadows, opposite this diminutive old lady in a long, grey cardigan, drinking tea, and eating slightly soggy biscuits. Lydia, her bright eyes lively with interest, asked Kate about herself and why she had decided to leave London and come to live in the cottage. Kate found herself telling her about her work, the forthcoming exhibition and even about Jake. Something about the way the old lady listened, asking questions now and again, made her open up to her as though she had known her for years. Then, having topped up their cups, Kate turned to the subject which had drawn her to come and see Lydia Campbell in the first place.

"Mrs Campbell, I found an old trunk in the cottage and in it were a wedding dress and veil, and some letters, which I haven't read, except to see that they came from my great aunt's fiancé. Who was he? Do you know?"

"Yes, his name was James Lovell. Such a tragedy, my dear. He was wounded in Italy in 1943, three weeks before they were due to marry. He had been given a week's special leave to come home for the wedding. Then his family got the telegram that he had been shot. He was invalided home but died from his wound not long after. Amelia helped to nurse him until the end. I don't think she ever really got over it. Never considered anyone else. And she was very attractive, you know. There were several young men who did come home, who wanted her. But she never looked at them. Then when the cottage in Tuckers Lane came up for sale, she bought it and moved out of the old rectory next door and went to live there so that she could be near where he used to live."

"You mean - Woodcote House?"

"Yes, James's family owned Woodcote and he was their only child. Once the parents died, the house was sold. It has a sad history that house. Amelia told me once that she was sure there was some sort of tragedy or scandal relating to it back in the nineteenth century, which also had something to do with Lavender Cottage. Of course, the house goes right back to Tudor times, so goodness knows what else its history holds. Then the latest owner - another tragedy when the wife was killed in a car accident."

Kate shivered. So there was a connection between Lavender Cottage and Woodcote House. An invisible thread of longing and tragedy. Was that why she had seen that face at the window on that first day?

"Are you alright my dear? You look pale." The old lady's voice interrupted Kate's thoughts. She gave herself a little shake.

"I'm fine. It... it's just so sad." She got up and took the cups to the sink and rinsed them out. "Can I come and see you again?" she asked, coming back to the table, where Lydia sat looking at her, both hands on the top of her stick.

"Please do," she said. "All my friends are gone now. I'm the last." She put up her hand and touched Kate's hair. "Ripe chestnuts, fresh out of the casing; Amelia's hair was just the same. You have the same colouring."

Kate bent and kissed her papery, old cheek. "Thank you for the tea," she said softly. "I'll let myself out"

62

Driving home, Kate felt her own cheeks wet with tears.

*

"Come on, let's go down the pub," Mimi said, hustling Kate and the others towards the door. "Coming, Geoff?"

Geoff shook his head. "Too much to do. So have you lot, really." He wagged a finger at the four girls. "You should be working all the hours God sends. I want this space filled." He swept his arm round the gallery which was being made ready for his next show.

"Well, as I told you, I've got quite a lot of stuff stashed at my mum's. Even though they're *soft* sculptures, they still take up a lot of space. Mum's going mad," Mimi protested. "And there's Bea's light boxes and Grace has got several tapestry pieces."

Kate said, "I've got some biggish paintings down at my house, the ones I didn't destroy! I *have* got a lot more to do though."

"Yeah, well, for the moment, you need to shake the straw out of your hair, Kate Atkins. Come on, let's see if any of the gang is at The Slug," Mimi said and turned to Geoff. "Are we done here?"

"Well, we can't make final decisions about things until all the work is on site, but I guess we're done for the time being. Remember, the deadline for completing your work is the twenty-fifth of May. The show opens on June the second, ready or not."

"And you'll put the carvings on display?" Kate asked anxiously.

"I will, I promise. I'll come down and meet your hermit as soon as I can get away and pick up some more pieces. You were right. His work is bloody good."

Kate had been delighted by Geoff's reaction when he had seen the carvings she had brought up with her. She had gone over to Zachary's that morning and together they had chosen a couple of pieces to show Geoff. A water vole, standing on its hind legs, its body twisted as it looked over its shoulder for signs of danger, and a sinuous little weasel with one paw raised, sniffing the air. Geoff had turned them over in his hands, recognising the work of a true artist and craftsman. He had readily agreed

63

to put them on display in the lobby of the gallery when it opened again after the refurbishment, and even suggested that Zachary could be allocated some space when Kate, Mimi, Grace and Bea had their show. Kate realised that the fact that Geoff was Grace's uncle ensured they got preferential treatment, but she couldn't wait to tell Zachary he had agreed to show his work. She would have to call round, though, as she wasn't even sure Zachary had a phone.

The Slug and Lettuce was crowded and noisy, but it was good to see several familiar faces, including Paul's, who came over and kissed her on the cheek. "Hello, lovely. How's it going?"

"Fine, how are things with you?"

"Great. Done some shoots on location- Hawaii, Norway."

"Brill. Who..." What she had been about to say died on her lips and, in spite of herself, her heart skipped a beat, as Jake's blond head came into view. When he saw her, he pushed through the crowd and stood looking at her for a long moment before sinking his hands into her hair and drawing her face to his for a lingering kiss on the lips. To her own surprise, Kate coped with it calmly. She tilted her head to the side and looked at him appraisingly. His face, once so familiar, seemed to be almost that of a stranger. When she spoke, her voice was steady.

"How are you, Jake? You look good. How's the work going? Has Straker installed the pods in his gallery yet?"

"It's scheduled for next week. When it's ready, you must come up again and see it. I'm working on a new installation - it's proving to be a pig of a thing to source the right materials, get them made to the right specifications." He stopped and slid both his hands around her waist.

"Come home, kid. I miss you. You're good for me."

Kate put her hand up to his cheek. "But you're not so good for me, Jake," she said, softening the remark with a smile.

*

Kate had been relieved to get back to the peace and solitude of her cottage after the trip to London.

She had stayed at Mimi's flat overnight, where a party of sorts developed after Mimi had texted various people with the message, "Come over to ours tonight, bring booze." She had drunk too much wine, stayed up half the night and had taken a train back bleary-eyed in the morning, with a splitting headache.

After a long soak in the bath, she threw on some old clothes and went for a walk down the lane to clear her head, intending to call in on Zachary to tell him that Geoff had liked his sculptures. Zachary had been quite sceptical when she had gone over to get them.

"He'll probably think they're not modern-arty and tell you to take 'em away," he had muttered, gruffly.

Now Kate was eager to tell Zachary about Geoff's proposal that his work should be shown with hers and her friends', and made her way down the path to his cottage.

He was sawing wood at the wood store at the side of the house and didn't appear to notice her until she came up to him, shouting triumphantly and without preamble, "He liked them! He's going to put them on display when the gallery opens again. He's having building work done at the moment."

"No kidding!" Zachary exclaimed, looking astonished as well as gratified.

"Yes, and he wants to come and see the rest of your work sometime. *And,*" she added, her eyes shining, "he suggested that you join us in our show. Have a section for your stuff!"

The thought of showing his sculptures in a London gallery seemed to be rather a lot for Zachary to take in. Though he appeared daunted by the idea, she could tell he was quietly pleased at the same time.

He blew the sawdust from the piece of wood he had just sawn and looked at Kate, clearly touched that someone should care about anything he did.

"Well, I'll be blowed. Who'd have thought it? Thank you, Kate," he said, a suspicion of moistness in his eyes.

On her way back a little later, passing Tim's house, Kate realised she still had not got a key to get in to feed the gerbil, but there seemed to be no-one at home yet, and she knew the children were away, so she decided to call round later. However, around seven o'clock, as Kate was making herself her usual cup of instant soup, there was a knock on the door. It was Tim, still in his city suit. He held out a key.

"The key to the front door," he said, "so you can get in to feed Socrates. I should have given it to you when you popped round."

"Oh, yes, thanks, I couldn't remember exactly when you were going."

"I'm off tomorrow morning, back on Saturday or Sunday, but Mrs B. will take over Socrates on Friday. She'll be back from Southend by the afternoon. The kids were picked up by their gran, Claire's mother, on Monday."

"Would...would you like some soup? Have you got any supper at home?" With Mrs B. away, she thought, he might not bother about supper.

"Well, that's nice of you - I..." He was interrupted by the sound of a car coming down the lane and the lights of a red Volvo came into view. It was Elaine Grainger. She glanced out of the car window and seeing Tim standing in the light coming from the open cottage door, stopped abruptly. Opening the car door she stepped out gingerly into the rutted lane in her stilettos, picked her way down the uneven path and came up to Tim standing on the doorstep. She had on a low-cut black dress that showed off her slim figure. Her blonde hair was waved artfully round her exquisitely made-up face. Kate caught a waft of expensive scent.

"Tim, darling, did you forget? Duncan's at my parents', so I've brought you dinner. Foie gras and beef Wellington." She looked at Kate. "I'm going to steal him away, I'm afraid."

"It's OK, he was just giving me the key so that I can feed Socrates while they are all away."

"I see. I could have done that, you know," Elaine said reprovingly to Tim. "Never mind, since it's all arranged, I'll let it go this once!" She smiled sweetly. "Come on, darling. I could murder a dry martini." She turned and made her way back to the car.

Tim glanced at Kate, a rueful little smile on his face. He murmured, so softly she could hardly hear him. "I think I'd rather have had the soup!"

The next morning, when Kate opened the door to bring in the milk, she saw the red Volvo bouncing back down the lane.

So she had stayed the night with Tim.

Kate had put aside the "Annie" triptych to work on some semi-figurative pieces she had been planning while still in Putney. They were going well, achieving startling illusions of space and depth on the two-dimensional surface. But she still hoped that Annie would call round some time, so that she could continue with the triptych.

The weather turned frosty that week, prompting Kate to go out and buy an electric heater, since her supply of logs was running low. When Bill Babbidge returned, she would ask him if he had a chainsaw - there was a fallen elm in the ditch at the end of the back garden that she hoped she could saw up.

On the Friday, early in the afternoon, there was a tentative knock on the front door. Opening it, Kate was delighted to see Annie Coulter standing there with the little boy, Darren, asleep in his pushchair, and the girl, Becky, standing clinging on to Annie's coat.

"Annie!" Kate cried. "How lovely to see you. Come in! I've been hoping you could get away. Is he...?" She stopped, worried at what she should say in front of the children.

"It's OK, he's out for the day. Gone off to the dog racing. Mags told me that you'd like me to come over. But why ever do you want to paint *me?*"

"You're just right for a three-part painting I want to do. Come in out of the cold."

Annie tipped the pushchair to get it over the threshold and down the little step into the sitting room. "Is it alright if I bring this in? It looks like it might rain."

"Of course. Let me take your coat. Hope it's not too cold in here. My great aunt must have been a hardy soul, with no central heating."

67

"No, it's fine. We're quite warm from the walk." Annie stood a little awkwardly in the middle of the room, Becky still clinging to her skirt.

"I'll make us some coffee," Kate said. "Sit down for a moment."

When she came back into the room with two mugs of coffee and a drink for Becky, Annie was sitting on the edge of the old sofa, looking round the little sitting room.

"This is ever such a sweet room," she said. "This cottage must be really old."

"About five hundred years," Kate answered, handing her the coffee and offering Becky the glass of orange juice. The child shook her head, so Kate put it down on the hearth and went to get some biscuits.

When Becky was munching happily, Kate went over to the corner and pulled out the painting she had started of Annie behind the glass. When she saw it, Annie gave a gasp.

"Oh, I didn't realise you'd already started it!" she exclaimed, getting up and standing in front of it, her coffee mug cupped in her hand. "It's amazing. And it looks like me even though it's all wobbly and broken up."

Kate was anxious to take some photographs before Darren woke up and started running around. She gave Becky some drawing materials and settled her on the sofa. Then she set up the sheet of Flemish glass rather precariously on the table, and got Annie to stand behind it. She had on a dark red jumper and her light brown hair was loose on her shoulders. The effect behind the glass, with the shadowy corner behind, was just what Kate was hoping for. She took a series of photographs, with Annie's face at varying distances from the glass, and her hand at different heights, up against the glass. The way the wavy glass broke up the figure behind it - in some parts clear, in others unrecognisable as part of a face or body - she found fascinating.

Next, she asked Annie to step back into the corner, so that her figure was only a blurred shape in the shadows, and took some more photos through the glass.

"I think I've got enough to be going on with," Kate said eventually.

She would have dearly loved to get on with painting Annie while she was there, but the little boy was starting to wake up and whinge in his pushchair and Annie went to take him out so that he could toddle about. Becky was getting restless, too.

"I wish I could start on some painting now, but it wouldn't be fair on the children," Kate said. "Maybe you could get away again another day."

"I may be able to come one morning when Becky is at nursery." Annie said, thoughtfully. "And perhaps Mags could mind Darren for a couple of hours if she's not working."

"That would be great," Kate exclaimed. "But don't for goodness sake do anything that would, you know, get you into trouble."

"I'll be careful," Annie smiled. "Anyway, it gets me out of the house. I'm still not sure why you want to paint me though," she laughed. "I'm no oil painting!"

"You've got a lovely face, Annie."

Annie grimaced. "I don't know about 'lovely'. Vince calls me a scrawny cow."

"Well, that's where Vince is wrong," Kate retorted.

Annie left soon afterwards, promising to try to come over again when Vince was away for the day and when Magda could look after Darren. When she had gone, Kate drove into town to get the photographs developed, wishing she had a computer so that she could print them out herself.

On her return, she lost no time in continuing with the "Annie" painting, putting aside the piece she had been working on that morning. When the light faded, she carried on by artificial light, not stopping till she realised she was famished, having only had an apple at lunch time. She put a match to the fire she had laid that morning and sat beside it, with her mug of soup a hunk of bread and an apple. She leaned back in the old armchair and looked across at the painting. Annie's face loomed from the shadowy background, seemingly hovering just behind the picture plane, through the gleam of the wavy glass. It was working!

Next morning, before getting down to painting, she took Tim's key

69

and made her way up the lane to the Crawford's house. She let herself in and stood for a moment in the hallway, letting the silence of the old house seep into her. Remembering the face at the window, she shivered slightly, then went down the hall to the family room at the back. Socrates was scuffling about in the wood shavings and shredded cardboard in his cage. When she opened the hatch and put a handful of seeds and nuts into his feeder, he immediately came to pick out a sunflower seed and started nibbling it. Seeing an empty cardboard tube beside his tin, Kate dropped it in, and instantly the little creature began shredding it to pieces with its razor-sharp teeth. Suddenly, she swung round, sure that someone was standing at the door.

It was almost a shock to find no-one there.

Chapter V

The sound of children's voices was immediately followed by a rap on the door, rousing Kate from her deep involvement in her painting. On the doorstep stood Tim, accompanied by both the children and the dog. Freddie was holding a box of chocolates, which he proffered to her a little shyly.

"For looking after Socrates," he said.

Amy held out a posy of russet-coloured flowers. "I picked them from the garden. They're called Rud... Rub.." She looked up at her father, her voice tailing off.

"Rudbeckia," Tim said, smiling down at her, then turned his smile on Kate, as he took in her slight figure standing at the door, her hair clasped any old how in some sort of claw comb, with wild tendrils of hair escaping all over the place. She had a paint brush in her hand, and was wearing an old, paint-stained shirt. There was a smudge of red paint on her cheek. He thought she looked adorable.

Kate took the flowers from Amy. "Lovely autumn colours," she murmured. "Thank you, and for the chocolates. You really needn't have. I only had to pop in a couple of times. Mrs B. looked in yesterday evening to say she was back. Oh, I'll get the key," she said stepping down into the room. "Come in. Would you like some coffee or something?"

"We're interrupting you working," Tim said apologetically.

Before she could demur, Freddie said, "We're going for a walk. Do you want to come?"

Kate hesitated. She had been painting solidly for three days and a brisk walk would do her good, she knew.

Tim was looking at the painting on the easel. "That's amazing," he said quietly. "Quite unsettling, actually. Who is it?"

"She's called Annie Coulter, from the village. I met her in the village shop and we got talking. She has a horrible partner called Vince."

71

She glanced at the children and lowered her voice. "I think he beats her."

"So you see her trapped and sort of eroded at the edges," Tim said, his eyes still on the painting.

"Yes, sort of." Kate was taken aback by his perceptiveness.

"Did you actually paint that?" Freddie said wonderingly, coming across to look at it. "It's awesome!"

Amy came over and stood examining the painting, with her hands on her hips, then pronounced, "You should paint fairies like I do. That lady's a bit scary."

Kate laughed. "Yes, I suppose she does look a bit strange with her wonky eye coming apart from her face."

Tim tore his eyes away from the painting. "Why don't you take a break and come out for a walk? It's a lovely afternoon. The clocks go back tonight and then it'll get dark much earlier."

"Oh, please come! We're going to the leaf-boat stream," Amy cried.

"We could have a grand championship," Freddie added enthusiastically.

Binky the Labrador, hearing the word "walk" again, had leapt up from where he had ensconced himself on the hearth rug, and was wagging his tail furiously.

"OK, you're on!" Kate stuck her brushes into a jar of white spirit and went to wash her hands at the kitchen sink.

Tim followed her. "You've got a bit of paint…" He came up to her and putting a drop of washing-up liquid on his finger, he tilted her face up to him and gently rubbed at the streak of Madder on her cheek. They were standing very close together. He had one hand on her shoulder, steadying her, as he worked the soap into the oil paint.

"There, I think it's gone. Some damp kitchen roll…" He still had his hand on her shoulder when their eyes met. Met and held for a long moment. Then Freddie came into the kitchen, calling out; "Come on Dad, let's go." He stopped for a moment, seeing his father standing so close to Kate. A mixture of emotions crossed his face. Then the moment passed and after a couple of minutes of confusion, with Kate pulling on boots and her coat and the dog getting under everyone's feet in the little sitting room, they all went out into the bright breezy afternoon.

Freddie, running ahead with the dog, led the way past their house down to the end of the lane and into the oak wood, waving to Bill Babbidge who was dead-heading dahlias in his front garden. As they came up to him, Kate paused by the garden gate.

"Hello, Bill. Did you have a nice stay in Southend?"

"Hello love, hello Tim. Yes, lovely thanks. The weather wasn't too bad. Mind you, it's always nice to get home again." Bill pushed his old gardening hat back on his balding head. He added, with a twinkle; "Lily and her sister could talk for England. I never get a word in edgeways." He said it affectionately, however.

"Bill, I was wanting to ask if you had a chainsaw I could borrow," Kate said. "There's a fallen dead elm at the end of my garden. Not very big, but I reckon it'll give me a good few logs." As she spoke, Lily came out of the front door, a flowery, pink overall over her clothes. Kate waved a greeting.

"I have indeed, love." Bill glanced at his wife, jerking his head in Kate's direction. "Kate wants to saw up a tree with the chainsaw:" He looked dubiously at Kate's slight frame. "But you better let me saw it up for you. That chainsaw's heavy and we don't want you chopping your foot off or something."

"I'm quite strong," Kate protested, not wanting to take advantage of Bill's kindness. Also, he was getting on a bit.

"Strong!" Lily snorted, her hands on her ample hips. "A puff of wind would blow you away. Bill can come over and start on it tomorrow."

"I'd be happy to saw it up for you," Tim interjected. He stroked his chin with mock pomposity. "I'm quite an expert you know. I helped Mario my gardener to saw up a big dead elm in our garden last year. Then we split the logs with an axe. Oh yes, I know all about logs."

"Tim, I couldn't," Kate began, but Tim put up his hand.

"No arguments. I'd feel terrible if you injured yourself. Dangerous things chainsaws."

Kate shot him a grateful look.

73

"Tell you what, we'll do it together," Bill said.

"Done!" Tim laughed, giving Bill's hand a shake, while Kate conceded defeat with a grateful smile.

Freddie came bursting out of the edge of the wood, calling impatiently. "Come *on*. We'll never get there at this rate."

Lily and Bill stood watching the little procession disappear among the trees, Kate and Amy giving a last wave over their shoulders.

"She's a lot better for him than that Elaine Grainger," murmured Lily to her husband, "even though there's quite a big age difference between Kate and Tim."

It was an exhilarating walk, first through the woods, where the brisk breeze made the tops of the oaks sway about, making a soughing sound through the tenacious brown leaves still thickly clinging to the branches. Passing quite close to Zachary's overgrown little field, Kate discovered that Tim had often seen his cottage through the trees when out on their walks, but had never met Zachary himself. He had also seen some of the carvings in the clearing and agreed with Kate about their quality.

But the children were too impatient to get to the 'leaf boat stream', so they did not stop to see if Zachary was there, continuing on to where the path met a bridleway. Turning into the bridleway, they followed it downhill to where the wood came to an end, and the path carried on between high hedgerows bordering fields of stubble and rough pasture. Kate heard a train in the distance and realised the railway line must be fairly near. Cotton wool clouds scudded by overhead and the sun was warm on their shoulders. Glowing red rose hips and hawthorn berries jewelled the hedgerows on either side of the bridleway, which was very muddy in places where horses' hooves had churned up the earth. Sloe bushes, blue with dusky fruit, grew in dense patches and soon Amy pointed off to the right. "There's the blackberry factory, 'cept I think the berries have all gone now."

Kate saw a mass of bramble bushes clustered on the right of the path, the shrivelled remains of a bumper crop of blackberries clinging to

74

the thorny branches, their leaves ranging from green through to purplish brown and deep red.

Freddie came running up, having seen them come to a halt.

"Mummy used to make bramble jelly with blackberries from here," he said. "And once she put a tiny little pot of it under that old tree trunk, with a label that said, 'Dear blackberry fairies, thank you for the fruit.'"

Amy nodded vigorously. "And do you know what? When we came back another day, the pot was there, but all the jam was gone, and so was the paper she put over it with a rubber band, *and* it was all washed and clean! The fairies must have done it."

"Claire got the idea from a poem by Walter de la Mare, called 'Berries'," Tim said. Freddie made a small, choking sound and turning suddenly away, started running off down the path towards a line of trees.

Kate glanced at Tim and, noticing his own eyes seemed to have tears in them, felt a lump rising in her throat.

"Best leave him for a minute," he said, his voice husky. "He would hate you to see him cry."

Amy put her small hand into her father's. "Do you think there are fairies in heaven, Daddy, or only just angels?"

"I expect there are both." He knelt down, there in the muddy lane, and hugged his daughter, his face buried in her silky hair. "Yes, I expect there are both," he said again softly.

The path had been sloping downward for some time and when they caught up with Freddie he was standing in the middle of a little bridge made of old railway sleepers, which spanned a small stream. The stream was bordered by long, tangled grasses and the dried seed heads of teasels and cow parsleys, which rattled dryly in the gusting wind.

Tim walked on to the bridge, putting his hand on his son's shoulder and giving it a little squeeze.

"Right, you organise the championships then. Leaves or sticks?"

Freddie's face broke into a grin. "Both. Leaves first." He turned to Kate. "It's a leaf version of Pooh Sticks, but it might not work 'cos of the wind. First leaf to come out the other side is the winner."

They all chose a leaf from the many fallen ones on the ground. The line of trees beside the stream was made up of a variety of species, and they all chose leaves from different trees. Kate chose a large oak leaf, brown and sere, Amy a golden sycamore leaf, Tim found a long willow leaf, like a canoe, and Freddie, searching along the bank of the stream, came running back with a deep orange beech leaf, curling up at the edges, like a miniature dinghy.

On Freddie's "Ready, steady, go," they all dropped their leaves into the water on one side of the bridge and anxiously watched their own "boat" fall into the sluggishly running stream. Kate thought her oak leaf was going to be blown away altogether. A gust of wind blew it up towards the grassy bank before it finally hit the water and started moving downstream. Tim's leaf landed broadside on to the current and spun round, before slowly starting to drift under the bridge. Amy's landed with a plop, flat on the water, spinning lazily as it vanished from sight, but Freddie's beech leaf-boat caught the wind and immediately took off, vanishing under the bridge at speed. He was sure he could even see a tiny bow wave.

They all dashed to the other side of the bridge, and Freddie let out a cheer as his leaf came sailing grandly out into the sunshine, the wind and the current combining to increase its speed. Amy's came next, still spinning slowly. Kate's oak leaf, having snagged on something under the bridge, finally appeared, but there was no sign of Tim's willow leaf. He lay down on the bridge and stuck his head over the edge. "I think I can see it stuck on a twig," he called, his voice sounding hollow from under the wooden planks. "No wait, here it comes, it's freed itself."

Seconds later his leaf arrowed out from the shadow of the bridge. The children's leaves had sailed on out of sight, but Kate's had got caught in an eddy and was floating in little circles near the bank. Tim's leaf got caught in the same eddy and they both swirled round and round, before finally being caught up in the overhanging grasses on the bank.

They had several rounds using sticks, which Amy was particularly lucky at, while the dog ranged up and down the bank, looking for rabbits, and they all got dirtier and dirtier, lying down on the bridge to see what had happened to their sticks, scuffling about looking for good twigs in the undergrowth.

They took a different route back, cutting through the fields in a wide arc, Amy insisting they visit the 'All Alone Tree', a mighty oak standing in the middle of a field, one of whose huge branches, itself the size of a tree, had broken off and lay beside it. Its rotting wood, Freddie informed her, was a haven for minibeasts.

"There are probably hundreds of invertebrates living in this old branch," he said, patting the rough bark. "Hoverfly and crane fly larvae, jewel beetles, stag beetles, wasps, and arthropods like millipedes and centipedes. Lots of food for woodpeckers." He pointed. "And look, bracket fungus. Cool."

"A whole ecosystem," Kate said, hugely impressed not only by Freddie's knowledge, but also by his intense interest and enthusiasm.

"The farmer who owns this land must be a conservationist," Tim said. "Come on, we'd better get going, it's starting to get chilly."

They carried on round the field and up towards the 'home' wood as Kate mentally dubbed it, that she could see at the top of the field. She thought she could see a smudge of blue smoke that was probably coming from Zachary's cottage.

She looked at the children running ahead with Binky.

"Freddie certainly seems to know his wildlife," she said to Tim, walking beside her, the sleeve of his coat occasionally brushing hers.

"He wants to be an entomologist. Where that came from, I don't know. He's always been fascinated by bugs and things."

"Well, it makes a change from kids who have their eyes glued permanently to screens."

"Oh, he likes computer games too, but he's just as happy with his head in a wildlife book or creating 'Sanctuaries' for creepy crawlies at the bottom of the garden. He takes a wicked pleasure in coming up to Elaine with some wriggling caterpillar he's found on the cabbages! It never fails to freak her out."

Kate laughed, but his reference to Elaine seemed to create a silence between them. She wondered, not for the first time, how serious Tim's relationship with her was.

The sun was setting behind the wood as they emerged into Tuckers Lane again and, waving at Mrs B. at her kitchen window, they tramped on down the lane.

"We've got some sausages in the fridge for supper," Tim said, a little tentatively. "Mrs B. doesn't usually come in on a Saturday evening. Poor woman needs some time off. So I usually hash something up. Why don't you come and join us? If you don't mind lumpy mash!"

"Now that's one thing I'm good at, mashed potato. Sometimes I put cabbage in it. You know - Colcannon, an Irish recipe."

"Sounds good. We've..." They had rounded the bend in the lane and Freddie let out a groan when he saw Elaine's red Volvo parked outside Woodcote. "Oh no, not *her* again. She's always..."

"Freddie!" Tim said sharply. "Be polite. Remember, she takes you to school every day." He waved and as they made their way down the lane, the driver's door opened and Elaine stepped out.

Elaine Grainger looked at the raggle-taggle little group coming towards her. The children were particularly scruffy and dirty, their Wellingtons encrusted with mud, and Tim wasn't much better. He seemed to have been kneeling in the stuff. But it was Kate that her eyes were riveted to, and her heart contracted with the same fear she had felt when she had first seen her.

Kate's auburn hair was even wilder than usual, blowing about in the wind, her cheeks were flushed and her green eyes sparkled. She looked very young. Too young. Elaine looked away and went up to Tim, lifting her face to give him a kiss on the lips.

"Tim, I tried to ring, but there was no reply. I thought you might be in the garden. Remember we said we might go and try out that new Italian restaurant for dinner tonight. Duncan is with Giles for the weekend, so I don't need a babysitter."

Tim clapped a hand to his forehead, "Oh God, yes, I remember now." Privately he thought: I don't know about *we*. It was entirely her idea. Then he exclaimed, "Oh, but the trouble is, I *do* need a babysitter."

"Perhaps Mrs B...?"

"That wouldn't be fair at such short notice. And she's just come back from her sister's yesterday."

Kate glanced at Tim. "I could babysit if you like," she said, her tone a little hesitant. It wasn't at all clear that Tim really wanted to go out to dinner.

Tim shot her a grateful look, though a rueful twist to his lips indicated he would have been glad of an excuse not to go.

"Well, that would be very kind, but you probably want to get back to your painting."

"Oh, that's OK. I wasn't going to do any more tonight."

"That's settled then," Elaine cut in, her tone a little stiff. She was torn between wanting to go to dinner with Tim, and resentment that Kate would be cosying up to Tim's kids. Mind you, they seemed to have been having a jolly walk all together anyway. God, they were filthy.

"You'd better have a good shower, Tim. You're covered in mud." She looked at the children. "So are you two," she added, ignoring Kate. She turned back to Tim. "I'll book a table, say for about eight? I'll come back about seven thirty. We'll go in my car, so that you can drink."

"Er, fine." Tim looked at Kate a little apologetically, feeling she had been steamrollered into babysitting. She *had* offered, but... "Are you sure that's OK?" he asked, and the slight softening of his voice was not lost on Elaine.

"Absolutely. I'll be over about a quarter past seven. And don't worry about the kids' supper. We can sort out the bangers and mash, can't we guys?" Kate said, turning to the children.

Both nodded enthusiastically, Freddie adding, "And baked beans, of course. You can't have bangers and mash without baked beans."

"Too right," Kate agreed with a grin. "Unthinkable!"

Elaine got back into her car, irritated at the easy rapport Kate seemed to have already established with the children: a rapport she had failed to achieve, even after more than a year ferrying them to and from school every day. She turned the car round and drove off, once again a little too fast.

Tim grimaced, muttering: "She'll damage a wheel in the potholes one of these days."

Later, after a bath, Kate made her way back down the lane, her sketchbook and pencil case tucked under her arm. Freddie let her in and led her straight to the kitchen. "I've started peeling the potatoes," he announced, pointing at the sink, which was full of potatoes and peelings.

"Excellent, I'll finish them off, if you can get out the sausages."

Amy came in, wearing pyjamas and a dressing gown, holding a piece of paper. "Hello Kate. I'm doing a menu. We're going to be having supper in a restaurant, called 'The Magical Castle Restaurant', look." She held out the piece of paper, on which was written in wonky letters:

The majicul Casle Restront
Menyoo
Sossiges
Mash
Baced Beens

Puding

"I don't know what's for pudding. I know, I'll put yoghurt or ice cream." She scurried back to the family room to add to the 'menu'.

Kate was in the middle of peeling the potatoes when she heard Elaine's voice in the hall.

"Tim? Are you ready?"

Freddie, cutting the potatoes into smaller pieces and dropping them into a pan of water, stiffened and muttered under his breath. "Just because she has a key, she thinks she can just come in without knocking." He went out into the hall.

"He's just having a shower. He was oiling the chainsaw and forgot the time." His tone was polite but a little cold. He came back into the kitchen, followed by Elaine.

"Freddie, could you go up and tell him I'm here. We want to have time for a drink before dinner," she said.

Freddie disappeared back into the hall and Kate heard his feet thumping up the stairs.

Elaine walked over towards Kate, her high heels clacking on the quarry tiles.

"Good of you to step in at a moment's notice. Tim, poor darling, is a bit absent-minded. Of course, it wasn't a firm arrangement, so I'd better forgive him." She leaned against the countertop, one hand toying with the gold chain round her neck. She had on a cream coloured, tightly belted trench coat in soft leather.

"So you're an artist, I hear. What sort of things do you paint?"

Kate glanced up from the potatoes. "It varies. Ideas come to me from what I see and feel about the world around me."

"Landscapes and things?" As she spoke, Elaine glanced towards the door and looked at her watch.

"Sometimes there are elements of landscape." Kate got the feeling that Elaine was not the slightest bit interested in the 'sorts of things' she painted.

"Are you intending to make your home here? I would have thought it's a bit quiet and dull."

"Actually, I love it. The poplars are so beautiful, and…"

"Poplars?"

"Yes, the trees all around the cottage and along the lane. They were the first thing I saw when I came down to see the house."

"Oh? I hadn't noticed." She hesitated. Her cool demeanour not quite masking what she really wanted to know about Kate. "Yes, but you must miss all your friends in London. There must be a boyfriend lurking somewhere."

The thought of Jake 'lurking' anywhere made Kate laugh out loud, but she was saved from answering by Tim and Freddie both coming into the kitchen together.

"Sorry, sorry. Got a bit side-tracked." Tim said, giving Elaine a peck on the cheek. He turned to Freddie. "Be good, and help Kate, won't

81

you? And bed by ten at the latest. I bet you haven't done your homework, even though you've had all of half term. It's back to school on Monday." He turned to Kate. "Amy better get to bed straight after supper, if you don't mind. They've both had baths."

Kate waved the potato peeler at him. "No problem. You go, it's gone half past. Everything's under control. Freddie'll tell me where everything is."

Tim smiled gratefully at her and went to say goodnight to Amy in the other room. Elaine clacked back out of the kitchen and headed to the front door, and soon Kate heard the door bang shut and they were gone.

By a quarter past eight, the sausages were cooked, the potatoes mashed and the baked beans warmed up. At Amy's insistence, Kate and Freddie had to pretend to be customers at the Magical Castle Restaurant, while she doubled both as waitress and customer. The first course having been demolished, the menu was produced again, and they were urged to choose between 'yogut or isecreem'. They all chose the latter, and Freddie went out to the freezer in the utility room adjoining the back porch leading off the kitchen. He came back with a tub of Neapolitan ice cream, with its stripes of three different flavours. "Only we always call it 'Napoleon' ice cream," Amy said solemnly. "And I only want the pink kind."

"You can't only have the pink kind," retorted Freddie, "or it'll make it uneven."

"How about if I only have vanilla and chocolate, that'll even it up," Kate suggested.

Freddie agreed, and after the ice cream was doled out and the tub put away again, they sat eating it, somehow getting on to the possibility of dragons, giants, goblins and other mythical creatures.

"Well, stories of giants may have come about because of the existence of people with some sort of overactive growth hormone," Kate mused. "I remember learning at school about the story of Goliath, in the Bible. He was supposed to be a nine-foot man who was fighting on the side of the Philistines against the Israelites. Mind you, it only took a stone from little David's sling to bring him down."

82

"And dragons may be sort of exaggerated versions of big lizards like Komodo dragons in Indonesia," Freddie put in eagerly. "Though I don't know where the fire breathing comes from. Maybe it's because of their toxic saliva."

Kate thought Amy was looking a bit apprehensive, and turned the discussion to fairies. Here Amy was on firm ground, being utterly convinced that there *were* such things, in spite of Freddie's scorn.

When the supper was cleared away, Kate took Amy up to bed, with a diversion to the bathroom for teeth brushing first. Keeping to the same theme as their talk downstairs, Kate read to Amy from a book full of stories about fairies - strictly the pretty, bewinged versions, not the darker bogles and kelpies of Celtic legend. When she saw Amy's eyelids beginning to droop, Kate closed the book and stood up. She bent down and gave the little girl a kiss on her soft cheek. Suddenly, both Amy's arms came up and grasped her round the neck in a hug.

"I like you," she said simply.

Kate's heart gave a lurch. "I like you too. Good night, Amy," she said, stroking the fringe out of the child's eyes. Then she went quietly out of the room, leaving the door slightly ajar.

Back downstairs, she found Freddie in the family room, watching a wildlife programme. She sat down and they watched it together in companionable silence. When it was over, Freddie sighed and dragged out his school bag.

"'Spose I better get this homework done."

"What is it?" Kate asked.

"Latin," he groaned. "Mind you, Latin's useful when it comes to learning the Latin names of species."

"Do you mind if I sketch you while you work?" Kate asked, adding hastily, "Just say no if you'd rather not."

Freddie pulled a face, but looked rather pleased all the same. "Do I have to keep very still?"

"No, just carry on normally. Ignore me." She went to fetch her sketchbook from where she had left it in the kitchen.

Though a bit self-conscious at first, Freddie soon relaxed and got involved in his Latin. Working with quick, lively strokes, Kate tried to capture the lean energy of the young boy. His wayward hair, the tilt of his head as he bent over his work, the bony shoulders and jutting elbows leaning on the table, the sleeves of his baggy T-shirt. Next she worked in the shadows cast by the overhead light, bringing out the 3D aspect of the drawing.

After about half an hour, Freddie flung down his pen, exclaiming, "Finished!" He looked over at Kate. "Have you finished your drawing?"

"Just about."

"Can I see?"

"Of course." She handed the sketchbook to Freddie.

Freddie took it, his eyes widening. "Wow! It's excellent. It really looks like me. Can I have it?"

"Yes, sure." Kate took the sketchbook and tore out the drawing, signing it with a flourish before handing it to Freddie.

"And now, it's gone ten, I think you'd better be off to bed," she said. "Are you too old to be tucked in?"

"Yes!" Freddie snorted. But he added immediately, "You could come and see my fossil collection."

"I'd love to," Kate said, getting up and tossing aside her sketchbook.

Freddie put the drawing down on the table. "I'll show it to Dad in the morning," he said, leading the way out of the room and up the stairs. Freddie's bedroom was at the side of the house overlooking where the lane curved round towards her own cottage. It was a typical young boy's room, with shoes, T-shirts and the odd football scattered about. On a desk by the window sat a computer and a games console, and a bookcase full of books on wildlife stood in the corner. On the broad windowsill was a large collection of fossils, which, unlike the rest of the room, was meticulously arranged.

"Mostly I've bought them from shops, but a few I've found myself, especially on the Jurassic Coast in Dorset, where Granny lives. This little ammonite I found on Charmouth beach, and this slab of slate I picked up in Kimmeridge. Look, you can see loads of little fossil shells stuck in it." His tone was animated, his enthusiasm palpable. "Here's a piece of petrified wood, and this," he picked up a smooth heart-shaped fossil with five arms of markings raying out from the centre, "I found on the gravel driveway at school. I just looked down, and there it was! It's an echinoid."

He went on pointing out other fossils, among them a mosquito in amber, a stone with the imprint of a fernlike plant, two or three trilobites, a beautiful nautilus, cut in half and polished, showing the internal structure. Kate was fascinated, as much by his knowledge as by the fossils themselves. Cupping a beautifully polished ammonite in her hands, Kate marvelled at the elegant spiral with its ever-decreasing ridges getting closer together towards the centre. The sheer age of the long dead creature in her hand was staggering. She thought of the millennia that had passed since it had sunk to the seabed and been covered by sediment, before finally being heaved to the surface again by earth movements, to end up in a young boy's bedroom on a windowsill in Surrey.

She looked up and saw Freddie watching her with an expression that was such a poignant mixture of eagerness, gratification at her interest, and something else, a sort of vulnerability, that her heart went out to him. She handed the ammonite back to Freddie.

"That's a very impressive collection. Thanks for showing me. They've given me an idea for a painting."

"Really?" His face lit up. "Cool." His expression then turned thoughtful as he added: "I wish Irina could have been more like you."

"Who's Irina?"

"She was an au pair that Dad got to look after us when Mum... when Mum died. At first, Granny Gwen and Gran and Gramps took it in turns to stay here, and then Irina came, but we didn't like her. Once when she had the evening off and she was going out, I passed her and she smelt like Mum. She had used Mum's scent from her dressing table. We still keep her things like she had them. And then her coat flapped open and I saw that she had one of Mum's dresses on. She'd just put it on without even asking. I recognised it straight away, because Amy and I sometimes..." He stopped and turned away, then said in a low voice which Kate had to strain to hear; "We sometimes go to her wardrobe to smell her clothes. They still smell of her."

Tears pricked Kate's eyes. She blinked them away as Freddie continued.

"Amy and I were very angry with Irina for using Mum's things, and so was Dad. He asked her to go, and then we got Kaja."

"What was she like?"

"She was quite nice. She was from Estonia, but after only about three weeks, her mother got very sick, and she had to go home to look after her and her younger sisters and brothers. Then Dad heard that Mrs B. would be able to look after us, and we love Mrs B.; so we decided not to have any more nannies or au pairs. The only trouble is, now we have to be picked up and dropped home by Duncan's mum instead of an au pair. I like Duncan, he's OK, but... his mum..." Freddie's voice tailed off, then he gave a rather unconvincing nonchalant shrug, adding; "Oh well, we have to put up with it, I suppose."

After saying goodnight to Freddie, Kate went thoughtfully downstairs again, musing on how hard it must have been for Tim in the weeks and months after Claire had been killed, trying to keep some semblance of normality for the children by sending them to school to be with their friends, to take their minds off their loss. And all the time having to cope with his own heartbreak. Mrs B. must have seemed like a godsend.

Going back into the family room, Kate picked up her sketchbook and began some rough drawings which incorporated spirals and segmented forms. She was so absorbed that she didn't hear the sound of the key in the front door or notice that Binky had got up and padded into the hall, and was startled when Tim and Elaine appeared in the doorway of the room. She jumped up.

"Sorry, I didn't hear you come in," she said, rather flustered. "Did you have a good dinner?"

"Yes, the food was excellent," Tim said. "Everything OK?"

"Absolutely fine. We too dined in a restaurant. The Magical Castle Restaurant. I can recommend the food, it was delicious!"

Tim laughed. "I must try it sometime."

"And Freddie's done his homework," Kate added, putting away her pencils.

"Been drawing?" Tim asked, looking over her shoulder.

"Yes, Freddie showed me his fossils and they've given me some ideas," Kate murmured, closing the sketchbook. "They're just scribblings."

Elaine had picked up the drawing of Freddie on the table. She felt a stab of envy when she saw the lively sketch, instantly recognisable as Freddie. So, now she's worming her way even further into their lives by doing drawings of the children, she thought, resentment welling up in her, the ambience of the intimate dinner with Tim in the softly lit restaurant evaporating swiftly. Tim saw her holding the drawing and, taking it from her, let out a low whistle of appreciation.

"It's Freddie!" he exclaimed. "Bloody good likeness. And you've really captured his... his... Freddieness! Have you given it to him?"

"Yes, it's only a quick sketch. Well, I'll be off." Kate looked around for her coat, then realised she'd left it on the coat stand by the front door.

"Listen, you must let me pay you the normal babysitting rate," Tim said, half embarrassed to mention money, but not wanting to take advantage of a struggling artist.

"No, no, I wouldn't dream of it!" Kate put up her hand in protest. "Anyway, I had a free dinner at the best restaurant in Surrey!"

"Well, I'll pay you in kind. We'll be round with the chainsaw to help Bill with the woodcutting operations tomorrow afternoon. Don't forget the clocks go back tonight, so we better start early. We'll be round about two."

Hearing this exchange between Kate and Tim increased Elaine's irritation. So Tim was going to be chopping wood for the wretched girl now! She turned to go into the kitchen, saying pointedly over her shoulder; "I'll make us that coffee, Tim. Goodnight, er..."

"Kate," supplied Kate, guessing correctly that Elaine could perfectly well remember her name.

She walked down the hall and retrieved her coat from the coat stand. Tim, following her, paused at the kitchen door. "Elaine, I'm just going to see Kate to her door. It's pretty dark out there," he said, and without waiting for an answer, he helped Kate into her coat and opened the front door.

"Honestly, there's no need," Kate protested.

"Nonsense! I'm sure it's perfectly safe, but I'm not letting you go wandering off into the night on your own. Anyway, it's pitch dark. Wait, I'll get a torch." He went back and grabbed a torch from the hall table and, calling to Binky, he pulled the door to and walked in front of her to the front gate, followed by the dog. As they came out into the lane, Kate stumbled on the rough ground and Tim took her arm to steady her. They started down the lane, the oval shape of the torchlight bobbing on the ground in front of them, Binky loping along beside them and Tim's arm still linked in hers. Kate felt a strange sense of contentment, of being somewhere she was meant to be. She was silent, not wanting to break the spell. Tim also said nothing and, too soon, they arrived at the gate of Lavender Cottage.

"Thanks for walking me back." Kate turned to him, just making out his face in the darkness.

"Thank *you,*" Tim said. He bent and kissed her on the cheek. "I'll see you tomorrow."

Kate turned and walked down the path to her door. Before she shut it behind her, she looked back. Tim was still standing at the gate and raised a hand in a wave. She waved back and closed the door, leaning against it for a moment, till her heart rate calmed down.

The woodcutting got under way the next afternoon. Tim and the children arrived at the door with Tim's chainsaw and a large axe, accompanied by Binky who was leaping about in the hope that another walk was in the offing. Tim had on a shapeless, tweed jacket, stout boots and a terrible old hat which he tipped as Kate opened the door.

"Art'ernoon, Miss," he said in a gruff voice, which made Amy giggle. "Want any wood sawing up? I've got a good team 'ere, an'...

88

ah!" He glanced down the lane at Bill Babbidge making his way towards them, pushing a barrow in which were his own chainsaw and axe. 'Ere's the guv'nor just comin' now, to direct operations."

Laughing, Kate led them round the side of the house to the where the dead elm lay half in the ditch at the end of the garden. Tim and Bill got sawing while the children and Kate, who had been put on log gathering detail, ferried the smaller logs from the branches to the lean-to log store against the outside of the kitchen wall, where Kate stacked them neatly. The larger ones would have to be split with the axe into smaller pieces before they could be moved. Soon, a sizeable pile was building up.

Halfway through the afternoon, Kate went in and made a large pot of tea. She had nipped out to the supermarket in the morning and stocked up on teacakes, which she toasted and buttered and took out to the garden. They sat on logs, munching on the teacakes, and drinking tea and Ribena. The children's cheeks were rosy with the exercise and the chilly wind which had started up, blustering in the poplars towering overhead, the last few leaves still clinging to the outermost twigs like filigree fringing. Bill sat sipping his tea, his flat cap pulled down over his bald head, while Tim, cradling his mug, stole a glance at Kate as she sat chatting to Freddie and Amy. He thought how young she looked. More like the children's sister than... Than what? he asked himself. How old was she? Twenty-two, twenty-three? That would make her fifteen years younger than himself. He was too old for her. And yet...

Kate looked up and their eyes locked for a moment, then Tim gave himself a mental shake and stood up. "Right, stand well back folks, the Mighty Quinn is going to do some log splitting."

By the time the short autumn day was drawing to an end, the tree was sawn up and most of the bigger pieces had been split and stowed away. What could not fit into the log store, they took and stacked in the corner by the fireplace.

"If you see any woodlice crawling out, don't kill them, will you?" Freddie said to Kate. "Just take them outside."

"I'll try," Kate said. "If they don't curl up in a ball and roll away."

89

Back outside, she looked round at them all affectionately as they stood lit by the last rays of the setting sun. "Thank you all so much. Now I won't freeze to death in the winter." She gave Bill a hug and, turning to Tim, said earnestly: "If you ever need a babysitter, you have only to give me a shout. Or if Mrs B. can't be there when the children get home from school." She turned back to Bill. "Just tell her to let me know if she needs me to do anything."

"I will, love," Bill said, patting her on the arm. "Oh, you can tell her yourself - here she is."

Lily had come around the side of the house, clutching her coat round her against the wind.

"Just came to say the supper's in the oven, Tim. Steak pie, and there's a trifle in the fridge. How have you got on? Ooh, it's cold out here and it's getting dark. Come on, Bill; you don't want your chest playing up, standing about in this wind."

"Yes, sergeant," Bill grinned, making a mock salute. He loaded his chainsaw and axe into the barrow, grasped the handles and, with a cheery wave, trundled off in the wake of his wife round the side of the house.

"I hope he hasn't overdone it," Kate said anxiously when they had gone. "He's getting on a bit, but he wouldn't stop until he'd sawn up the whole thing."

"He'll be fine," Tim assured her. "He's a tough old boy, for all his roly-polyness. He's got stronger hands than I have."

"I don't know... your log splitting was pretty impressive," Kate said. "I hope *you* haven't strained anything."

Tim flexed his arms. "The old muscles may be a bit stiff tomorrow, but nothing too bad. Well team, we'd better be getting home." He picked up the heavy chainsaw and the axe.

"Thank you again," Kate said. "And thank you Freddie and Amy, for all your help."

When they too had disappeared round the side of the house, Kate surveyed the neat pile of logs stacked by the kitchen door with a sense of satisfaction. Then she went inside, shutting out the cold, windy, autumn evening.

Chapter VI

The weather turned much colder that week. Kate tried not to light the fire until the evenings, making do with the electric heater on a low setting during the day, though she still worried about the amount of electricity she was using. From Lily Babbidge, she found out the name of a coal merchant, and ordered five bags of coal to be delivered, since the logs seemed to burn down very fast on their own. The cost made her blanch a bit, and she worried about how long her great aunt's bequest of £20,000 would last, what with council tax and other utility bills. She would have to hope that at least some of her paintings sold when the show finally opened.

Having taken the middle panel as far as she could without Annie being there, Kate started on the first panel of the triptych, working from the photographs she had taken. It was not ideal, however, so she was overjoyed when, on the Wednesday morning, Annie appeared at the door, on her own.

"Do you want me to sit for you today?" she asked. "Vince said he was going to be out all day and Magda said she could have Darren for a couple of hours. I've just dropped Becky off at nursery."

"Oh yes! Brilliant!" Kate drew her into the little sitting room. "I've just got to a point where I really need you to be here."

Annie had thoughtfully put on the same clothes she had worn on her previous visit. Kate lost no time in setting up the glass and positioning Annie where she wanted her. Soon she was lost in the painting, her eyes darting from Annie to the canvas and back again. Annie stood, motionless and quiet and Kate got the feeling she was almost revelling in just being able to be still for a moment, without the kids grizzling or Vince berating her about something. But her thin body remained tense, as though she knew she was doing something that would enrage Vince if he found out, and that she was still in a trap from which she did not have the means to escape.

After what she thought must be over an hour and a half, with a few five-minute breaks, she stirred and said apologetically, "What time is it, Kate? I'll have to go and get Darren. Magda's got to go to work at eleven."

"Oh God! I'm so sorry Annie, I completely forgot the time." Kate glanced at her watch. It's nearly twenty to eleven. Have you got time for a quick coffee?"

"No thanks, I better be off. It'll take me ten minutes to walk back."

"Well, you must take this. I wish it could be more." Kate pressed a ten-pound note into Annie's hand. Annie protested, but Kate was adamant. In the end, Annie tucked the note away deep in her pocket, to add it to the small but growing "emergency" hoard she had been saving for months.

By the end of the week, working solidly every day, Kate was ready to start on the third panel. This was going to be the most difficult. She wanted to have Annie's face emerging through the glass, which melted away from her face, almost as though it was coming through a barrier of water. She needed a mannequin to stand in for Annie, which she was sure she could get on eBay. But for that she needed a Wi-Fi connection for her mobile, something that the cottage did not have.

That evening, after she had seen the lights of Tim's car going past the gate, she walked up to the Crawfords' house and Tim, hearing her problem, willingly gave her his Wi-Fi number so that she could use her phone to connect to the internet. She soon located a mannequin on eBay that she thought looked most like Annie and ordered it, as well as a long light brown wig.

As Tim saw her to the door he seemed to be about to say something, but Freddie came charging down the stairs, closely followed by Amy, and the resulting flurry of conversation and Kate's departure soon after, prevented him.

Within two days, the bulky box containing the mannequin arrived on Kate's doorstep. Excitedly, she took it upstairs and dressed it in a red jumper and long brown skirt and put the wig on its head. She laid it in the bath and ran the water until it was halfway up the face, the water being an approximation of the wavy glass she had used for the other panels. It looked rather macabre, with the face and one hand emerging from the water and the hair floating out round the face. Kate had wanted the painting to give the impression of someone breaking out into freedom, rather than a drowning woman reaching out for succour. But then she stopped and thought, *Maybe it could be ambiguous. Maybe it could mean either*.

There was no room to set up the easel and the large canvas in the cramped little bathroom, so she took several photographs and then got her sketchbook and did some watercolour sketches, feeling like John Everett Millais painting Elizabeth Siddal in the bath for his painting, *Ophelia*.

"At least mannequins can't catch pneumonia," she thought wryly.

This third panel proved to be a real challenge. To get the effects Kate wanted was no easy task. First she had to adapt the horizontal position of the mannequin, so that it seemed to be standing upright. She worked and re-worked the image until she began to capture the effect she was trying to achieve - Annie's face and hand emerging into clarity, with the rest of the body still seemingly behind the glass, blurred and distorted. But she really needed Annie to come back for a final session.

By mid-November, Kate had done all she could to the triptych without another sitting with Annie. She had hoped to bump into Annie in the village shop, but there was no sign of her, and she dared not go to her house. However, one rainy afternoon, hearing a knock, Kate opened the door to find Magda McLeary standing under the little porch roof, shaking the rain off an umbrella as she collapsed it.

"Magda!" Kate exclaimed, surprised, then suddenly apprehensive. "Is Annie alright? Come in. Gosh, it's tipping down."

Magda left the umbrella propped by the front door and stepped down into the sitting room, wiping her soaking shoes on the rug just inside the door.

"Annie's OK, but Vince knocked her about a bit because little Becky said something about a drawing she had done at the 'painting lady's house'."

"Oh my God!" Kate cried, horrified that she had been the trigger for Vince's violence.

Magda put a hand on her arm. "Don't blame yourself, love. If it wasn't that it would have been something else that set him off. Anyway, Annie enjoys sitting for you. Gave her quite a boost, that someone saw something interesting in her. I've just been doing the cleaning at Tim's, and stopped by to tell you that Vince told Annie he would be out all day tomorrow, so I said I'd have Darren for a couple of hours again while Becky was at nursery. Do you want her to sit for you again?"

"Yes, I do need her at least one more time," Kate replied eagerly, but added anxiously, "But only if Vince doesn't find out and beats her again."

"No reason why he should, if the kids don't know, they can't spill the beans." She paused, glancing towards the easel in the corner of the room. "Can I see the painting?"

"Of course." Kate went over and pulled out the first two panels, the last one being still on the easel." It's three paintings actually - a sort of triptych."

Magda stood looking at the paintings thoughtfully. Finally, she said quietly, "That's Annie's life alright. I've always felt that she was trapped in that relationship and wished she could be free, either by Vince going off for good or that she and the kids could get away somehow." She looked again at the third panel. "The effect of her face and hand coming through the glass - or is it water? It makes me think of a butterfly coming out of its chrysalis. Or a bird breaking out of its shell." She paused, her broad, strong face troubled. "But she has nowhere to go. It's no good her coming to me or anywhere Vince can find her, and she has no family that she knows of. She was in foster care most of her childhood. Then she gets into this situation and doesn't know how to get out. I've told her about women's refuges, but she doesn't want to live anywhere else. It's the only place that she's ever been able to call home and, anyway a refuge would not be a long-term solution."

Kate thought of her good fortune in having been left Lavender Cottage, so that she could escape a relationship which, though in no way comparable to Annie's abusive one, was nevertheless restrictive in a different way. It wouldn't be a solution to ask Annie to come to stay with her temporarily. If Vince found out, which he probably would, she shuddered to think what he would do.

Magda interrupted her thoughts. "Well, I'll tell her to come along after she's dropped Becky off, shall I?"

"Yes, thanks. Look, let me give you my mobile number," Kate said, scribbling it on a piece of paper. "In case you need to contact me."

Magda took a last look at the painting on the easel. "Let's hope your painting comes true," she added, as she turned to leave.

When Annie arrived the next morning, she still had the traces of a cut lip and a bruised cheekbone.

Seeing Kate's concerned expression as she opened the door to her, Annie said, "You know about Vince hitting me." It was more of a statement than a question.

"Yes, Magda told me - well, she more or less had to. And, Annie, I'm so sorry."

"Don't blame yourself. I enjoy sitting for you. Really."

Getting down to the painting, Kate found herself incorporating the tell-tale signs of violence into the painting of Annie's face emerging from the glass, feeling a little ghoulish to be doing so, but thinking that they told their own story.

By the time Annie had to go, Kate felt that she had enough to be able to carry on without Annie having to be there. Annie stood looking at the painting, noticing the cut lip and the bruising.

She touched her face. "You've put the marks in."

"Yes, I hope you don't mind."

"Well, it's the truth, isn't it?"

Kate nodded. "It is. I hope to God he doesn't find out about today."

But as Annie hurried out of Tuckers Lane and crossed the road, a dirty white van was approaching from the right. The ferrety man at the wheel muttered to the bull terrier sitting beside him on the passenger seat,

"Oi, oi, that's Vince's Annie. Where's she been, scurrying along like that? And without the kids too. Vince'll want to know about this."

That night Kate slept fitfully and towards morning she woke from a deeply disturbing dream. She had dreamed she was in a room with curved, windowless, white walls, which seemed to have blood vessels snaking across them. Her feet were entangled in something and looking down, she saw that thick sinewy tendrils were wrapping themselves around her ankles and feet. The tendrils started winding up her body, trapping her arms and the more she struggled, the tighter the sinews became. Gradually, she realised that it was not herself that was trapped, but that she could see a shadowy figure tangled in the white strands, a figure which seemed to be screaming soundlessly. And then she was receding from the figure, which got smaller and smaller with distance. She woke with a start, the horror of the dream still a palpable presence. The first streaks of dawn gleamed through the tossing bare branches of the poplars beyond the window and the wind sobbed in the chimney. She snuggled down under the covers again, but the dream had woken her thoroughly.

She got up, shivering in the cold bedroom, and went downstairs to get a coffee to warm herself up.

Standing at the window of the small sitting room, warming her hands round her coffee mug, she kept re-living the dream. The figure had seemed to be in a curved, enclosed space; organic, like a womb or an egg. Magda's words came back to her, about the third panel reminding her of a bird breaking out of its shell. Only, in her dream there had been no breaking out. The figure had remained trapped. She put the coffee mug down and pulled out one of the canvases Bill had made for her. Still in her pyjamas and a thick, old cardigan, she began to sketch in the main compositional elements of a new painting.

An hour later, her mobile rang. It was Magda.

"Kate, love, it's about Annie. Vince found out about her coming to sit for you. He came back drunk last night and knocked her about something awful. I heard all the commotion and Mike and I went round there. He was in a terrible strop and poor Annie's got another black eye

96

and a cut head where he banged her against the door frame. Mike called the police and they came and hauled Vince off and put him in a cell for the night. I'm round at Annie's house at the moment, but she's refusing to go to the hospital to get them to look at the cut on her head, and now she's saying she's not going to press charges. So they'll have to let him go." Magda spoke in her usual calm voice, but Kate could sense the anger behind her words.

"Oh my God! It's all my fault. How did he find out about her coming here?"

"That Reg Perkins, Vince's friend, saw her coming away from your house and he told Vince. Vince hit her till she told him where she'd been."

"Magda, I'm coming round now," Kate said, horrified at the turn of events. "We must persuade her to go to a women's refuge until the council can rehouse her. Surely she doesn't mean to stay with Vince after this?"

"I wish I could be sure. She seems to think he'll come and find her wherever she is. And Kate," she added, "can you bring your camera? I want to take pictures of her in this state. For evidence."

"I will, but I'm sure the police will take photos anyway."

"Yes, you're probably right. Well, see you shortly."

"Yes, see you in a few minutes."

When Kate got to Annie's house, she saw a police car parked beside the gate. Mike was coming out of Magda's house next door. He greeted her over the fence.

"Hi, Kate. Mam's next door with Annie. There's a policewoman there now. We all gave statements to the police last night, but I think they're deciding what Annie better do now."

"Thanks Mike, I'll go in and see Annie. I feel terrible she was beaten up because of me."

When Kate rang Annie's doorbell, Magda let her in and led her to the kitchen. Annie was sitting at the kitchen table with the little boy Darren on her knee. The young policewoman stood with a notebook in her hand, leaning against the sink. She acknowledged Kate with a wave of her pen.

Annie's face was a mess. One eye was swollen nearly shut and the cut on her lip had opened up again. She had obviously made an effort to wash the blood off her head, but some was still visible matting the hair just above her temple. Becky was standing clinging on to her mother's arm and sucking her thumb. Both children seemed subdued and cowed.

Seeing Kate, Annie made a gesture as though to cover her eye, but realising the futility of it, she dropped her hand back onto the table. Kate went over to her and put her arm round her thin shoulders.

"Annie, this is all my fault," she said wretchedly. "I'm so sorry. If I hadn't…"

"No, no. I didn't have to sit for you. I wanted to," Annie said. "And you paid me. Vince would have found some other reason to lash out. He usually does when he's drunk. It's just a bit worse than usual this time."

"Annie, you can't stay with him. If he…think of the children."

The policewoman looked up from her notebook and addressed Kate. "You must be the artist she was sitting for. Have you come across Vince Dobbs?"

"I've met him once." Kate looked at Annie, then back to the policewoman. "Don't you think Annie ought to go to a safe house or something? She can't stay here with that man!"

The policewoman also glanced at Annie. "She's a bit stubborn! Wouldn't come to the police station last night to get checked over or go to the hospital, won't press charges against Dobbs. I'm trying to persuade her to go to Prestley House. It's a women's refuge not far from here. Just for a while, till they can find somewhere else for her and the kids. And she really needs to have that cut on her head looked at."

"But I like it *here*. I like the village and Becky's settled at nursery. And Vince'll kill me if I leave. He'll come and find me!" Annie's voice rose in distress and tears sprang to her eyes. Becky buried her face against her mother's arm and Annie, with an effort, said more calmly, "He'll get over it. He calms down and he's not too bad when things are going well for him - if he's won on the dogs or something…"

The policewoman interrupted her. "You could just go to Prestley House for a little while. It may be that you could come back here and we could put a restraining order on your - husband? - to keep away from you."

Magda gave a snort. "That's not going to stop him turning up one night and lamming her again."

"We're not married," Annie said, dully. "Never got round to it somehow." She sighed, putting her arm round her little girl and holding both the children close. "Well, I suppose we could go to this place for a while. I don't want the kids frightened like that again."

"Good," the policewoman said. "I'll just contact the refuge, make sure they have a room for you. You'd better pack a bag. Take stuff for the children, toys, nappies, if he's still in them." She gestured towards the little boy, then went outside to make some phone calls.

Annie sat the toddler down on the ground and stood up, wincing slightly, holding on to the table to steady herself. She put on a bright smile and said to Becky, "Come on, love, we're going on a little holiday. Let's go and pack your things." She turned to Magda. "Could you watch Darren for me?"

"Of course, dear. I'll make us all a nice cuppa in the meanwhile."

Before Annie went upstairs, Kate touched her arm gently. "Annie, will you let me take some photos of you – as evidence, just in case you change your mind about pressing charges?"

Annie's hands shot up to her face. "Oh Kate, I don't know. I'd rather not!"

Magda interrupted in a quiet but firm voice. "Annie love, it's just in case. Please let her."

Annie dropped her hands resignedly and Kate took a number of pictures of Annie's damaged face and a huge bruise on her arm. Then Annie took Becky's hand and went up to pack a bag.

Kate kept the little boy occupied while Magda made the tea, giving a mug to the police officer when she came back into the kitchen.

"It's all arranged. They've got space at the refuge. I'll run her there now." She added in a low voice, "It happens so often, the wife…or

99

partner...refuses to press charges. Scared of repercussions... or scared of change...whatever reason, and the abuser often gets off scot-free." Seeing the camera in Kate's hand, she added, "Been taking photos of her?" Kate nodded.

"No need, I was about to do just that."

Magda said, "Can we go and see her at the refuge?"

"Yes, I'll give you the address. But keep it absolutely secret. Don't let Dobbs get hold of it."

She scribbled the address on her pad and tore off the sheet, handing it to Magda. "Men are not allowed to visit, by the way."

When Annie came back down, lugging a bulging holdall, followed by Becky clutching a teddy, Magda made her sit down to drink her tea and eat a couple of biscuits, which she did with some difficulty, through her swollen lips. Then the police constable, who they discovered was called Jane Leadbury, said briskly to Annie, "I'll just take some photos of your injuries, then we'd better be off. We had to release Dobbs this morning. He was picked up by one of his mates. He would normally have been released last night, since you didn't press charges, but we kept him in till we had a chance to get you to safety. He's likely to turn up here at any moment. We've got to get you away before that. I do advise you to press charges, so that we can recommend to the Crown Prosecution Service that a criminal prosecution for Actual Bodily Harm be brought against Dobbs. You should also apply for a civil injunction to stop him coming near you."

Annie looked dubious and confused at the same time, but made no comment other than, "I'll think about it."

"Don't leave it too long," the policewoman cautioned. "The sooner you do it the better."

For the second time, Annie's injuries were photographed, after which the policewoman indicated that they should leave.

Kate hugged Annie, carefully, in view of her injuries. "Magda and I will come and see you," she said, her own eyes welling with tears at the sight of the forlorn little family, forced to leave their house.

Annie took her hand in both hers. "Promise you won't blame yourself. Maybe it's good that it's out in the open now. It's been going on

100

for years." She turned to Magda. "I'm ever so worried about you and Mike. Vince's bound to know it was Mike who called the police. Vince might come round and..."

Magda gave a short derisive laugh. "I'd like to see him try anything. Mike's a 5th Dan Karate black belt." She squared her shoulders and crossed her strong arms. "And I reckon I can give as good as I get. Just let him try!"

The policewoman ushered Annie and the children out to the police car. Kate and Magda followed, Magda carrying Annie's holdall, which the policewoman stowed in the boot. They stood watching as Annie and the children got in the car. As it pulled away, they saw Annie's poor battered face looking back at them and at the house as she gave a little wave.

No sooner had the police car vanished around the corner, when a dirty white van turned into the road and drew up at Annie's gate. It had barely stopped moving when the passenger door opened and Vince Dobbs leapt out and came storming towards them. He was unshaven, dressed in grubby jeans and T-shirt and had a can of lager in his hand, which he drained, then proceeded to crush before throwing it down on the pavement. He approached them menacingly as they stood by Magda's gate.

"I've just seen Annie being driven off in a cop car. Where the hell have they taken 'er?" he shouted, bunching his fists and coming so close that they could smell his sweat and the beer on his breath. The driver of the van slid out and came to stand next to Vince, the eyes in his ferrety face darting between the two women.

"Never you mind Vince Dobbs. Somewhere you can't knock the living daylights out of her," Magda said, looking squarely at him, her arms folded.

"And what's it got to do with you, you interfering cow?" Vince snarled. His eyes swivelled to Kate. "Or you? What the fuck are you doing 'ere? It's all because of you, with your arty farty crap, that she's been getting ideas. Why don't you mind you own fucking business?"

Kate felt her heart pounding against her ribs, but she drew herself up to her full height, though that was not saying much, she thought ruefully, and gave him a steady stare.

"All she was doing was sitting for me. That's hardly a crime."

"What do you want to paint a scrawny ratbag like 'er for anyway?"

"She's not a scrawny ratbag. She's got a lovely face, or she did before you got to work on it."

Vince took a step towards her, a murderous expression on his face.

Magda put a warning hand on Kate's shoulder. "I think you'd better be off, love," she said quietly. "There's nothing more you can do here. I'll give you a ring later."

"But you... He might..." She glanced at Vince.

"I'll be fine. He won't dare try anything. We've got witnesses!" She swept her arm up and down the street. It being a Saturday, there were a number of people around. In several of the houses, curtains twitched and people stood watching at their gates, curious as to the circumstances of this particular "domestic". Mike emerged from his house and joined Magda and Kate, looking steadily at Vince, with his hands casually in his pockets.

The ferrety man stepped up and grabbed Vince's arm. "She's right, mate. I'm not going to make a habit of picking you up from police stations. I like to stay as far away from 'em as possible."

Vince grunted. "I'll find 'er. I'll find 'er and make 'er come home. Who's going to cook me dinner now?" He turned away, muttering under his breath to his companion.

Magda walked with Kate to her car, murmuring: "Could we go and see Annie tomorrow? I don't have to work till the afternoon."

"Yes, we'll go in my car. Do you know where the refuge is?"

"Not exactly, but I know the road on the address. Mike could run us there if you like."

"No, that's fine, I'll drive us there. I'll pick you up about ten?"

That agreed, Kate got in the car and started the engine, aware that the two men were still standing on the pavement a few yards away. She drove the short distance to the end of the cul-de-sac where she could turn and as she drove back past, she caught a strange expression on Vince's face as he peered into the car at her. It was an expression that sent a cold shiver down her spine. His lips were twisted into a half snarl, half leer, and his eyes were narrowed as though a particularly unpleasant thought had just occurred to him.

It was just as well she didn't hear what he muttered to his friend, as the two men turned away and went down the path to the house.

"Seems like little miss arty-pants needs to be taught a lesson about interfering in other people's business. And I know just the sort of lesson I could give 'er, if you get my meaning." He glanced sideways at his scrawny companion, who sniggered knowingly as he shut the door.

*

The next morning, Kate and Magda found the refuge without trouble. The woman who opened the door asked several questions of them before she would let them in. Then they had to wait in the hallway while she went to speak to Annie. "OK, you can go up. Sorry, but we have to be careful." She smiled, "First door on the left."

Annie was delighted to see them. Her face, if anything, looked worse than the previous day. The bruising had come out fully, and the whole of her eye and cheekbone were a purplish blue. Her cut lip was still swollen, and her hair still had traces of blood caked in it.

"Oh, I'm so glad to see you," Annie cried, a quiver in her voice. "They're very nice here, but they're all strangers."

Kate looked around. The room was a reasonable size, containing two single beds, a cot, a wardrobe and a chest with a mirror on it and a couple of chairs. There was a wash basin in one corner. The two children were playing on the floor, Becky trying to do a jigsaw, and Darren immediately taking it to bits again, which was causing some conflict.

"I promised them I would take them down to the playroom later. They're getting a bit bored up here." Annie said, taking some clothes off the chairs so that they could sit down.

Magda went across, and tipping Annie's face up, said, "Has anyone had a look at this eye? And I'm sure you need a stitch or two in that head wound."

103

"Oh, it'll be fine. I just don't want to wash my hair yet, in case it starts bleeding again."

"What happens now?" Kate asked. "How long can you stay here?"

"They said I can stay until they can arrange for accommodation for me, or else I'll go home and they'll get a restraining order on Vince to keep him away from the house. I'll have to pay rent here, but they'll arrange benefits for me, so I can pay."

"What do you do about meals?" Magda asked, picking up Darren, so that his sister could do her jigsaw in peace, and sitting down beside Annie on the bed.

"We all share the kitchen, and we can make our own meals, or we make enough for everyone to share. And we have to share the bathrooms as well." She stopped, the tears she had been holding back suddenly spilling down her cheeks. "I wish we could be back in our own house. I know we're safe here, and everyone is so kind, but..."

Magda put her arm round Annie. "But don't you want them to re-house you somewhere Vince can't find you?" The little boy reached out for his mother, and Annie took him from Magda and hugged him close.

"I'd rather come back home. I'd hate not having you next door, Mags, and I'd have to get Becky into a new school. It's not right that I should have to be the one to leave." She dabbed her eyes with a crumpled tissue and looked at Magda. "But he's there, isn't he? I saw him coming back in Reg Perkins' van as we were leaving yesterday. He gave me such a filthy look."

"Yes, he's there. We had a few words! He tried to find out where they'd taken you." Magda paused. "Anyway, I think you'd better stay here for a while, till we get things sorted out. But if you do come back, they can get a protection order issued, to make him keep away from you and the kids."

"They'd have to get him out of the house first." Kate put in. "That might not be easy."

"Well, I know it's not the same situation, but after my Jim died, I got an occupational order, and I was allowed to stay on in the house, so you should be able to stay if Vince was ordered out," Magda said. "I still don't

104

think any court order will keep him away though."

There was a knock, and the woman who had let them in put her head round the door. "You can take them down to the kitchen and give them a cup of tea, love," she said to Annie.

Thanking her, Annie stood up and led them down to the kitchen. There they met two other women who greeted them with friendly smiles. But Kate noticed the same haunted quality in their faces that she had seen in Annie's.

Back at home later that day, Annie's situation continued to prey on Kate's mind. She could not help thinking that Annie would still be in her own home if she, Kate, hadn't wanted to paint her. Yes, she was safe for the time being from the physical and emotional abuse, but she still seemed to be trapped in another kind of cage. One in which she had to remain if she and the children were to be safe. She had sensed a quiet desperation in Annie that recalled the dream she had had the night before.

She lit the fire and went and stood in front of the painting she had begun that morning. Then, taking up her brushes, she began to paint. The evening started to draw in and she turned on the light, leaving the curtains open as usual. Drawn curtains always made her feel slightly claustrophobic, and she was not overlooked by any houses.

The tall poplars, almost leafless now, stood sentinel in the field beyond the garden, and a frost had begun to rime the dry grasses and the hedgerows. It was very still.

The warm light of the sitting room shone out into the darkness, with Kate standing painting near the window.

It was quite late before the shadowy figure which had been standing unseen in the field on the other side of the fence, turned and left its vantage point opposite the window, and made its way back out of the field and into the dark lane.

*

105

Kate turned the car into Tuckers Lane, her mood much lighter than it had been of late. She and Magda had just been to see Annie again and with each visit Annie's face had looked better. The bruising had faded considerably and her head wound, which had had to be stitched after all, was healing well. Only the cut on her lip still looked very sore, Annie complaining that it kept splitting again every time she smiled. And she *was* smiling more. She had made some friends at the safe house and they all seemed to get on well as a little community, sharing the cooking and other chores, and helping to look after each other's children. Kate also gave Annie the photographs she had had developed of Annie's bruised face, in case they were needed in the future.

As she rounded the bend in the lane and the cottage came into view, she was surprised to see a large, blue van parked on the verge outside the gate. She pulled up behind it and as she got out, she saw through the overgrown hedge, a figure coming back down the path from the front door. Jake! He must have bought himself a van.

She opened the gate and stood looking at him in astonishment. One part of her was actually quite pleased to see him. She had been leading a fairly solitary existence lately. She had seen nothing of Tim and his family since she had asked to use his Wi-Fi connection and apart from her visits to Annie with Magda, she had hardly spoken to a soul except the people in the shop and a telephone conversation with her father up in Yorkshire. She had been working almost constantly, but she knew that any chance of doing more that afternoon had now evaporated.

She found her voice. "Jake! What are you doing here?"

"I've come to abduct you, kid. I want you to see the pods in situ and I thought you'd probably procrastinate and make excuses if I phoned, so I thought I'd just come and carry you off."

"How did you know where I live?"

"I bumped into Mimi in the pub last night. I had to nag her a bit. She didn't know if she should give me your address, but I said I was sure you would want to see my stuff in the gallery of the mighty Straker."

"Well, yes, I do. Of course I do. I was going to come up soon anyway, once I'd rung you and found out if it was installed. Did it go

106

smoothly?"

"A few hitches. The movement sensor of one of the pods wasn't working. Then the sound system in another, etc. I've had to get my electrical guy along several times to troubleshoot. Bloody visiting public keep touching the things." He changed the subject. "Like the van?"

"Yes, it's…big. Is it yours?"

"Yeah. I really needed it to hump stuff about. Got a good deal on it. It's only four years old." He glanced towards the cottage. "Well, aren't you going to show me round your country residence?"

"Yes, of course, come in Jake." She led the way down the brick path to the front door, wishing the garden wasn't so bedraggled-looking. "Don't look at the garden. I haven't got round to tackling it yet," she said, unlocking the door and stepping down into the sitting room. Jake followed, dipping his head to get his tall frame under the lintel. He stopped and looked around the room, taking in the inglenook fireplace, the sagging sofa and chair, his gaze coming to rest on the large painting on the easel.

He stood staring at it for a long moment. The predominant colour of the painting was an icy blue-white, deepening into shadow at the edges, as though the sides were closing in. In the centre, a shadowy figure seemed to be suspended in space, entangled in membrane-like strands, which stretched to the sides of the illusion of curved space within the picture. The figure was a blackish red, with vestigial features, and the mouth seemed to be open in a silent scream. Thin red lines, like blood vessels, snaked round the curved walls. Winding among the membranes, written in black paint, were the words - *Quiet shell - now I know- what the bird in the egg must undergo.*

"What's all this about?" Jake wanted to know, stepping back to view the painting from further away. "Bit of a departure for you. A bit psycho!" Not waiting for a reply, his gaze shifted to the canvases propped in the corner. He pulled out the last panel of the triptych.

Kate had been standing somewhat uncertainly near the fireplace, anxious, in spite of herself, that he should not be dismissive of the new paintings. She came forward and pulled out the other two panels. "It's a

107

triptych. They go in this order." She lined them up against the wall and stood back so that he could see. Jake stood looking at the triptych through slightly narrowed eyes, his face giving nothing away. Finally, he turned to her. "Explain," he demanded. But before she could answer, continued; "I mean, I can see that it's someone breaking through a barrier, maybe breaking free. But is it imagined or is it someone real?"

"It's someone real. She's called Annie." Kate found herself telling Jake about Annie's situation, trapped in the destructive relationship with Vince Dobbs. When she had finished, Jake nodded. "I suppose that's why they work. They ring true."

Kate knew that for Jake that was high praise indeed and couldn't help feeling gratified. Whatever else he was, she knew Jake was artistically brilliant and she valued his opinion. He even said he liked the painting of the poplars through the window, approving of her treatment of light and the tonal contrast of the window frame.

"Well, who's been a busy little beaver, eh?" Jake said finally, sprawling on the sofa and adding, "Listen, kid, it's a bit late to go back to London today. Can I crash out here, and we can go up in the morning?"

Kate hesitated. "Yes, I...I suppose so. We can have baked beans on toast and I might have a bottle of wine somewhere."

"Great! It'll be like old times!"

Kate wanted to say; "Not quite like old times." She wasn't sure how she was going to handle things when it was time to go to bed, but she put off thinking about that for the time being and said nothing.

"Show me the rest of the house, then maybe we can go out for a drink," Jake said, standing up. "What do they do on a Friday night around here? I thought I saw a pub up the road."

"Yes, there's one in the village, by the green. The Jolly Farmer."

Kate led the way up the little staircase and showed Jake the bedrooms and bathroom. He had to duck his head to go through the doors and he seemed to take up most of the space in the small rooms.

"Very quaint," he said. "But I think I would brain myself regularly on all these beams and low door frames if I lived here." Kate saw him glancing at the bed in her room and her heart sank.

"Let's go to the pub," she said briskly, starting downstairs again. "We'll go in Trog."

As they walked into the pub, Kate saw Mike sitting at the bar with a pint talking to Dave who was serving behind the counter. They both greeted her, giving Jake the once over as he came up to them.

Kate introduced them. "Jake, this is Mike and that's Dave. Jake's popped down from London, so I thought I'd show him my local."

"Hi, Jake. You an artist too?"

"Yeah. Sculptor. How about you?"

"I work at the garage." Mike turned to Kate. "Car behaving itself?"

"Going like a dream, touch wood." Kate turned to Jake. "Mike sorted out Trog's spark plugs."

"How are Mimi and the others?" Mike asked, a gleam of interest in his eye.

"Fine, I think." Kate answered. "I haven't seen them for a while, but I'm going up tomorrow, so I'll probably catch up with them then."

Jake looked puzzled. "How come you know Mimi and co?" he asked Mike.

Kate laughed and answered for him. "Mimi, Grace and Bea suddenly turned up one day, and Mike had booked to pick up my car while they were at the cottage, so Mimi - you know what she's like - decided we should have a house-warming and asked Mike and Dave along!"

"Huh! I didn't get asked to any house-warming party!" Jake said putting on an affronted air.

"It was just an ad hoc thing, impromptu," Kate said. "Come on, what are we drinking?"

Later, back at the cottage, after a supper of beans on toast washed down with a bottle of wine, they sat talking by the fire. "Oh! I haven't told you yet," Jake said. "I've moved flats. Found a place in Hackney, near the studio. It's only five minutes' walk. I'll take you there when we go up. You must come to the studio too. See the new stuff."

"Wow! You've been busy! Did you buy the van before you

109

moved?"

"Yeah. Well, I needed it anyway, but it was very useful for taking all my gear to the new place. I leave it at the studio, since there's nowhere to park near the flat. Parking's included in the studio rent."

Kate asked about Jake's new work and she in turn told him about Zachary, and Geoff agreeing to display some of his pieces at the gallery. "Oh, Jake, before we go tomorrow, can you come and see Zachary's work? You'll love his stuff."

"Yes, we can do that, as long as we get to Straker's by early afternoon."

Looking at Kate, sitting opposite him, her face animated and with the warm glow of the fire glinting on her hair, Jake began to realise that she had changed. She had always been her own person, but now she seemed stronger, more independent. She was slipping away from him and it was his own fault. That morning, waking up in Lucinda's bed, he had felt a sudden need to see Kate. Looking at the sleeping face of the girl next to him, her long blonde hair spread out on the pillow, he realised how much he missed waking to see Kate's crazy, tousled mop beside him, her thick dark eyelashes lying softly on her cheeks as she slept. He compared Lucinda's sophistication and rather aimless existence with Kate's creative fire and passion for her art; a passion he could identify with.

So, he had extricated himself from a party he had been due to go to at the flat of one of Lucinda's friends and had gone in search of Mimi to get her to tell him how to find Kate's cottage.

And now it was getting late. He wanted to take Kate up to bed, but suddenly he felt unsure of himself. It wasn't a sensation he was used to and it threw him. He yawned exaggeratedly and stretched.

"Time for bed, I think," he said, standing up and putting out his hands to pull Kate to her feet.

Kate took his hands and stood up. She faced him squarely, her face lifted up to his.

Softly, she said, "Jake, I need you to sleep on the sofa tonight. It's not right at the moment. I… I'm sort of in a different place. I'm in alone mode. Can you understand?"

Jake looked down at her. He traced her slightly parted lips with his forefinger. Then he bent and kissed them lightly.

"OK kid, it's not what I want, but I was kind of expecting this. You're different somehow. But never say never."

"Thank you, Jake. And yes, never say never."

With that, she found a blanket for him and gave him a hug before going up to bed.

Lying in the darkness, gazing out at the shadowy branches outside the window, Kate knew that her decision to sleep alone was not just because of Jake's cheating ways, not just about the life she now had here in the cottage and the new impetus she had with her work. It was also to do with how she felt about Tim. She told herself yet again that Tim's affections were otherwise engaged, that he and Elaine were an item, that he must be about fifteen years older than herself, that he probably regarded her as some urchin girl, who got on well with his children and was good for babysitting. But she couldn't help remembering, with a lurch of her heart, the way their eyes had met during the woodcutting exercise, that windy, sunny autumn afternoon. And it was Tim's face she saw when she closed her eyes and drifted into sleep.

Chapter VII

When she came down the next morning, Jake was still asleep, his lanky body sprawled out with his head on one arm of the sofa and his feet on the other, the blanket all tangled up around him, and the fire dead in the hearth. She felt a bit guilty, making him sleep in such discomfort, but she knew he had slept in worse places while a student at art school.

He stirred and opened his eyes, yawning massively. Kate bent over the back of the sofa and ruffled his hair. "Were you horribly uncomfortable? And you were probably freezing once the fire died down. You could have put some more logs on."

"I wasn't cold, and I slept like the aforesaid logs." He yawned again. "Any chance of a cup of coffee?"

"Just going to make it. Want some toast?"

"Definitely!"

"With Marmite?"

"You remembered!"

"How could I forget! It hasn't been that long."

"It feels like it. You left a hole in my life by going off like that."

Kate looked at him sitting there, his hair tousled, that blur of blond stubble on his chin and just for a moment, felt her resolve weakening. He must have seen something of it in her face, because he got up and came over to her and put his hands on her shoulders. But the moment had passed. Kate reached up and planted a sisterly kiss on his stubbly cheek and said briskly, "Breakfast. And I must phone Mimi and co. I'll tell them I'm coming up. Maybe they could come and see your pods too."

She went off to the kitchen, and Jake stood for a moment, looking out of the window, his thumbs hooked into the back pockets of his jeans. *She'll come round*, he said to himself. But there was an element of doubt in his mind.

112

Tim stood indecisively in his study, cradling a mug of coffee in his hands. The idea he wanted to put to Kate seemed eminently sensible, but he didn't want to sound patronising or put Kate under any obligation if she accepted his offer. He had not seen anything of her since she had turned up on the doorstep and asked for the use of his Wi-Fi connection and assumed that she was immersed in her painting. Mrs B. had not seen her either, but Tim had been disturbed to hear what Magda had told Mrs B. about the Annie affair. Vince Dobbs sounded a nasty piece of work and he hoped Kate would have no more dealings with him. He wondered if he should nip over to see Kate to tell her his idea, but then he remembered that he had seen a large, blue van parked outside her cottage when he had driven past the night before. It looked as though she had a visitor.

Tim went to the kitchen and put his empty mug on the draining board. Lily was washing a lettuce in the sink and said over her shoulder, "Are you off to do the weekend food shopping now? I've left the list on the table, but I don't know what else you want. There's some salad and quiche you can have for supper, and I'm doing you a steak pie for you to warm up tomorrow. "

"Thanks Mrs B, that's lovely. I'll take the kids to the pub for lunch later, after doing the food shop." He picked up the list, then paused. "Lily, I wanted to ask your advice about something."

Lily glanced at him, her hands still busy washing the lettuce leaves and putting them in a colander. "Yes dear? What about?"

"You know that big loft space over the garage? The people before us used it as an office, but Claire always said it would make an excellent artist's studio, with those big dormer windows."

Lily's face lit up. "Ooh, I know what you're going to say. Kate could use it as her studio!"

Tim grinned at her. "You've got it in one! I had the idea some time ago, when I saw how little space she has in the cottage for all her canvases and stuff. Do you think I should put it to her?"

"I think it's a lovely idea," Lily said, beaming. "But…" she paused, then continued. "Knowing you, you'll not charge her anything for

113

using it, and no doubt she'll feel that she should pay you something. She probably can't afford to."

"I've thought of that. I could ask her to give the kids art lessons in lieu. She'll see through that, but it may help her to accept the offer."

Lily looked quizzically at him, her head on one side. "And what is her ladyship going to think of that little arrangement?"

Tim looked puzzled. "Her ladyship?"

"You know who: Elaine."

"What's it got to do with her?"

"Oh, come on Tim, you know she's got her sights on you, and she's not going to be exactly delighted that you're giving the use of a studio to a beautiful young girl like Kate."

"Look, Kate's probably got some bohemian artist boyfriend in London or somewhere. She's not going to be interested in a thirty-five-year-old father of two who works in the City."

Something about the way Tim said this made Lily look at him sharply. It was as though he was talking more to himself than to her. Lily was very fond of Tim, and her heart often ached for the young widower, left with two children to bring up. The last thing he needed was to lose his heart to a woman, not much more than a girl, who, as he himself said, was used to a lifestyle so different from his own. *Mind you*, she thought to herself as she shook the water from the lettuce, *if it's a choice between Kate and that Elaine, I know who I would choose for him*.

Lily started putting the lettuce into a plastic container. "Well, there's no harm in mentioning it to Kate, see what she says."

"Yes, I will. Maybe I'll call in on the way to Sainsbury's." He went out into the hall. "Kiddos, we're off to Sainsbury's. Come on, get your coats on, it's cold outside."

But there was no need to call in on Kate, because as Tim and the children came out of the front door to go to the car, they saw Kate coming down the lane towards them, accompanied by a tall, blond, young man who loped along beside her, his shoulders hunched against the wind and his hands thrust into his pockets.

Kate's face lit up when she saw them and Amy ran over and took

114

her hand. "I haven't seen you for *ages,*" she squealed delightedly. "Can you come and babysit again soon?"

Kate laughed and came to a stop as she and Jake drew level with Tim and Freddie, Amy still hanging on her arm. "This is Jake," she said, introducing him. "Jake - these are my lovely neighbours, Tim, Freddie and this fairy child is Amy."

"No, *you're* the fairy," Amy said, "'cept you're a fairy witch, because of your fairy witchy hair."

Everyone laughed, which made Amy go all shy and hide behind her father.

"Actually, I was just about to drop by," Tim said to Kate. "Have you got a minute? I want to show you something."

"Oh? What?" Kate looked mystified, and added, "We're in no hurry, we were just going to walk over to Zachary's so that Jake can see his carvings. Then we're going up to London to see Jake's installation at Straker's gallery."

Tim had felt a sinking of the heart when he had seen Kate with Jake. So, she did have a bohemian artist boyfriend. A sculptor or whatever people who made installations were called. And why did he have to be so staggeringly good looking?

"It's just here, over the garage," Tim said, impatient with himself for being dismayed by the existence of Jake. He led the way round to the side of the garage to a door which, when opened, gave straight onto a staircase leading to an upper floor. Followed by Kate, Jake and the children, he went up the stairs and flung open the door at the top, standing aside so that Kate could go in. She stepped into the large, light, airy space above the double garage and gasped with pleasure.

"Wow! Look at all this *space!* What do you use it for?" she exclaimed, then stopped short, as if immediately realising the stupidity of the question, because, apart from a dilapidated desk in one corner, a sink in another and a couple of old office chairs, the room was empty, with a bare chipboard floor.

"Well, that's just it. We don't use it for anything. It seems a bit of a waste, and it occurred to me that you might like to use it as a studio.

You don't have much room in your cottage for all your canvases. Look, there's even a sink to wash your brushes in."

Kate stared at him, her eyes wide with surprise and incredulity. "Oh, I couldn't possibly! I... I'd make a mess, get paint on the floor or something. And I ..." She stopped, then blurted out: "I couldn't use it for free, and I can't afford to pay you rent or anything."

Tim held up a hand. "Hang on, hang on. I was wondering if you could give the kids art lessons in lieu. I think Freddie's got some talent, and I was hoping he could try for an art scholarship to Charterhouse when he leaves Latham House. Maybe he could do some extra work with you. And Amy adores messing about with paints and things."

Kate looked at him with a wry smile, then gave his shoulder a playful shove. "You're just trying to make me feel better about it."

Tim looked affronted. "No, really." He turned to Freddie. "You *are* good at art, aren't you?"

"Well, my art teacher says I am, and that I should try for a scholarship to my next school."

Tim gave Kate a smug 'I told you so' look, and she laughed.

"Well, I must say it *is* very tempting." She flung her arms wide and said again, "All this space." She walked to the window at the far end of the room, which overlooked the lane, delighted that she would still be able to hear and see the poplars, since the line of them stretched the whole length of Tuckers Lane.

Jake, meanwhile, had been prowling around and peering through the windows. The ones on the right overlooked Woodcote House and the lane, while the windows on the left gave onto the wood that bordered the garden, the tawny branches of the oaks filling the view, tossing in the chilly wind.

Another large window on the end wall faced north and the poplars across the lane, with the Babbidges' cottage visible off to the left.

"It's an offer you can't refuse, kid," Jake said with a slight shrug and a tilt of his head. He looked curiously at Tim, the thought occurring to him that his offer might not be quite as altruistic as it seemed.

"There you are! Very sound advice," Tim said triumphantly, not

116

noticing Jake's quizzical stare. "And as for the floor, we can put down some vinyl or something, which you could muck up as much as you like."

"Well, it would make a wonderful studio, of course. It *is* rather cramped in the cottage, and the light is not too good, with only the two smallish windows. And I'd love to do some art with the children." She looked from Freddie to Amy. "We could do some cool stuff."

Freddie grinned at her. "Great. Can I paint a real, proper canvas? With oil paints?"

"Sure! Maybe you could get one or two from an art shop. Or maybe Mr B. could make them for you, like he made mine."

Amy skipped up to her. "Can we do some clay things? I want to make a fairy castle."

"Absolutely. You two could do your stuff at this end," she indicated the area nearest the door, "and I could set up my stuff over there." She walked to the further end, revelling afresh in all the light and space.

"Well, that's settled then," Tim said with satisfaction. "Just give me time to get some vinyl floor-covering down. I've been meaning to put something down ever since we came here. You could use that old desk as your painting table and we'll find some furniture that the kids can use." He looked at the children. "But you are only to come up here when it's your lesson. You mustn't keep coming up here pestering Kate when she's trying to work."

"Oh, that's OK," Kate began, but her attention was diverted by the sight through the window of a red car pulling up in the lane. A woman got out, followed by a boy who emerged from the passenger side, just as Lily Babbidge came out of the front door of Tim's house with her coat on. Kate recognised Elaine and her son and watched them stop at the gate while Elaine exchanged a few words with Lily, who pointed towards the garage. Elaine glanced up towards the windows of the garage loft.

"You've got visitors," Kate said to Tim, who came to the window and looked down at the two figures walking towards the open door at the side of the garage.

There was a call of, "Hello, Tim?" followed by the sound of two sets

117

of footsteps coming up the stairs. Seconds later, Elaine's blond head appeared, slightly disarrayed by the blustery wind. She stepped into the room and surveyed the scene with cool appraisal. Duncan followed her through the door and walked over to talk to Freddie.

"Mrs B. told me she saw you all coming up here," Elaine said, going over to where Tim was standing and giving him a kiss on the lips. She glanced at Kate, a flicker of hostility in her eyes. Then her gaze fell upon Jake, lounging against the desk, and she did not miss the look of appreciation with which he was regarding her. She turned back to Tim.

"Mrs B. said that you were suggesting that, er... Kate here could use this room as a studio. I thought Freddie was hoping to have it as a table tennis room," she said with an air of studied surprise. "He and Duncan were getting quite excited about it."

Tim caught the look of dismay and embarrassment that Kate shot in his direction and said hurriedly, taking an involuntary step towards her, "No, we've changed our minds about that. We're going to do up the old barn at the bottom of the garden as a proper games room instead. Much more suitable, isn't it, Fred?"

Freddie nodded vigorously. "Yes, and we're going to have a table tennis table and a table football game and an exercise bike and things." He turned to Duncan. "I didn't tell you because it was going to be a surprise. Never mind, you can help plan it out."

"Cool," Duncan said, grinning. The two boys went off into a huddle, chattering about the proposed games room.

Elaine arched an elegant eyebrow. "It'll cost you a pretty penny. That old barn looks as though it's about to fall down."

"Not at all, it's structurally very sound. Just needs some work on the roof and of course the whole of the inside will have to be gutted."

"As I said, it'll cost an arm and a leg." Elaine, tiring of the subject, turned to Jake, and held out her hand.

"We haven't been introduced. I'm Elaine."

Jake shook her hand. "Jake," he said, a lazy smile touching his lips.

"Where do you live Jake?" Elaine murmured. "Are you down for the weekend? I was just going to see if Tim and the children wanted to go to the pub for lunch. Perhaps you could join us?"

"No can do I'm afraid," Jake said, still leaning against the desk, his hands back in the pockets of his scruffy jeans. "I've got to get back to London. Kate's coming up to see my installation at Straker's gallery."

Any ideas that Elaine may have had of making Tim jealous by flirting with Jake over lunch were dashed by this piece of information. But her mind was put at rest somewhat by the fact that Kate and Jake seemed to be involved with each other. She was still unsure of Tim, and Kate's arrival on the scene had been causing her some disquiet ever since she had set eyes on her. If Kate was in a relationship, she might not be so much of a threat.

As for Kate, she too had seen the gleam of interest in Jake's expression when he looked at Elaine, and was gratified at how indifferent she felt about it. What *had* caused her a stab of irritation was the possessive way Elaine had kissed Tim when she had come into the room. She said to Jake, "We'd better get going if we're going to pop in on Zachary. I hope he's there."

She looked round the room again and turned to Tim. "Well, if you really are sure about this, I'd love to work up here. You must let me pay for the vinyl flooring at least."

"Never mind about that now. And I'll let you know when it's ready for you to set up shop." He smiled at her. "You can be our artist in residence."

Elaine, digesting the implications of this last exchange between Kate and Tim, felt a tightening in her gut. Her mind baulked at the thought that Kate was going to use Tim's garage loft as a studio, bringing the two of them into frequent contact. Who knew what that would lead to, Jake or no Jake. She flashed a look of hostility, almost hatred, towards Kate as they all clattered back down the stairs, Freddie and Duncan bringing up the rear, still busy with plans for the games room. Back outside again, Kate and Jake took their leave of the others and began walking up the lane, to the path that led through the wood towards Zachary's cottage. As he watched them go, Tim saw Jake drape his arm across Kate's shoulders. Elaine's sharp eyes did not miss the almost imperceptible tightening of his lips.

When they reached Zachary's clearing, Kate eagerly pointed out the deer and other animals dotted about amidst the long dry grasses. Jake ran his hands over the deer's back and stooped to examine a badger, which had obviously been there a long time because the wood was weathered and starting to crack.

"These are staggeringly good," he said. "But why does he leave them out here to deteriorate?"

"I think he likes having some outside in a natural setting," Kate said. "He's got loads more in that shed over there."

They heard Zachary's deep voice behind them as he emerged from his cottage. "Kate! Haven't seen you for a while. How's it going?"

"Hi, Zachary. We popped over because I wanted to show Jake here your sculptures. He's a sculptor, too."

Zachary came forward, his hand extended, and Jake shook it. "What I've seen so far is very impressive," he said. "I couldn't do such stuff in a million years."

Kate interjected; "Your work is completely different, Jake." She turned to Zachary. "He uses materials such as fibreglass and resin and electronics, and his stuff is often quite conceptual. You can't compare the two."

Jake nodded, then said "Kate says there's more of your work in the shed. Can I see?"

When Jake saw Zachary's work, he was as astonished as Kate had been when she had first seen all the pieces in the shed.

"Man! You can't keep all this shut away in here! People have got to see it. It's a treasure trove."

"That's what I told him," Kate said, delighted at Jake's reaction. "As I told you, Geoff suggested that he comes in on our exhibition next year. I'm sure he'd sell loads."

"Definitely." Jake picked up an outsized snail, the whorl of its shell echoed in the polished grain of the wood, then a field mouse, nibbling on a wheat seed. "My work may be modern," he said to Zachary, "but yours is

120

alive."

Kate went up to London in Jake's van, dropping off her car near the station on the way, to pick up on her return later. They went first to Jake's studio to see the projects he was currently engaged in. An assistant was at work at the far end of the room, welding something, while nearby, large spheres of transparent resin lay nestled in boxes, each with a thin strand of clear cord protruding from them.

"They're going to hang from a false ceiling, at varying heights, like rain falling," Jake said. He showed her his drawings of what it would look like. "As you see, some have hit the ground, making concentric ripples in these resin 'puddles'. You will be able to walk among them and there'll be the sound of rain falling and some isolated notes played on a harp. The sourcing of the materials, and getting the globes made with the strands embedded in them - it all took time. It's going to be a pig to install, but Straker likes it, thank God." He stopped. "I just don't know what to call it. I don't just want to call it 'Rain'."

Kate stood gazing at the drawing. Then it came to her. "'The Quality of Mercy'," she said softly.

"What?"

"From Shakespeare. The Merchant of Venice. Portia's speech:
The quality of mercy is not strain'd
It droppeth as the gentle rain from heaven
Upon the place beneath."

"That's it!" Jake cried, hugging her. "'The Quality of Mercy'. Excellent! You see, you *are* my muse!"

"And you're a genius. "This piece is going to be stunning." Kate went and picked up one of the resin spheres. It was about a third smaller than a football and slightly greenish in colour. To walk into a whole roomful of them hanging at varying heights, some half dissolved in puddles on the floor, accompanied by the sound effects, would be an amazing experience.

"What's happening down that end?" she asked, indicating the assistant, his face covered with a visor, who was using a blowtorch to weld

121

metal to a freestanding metal slab that looked like a door with a number of large keyholes in it.

"It's called 'Watching Me Watching You'," Jake said, as they walked towards it. "Each keyhole will have a small TV screen behind a shutter and, when you press a lever, the shutter opens, revealing a video of a large eye."

"A bit unsettling!" Kate said, a little dubiously.

"That's the idea. At the same time, a recorded voice will ask a question, such as 'Who are you?' 'Why have you come?' 'What do you want?' - things like that."

"Spooky!" Kate gave a slight shiver.

Jake went over to the technician, who turned off the welding torch and lifted his visor to talk to him. Kate wandered round the studio, examining working drawings which were stuck up on the walls, and various anonymous lumps of plaster and metal which were littered about.

A sheaf of drawings on a table caught her eye. They seemed to be developments of one theme: a large, central, amorphous shape had smaller shapes attached to it by attenuated strands and the smaller shapes also had offshoots which were connected by strands to other offshoots so that the whole formed an interconnecting matrix. She heard Jake come up behind her to look over her shoulder.

"Ah, now this one I do have a name for," he said: "'Cogito ergo sum' – 'I think, therefore I am'. It's based on the neurons in the brain. The idea is that there are going to be lights coming on randomly in the globules, like neurons firing in the brain, and the light travels down the fibre optic strands and triggers off other lights and so on. I've got to work out how to do it though."

"Will it be spread out on the ground?"

"Not sure yet, I may scrunch it up into a big ball or something, but I'd prefer to see it spread out with the light travelling down the strands. Of course, it's not supposed to be an accurate model of neurons and synaptic connections – they're just the starting point."

"It could be fixed to the wall – mounted vertically."

"Yeah – that could work too – like a sort of mind map." Jake paused and looked at his watch. "Well, if we're going to Straker's we'd better get going, because I want you to see my new flat first while we're here. It's just up the road. Did you say you were going to meet Mimi and co at Straker's?"

"Yes, I said we'd be there about four."

They left the studio, waving to the assistant at the far end of the room, and once out in the street, began walking in the direction Jake indicated.

Kate looked quizzically up at Jake. "How on earth are you funding all this? I know Straker's paying for the studio space through his foundation, but assistants, materials, electricians, programmers – he can't be paying for all that."

Kate detected a slight hesitation in his reply and a somewhat studied casualness. "Well, the pieces I sold at the show have gone a long way towards it, and I've had a substantial loan as well."

"Oh? And who might that be from?" Kate asked mischievously, having a very good idea who the benefactor might be.

Jake glanced down at her, then broke into a grin. "Yes, as you have obviously gathered, Lucinda lent it to me. Well, it's more like an investment. She thinks I'm destined for fame and fortune. Anyway, she might as well put all her loot to good use!"

Kate had to agree with that.

Jake's flat was on a relatively quiet side street above a tailor's shop. It did not look very promising from the outside but proved to be quite spacious and in good decorative order, if in a state of some chaos. Kate well remembered Jake's inability to put anything away. The bathroom had wet towels on the floor and the bed was unmade in the bedroom. Kate noticed a gold high-heeled shoe lying by the bed. Jake saw her glance and putting his hands round her waist, turned her towards him.

"Kid, she's useful to me. I admit I am using her." He tilted her face up to him and suddenly his lips were on hers, hard and hungry, and for a brief moment Kate responded, her hands buried in his curly hair, her body remembering the contours of his. But out of nowhere came the thought of how it would feel to be kissed by Tim like this. She pulled away and went to the window, leaning her head against the cool glass. Jake stood for a moment in the centre of the room, cursing inwardly, then gave a short laugh. "Is this to do with Mister big-shot-in-the-city? If so, you've got some competition from the buttoned-up blonde."

"Don't be silly, Jake. I hardly know him."

"You know him well enough for him to offer you the use of studio space."

"It's just a kind and thoughtful gesture. Come on, Mimi and the others will be waiting for us."

Jake went over, put an arm round her shoulders and gave her a hug. "OK then kid, let's go."

They walked to the tube station together but somehow apart, each lost in their own thoughts.

In the foyer of the gallery, Kate immediately spotted Mimi's spiky, magenta hair among the cluster of gallery-goers near the door, and as she made her way over with Jake, Grace and Bea got up from a nearby bench. The usual flurry of greetings over, they proceeded into the gallery, heading straight for the room where Jake's pods were installed.

Kate caught her breath when they went in and the others also stopped dead to take it in. It was a bigger room than the one in which they had been installed at Jake's show and the lighting was dim. The seven pods, each around five feet in height, tapering towards the top, stood dotted about the space, their smooth, black outer surfaces gleaming dully. They looked like spectral flower buds in the low light, but as they stood there, another gallery visitor walked past one of the pods and it slowly started to open, its five segments separating outwards from the top, revealing a soft greenish light, which appeared at first as chinks between the opening parts, then revealing itself to be a cone of light shining upwards and emanating from deep within the base. At the same time, a musical note sounded electronically, reaching a crescendo when the segments were fully open in a chalice shape and fading as they started to close again.

Kate and the others started walking among the pods, setting off the

124

movement sensors on their outer surfaces, and causing them to open and emit their light, each one having a different coloured light and a different note of music. When all the pods were at different stages of opening and closing, the various colours and notes created an extraordinary, dreamlike effect. Kate had known what to expect, since she had seen the installation many times during its construction and finally completed at Jake's show, but in this setting, with everything working perfectly and the light at just the right level of dimness, she was entranced anew. Looking at the faces of her friends and the other members of the public who had come in, she knew they too had come under its spell.

She wandered back to where Jake was leaning against the wall near the door, his arms folded, watching them. She put a palm against his cheek, looking up at him with shining eyes.

"It's amazing Jake. A triumph."

Jake grunted, inwardly pleased at her reaction, but said; "When it all works properly! We've had endless glitches, with the sensors not working on some or the music circuits packing up or the opening mechanisms getting stuck. At least it all seems to be OK today!"

Before they left the gallery, they went to see Jake's other pieces that Straker had bought at the show, set up in another room. The 'Through a Glass Darkly' piece looked particularly effective, situated in the centre of the room, the shadowy shapes moving lazily within the large smoked-glass globe.

"Well, I think we all ought to celebrate Jake's great fame by going to the pub!" Mimi announced as they came out into the street again. "I've been working like a galley slave for weeks, I don't know about anyone else."

Jake went with them to a wine bar around the corner from the gallery, where they polished off a couple of bottles of wine and had something to eat. Mimi was on good form, entertaining them with anecdotes about the sixth form college where she taught art part-time. Kate found it hard to picture Mimi in a teaching capacity, with her wacky clothes and irreverent personality, but she seemed to enjoy it and could relate to the students well, being not much older than they were. Bea seemed more relaxed and less intense than usual, having just completed an ambitious piece involving stained glass. Grace was her usual dreamy self, looking like a sixties flower child as she sat sipping wine and doodling on a napkin.

Kate looked round at her friends and did feel a pang of regret that she so seldom made the effort to come up and just spend time with them. When she was in London with the old crowd, her life down in her little cottage seemed as though it belonged to another person. So it was with some reluctance that she looked at her watch and decided that she ought to be making her way to Waterloo to catch the train back.

They parted at the tube station, Mimi going back to Camden, Grace to Richmond and Bea to Hammersmith. Kate waved as they went through the ticket barrier and disappeared into the crowds. She turned to Jake, reaching up to draw his head down to give him a kiss on the cheek.

"It was good to see you Jake, and the stuff you're working on. And your pieces look fabulous at Straker's."

"I could come down again sometime?" He said it as a question, with a slight uncharacteristic diffidence.

"Of course, any time;" she said, with well-disguised reluctance. Jake tended to complicate things. Hopefully he would be too busy to come down for a while.

Any regrets she might have had about leaving London for her new life disappeared as soon as she got home and parked her Mini in the lane outside her cottage. It was a frosty late November night, and the cottage was wrapped in darkness, the leafless poplars towering protectively overhead with a starry sky as a backdrop. It was so quiet and beautiful that she lingered for a while, her head thrown back, gazing up at the trees and drinking in the stillness. Then she unlocked the front door and let herself in.

*

Things moved swiftly in regard to her proposed new studio in Tim's garage loft. He lost no time in getting some vinyl floor covering laid down and, on a Saturday morning a couple of weeks later, he turned up at Kate's door with the children and the dog, holding up a key.

"Your studio awaits you. The floor covering is down and some bits of furniture, so it's all ready whenever you want to move your stuff in." Tim looked at her a little anxiously. "You did really want to use it, didn't you? I mean, just say if you've changed your mind."

The expression on Tim's face, half worried, half pleased to be able to help, caught at her heart. Looking from him to the children's eager faces, she couldn't help flinging her arms wide to gather them in a group hug. She kissed Tim lightly on the cheek. "Oh Tim, thanks. Gosh, you didn't waste much time!" She drew them into the house, gesturing to her painting corner, cluttered with canvases, her easel and her painting paraphernalia.

"As you can see, I'm getting a bit conglomerated in here. It'll be wonderful to have more space. Also, I like to stand well back from a painting sometimes when I'm working on it, and I can't in this little room."

"Well, do you want to start shifting your stuff now? We've got the rest of the morning free."

"We can help," Freddie interjected. "We'll be very careful with everything."

Amy, not to be outdone, piped up, "I can carry this pot of brushes. Wow! you've got *millions* of brushes. But I can *easily* carry it," she added hastily, picking it up with both hands and marching to the door.

Kate chuckled. "It looks like it's moving day!" she said, grabbing her coat off the hook and shrugging into it. "Lucky it's not raining."

"Shall I take these two big canvases to start with?" Tim asked, pointing to the stack leaning against the wall.

"Yes please, and I'll take this one on the easel, it's still wet and may muck up your clothes." She lifted the third panel of the triptych off the easel and Freddie helped her fold the easel up for easier transportation.

They trudged off up the lane, Freddie struggling a bit with the large easel, but refusing any help.

127

When they got to Tim's garage, Tim, with great ceremony, stood aside so that Kate herself could unlock the door and go up the stairs first. When she got to the top, she gave a gasp of pleasure. The room seemed transformed. The floor covering was a deep blue, contrasting with the stark whiteness of the walls. The watery sun, slanting in through the windows fell across the floor. At the far end stood the desk that had been there before, but now there was also a formica topped table, an old armchair, and another small table under the window with (a thoughtful gesture which touched her) an electric kettle, a couple of mugs and a jar of coffee on it. On the desk sat a computer, and when Kate saw it, she looked enquiringly at Tim.

"Oh, yes, I meant to tell you. I treated myself to a new computer, so I decided to put the old one in here, in case you wanted to show the kids stuff about artists or something. And of course, you are welcome to use it for your own needs. It's got its own server and everything."

"That's fantastic! Thank you!" Kate said gratefully, overwhelmed by Tim's thoughtfulness and generosity. She continued her inspection of the studio.

At the nearer end of the room was another old table, which had once been painted white and was now rather scuffed and scratched, and the two office chairs.

"That's where we are going to do *our* art. When are we going to start our lessons?" Amy said, carrying the pot of brushes to the table at the far end of the room.

"Amy, don't pester. Let Kate settle in first, there's no hurry," Tim chided her.

But Kate said quickly," Well, you're at school during the week, so how about next Saturday morning? I'm sure I'll be well settled in by then."

"Cool," Freddie said, struggling with wing nuts as he tried to put up the easel.

Kate gave him a hand and set the painting she had carried over back on the easel. For the first time she was able to stand well back from it and realised with a slight shock that the effect she had wanted to create was

128

now almost captured and needed just a few adjustments, which she itched to tackle. Annie's face and one hand seemed to emerge from the glass-like surface, the rest of her body still distorted by the effects of the wavy glass. They all stopped and gazed at the painting in silence. Then Freddie said; "How do you get that effect - as though the woman is coming out of the picture? It's awesome."

Then Amy made them smile by commenting sternly, "But the lady's got a cut lip. She'd be more prettier if you painted lipstick to cover it up."

They made several journeys back and forth, carrying canvases, paints, sketchbooks and other bits and pieces, until everything was in situ in what they were all already calling The Studio.

Amy disappeared for a few moments, coming back up the stairs with a children's paint box and a wallet of felt pens, which she solemnly placed on the nearer table.

"Go and get your paints, Freddie," she commanded. "If you use mine, you'll make my colours all dirty."

Freddie grimaced. "My paints are a bit rubbish and anyway, I want to paint in oil paint like Kate. Can we go and get some today, Dad?"

"Well, I'm a bit clueless when it comes to such things," Tim said ruefully. He turned to Kate. "Could you give me some idea as to what to get?"

Kate thought for a moment. "It would be better if I came along to the art shop with you really," she said. "There's so much choice these days, it's quite confusing."

Tim's eyes lit up. "Tell you what, how about we all go out and have some lunch, then we can go on to the art shop afterwards!"

Amy squealed and grabbed Kate's hand. "Oh yes, please come, Kate!"

Kate looked from her to Freddie's eager face and then to Tim's, which had an expression on it very similar to his son's.

"OK! Let's do that then." She was torn between wanting to get on with her painting yet wanting to spend more time with Tim and the children. "Just let me go and change these disreputable jeans."

"We'll pick you up at the cottage in about ten minutes then," Tim said.

Kate gave a last glance round the studio. "Thank you so much for helping me move in, and... well, for everything, right down to coffee and a kettle!"

They had lunch in a little restaurant off the High Street in Guildford, Tim sitting next to Kate, with the children opposite. Sipping her wine while they waited for the food to arrive, it occurred to Kate that they must look for all the world like a husband and wife with their two children, not realising that in fact she looked more like the children's sister. Amy was captivated by the Christmas decorations around the restaurant and the twinkling Christmas tree in the corner, her shining eyes reflecting the fairy lights festooning the walls.

"What are you doing for Christmas?" Tim asked Kate, during a brief lull in Amy's chatter about letters to Santa and a grilling as to when they were going to go and buy their own tree. "You are very welcome to join us for Christmas lunch. My mother will be with us and will be doing the cooking."

"Yes, and I'm going to help Granny make the mince pies," Amy said importantly. "I'm the one who puts the pastry stars on, like Mummy used to."

Kate smiled at her, and turned to Tim. "Sweet of you Tim, but I'm going up to Yorkshire, to spend Christmas with my father in Scarborough, where he moved after he married again. I haven't seen him since last Christmas. To tell you the truth, I don't feel too comfortable there. His second wife, Doreen, is good-hearted, but incredibly house-proud. Everything is immaculate and spotless, every saucepan burnished. Not a speck of dust is allowed to settle anywhere. I think she regards me as a messy puppy, mucking up the place. If I put a glass down, it's whipped up and a coaster popped under it."

"How exhausting!" Tim laughed.

"I'm sure she's very fond of Dad, "Kate continued. "But he's only allowed to smoke his pipe in his study, only wear slippers in the house, etc. But he takes it meekly, and seems happy. He was like a rudderless boat when Mum died, a lost soul, and she came along and sort of took him over. She's from Yorkshire. She met him when she went down to Bournemouth for a holiday. Anyway, I'll be driving up on the twenty third, and coming back about the twenty eighth. But thanks for the offer."

Tim, clearly thinking of the dilapidated state of Kate's Mini, said with a touch of concern, "You don't think it would be wiser to go by train? They say it's going to get much colder next week, with the possibility of snow."

"It probably would be wiser. Poor old Trog is getting on a bit, but what with Christmas presents and stuff, it's easier just to fling everything in the car."

"Well, it's a lovely part of the country anyway," Tim said, moving his glass out of the way as the food arrived.

It was a jolly little meal, snug in the cosy restaurant, while a cold wind started up outside, whipping at the scarves of the Christmas shoppers passing by on the street beyond the window. Kate felt a warm contentment deep within her, a feeling that she was somehow at home, that something had come to meet her, and had enfolded her. And that feeling was bound up with the man sitting beside her on the bench seat. Because he was not sitting opposite, their eyes did not meet often, but when they did, their gaze held a little longer than necessary.

Freddie, munching on his tortilla wrap, noticed how they looked at each other and for the first time since his mother died, he felt the hard, little knot of misery deep in his chest, begin to loosen. He had never felt that when he had seen Elaine draping herself over his father. Rather, the knot had seemed to tighten.

At the art supplies shop, Kate selected some equipment to get the children started - oil paints and related equipment for Freddie, sketchbooks, some tempera paint for Amy and a bag of air hardening clay.

"You don't need a kiln for this stuff, you just paint it with hardener and then paint. Of course, you can't get it wet, so you won't be able to make pots to contain liquids. You need a kiln and proper clay for that,"

131

Kate said. "But it's good for modelling figures and things."

"Yes, we use it at school sometimes," Freddie said. "But we do have a kiln at school as well."

They lugged their booty back to the car and on the way home Tim stopped the car outside a second-hand furniture shop.

"We need a cupboard or something to stash all this stuff in," he said. "Let's see if they've got anything suitable."

Half an hour later, Tim had bought a low two-door cupboard and another table, both of which he had to leave at the shop for the time being since they would not fit in the car with everyone in it. Having arranged with the man in the shop that Tim would come back later with the empty car to pick up the items, they drove home,

The short winter's day was drawing in when they got back. Big, black clouds were rolling in over the horizon and there was the sting of cold rain in the air. Kate and the children went straight back up to the studio and started unpacking their purchases while Tim went back to the furniture shop. When he got back, they managed, with much difficulty, to get the table and cupboard up the narrow stairs. The children took charge of putting the stuff away, not without a few arguments as to where things should go.

"The new table is for messy stuff like clay," Freddie said, "and it has to be near the sink here."

"Actually Daddy, we need *another* table," Amy said, "to put things on after we've made them."

Tim laughed. "We'll gradually add to the equipment, don't worry. We can't do everything at once."

Kate groaned. "You'll be regretting this art lessons idea. All this stuff you've had to buy."

"I think it's great. It's the sort of thing Claire would have supported a hundred percent."

"Well, I think it's great too. But then I would!" Kate said. She turned to the children. "So we'll have our first lesson on Saturday – about ten?"

That arranged, they switched off the light and clattered back down

132

the wooden stairs.

Kate locked the door at the bottom and turned to Tim. "Well, we got a lot done today. Tim, thank you. I'm so looking forward to working up there."

At the gate of Woodcote, the children walked down the path to the front door, just as Mrs B. was coming out. Seeing them, she jumped slightly.

"Ooh! You gave me a fright! I wondered who it was for a moment!" She peered out into the darkness where Tim and Kate were standing at the gate. "Tim? I've left a casserole in the fridge for tomorrow. Is that you, Kate?"

Kate waved. "Hi, Mrs B. We've been getting the studio ready."

"Thanks, Lily," Tim said as she came up to them. "Oh, by the way, do you think Bill would be able to put some shelves up in the studio? We need more places to put things."

"Oh, I'm sure he would. I'll get him to pop along tomorrow and have a look."

"Great. Of course I'll pay him for his work. Thanks again, Lily. Bye for now."

Lily Babbidge disappeared into the darkness, the light from her torch bobbing along on the uneven surface of the lane.

"Night, Tim," Kate said. "Thank you for lunch."

Tim bent and kissed her cheek. "And thank you for helping to buy the art stuff." A gust of wind blew a strand of hair across Kate's cheek, and he gently brushed it away. Then he turned rather abruptly and went in through the gate. Kate gave a wave but before she started off down the lane, she involuntarily glanced up at the bedroom window. Surely it was her imagination that she saw the pale oval of a face behind the dark pane of glass?

Chapter VIII

Much as she wanted to go straight to her new studio the next morning, Kate felt she couldn't settle down to work with a clear conscience until she had paid Annie a visit at the refuge. She had not seen her since the day she had come back and found Jake on her doorstep, and being Sunday, Magda would not be working and might want to come too. Magda agreed with alacrity when Kate phoned her and, having arranged to pick Magda up, Kate drove round to her house. Mike came out to say hello as his mother got in the car, coming around to the driver's side, leaning his arms on the roof and bending down to speak to her as she opened the window.

"Hi Kate! How's it going?"

"Mike! Good to see you. Great, actually. I have a new studio! It's above Tim Crawford's garage. There's a lot more space and I can use it rent free in exchange for giving his children art lessons."

Unseen by Kate, Magda's mouth twitched in a covert little smile as she fastened her seatbelt, but if Mike thought there was any hidden agenda in the arrangement, he gave no sign of it.

"Well, I must admit, I did think your little sitting room was going to be a bit on the small side for all your canvases and things."

"I was intending to stash some in the shed, but this is much better, and there's much more light as well."

She stopped and glanced over her shoulder towards Annie's house next door. "Seen anything of the delightful Vince?"

"Not to talk to, but I've seen him on several occasions walking off down the road at night. God knows where he goes off to."

"Up to no good I shouldn't wonder," Magda interjected tartly. "And that ratty little friend of his is always coming and going, cluttering up the road with his filthy van. Come on love, we better get going," she said to Kate.

134

Waving to Mike, who gave two smart taps on the roof of the car, Kate drove off, relieved that Vince was nowhere to be seen.

When they arrived at the refuge, they found Annie in the playroom with the children. She had news for them.

"I've started to apply for a Protection Order – well, two actually. Something called a non-molestation order and another one called an occupation order – that's to stop Vince coming to the house when I go home." The words tumbled out breathlessly even before she had finished hugging them, and she drew them over to a couple of armchairs near to where the children were playing on the floor. "But first I have to talk to a solicitor who'll arrange it for me."

Magda put a hand on her arm. "Hang on, how will you pay for a solicitor?"

"I contacted the Citizens Advice Bureau and they are going to find me a solicitor who will apply for Legal Aid for me. They were ever so helpful. And also," Annie went on in a rush, "the police came to see me and I've decided to press charges against Vince. The police are going to recommend to the Crown Prosecution Service that a criminal prosecution for Actual Bodily Harm is brought against Vince."

Kate looked at Annie in amazement. She seemed a different person. For a start, her face had almost completely healed; the black eye was gone and her lip bore only a trace of the deep cut Vince had inflicted. Her hair had been newly washed and fell in soft waves to her shoulders. But it was her demeanour which was the most startling. The tenseness in her shoulders had gone and the way she spoke seemed infinitely more confident and assured. A few weeks without the malevolent presence of Vince had done wonders for her morale.

It was evident that Magda was thinking the same, because she said: "Well, Annie love, you seem to be coping with everything brilliantly. And you look so much better."

"I feel much better," Annie said, with one of her luminous smiles. "But oh Mags! I'm so looking forward to coming home. I hope I can get the injunction sorted out quickly. I'll probably have to go to court. That scares me something awful. But I'm determined to go through with it."

"Good for you, love," Magda said. She looked down at the two children playing on the floor. "The kids look well. Hello Becky, sweetheart. Hello Darren. Are you being a good boy?" The toddler nodded, barely looking up from the toy mobile phone he was playing with, but Becky came over and leant against Magda's knee affectionately.

"So you haven't forgotten aunty Mags, then Becky?" Magda murmured, putting her arm round the little girl.

"Of course she hasn't, don't be daft!" Annie laughed.

"Have you got her into another nursery?"

"No, I keep hoping we can go home soon, and she can go back to her old one."

"It may take quite a long time before you can go to court," warned Magda. "Susan Kelly down the road had to wait ages for her case to be heard."

Annie sighed. "Well, I suppose I could ask the nursery school round the corner if they could take her for a while." A thought struck her. "Mags, could you take my house key and dig out some more clothes and things? I'm sick of washing and wearing the same stuff and the kids need some more clothes too. We'll need something decent to wear since we'll be here for Christmas. If you could bring them next time you come, I'd be ever so grateful, but don't come specially. And don't let Vince catch you, for heaven's sake!"

Mags smiled grimly. "Don't worry, he won't. And even if he does, he can't do a lot, since you'll have given me a key and I'll have a perfect right to be there."

Annie looked alarmed. "But please be careful Mags. He's got such a temper on him."

Magda patted her hand. "Don't worry, I'll be careful. You go and get the key."

After Annie had come back down with her front door key, they chatted over mugs of coffee, Annie asking Kate how the triptych was coming on.

"It's getting there. And I've got a new studio!" Kate went on to tell

Annie about the new arrangement, including how she was going to give art lessons to the children.

"It sounds like a good plan all round," Annie said approvingly.

"Well, maybe not everyone will be so happy," Magda said. Then, responding to Annie's and Kate's inquiring glances, added: "That Mrs Grainger won't be too pleased with the situation I shouldn't wonder. She's got her sights set on Tim Crawford, so Lily seems to think. And she won't be happy that a lovely young artist has set up a studio over his garage!"

Kate, rather flustered by this remark, got up hurriedly, collecting the coffee mugs. "I don't suppose I'll see much of Tim – he's in London all week, and I'll try not to get in the way at the weekend, apart from giving the children their lesson. Well, Annie, I think we'd better be off. I'll just take these back to the kitchen."

Annie and Magda exchanged knowing smiles as she disappeared out of the door.

Having dropped Magda home and popped into the village shop for some groceries, Kate collected a few more bits and pieces from the cottage and started off down the lane towards the studio. As she walked, she could hear the sound of the poplar branches swaying in the bitterly cold east wind. Going past the Crawfords' house, she went round the back of the garage, unlocked the door, and went up the stairs. Entering the studio, she gave a sigh of pleasure. The room was bathed in light and the radiators under the windows made the room feel pleasantly warm after the icy wind outside. It was very quiet, the only sound coming from the wind in the trees and the occasional cawing of rooks in the wood. She sank down in the old armchair Tim had so thoughtfully provided, and for a moment sat still to drink in the peaceful, light-filled space. Then she stood up and started to work.

*

As the week went on, the cold intensified, with snow flurries blown in on the wind, which had veered round to the north, interspersed with

137

wintry sunshine. Kate would get to the studio early, bringing a sandwich for lunch, and work through till seven or eight o'clock in the evening.

On the Thursday, however, Magda phoned, telling her that she had managed to get into Annie's house and collect the clothes and things that Annie had wanted.

"Would you be able to drop them off to Annie sometime? I don't like to ask, I know you're busy painting."

"No, that's fine Mags. But I just want to get little Christmas presents for Annie and the children. If I go now, I can pick up the stuff from you this afternoon, if you're in."

Later on that morning, having found some suitable gifts in the village shop and wrapped them, she drove to Magda's house, glancing apprehensively at Annie's next door, for any sign of Vince. Magda came out, lugging a bulging holdall and a carrier bag.

"Sorry I can't come with you love, I have to go to work in a minute. I was afraid I'd miss you."

"That's fine, Mags. I'll just say a quick hello to Annie and drop the bag off. "

"In this carrier bag are some presents for them. Together with your presents, at least they'll have something to unwrap on Christmas Day."

Kate glanced next door. "You didn't bump into *him* then – when you went to get the stuff?"

"No, I waited until I saw him go off with that horrible little friend of his. I had a quick snoop around. Ugh! You should have seen the state of the place! Annie used to keep it so spotless, now it's a tip. Dirty dishes all over the kitchen, beer cans on the sitting room floor, takeaway cartons strewn about. Disgusting!"

Kate shuddered. "Annie would have a fit! Well, I'll be off. See you soon, Mags."

At the refuge, she dropped the clothes and the presents off to a grateful Annie. The tears started to her eyes when she saw the wrapped presents. "You're such good friends to me, you and Mags!" she said with a little choke in her voice.

Kate hugged her. "Don't forget how you helped me with my

138

painting! You've been a good friend to me too!"

Giving the children a little bag of sweets each, Kate left, and after grabbing a sandwich back at the cottage, went to her studio and was soon immersed in her work.

On the Friday evening, walking back towards the cottage, she saw the lights of a car bouncing down the lane towards her. It was Tim and seeing her picked out in the beam of his headlights, he stopped and wound down the window.

"Kate! How are you getting on up there? Everything alright?"

Kate stopped by the driver's window. "Hi Tim. Yes, it's brilliant. I love working there and I've got quite a lot done this week."

"Good. The kids are looking forward to their lesson tomorrow. Amy can't wait to make her fairy castle out of clay!"

The wind blew a flurry of tiny snowflakes into the car window and Kate shivered.

"I won't keep you standing out in the cold. And I'm late back tonight. I've got to get home. I phoned Mrs B. to ask her to take the kids to her house if she had to go back to get Bill's supper."

A thought struck Kate. "Tim! They can always come up and wait with me in the studio till you get back," she exclaimed. "Please, it's the least I can do."

Tim smiled gratefully. "Well, that would certainly take a weight off my mind. Sometimes I can't avoid a late meeting and I don't like to impose on Lily too much. She's not as young as she was. And she's got Bill to think about as well as my lot."

He looked at Kate standing there in the lane, hugging her coat round herself. "Now you get yourself home or you'll freeze to death."

Kate gave a grin, waved, and disappeared into the darkness, while Tim put the car in gear and drove off down the lane.

The bulky figure which had ducked down into the ditch when Tim's car had appeared scrambled out just as Kate went into the cottage, closing the door behind her.

The next morning, Kate was in the studio, getting ready for the children's lesson. She first wanted to assess their potential by asking them to do some drawing from direct observation, so she set up a still life of some Bramley apples together with a chunky jug she had found among her great aunt's crockery in the kitchen. Then she put out some charcoal and some inexpensive paper. When the children came clattering up the stairs just before ten, followed by Tim, she was ready for them.

At first Freddie seemed a little disappointed to see the drawing materials set out.

"Oh! I thought I would be starting on an oil painting!" he exclaimed, going up to the table and picking up a stick of charcoal.

"We will soon, don't worry," Kate reassured him. "I just wanted to see what your drawing style is like. And drawing is tremendously important. You just can't do enough of it. It trains your eye like nothing else."

"Am *I* drawing the apples as well?" Amy asked, eyeing the paper set out at the other end of the table and gazing critically at the still life.

"Yes, you too," Kate said briskly. "Next time we can start on your clay castle." She turned to Tim, who was standing a little awkwardly near the door. "I'm afraid I won't be here next Saturday. I'll be driving up to Yorkshire on Thursday to spend Christmas with Dad and Doreen."

"Well, I didn't think you'd be giving them a lesson so close to Christmas anyway," Tim said. "And it'll be nice for you to see your father."

"Yes, it'll be great to see Dad, and Doreen's lovely really, in spite of all the cleaning and tidying.

Tim looked out of the window, then said seriously. "Are you still determined to drive up? They say heavy snow is on the way tomorrow."

"Yes, I was going to drive, though I'm a bit worried poor old Trog is going to conk out in the middle of nowhere in a snowdrift!" She shrugged. "I'll just have to hope the roads aren't too bad by Thursday." Then turning to the children, she said brightly, "Now you guys; shall we

140

get started?"

"I'll leave you to it," Tim said. "Be good you two, have fun." He gave Kate a wave and disappeared down the stairs.

The two-hour lesson went by quickly. Kate first got the children to do some loose, free sketches of the objects, to try to capture the lumpy solidity of the apples, the curves of the jug, the way the shadows described the forms. Then she got out some blue sugar paper and charcoal, and they started on more detailed drawings.

Freddie was soon engrossed and right from the start, Kate could see that he had an excellent eye, and his mark making was assured yet sensitive. He achieved the ellipse at the top of the jug and the symmetry of the sides fairly accurately, and his apples had a sense of weight and mass. Amy's drawing had a quirky eccentricity and unusual viewpoints that gave it an almost Cubist quality. However, she tired of it after a while and spent the rest of the time planning out her fairy castle.

By the time Tim came clumping up the wooden stairs in his gardening boots two hours later, Freddie had completed a striking charcoal still life, with some subtle tonal effects achieved by smudging the charcoal, and the highlights picked out in white chalk.

"Freddie, that's marvellous!" Tim said, regarding it appreciatively. He turned to Kate. "So do you think he has talent?"

"Most definitely! Well, look at what he's done. I think it's pretty impressive."

"Look at mine, Daddy," Amy interrupted, holding out her drawing.

Tim's eyes widened in admiration. "That's brilliant, sweetheart! Gosh, if your name was Picasso, you could sell it for millions!"

Amy preened, then insisted on giving him a detailed explanation of how she was going to make her castle. Kate looked at their two heads bent over the plans and her heart gave the by now familiar little lurch that she often felt when she saw Tim with his children. Though it was not *only* when she saw him with his children.

*

141

The snow started falling in earnest late that night. Kate was huddled by the fire in her little sitting room, working up some of the sketches she had made based on Freddie's fossils, when a gust of wind blew a flurry of flakes against the window. Getting up, she peered outside with her forehead against the icy glass, and was surprised to find the ground already white, and the air filled with driving white flakes, whipped up by the strengthening wind. Shivering, she made herself a hot drink before banking up the fire and putting the guard firmly round it. She went up to her bedroom, which was not as cold as it could have been, due to the fire in the room below and the warmth of the chimney that went up through the middle of the house.

All night the storm raged, with the wind moaning in the chimney, and the driving snow flinging itself against the window. With the dawn, the wind dropped, and the silence folded itself round the cottage as the pale unearthly light crept across the snow-blanketed fields.

Kate woke in the first light of dawn and, snuggled in the warm cocoon of her bed, looked towards the pale rectangle of the window, against which little drifts of snow had built up. She watched as the sky brightened beyond the branches of the poplars and turned a wonderful salmon pink with the sunrise. Shivering, she got out of bed, thrusting her feet into her sheepskin slippers. Pulling on a thick woolly cardigan, she went to the window.

A magical world greeted her. The sun was breaking through the tattered remnants of the storm clouds, and its low rays shafted across the field beyond the poplars, glittering on the pristine blanket of white. The wind had caused the snow to drift up against the trunks of the trees like waves lapping at their bases. Kate opened the window, dislodging a shower of snow crystals, and breathed a great gulp of icy air before hurriedly closing it again and going downstairs to see if the fire still had an ember or two which she could bring to life again.

The snow was beautiful, but turning on the radio, Kate discovered that the whole of the south of England had been brought to a virtual standstill, though the snow ploughs had been out in force all through the night. She began to wonder if it would be feasible to drive up to Yorkshire after all, and whether it would be better to put off her visit till the roads improved.

Meanwhile, she was determined to enjoy the snow, and later, dressed warmly in several layers of clothing, she found her camera and let herself out, kicking aside the drift of snow which had accumulated against the front door. The garden path had completely disappeared and the unkempt hedge bordering the lane was weighed down with at least six inches of snow. The upward sloping branches of the poplars had not accumulated much snow, but a fine sprinkling of tiny crystals drifted down as the slender twigs stirred in the icy breeze. Luckily, the gate, still hanging drunkenly on its one hinge, had been left open, or Kate would have had to scrape away snow before she could get out. Her Mini, tucked up against the hedge, was encased in a smooth blanket of white, its outward-facing wheels hidden under a deep drift.

Kate started off up the lane, her booted feet making squeaking sounds in the dry powdery snow, which came up almost to the top of her boots. As she drew abreast of Woodcote House, an upstairs window was flung open, and Freddie stuck his head out, calling, "Kate! Wait! We were just going to come and ask you if you wanted to go for a walk to the top of the hill, so that we can go tobogganing."

Kate stopped and looked up, smiling. "Great! I was just going for a walk anyway, to take some photos. It's so magical!"

"Hang on then, I'll come down."

Freddie shut the window and shortly after, the front door opened and Binky came bounding out, scampering like a mad thing in the strange, cold, white stuff which seemed to his doggy brain to have the potential for some excellent fun. Freddie was in the inner porch, putting on his anorak and stuffing his feet into wellingtons.

"I'm just going to get the toboggan from the shed," he called, and disappeared round the side of the house, lifting his feet high to trudge through the snow. Meanwhile, Amy emerged from the front door, well wrapped up in a pink anorak, a fluffy hat and wellingtons with pink flowers all over them.

143

She came down the path towards Kate, looking back at the footprints she was making, just as Tim appeared in the doorway, also dressed warmly in a fleece-lined Barbour, flat cap and wellingtons. A canvas bag was slung over his shoulder. He waved a greeting to Kate, and pulling the door shut, called out: "I'll just go and help Freddie excavate the toboggan. I think it's under a pile of garden chairs."

Before long they reappeared, with Freddie dragging the toboggan behind him on a rope.

"Well, let's go on an Expotition to the North Pole!" Tim cried, pointing dramatically down the lane towards the wood.

"Yes! Like Winnie the Pooh and Christopher Robin!" Amy squealed delightedly.

"Oh! But we haven't brought any provisions!" Freddie said, stopping dead. "Pooh and co always brought provisions, so did all Rabbit's friends and relations."

"Eeyore didn't bring any. He had to eat a thistle," Amy said solemnly.

Tim held up a hand, then patted the canvas bag. "Of course we have provisions!" he said triumphantly. "What kind of Expotition would it be without provisions? We've got a bag of Mrs B's flapjacks and a flask of tea."

That important matter having been resolved, Freddie set off down the lane behind Binky who had bounded ahead, leaving a scuffed trail of footprints behind him. The others followed, soon coming abreast of the Babbidge's cottage, its immaculately clipped box hedge looking like an iced loaf cake, and a homely spiral of smoke curling up from the chimney.

Bill had already scraped the snow away from the path and was stamping his boots on the doorstep as they passed. He gave them a cheerful wave, his beaming face looking rosier and shinier than ever in the frosty air.

"Lucky it's a Sunday," he called. "Roads are very bad, especially the side roads. Have you tried to go out in the car Tim?"

"No. I'm sure the Land Rover can handle it, but I don't need to go out today anyway."

Bill eyed the toboggan. "Going up to the hill are you? Well, have a good time!"

"Bye Bill, and tell Mrs B. that she's not to worry about coming out in the snow to sort out lunch. We'll make do with stuff from the freezer or something."

"Will do, Tim, if you're sure."

"Absolutely. Bye!"

Waving goodbye, they entered the wood, and gave a collective gasp. Here in the relative shelter of the wood, the wind had not shaken so much of the snow off the branches, and it lay on every branch and twig, creating an exquisite filigree tunnel of white and deep sepia brown, with shafts of sunlight casting blue shadows across the path.

Kate took photo after photo, and when they emerged from the wood at the top of the hill, they all stood looking around in wonderment at the glittering panorama of sun-gilded snowy fields. The children immediately started taking it in turns to toboggan down the slope that they had walked up that autumn day when they had played leaf boats. Remembering that day, Kate glanced at Tim, just as he turned to look at her. His eyes, crinkled against the dazzling whiteness, looked very blue.

Tim in his turn, caught his breath as he looked at Kate. She had an old green bobble hat rammed down over her unruly auburn hair, which was escaping in all directions. Her face was completely devoid of make-up, her cheeks flushed with the cold, and her green eyes sparkled. Their glance held for a second, then she looked down, the thick dark lashes shading her eyes.

Freddie came panting up the hill, dragging the toboggan. "Do you want a go Kate? It's brill!"

"Ooh! Yes please! Can't resist!"

Kate handed her camera to Tim to hold, then settled herself on the toboggan. Freddie gave her a push, and she started to move, gathering momentum, till she was going at a fair speed down the slope, with Binky scampering after her, barking wildly. Nearing the bottom, the toboggan hit a hump and tipped sideways, throwing Kate into the snow, where she lay slightly winded and laughing helplessly.

She heard Tim shouting from the top and clambered to her feet, giving a reassuring wave before trying to dust off some of the snow which seemed to envelop her from head to foot. Grabbing the rope, she started back up the slope, dragging the toboggan behind her. At the top, she collapsed on the ground, panting from the exertion of struggling up in the deep snow.

"Crumbs! I'm boiling hot now, except my hands, which are freezing!" she gasped, pulling off her damp gloves and blowing on her hands.

Next it was Tim's turn. He folded himself with some difficulty on to the toboggan and took off down the slope, the impacted snow and his extra weight causing the toboggan to gather speed quickly so that it careered down at quite a rate.

After several more goes by the children, Tim reached for the canvas bag.

"Time for the *provisions,* I think," Tim said, opening the bag and pulling out a thermos flask and some plastic cups. They all sat down on a snow-covered fallen tree trunk, while Tim poured out the steaming hot tea and handed round the flapjacks. Sitting there with the three of them, warming her hands round her mug of tea, Kate experienced the same feeling of belonging that she had felt when they were having lunch in the restaurant in Guildford. It was as though this was where she was meant to be. As though she fitted into a space that was shaped like her. And yet, how could that be? She was an imposter. Claire, Tim's wife, should be here, with her children, with her husband. She had been snatched away from them, leaving them bereft. How could she, Kate, presume to put herself in Claire's place?

She was jolted out of her reverie by Amy saying plaintively: "Daddy, I'm getting cold, especially my bum."

Tim laughed and started stowing things back in the bag.

"Can I have just one more slide?" Freddie pleaded, and at the nod from his father, was soon off down the slope again, beating his previous longest slide by several feet, much to his jubilation.

When he came back to the top, they started back through the wood,

146

running the gauntlet of dollops of snow which, loosened by the wind and the warmth of the sun, came cascading down, often going down the back of their necks.

Back at Woodcote, at the insistence of the children, Kate agreed to help them make a snowman in the back garden. The snow was less powdery and dry now, so they were able to make it quite tall, with Tim placing the head on as he was the only one who could reach. Freddie fetched the coal for the eyes and mouth, and Amy raided the fridge for a carrot nose. They stood back to survey their handiwork, hands aching from the cold, then hurried into the house.

After some foraging from Tim in the kitchen cupboards, Kate rustled up a lunch of pasta carbonara, which they ate hungrily in the family room, looking out at the snowy garden and the snowman, whom Amy had named Mr Carrot.

Tim looked across the table at Kate. "You're not seriously still considering driving up to Yorkshire for Christmas with all this snow, are you?"

Kate gave a small grimace. "Well, I must admit, I'm beginning to have my doubts," she said. "It depends on whether there's a thaw in sight. I wonder what the forecast is."

"I'll look it up on the computer," Freddie said, getting up and turning it on.

The forecast was for it to freeze that night, followed by a cold fine day, but there was a strong possibility of snow further north later in the week.

"I'll phone my Dad and talk to him about it," Kate said. "It does look a bit dodgy."

"Remember, if you don't go, you're very welcome to have Christmas lunch here," Tim said a little hesitantly. "Or would you want to be with your, er, friends?" He had nearly said "boyfriend" but he was not at all sure what the situation was with Jake. She did not seem to see that much of him, and yet Jake had acted quite possessively towards Kate that day when he had come down to see her, and she had gone off to London with him. Maybe they were both too busy with their work to see much of one another, even though they were technically together.

Kate noticed the hesitation, and guessed what he meant. She longed to say; "It's not what you think, I'm not with Jake anymore," but instead she said, "No, I think everyone will be spending Christmas with their families, so I would just stay here."

"Oh! Please come here for Christmas lunch then," Freddie said eagerly. "We need more people to play silly games and things."

"Pleeeeease Kate!" Amy interjected pleadingly.

Kate felt doubtful. The last thing she wanted to do was intrude on their family Christmas. Tim glanced at her and said quickly; "Actually, if you could give my mother a hand with the meal, it would be a real help. Claire's parents are going to be with Claire's sister and her family."

Kate looked at him, trying to decide if he was just saying that about helping his mother to put her mind at ease. She looked at the bright, expectant faces of the children and smiled.

"Well, if I can be of use, I'd love to come! That's if I don't go up to Yorkshire after all."

Amy clapped her hands delightedly and Freddie gave her one of his lopsided grins.

"That's settled then," Tim said with satisfaction. "I think you and my mother will get on like a house on fire."

"Well, as long as I don't actually set the house on fire," Kate laughed.

The phone rang in the hall, and Tim got up to answer it while Kate and the children took their plates back to the kitchen. Tim came in while they were stacking the dishwasher. "That was Elaine. Her car's stuck in her garage and her drive is impassable. She wants me to flatten down the snow with the Land Rover so that she'll be able to get out in the morning. You'd better come with me, kids. Freddie, you and Duncan can do some snow clearing for her."

"But Daddy, I don't want to go. Can't I stay with Kate?" Amy said plaintively.

Before Tim could demur, Kate said quickly: "I'll look after her. We could go up to the studio." She looked at Amy. "Maybe you could start

148

on your castle."

"Ooh! Yes, can I?" she squealed. "Come on, let's go now." She grabbed Kate's arm and started pulling her towards the door.

"Calm down, Amy. Alright, if Kate is sure, you can stay with her." Tim turned to Kate. "Have you got the key of the studio with you? If not, I have a spare one."

"Yes, I have, it's on the key ring with my front door key. Come on then, Amy, put on your boots and things." She turned to Tim. "I hope the roads are driveable."

"Oh, the Landy has no problem with snow," Tim said confidently.

Kate and Amy trudged across to the garage and watched from the window of the studio as Tim, with Freddie beside him, backed out the Discovery and went off down the lane, leaving deep tyre tracks in the snow.

Later that afternoon, keeping to the tracks the Land Rover had made, Kate walked back down the lane to her cottage in the blue twilight as the short winter's day drew in. The sky was completely clear and the temperature was dropping fast.

She and Amy had spent a companionable afternoon in the warm studio, with Amy pottering contentedly with lumps of clay which gradually started to resemble a round tower. They had decided that a fairy castle might be a bit of a tall order for a first attempt, so they opted to make Rapunzel's tower instead, complete with pointed roof, with Rapunzel leaning her round face out of a window at the top, and her hair hanging down in a long plait to the ground.

Amy had been mightily pleased with her handiwork, standing back to admire it with her clay-caked hands clasped behind her. Glancing at her from the other end of the room, standing there with her little straight back and messy hair, Kate had longed to hug her close, as Amy's mother would have done, if Amy had said to her, "Is this good, Mummy?"

Unbidden, the tears had started to her eyes. Though she had been much older when her own mother had died, she had felt her loss acutely when she had achieved something and had known how proud her mother would have been. And then Tim had come back with Freddie, expressing wonder and amazement when he saw the wonky little tower.

He examined it from all angles, while Amy explained how she had marked out the stones and plaited the princess's hair. Looking at Kate over Amy's head, Tim had seen the tears shining in her eyes and was struck by the difference between the expression on Kate's face and the quickly concealed flash of fury in Elaine's eyes when Freddie had earlier enthused about the "ace" time they had had with Kate in the snow.

Kate let herself into the cold, dark cottage and quickly set about lighting the fire and switching on the fairy lights she had draped on the mantelpiece. She had arranged them among some cypress branches she had cut from the stunted tree near the gate. It made the little room look quite Christmassy and that reminded her to phone her father.

Doreen answered the phone and Kate exchanged a few pleasantries with her before being passed on to her father. He had seen the coverage on the news about the disruption the snow had caused and had been half expecting Kate's call.

"Don't come, Kate," he said worriedly. "You know I'd love to see you, but I would never forgive myself if something happened to you on the icy roads. They say it's our turn for the snow this week."

"Yes, I heard that. Looks like most of the country will be having a white Christmas!"

"Come up when the weather gets better. You know how you love walking round here. You couldn't do that in the snow."

"What if there's a sudden thaw?"

"Look, you were going to come up on 23rd, weren't you? I can't see it improving dramatically before then."

"Well..." Kate hesitated, then made her decision. "Okay, Dad, but what about my presents to you and Doreen? They'll never get there in the Christmas post at this late stage." Kate didn't add that she had not yet bought them, having meant to do so in the coming week.

"Well, the same applies to our present to you," her father replied, "though actually, we were just going to give you a cheque, because we don't know what you want or need."

Kate smiled with relief, thinking back to some of the hideous garments her father, and latterly he and Doreen, had given her in the past.

"And I'll bring your presents up next time I come", Kate said, and ended the call with a promise to phone again on Christmas Day. She then sat for a long time gazing into the fire, remembering the day just past: Freddie with his freckled nose rosy with the cold, yelling as he sped off down the hill on the sled. Amy, engrossed in her Rapunzel tower, prattling away as she worked. And Tim. Tim looking at her with that softening in his eyes. A look that filled her with an ache of longing.

She was glad that she had made the decision not to go up to Yorkshire. The following week continued to be cold, with only a slight thaw during the day due to the bright sunshine, and frosty nights, when the melting snow on the roofs froze into long icicles. As predicted, the north of the country had been blanketed by snow in its turn, paralysing many of the roads.

On the Monday before Christmas, determined to try to get into town to do some Christmas shopping, Kate opened the shed door with difficulty against the piled up snow and got out a spade. She set about digging her Mini out of the cocoon of the drift which still covered it. It was hard work and she had not made much progress when she heard the crunch of wheels on the snow, as Tim and the children drew up in the Land Rover.

Getting out and coming round to the front of the car, Tim surveyed her efforts.

"That's going to take you ages. Do you want to go somewhere?"

"I wanted to go into town to do some Christmas shopping," Kate said, brushing a damp tendril of hair out of her eyes.

"We could take you. Then we'll help you dig your car out later. We're going to do some Christmas shopping too, and then we're going to Sainsbury's. We're also getting some shopping in for Mrs B. She won't let Bill out on the roads."

"Well, that would be great…are you sure?" Kate looked ruefully at her paltry efforts at digging out her car. Then a thought struck her. "How come you're not at work?"

"Apparently the trains are still disrupted - half of them aren't running. Wrong kind of snow!" Tim grinned. "So I'm taking the day off."

"Okay, give me two minutes," Kate said and hurried into the house to collect her bag and change into a less scruffy coat.

The smaller roads were still mostly uncleared, but the main road into Guildford was not too bad, and there was a fair bit of traffic about. Once they had parked, Kate went off on her own to do her shopping, meeting the others back at the car two hours later. Then, with the bags of presents cluttering up the back of the Land Rover, they drove to the supermarket and piled it up more with all the groceries, Kate taking the opportunity to stock up her store cupboard. On the way home, they went to the nursery and bought a large Christmas tree for Woodcote. They drove home with it tied to the roof rack, singing Christmas carols at the top of their voices.

Later that afternoon, Tim and the children came over and together they cleared the snow from around the Mini so that Kate could get it out if she needed to, though she wasn't sure how she would fare on the lane itself. Then she built up the fire and they sat in front of it drinking tea and hot chocolate and eating the crumpets she had bought earlier.

"When are we going to decorate the tree, Daddy?" Amy asked, swallowing a mouthful of buttered crumpet.

"Well, I've got to put it in the stand, which is a bit of a palaver. Then I must do some work this evening - I've got emails and things to deal with."

"Oh, but Daddy, I want to decorate it tonight!"

"I've got to go and get the decorations down from the loft first. Then maybe you could decorate the tree in the morning with Mrs B."

Freddie suddenly turned to Kate. "Can *you* help us decorate the tree?" he said, with an expression on his face which was a mixture of pleading and anticipation.

Kate looked at Freddie and then at Tim and said diffidently: "I was going to ask if you would like me to look after the children tomorrow.

Save Mrs B. having to slide about in the ice on the lane. You saved my bacon today, let me do something to help." She turned back to Freddie. "And we can decorate the tree as well."

The children whooped with delight, but Tim put up his hand in a staying gesture. "Hang on, kids. Kate, you'll want to get on with your painting. I'm not going to start taking advantage of you and expecting you to babysit my children."

Kate's eyes flashed. "Tim, you've done so much for me. The studio, chopping wood, clearing snow, you must let me do my bit and I'd love to help decorate the tree. I haven't done it since Dad got married. Doreen's always done it about three weeks before Christmas."

Tim looked at her, an unreadable expression on his face. She sat there, cupping her mug of tea in her hands, her hair aflame with the light of the fire, and held his gaze defiantly.

Suddenly, he smiled, his eyes crinkling mischievously. "Well, you asked for it. Good luck with disentangling the nine million tree lights which nearly drive me mad every Christmas. On your own head be it!" Then more seriously, he added. "Are you sure you can give up your day? You could take them up to the studio in the afternoon and get on with some work."

"We'll see. Or we might make some gingerbread stars to hang on the tree!"

Amy got up, put her plate down on the hearth rug, and walking over to Kate, she plonked herself down on her lap and putting her arms round her neck, hugged her tightly. Taken completely by surprise, Kate hugged her back, stroking her silky hair. For a moment there was a silence broken only by the crackling of the fire. Then Amy pulled away slightly and looked at Kate's face. She ran a finger down her cheek and said wonderingly: "How did you know about the stars?"

Later, watching the little family trudging off down the snowy lane as the light was fading, Kate thought of Amy's question and Freddie's explanation that their mother had always made iced gingerbread stars to hang on the tree. Kate herself could not explain her own remark, as she

153

had never made gingerbread in her life, let alone stars to hang on the tree. She would have to find a recipe on the internet. She shut the front door and went back to the fire deep in thought.

When Kate got to the Crawford's house early the following morning, Tim was getting ready to leave for work. The children were still eating their breakfast in their pyjamas, as per their more relaxed school holiday routine. There were dirty dishes piled in the sink and Binky had come in from the snow and left melting puddles all over the kitchen floor. Tim started to apologise for the chaos, but Kate waved him off briskly and returned to the kitchen.

"Right team, if you've finished breakfast, why don't you go and get dressed and as soon as we've cleared up in here, we can get started on the tree."

"Cool! Dad found the box of decorations and he's put up the tree in the sitting room," Freddie said, getting up and putting his cereal bowl in the sink.

Amy looked with distaste at the soggy remains of her cereal and wrinkled her nose. "I don't want any more," she said. "It's gone all yucky."

"Never mind, leave it and go and get dressed."

"But my tights have all gone into spaghetti!" Amy protested, dragging Kate into the utility room and pointing at the laundry basket. "Daddy took them out of the tumble dryer, and they're all tangled up!"

Kate laughed and they both started to disentangle the colourful ball of woolly tights, often finding that they were both trying to free the same pair.

Later, with the children finally dressed and the kitchen tidied, they got to work on the tree. Tim had been right. The fairy lights were in a jumbled heap, and for the second time that morning, Kate found herself in disentangling mode. At least they worked when she plugged them in.

The next hour was spent decking the tree with a superabundance of tinsel, baubles, angels, icicles and various dog-eared decorations that the children had made over the years. Any ideas that Kate may have had

154

about tasteful minimalism were forgotten and she was soon piling on the glitter with enthusiasm.

A glimpse of red in the corner of her eye made Kate glance out of the window. Elaine Grainger's red Volvo had drawn up in the lane and Elaine and Duncan were getting out and coming towards the gate. Kate went to open the door.

The combination of surprise and hostility on Elaine's face when she saw Kate standing there was quickly replaced by a chilly smile.

"Oh, hello. No need to open the door for us. I have my own key – for when I bring the children home from school. I thought Mrs B. would be here with the children, or that perhaps Tim had stayed home again." She brushed past Kate, followed by Duncan, who had been standing behind her. "Is he here?"

"No, he's gone into work, so I said I'd stay with the kids today - give Mrs B. the day off."

Amy appeared at the drawing room door. "We've been decorating the tree with Kate," she said. "Come and see it!"

As Elaine followed her into the room, she fought to keep her face impassive. So the little ginger cow was still trying to worm her way in to the family, making herself indispensable, getting all buddy buddy with the children.

She stopped and stood surveying the tree in all its gaudy, blazing glory, and the mess of tinsel and boxes on the carpet and gave a visible shudder. Duncan edged past her into the room and grinned at Freddie.

"That looks wicked," he enthused. "Mum won't let me do our tree. And it's only allowed to have red bows on it."

Elaine turned to Kate. "I would have thought as an artist, you would have encouraged them to decorate the tree more tastefully." She gave a little laugh, as though to imply that she was joking, but it did not come across that way.

Kate, however, said light-heartedly: "Oh, I think the children should decorate it how they want. It's their tree!"

Elaine's lips tightened for a second, then she gave a shrug. "Ah, well, I suppose you're right. Anyway, I came to ask if I could leave

155

Duncan here for a while. I really must go to London and do some Christmas shopping. The roads seem to be better today and I think the trains are running almost normally. But if Mrs B. isn't here..."

"No, that's fine. Duncan can help us finish the tree and make some gingerbread stars." She looked at Duncan, whose face had lit up at her words. "I can give him some lunch, so you don't have to hurry back."

In spite of herself, Elaine gave Kate a grateful look. "Could you? Well, that *would* be a help. Thanks. Don't worry, I'll see myself out. We're quite at home here." She turned towards the door, calling over her shoulder; "Bye, Duncan, see you later." Then she was gone, snapping the door shut behind her, just as the phone rang. It was Lily Babbidge.

"Hello, Kate, love, it's Lily. Tim told me you were looking after the kids today. Really, you didn't need to. I was all set to come over. What are you doing about lunch? There's fish fingers in the freezer, or you could do baked potatoes and beans."

"Don't worry, Mrs B. I'll rummage around and find something. They won't starve. Tim bought all sorts of stuff yesterday. We've got Duncan here as well. Elaine has just dropped him off so that she could go shopping."

"Ooh! What a cheek! She's done that on several occasions when I've been there. I know she does the school run, but it's a bit much to ask *you* to have him."

"Oh, I don't mind. He's a nice boy actually," Kate said, dropping her voice, though judging by the chatter in the other room, Duncan would not have heard her talking about him, then added with a chuckle, "Surprisingly!"

Lily chuckled too. "Yes, he's alright, is Duncan. I feel sorry for him really. I think his dad is so preoccupied with his new wife, he doesn't seem to have much time for the child when he goes to stay with them. He seems to do nothing but watch television and play computer games, from what he tells me."

"Well, I'd better go and clear up the drawing room. We've been decorating the tree, and it looks like a tornado has been through the room!"

"Well, don't worry too much. Magda goes in to clean later. She'll tidy up."

"And I promised we'd make gingerbread stars to hang on the tree. Haven't the foggiest idea how to make them! Have you got a recipe?"

Lily reeled off the recipe to Kate, which she jotted down on the pad beside the telephone. "You'll find all the ingredients you need in the kitchen cupboards and the fridge. Good luck!" She rang off and Kate returned to the children.

They spent ten minutes doing a cursory tidy up of the debris in the drawing room, and then they all decamped to the kitchen and set to work on the gingerbread making. When Magda arrived to clean later that morning, she stood at the kitchen door and burst into fits of laughter at the sight that greeted her. There was flour everywhere, including all over the children's clothes, hair and faces. Even Kate had a white dusting in her hair due to over-vigorous mixing by Amy. There were dirty bowls, rolling pins, star cutters, spoons and packets of ingredients all over the kitchen table and on every surface. But there was a warm spicy baking smell in the air and on a cooling rack beside the oven were serried ranks of gingerbread stars, each with a hole for hanging up with string.

Freddie pointed them out proudly. "All the holes joined up, so we had to poke them again while they were still hot" he explained solemnly, while Amy piped up,

"I cutted eight stars. But Freddie and Duncan cutted *millions*. Would you like one? They're yummy."

Magda wiped the tears of laughter from her eyes and said, "Mmm... yes please." She took one and having pronounced that they were indeed yummy, packed the children off to play while she and Kate cleaned up.

After a lunch of pepperoni pizza that Kate had unearthed from the freezer, they took turns at icing the gingerbread stars and scattering them with silver balls. Then they all went outside to make another snowman, or rather a snow woman, which, being smaller than Mr Carrot, was promptly dubbed Mrs Carrot by Amy. Then of course they had to make Baby Carrot, by which time they were thoroughly chilled and had to come inside to warm up.

Magda, having finished her work, put on her coat to go. Kate walked with her to the door.

"Annie phoned me yesterday," Magda said in a low voice. "She's been granted legal aid to bring her case to court. She's also going to try to get the rental agreement for the house put in her name so that she can come home, plus housing benefit. And she's got a restraining order to stop him coming near her. If he does, he'll be arrested." She shook her head, a dubious twist to her mouth. "I don't know. I think she should go away, where that beast can't find her. He's bound to get at her sometime unless he's actually put in jail. Even if he is, what happens when he's released?"

"I know, but I can understand her wanting to come home. You said that it's the only real home she's ever known."

Magda sighed. "We'll just have to wait and see what happens when the case comes to court."

She buttoned up her coat and wound her scarf round her neck. "I'll be off now. I'm just going to pop in to have a cuppa with Lily."

Kate waved her off and shut the door on the icy afternoon air.

Elaine, letting herself in when she returned about six thirty, found them all in the family room, busily engaged in making snowflakes from paper purloined from Tim's printer, some of which they had already stuck on the windows. They had not heard her, because the CD player was playing Christmas carols very loudly. There were bits of cut paper all over the table and their heads, bent over their work - Duncan's white blond, Amy's pale gold, Freddie's mousey brown, and Kate's auburn mane, formed a pleasing colour combination. Yet the feeling that this little group of people were sharing something from which she was excluded made angry tears prick her eyes.

Masking her irritation, Elaine put on a bright smile just as Amy looked up and saw her.

"Kate showed us how to make snowflakes. Look, you cut a circle and fold it three times, then you cut little shapes out," she said schoolmarmishly. "Then you open it out again!" She picked up a finished one, while Kate said laughingly, "Here's one she made earlier!"

158

Elaine managed another brittle smile, then taking off her coat, she sank down on the sofa.

"Oh, my feet! I've been up and down Bond Street and Knightsbridge, and all over the place."

"Would you like some tea?" Kate asked, eyeing the uncomfortable-looking high-heeled ankle boots which Elaine had kicked off,

"No thanks, but I could murder a glass of wine!" Elaine said, leaning her head against the back of the sofa. "There's probably an open bottle in the fridge door. Would you mind?"

Tim, returning half an hour later, stopped on the garden path and looked in through the drawing room windows. The main lights were off, but the tree blazed in the corner of the room, a shimmering, glittering pyramid of colour and light. He could almost imagine Claire sitting at the piano, playing a nocturne, her sleek, dark hair shining in the light of the tree. For a moment, he closed his eyes dreading the wash of pain and loss that always enveloped him when caught unawares like this. And the loss was there, just as strong, but somehow there was an easing of the pain, as though a balm had been laid gently on his heart.

He put the key in the lock, and let himself in. Putting down his briefcase he went towards the family room, but passing the kitchen, he saw Kate putting a tray of fish fingers into the oven.

"Oh! Hi, Tim. I'm just doing some supper for the children. Then I'll be off. Elaine and Duncan are here. Elaine asked if Duncan could stay here while she went shopping in London." Tim's sudden appearance had caught Kate off guard, and she found herself gabbling.

Tim's eyes darkened momentarily in annoyance. That was too bad of Elaine, expecting Kate to babysit her son.

"Sorry about that," he muttered, glancing at the door. "Hell of a cheek!"

"No, it was fine, really. We had good fun, and he's a nice chap." She turned to the oven. "There are baked potatoes in here which are nearly done and peas in this saucepan."

Elaine came into the kitchen in her stockinged feet, carrying her

159

empty wine glass.

"Tim, darling! I didn't know you were home!" She gave him a kiss on the lips and stood close to him. "You're early! We could have come back on the same train. I only got back half an hour ago myself." She paused and looked down into her glass. "What does a girl have to do to get a refill around here?"

"You're driving Elaine, no more for you," Tim said firmly, taking her glass and putting it by the sink.

Elaine sighed and glanced at Kate. "He's so protective. Keeps me on the straight and narrow." She gave Tim a sidelong glance. The wine seemed to have loosened her tongue somewhat and Kate noticed her demeanour was less *buttoned up* - a description Jake had used about her.

Suddenly, Kate felt that she must be out of there. Elaine's flirtatious intimacy with Tim, the way she treated his house as a second home and most of all the signals that Elaine was sending, which only another woman would read - that she and Tim had been and still were, lovers - all these combined to dissipate the enjoyment of the day she had spent with the children.

Kate opened the oven and gave a potato a squeeze. "They're ready now. So you can eat when you want. I think I'd better be off. Get the fire lit and warm up the cottage."

Elaine saw Tim looking at Kate's retreating back as she went to say goodbye to the children and something in his expression struck a chill in her heart. It was a chill which stayed with her long into the night, as she lay alone in her king-sized bed in her immaculate, white bedroom.

Chapter IX

Christmas Eve saw more flurries of snow, blown in on a northerly wind which chilled to the marrow. But Kate was glad. She always hoped for a white Christmas, and since her father had moved to Yorkshire, she had experienced one or two, but it hardly ever happened down south.

She had managed to extricate her car the previous day and had bumped her way down the frozen snow ruts in the lane, determined to go into town to do some more shopping and to stock up on groceries at the out of town supermarket. While in Guildford, she treated herself to a new dress to wear on Christmas Day, thinking she ought to look as though she had made an effort. She wasn't sure how much the Crawford family dressed up for Christmas, but she thought she should err on the safe side.

Having spent Christmas Eve morning making a batch of mince pies, Kate put some in an empty biscuit tin to take to Zachary. She wanted to tell him that Geoff had phoned the night before to say that he intended to come down and see his work and take away some more pieces to put in his gallery. She also wanted to take presents to Lily and Bill Babbidge. Well wrapped up, she set off down the lane, glancing in at the Crawfords' drawing room windows as she passed. The tree twinkled in the window and smoke rose from the chimney, and she could hear Binky barking somewhere behind the house. There was a spanking new blue Mini parked near the garage next to the Discovery, which Kate realised must belong to Tim's mother.

She called at the Babbidges' cottage and spent a pleasant half hour chatting over coffee. The cosy little kitchen was redolent with the aromas of baking and of a ham simmering on the stove. Lily plonked a plate of mince pies in front of her.

"Oh, dear!" Kate said, ruefully eyeing their fluffy perfection. "You should see the pathetic ones I've just made. I'm taking a few to Zachary. I hope they're not too disgusting! I'm afraid I'm not very good with

161

pastry."

Lily tutted reprovingly. "Don't do yourself down. I'm sure they're delicious. And it's a lovely thought. I'm sure the poor man hasn't had anyone make him mince pies or anything else for a very long time."

Kate took three parcels out of her rucksack. She had bought some talcum powder for Lily and tobacco for Bill's pipe, and the third parcel, to them both, was a watercolour of apples she had taken out of her sketch book and had found a frame for in Guildford.

"Just little pressies to open on Christmas Day."

Lily gave Kate a hug. "You shouldn't have, dear," she scolded affectionately. "But it so happens I have something for you!" She bustled off and returned with a squashy parcel, which she tucked into Kate's rucksack. Kate hugged her in turn, then put on her coat.

"I'd better go and take Zachary his wonderful gourmet mince pies," she said laughing. "I hope he doesn't break his teeth!"

Due to the covering of snow, it was quite hard to find the indistinct path in the woods which branched off from the main one. The smell of wood smoke guided her, however, and the snow was trodden down a little where the smaller path began. Soon she was standing in the clearing beside Zachary's cottage. The snow had flattened down the long grasses and nearly covered most of the smaller carvings dotted about. Only the doe and her fawn stood clearly visible, their backs covered with a layer of white.

She followed the pathway of trodden down snow and knocked on the door. Zachary opened it, his face breaking into a grin when he saw her.

"Kate! Good to see you! How've you been? Come in out of the cold. I've got a fire going."

Kate stepped into the cottage and gave a small gasp as she looked around. She had never been inside the cottage before and, whereas the outside looked almost ramshackle, the inside was neat and tidy with a big open hearth in which burned a cheerful fire. But it was the beautifully made furniture which made her catch her breath.

162

Beside the fire was a big rocking chair with fat red cushions and a graceful curved back. On the other side of the hearth stood a squat rustic armchair, made of knobby branches, polished to a silky sheen, also with plump cushions on the seat and against the back. At one end of the room was a table made from what looked like reclaimed wood, with chunky legs, and two crazy looking chairs with asymmetric backs of stripped willow wood. Wherever she looked there were unusual and beautiful wooden objects. A bowl made from a root ball, carved bookends, a little table with the tree rings beautifully delineated on the round top.

Kate walked about peering at the treasures, while Zachary put the kettle on and made tea. Kate accepted it gratefully, even though she had just had coffee with Lily and Bill. It was a cold day.

She pulled out the tin of mince pies and handed it to Zachary.

"I made you some mince pies, but I'm rubbish at pastry, so I don't know how edible they are. Happy Christmas!"

Zachary took the tin and removed the lid. The pies had got a bit crumbly from being transported and looked rather forlorn. Zachary looked at them and then at her with a strange expression on his face. He walked to the table to put them down and stood for a long moment with his back towards her, looking down into the tin. Then he cleared his throat, and turning, said in a husky voice. "Thank you, Kate." He came over to her and put his hands on her shoulders. Bending, he planted a kiss on her forehead. Then he went back to the table, picked up a mince pie and bit into it.

"Delicious!" he pronounced, with an exaggerated smacking of his lips, masking his initial emotional response to Kate's homely little gift.

Kate laughed, relieved that the slight awkwardness had passed, but touched by a sense of the loneliness of the man as she had watched him standing with his back to her at the table.

She said brightly; "Geoff says both your pieces have been sold and he wants to know how you want to be paid."

Zachary looked surprised. "Both sold? Well I'm blowed!" He hesitated. "I don't have a bank account, so it'll have to be cash I'm afraid. But there's no hurry. Any time will do."

163

Kate gave a sigh of mock exasperation and said sternly, "What am I going to do with you? You need a business manager! You'd probably *give* your work away if you had half a chance!"

"Oh, don't worry, when I need money, I take stuff along to the market. Sufficient unto the day!"

"Well, anyway, Geoff wants to come down early in the New Year and take more of your work away. He's got increased display space now in his foyer area, and there has been a very favourable reaction to your work."

"Well, I've got you to thank for that, Kate," he said, handing her a mug of strong tea and gesturing that she should sit down by the fire. "And I do appreciate it."

Kate sat down on the knobbly chair, which turned out to be extremely comfortable, while Zachary folded his lanky frame into the rocking chair. She remembered one of the reasons she had wanted to come and see him.

"Oh, by the way, I want to buy a small piece from you as a Christmas present for someone. Can I have a look in the shed?"

Zachary looked at her levelly. "No way are you going to pay me money. Not after what you've done for me. You can have what you like for free."

Kate took a scalding sip of her tea. She raised her chin stubbornly. "In that case, I can't take anything! And I was relying on getting something from you!"

Zachary stroked his chin thoughtfully. "How about if we called it your commission for finding an outlet for my work? Anyway, you're a bit stuck now. Too late to get a present anywhere else!" He spoke seriously, but with a wicked twinkle in his eye.

Kate rolled her eyes in exasperation. "We could sit here arguing all afternoon! Let's just go and see if there is a small piece you wouldn't mind parting with."

"Come on then, bring your tea with you."

Kate had trouble choosing; every piece was a gem. She wanted to give it as a present to Tim, but was unsure what he would like best. In the

164

end she settled for a young otter, turning in a fluid curve to look over its shoulder, one paw raised, its nose snuffing the air.

Her renewed protestations about payment were met with an implacable refusal from Zachary and, making her feel even more obligated to him, he disappeared into the house, returning with a small, wrapped parcel which he put in her hand.

"My present to you," he said. "I was going to nip down and give it to you. It's only a little thing," he added, seeing her expression.

Kate decided to accept gracefully and, reaching up, gave him a peck on the cheek. He smelt of woodsmoke and pine resin.

"I know I'll love it. Thank you, Zachary. And for the otter. It's beautiful." She put both carefully into her rucksack and turned to go. As she reached the other side of the clearing, she stopped and looked back. Zachary was still standing by the door of the shed, a solitary, attenuated figure in the snowy landscape. She waved and set off back along the path.

As she approached the Crawfords' house, there was a flurry of activity as the children, Binky, Tim and a woman who looked to be in her mid-sixties emerged from the front door. Spotting Kate coming down the lane, the children grabbed their grandmother by the arm and dragged her to the gate to introduce her to Kate.

Gwen Crawford was a thin, fairly tall woman with greying fair hair bundled into an untidy bun at the nape of her neck.

"Heard a lot about you. Apparently you are a fairy witch, paint cool paintings and are excellent at making snowflakes. As though we need any more!" she laughed, as a fresh flurry of snow swirled around them.

Tim came up to them, putting on his gloves. "Last minute emergency shopping expedition. There's always something that gets forgotten."

"Cranberries!" his mother said crisply. "And nuts, and smoked salmon, and satsumas. Entirely my fault. I said I'd bring everything, but I left the smoked salmon in the freezer and the rest must have been forgotten in a bag somewhere in my kitchen. Never mind. Sainsbury's will still be open."

Tim started off towards the Land Rover to back it out, but stopped and turned to Kate. "We're going to Midnight Mass tonight. Want to join us?"

Kate had been thinking of going herself, and accepted enthusiastically, inviting them to come back for a glass of mulled wine afterwards. She had bought a couple of bottles just in case she needed them. Agreeing that the Crawfords would pick her up at eleven that night, they went their separate ways, Kate trudging back down the lane to spend the rest of the afternoon tidying up and wrapping presents. She had taken to Gwen Crawford immediately. She seemed a cheerful, slightly scatty woman who, she was sure, would be easy to get along with.

This feeling was reinforced that evening, when they all squashed into the village church, their noses red from the cold, and sang carols lustily with the rest of the congregation. Gwen, her woolly hat askew on her head, belted out *Hark the Herald Angels Sing* and *O Come All Ye Faithful* in a rich contralto and seemed to enjoy herself immensely.

Later, Tim left the Land Rover right in the middle of the lane outside Kate's cottage, knowing no-one would be coming past, and, stamping the snow off their boots, crowded into her small sitting room to wish each other Happy Christmas with mulled wine for the adults, and pretend mulled wine of warm blackcurrant juice for the children.

With some trepidation, Kate brought out her mince pies.

"I'm afraid they're not a patch on Mrs B's," she said, handing them round hesitantly.

"Nonsense, my dear," Gwen said robustly, biting into a slightly singed offering. "They're better than mine, that's for sure." She looked at Kate with a conspiratorial grin. "I hope you're a better cook than me. I hear you're going to help me with the lunch tomorrow!"

"Well, I hope I'll be a help and not a hindrance!" Kate laughed. "I used to do Christmas lunch for my father after my mother died, and before he married again, but it was more a matter of making it up as I went along and trying to remember how Mum did it."

"Well, I've been doing it for forty years, and I still manage to have the odd disaster. One year I dropped the entire turkey on the floor as I was getting it out of the oven. There was turkey fat *everywhere*. Thank heaven it was in my own kitchen!"

"Yes," Tim put in. "That was one of your more spectacular efforts. And then Mr Stubbs came running in, tore a leg off the bird and ran off with it!"

He burst out laughing at Kate's horrified expression. "Mr Stubbs was Mum's dog, not a very hungry house guest!"

"He was called Mr Stubbs because of his stubby tail," Freddie explained helpfully, as Kate dissolved in laughter.

There was more hilarity on Christmas Day. After phoning her father and Doreen to wish them Happy Christmas, Kate had opened the gift from Zachary, a lovely little paperweight in the form of a snail, the elegant whorl of its shell echoing the wood grain, and the parcel Lily Babbidge had given her – a long, knitted scarf in the softest yarn. She had then gone over to the Crawfords at ten thirty as promised, enveloped in her new scarf. She found Gwen in the kitchen, dressed elegantly in a soft grey dress, but with an old apron on and her hair standing on end as she crashed pots and pans around in a seemingly random fashion.

Together, somehow, they got everything simmering and roasting, while having their glasses topped up with champagne by Tim at frequent intervals. When the time came to check how the turkey was getting on, they found its legs had burst through its covering of foil in the roasting pan. Gwen gave a shriek of laughter.

"It… it looks as if it's trying to escape and do a runner!"

Slightly drunk as she was, this struck Kate as being excruciatingly funny, and Tim, coming into the kitchen with a champagne bottle in his hand, found the two of them clutching each other in fits of giggles. The sight of his mother in her incongruous attire of cashmere, pearls and an apron which sported the legend *Too many broths spoil the cook* and Kate, with his own voluminous 'Barbecue' apron wrapped twice round her slender frame, hooting with laughter, immediately set him off too, and it was this scene which greeted Elaine as she came to the kitchen door a moment later. Freddie had let her in, since the racket in the kitchen had prevented Tim from hearing her knock at the door.

167

Kate saw her standing in the doorway, and the look of dismay on Elaine's face as their eyes met made her heart go out to her in spite of herself. The look quickly suppressed, Elaine walked across to Tim and kissed him. She was holding a pile of wrapped presents.

"Merry Christmas, Tim. You did say to pop in for a drink on my way to lunch with my parents, didn't you? And I wanted to drop your presents off."

"Yes, of course. And we have yours and Duncan's presents to give you. Is Duncan here?"

"No, he's with his father this year. No doubt he'll be stuffed full of junk food for four days." She turned to Gwen. "Hello, nice to see you again. I see you have a sous chef to help you this year." She gave Kate a cursory nod of greeting.

"More like a comrade in arms," Gwen retorted. "We may well get the lunch on the table before four o'clock!"

"Come on, let's all go and have a civilised drink in the drawing room," Tim said, guiding Elaine out of the kitchen. "Old Turkey Lurkey won't come to any harm for a while."

"I've got some smoked salmon canapé thingies in the fridge," Gwen said, taking off her apron and trying to smooth down her hair. Kate took off her own apron and, carrying the canapés, followed Gwen into the drawing room where the children were sitting on the window seats, playing with the presents they had got in their stockings. Elaine was standing beside the fire, a glass of champagne in her hand, and Kate had to admit that she did look stunning. Her hair framed her face in elegant blonde waves, and she wore a wrap-around dress of red crêpe silk with a plunging neckline, set off with ruby earrings and red stilettos. How she managed to negotiate the snowy ground in those was a mystery to Kate. Tim was opening Elaine's present to him, which turned out to be a silk Gucci tie. He got up and gave her a kiss on the cheek.

"Thank you, Elaine, it's perfect. And here's my present to you." He handed her a small parcel, professionally gift wrapped.

Elaine unwrapped it, revealing a velvet jewellery box. Her eyes glittered as she glanced up at him. Opening the lid, she revealed a gold

168

bracelet, set with turquoise stones.

"Tim, it's beautiful." She slipped it on her wrist then put her hands on his shoulders and kissed him on the lips, whispering, "Thank you, darling," as she pulled away and wiped the lipstick off his mouth coquettishly with her fingertips.

"And thank you for all the help with school runs and things;" Tim said seriously. "We'd be in a bit of a fix without you!"

Elaine stiffened slightly. "Well, I hope that's not why you gave it to me," she said in a low voice, and then brightly, "Pity I can't wear it today, not with red!" She slipped the bracelet off and put it back in its box. "And now you two," she said to Freddie and Amy; "here are Duncan's presents to you."

As Kate watched the children open their expensive gifts from Duncan and in turn hand Elaine their own present to her son, she suddenly felt ashamed of the homemade presents she had brought for the children. She had left her gifts on the hall table as she came in, intending to give them out later on. Now she thought she would wait until Elaine had left.

She was still holding the plate of smoked salmon canapés, and proffered it to Elaine, who extended a red-taloned hand and took one delicately.

As Kate turned to offer the plate to Tim, Elaine felt again a flicker of fear. She had never seen Kate looking like this, and by the look on Tim's face, neither had he. Freed from the enveloping apron, her figure was shown to perfection by the simple, green, long-sleeved jersey dress which fell in soft folds to her ankles. Round her neck was a pendant of amber glass on a leather thong, and her hair, usually scrunched up in a messy bundle or ponytail, now framed her face and cascaded down her back in all its russet glory.

Gwen, watching the little tableau from where she sat, resting her feet from the exertions of the morning, took in the situation at a glance. She had felt an immediate rapport with Kate, thinking she already knew her better than she knew Elaine, in spite of the fact that Elaine had always been gushingly friendly to her on the occasions they had met.

Now she noted the tense set of Elaine's shoulders as she picked up

169

another parcel and came over to her.

"And this is for you, Gwen," she said with a brittle smile.

"Oh, my dear, I haven't got anything for you!" Gwen said in dismay. "You really shouldn't have!"

"Not at all. It's my pleasure. Go on, open it."

Gwen undid the wrapping to reveal a Hermès scarf. Hiding her irritation at the ridiculously extravagant present, Gwen waxed lyrical over its gorgeousness, while Kate thought ruefully about the box of three handmade soaps she had bought for Gwen.

"Well," Elaine said, draining her glass. "I suppose I'd better be going. It'll take me at least half an hour to get to Dorking. Don't forget, Tim, you and the children are coming over to us for dinner on New Year's Eve." She looked at Gwen. "If you're still here, of course you are invited."

With barely a glance at Kate, she waved to the children and walked out into the hall, with a beckoning look to Tim. He followed her out and helped her on with her coat.

"You *will* come on New Year's Eve, won't you, Tim?" Elaine pleaded, putting both hands on his shoulders and looking up into his face searchingly. "Or will you be entertaining your little artist again?"

Tim moved away from her and opened the front door.

"We'll be there, Elaine. I hadn't forgotten. Though I think it'll be rather late for Amy to stay up."

"Oh, she can always go to sleep upstairs till it's time to go home." Elaine pulled on her gloves and gave him a lingering kiss on the lips. When she turned at the gate to wave, she thought his smile looked a little forced.

Driving off down the lane, Elaine felt heartsick at the thought that Kate would be in Tim's company for the rest of the day, joining in their family Christmas, cosying up to the children – and Tim as well probably – and ingratiating herself with Gwen. She couldn't banish from her mind the sight of Kate, Tim and Gwen hooting with laughter in the kitchen earlier on. She had gone to a lot of trouble to choose that scarf for Gwen, and it had cost a fortune. Gerald's divorce settlement was generous – well, he could afford it – but nevertheless, at two hundred and fifty pounds, it had taken a chunk out of her monthly allowance. However, if it helped to get Gwen on her side...

Allowing herself some satisfaction that Kate would not have been able to afford such an expensive gift, Elaine sped off towards her parents' house. There the three of them ate their roast duck in the sepulchral calm of the elegant dining room, after which her father fell asleep by the fire and her mother sat glued to something on the television, while Elaine polished off the claret and dived straight into the brandy. God, she would be glad when Christmas was over.

Meanwhile, chaos reigned in the Crawfords' kitchen, as Kate and Gwen scurried about with pans of Brussels sprouts, parsnips, gravy and trays of roast potatoes, while the pudding steamed away, making all the windows mist up. Binky padded about, getting in everyone's way, hoping for some handouts of sausage wrapped in bacon, while the children tore open boxes of Christmas crackers to put on the table. Tim, busying himself getting the wine uncorked, suddenly looked at his watch and exclaimed; "It's nearly three o'clock. Can you put everything on hold while we watch the Queen's speech?"

When they finally sat down to eat in the dining room, which faced the front of the house, it was half past three. The short December day darkened and the light from the candles in the candelabra on the table touched their faces with a soft glow as they did justice to the turkey, which, though rather overcooked, was eaten with relish by everyone. Then Tim marched into the room with the pudding and having poured brandy over it, set it alight to cheers and clapping.

By the time they had pulled crackers and read out the execrable jokes inside them, it was pitch dark outside, and the wind had got up, buffeting the windows of the old house, letting in tendrils of icy air.

Gwen looked at Tim. "Do you still not close the curtains? Even though..." Her voice trailed off.

"No, we always leave them open," Freddie said, getting up and going to stare out into the darkness. "Mummy always wanted the house to have open eyes."

In the silence which followed his words, the grandfather clock in the hall struck six silvery chimes and Gwen stood up.

"Well, I suppose we'd better get all this stuff cleared away, then we can forget about it."

When everything was tidied up and the dishwasher was humming away, they all settled down in front of the fire in the drawing room, and Kate at last rather diffidently fetched her presents for the family. She gave Gwen hers first, who seemed genuinely delighted with the three bars of soap scented with rose, jasmine and lavender respectively.

"I *adore* lovely soaps," she said, sniffing them. "Thank you, Kate. And here is a little something for you that I took from my bookcase at home when Tim told me you were going to be here." She handed Kate a package, which turned out to be a small leather-bound *Golden Treasury*.

Kate gave an exclamation of pleasure. "Gwen, it's perfect. I've got various poetry books, Daddy being an English teacher, but I haven't got a Golden Treasury. Thank you." She got up and gave Gwen a kiss on the cheek, then gave Freddie and Amy their parcels.

Amy tore hers open and gave a squeal of delight at the framed watercolour painting of a fairy-tale castle, perched precipitously on a crag, complete with an abundance of turrets and towers. Kate had worked on it in the evenings after coming back from the studio and had found a ready-made frame to fit it in Guildford. She had done the same with Freddie's present – a pen and wash drawing of a stag beetle. Freddie had opened his more slowly and his luminous glance up at her when he saw it made her heart contract. Tim, looking at the three of them, was struck anew at how Kate was able to have such an instinctive understanding and connection with his children.

Amy came over to Kate and flung her arms round her neck. "Thank you for my lovely picture. I'm going to have it in my bedroom where I can look at it when I go to sleep."

Freddie also came over and shook her hand shyly. "You've got the reddish colour of the antlers just right," he said. "It's really cool!"

Kate smiled and picked up her last parcel. "And this is for you

172

Tim," she said, getting up and handing it to him.

When he saw the otter, Tim turned it over appreciatively in his hands, enjoying the feel of the wood and admiring the craftsmanship.

"Exquisite," he murmured. "One of Zachary's, I presume." He looked up. "Thank you, Kate. He shall take up his position here on the mantelpiece." He pushed aside some Christmas cards and placed the otter next to the photograph of his wife. Then he went over to the Christmas tree and picked up the last parcel left underneath.

"For you," he said, handing Kate the flat package.

It was a book of Norman Ackroyd's wonderfully atmospheric aquatints of the stormy seas and wheeling gulls around lonely Scottish islands, accompanied by the poems of the Scottish poet Douglas Dunn. Kate looked up at Tim with shining eyes.

"Oh Tim, you must be psychic! I love Ackroyd's work and poetry is hugely important to me – so the two combined…! Thank you!"

She got up and kissed Tim on the cheek. He put his hand briefly on her waist as she did so.

"I'm totally clueless about art," Tim said ruefully; "so I asked a colleague at work who's very in the know, and he suggested this book."

"Well, it was a brilliant choice!" Kate said, sitting down to turn the pages of the book, revelling in the reproductions of storm-tossed-seas, wheeling gulls and misty Scottish islands and reading snatches of the poems.

But she was not allowed to browse for long. The children insisted on a game of charades followed by another of consequences, and before they knew it, it was ten o'clock, and Amy's eyelids were beginning to droop.

Kate felt it was time to go and she stood up, stretching, reluctant to leave the roaring fire and go out into the snowy darkness.

"I think I'd better wend my way back," she said, turning to Tim. "It's been such a lovely day, thank you for having me."

"Hang on, Kate," Tim said, also getting up. "Let's get Amy to bed, and Freddie too, probably - it's quite late. Then we can have a nightcap before I see you home."

173

Kate didn't need much persuading, and having hugged the children goodnight, sat back down on the sofa and gazed into the fire while Gwen went up with the children, who were both clutching Kate's pictures, to supervise Amy's tooth brushing operations. Tim disappeared and returned with three Whisky Macs on a tray which he put down on the coffee table, before going up to say goodnight to the children. Both Gwen and Tim came down together and the three of them sat companionably sipping the fiery whisky and ginger wine combination. Then Kate got up again. "Now, I really had better be going!" She looked from Gwen to Tim. "Thank you for my books; I love them."

"And thank you for my soaps. And for helping me with the lunch."

"Helping, or hindering?" Kate grinned, going up to Gwen and kissing her affectionately. She turned to Tim. "There's really no need for you to come out in the cold. It's only a hop, skip and jump to the cottage. I won't do a Captain Oates!"

"Not a bit of it. Wouldn't dream of sending you out in the freezing dark by yourself."

They went out into the hall, where Tim helped Kate on with her coat, and pulled on his shabby gardening jacket. In the porch, Kate slipped off her flat pumps and put on her wellingtons, while Tim put on his own boots, and they went out into the icy night air.

Once their eyes adjusted, they found it easy to see because the light of the rising moon reflected off the snow-covered ground and there was no need for the torch Tim had brought. He turned it off and put it in his pocket. As they started off down the lane, Kate felt a little lightheaded due to the effects of the Whisky Mac. Their boots crunched on the frozen snow and Kate stumbled in the ruts made by the Land Rover tyres. Instantly, Tim's arm was around her waist, steadying her. He kept it there a little longer than necessary as they continued down the lane, and soon – too soon, Kate thought – they arrived at her cottage.

Taking her keys from her pocket with fingers numb with cold, and encumbered with her presents and her shoes, Kate dropped the keys in the snow. Tim bent to pick them up, and when he straightened up, they found themselves very close together, there on the doorstep. For Kate, the combination of the whisky and Tim's proximity, the sound of the wind in the trees overhead and the icy moonlit night, all combined to imbue the situation with a dream-like quality.

Fumbling the front door key into the lock, Tim opened the door. He stepped back, and Kate turned to face him. The pale oval of her face in the dim, cold light gave it an ethereal, ghostly quality. Her nearness was almost more than Tim could bear. He longed to take her in his arms, but his natural reticence, his worry that she did not think of him in that way, the existence of Jake, all combined to prevent him from doing so.

"Goodnight Tim, and thanks again," Kate said. She reached up to kiss him on the cheek, but at the last second, it was their lips that connected and for one drowning moment, they were lost in each other. Then, Elaine's stricken face when she had come into the kitchen that morning, flashed into Kate's mind, and simultaneously into Tim's, came the image of Jake walking off down the lane with Kate, with his arm draped over her shoulders.

They pulled apart, the vapour from their breaths clouding the air between them. Kate, shaken by the thudding of her heart, stepped backward down the step into the house and with a last "Goodnight", watched Tim turn and walk away to the gate, to disappear down the snowy lane.

*

During the next few days, Kate mainly kept to the cottage, only venturing out to the village shop to get a few groceries. She suddenly felt nervous about seeing Tim and put off going to the studio. Again and again she relived their kiss on the doorstep, wondering if she was reading too much into it. Had he felt anything of what she had felt, and was still feeling? With Jake, passionate though their relationship had been, it had not really touched the core of her. Tim's kiss, on the other hand, had given her a brief glimpse of something which answered a need in her she had not even known existed.

But there was Elaine. Though she found her hard to like, Kate sensed in her a vulnerability under the brittle exterior. She had always found it difficult to shut herself off from the feelings of other people and couldn't help putting herself in Elaine's place. How would she feel if she had been having a relationship with Tim, and Elaine had come along and begun to play an increasing part in his life? On two occasions since Christmas Day, she had seen Elaine's car coming down the lane, splashing through the puddles caused by the slow thaw that had begun to melt the snow on Boxing Day evening.

However, Kate did venture out for a solitary walk one afternoon, to deliver thank you notes to the Crawfords, to Bill and Lily Babbidge, and to Zachary.

At Woodcote, she didn't knock on the door, but merely dropped her letter through the letterbox. Since she did not hear Binky barking, she assumed the family must be out.

Mrs B. however was in her kitchen and spotted Kate coming down the path to their cottage.

"Hello Mrs B!" Kate said, giving her a kiss when she opened the door. "I hope you're having a bit of a rest while Gwen holds the fort at the Crawfords."

Lily smiled with pleasure when she saw Kate wearing the scarf she had knitted for her. "Hello dear, lovely to see you. Did you have a good Christmas? How did you and Gwen get on with the turkey and that?"

"Fine! Well, it was edible anyway! I've just popped round to give you this little thank you note." She fingered the scarf. "It's beautifully warm."

"And thank you for our presents, dear. We love the picture especially." She stepped back. "Come in for a bit. I know there's a thaw on, but it still feels terribly raw out there."

"Thanks Mrs B, but I'm just popping round to thank Zachary for his present. He gave me one of his beautiful carvings."

Taking her leave of Lily, Kate let herself out of the gate, and started down the track through the dripping wood, turning off the main path when she drew level with Zachary's cottage. When she got to the clearing, there was no sign of Zachary, and when her knock on the door received no

176

response, there being no letterbox, she stuck her note under the door and started back, giving the roe deer sculpture a pat on the nose as she went past.

The day before New Year's Eve, Mimi phoned, insisting that she come up to see in the New Year with them.

"We're sending Paul down to abduct you – no arguments. Or are you going to be singing Auld Lang Syne with the City slicker?"

"I keep telling you, he's in a relationship," Kate retorted, a little too quickly and Mimi's sharp ears picked up the edge in Kate's voice. She knew better than to quiz Kate further.

"Okay! Keep your hair on. What did you do for Christmas? Did you go to Yorkshire?"

"No, I... the snow. I just stayed here."

"What, all by yourself?"

"No, if you must know, I helped the City slicker's mother make the Christmas lunch at their place."

A delightedly facetious remark rose to Mimi's lips, but she suppressed it, sensing that here was something she could not treat with her usual irreverence.

Instead she said; "Good, at least you weren't on your own. Anyway, what about tomorrow? Party at my place. Resistance is futile!"

Kate did not need persuading. In the past few days, she had been restless and unable to settle to anything except working through some ideas in her sketchbook, and she felt in need of something that would distract her from brooding about Tim. After chatting to Mimi, she rang off, and immediately called Paul. He sounded pleased to hear her voice.

"Kate! I was going to give you a call shortly. I've been commanded to come and carry you back for the New Year shenanigans. You up for it?"

"Yes, sounds good. But you don't need to come all the way down to get me. I'll just jump on a train."

"No! It's more than my life's worth. Mimi would kill me if you changed your mind at the last minute and decided not to come. Mid-

177

afternoon be alright for me to get there?"

"Yes, that's great Paul. How are you anyway? Long-time no see!"

"Yeah, sorry not to be in touch. Been all over the place. We'll catch up when I see you. Bye, beautiful."

"Bye, Paul, see you tomorrow."

Kate also rang Geoff and he agreed to come down the following week to view Zachary's work and take some more pieces away with him to sell in his gallery. He told her that the foyer area of the gallery was complete and refurbished now, but the exhibition rooms were still not ready. Then he would have to work through the backlog of shows before Kate and co. could put on their own exhibition. Kate knew that they owed Geoff a debt of gratitude for taking a chance with four unknowns, and she also knew that it would probably not have happened if Geoff had not been Grace's uncle. Nevertheless, it was good of him to let Grace's friends exhibit in his gallery. She realised how lucky they were to have the opportunity of putting on a show in the trendy environs of Notting Hill.

When Paul arrived the following afternoon, he demanded to see the work she had been doing, so they squelched up the lane in the muddy slush to the studio, and Kate could not help glancing towards Woodcote House as they went past. Gwen's blue Mini was still in the space beside the garage, but all was quiet, and Kate unlocked the door that led up to the studio without seeing anyone.

Paul, with his default mode of giving things his full attention, examined her work with intense interest, especially the triptych of Annie.

"Is this autobiographical?" he asked speculatively, as he stood staring at the three panels. "The girl doesn't look like you though."

"No, it's someone I know in the village. Lives - or rather, used to live - with an appalling man who beat her up. She's now in a women's refuge with her kids, waiting for her case for assault to come to court. I feel terrible, because it was her sitting for me that led to the last thrashing, which caused her to have to leave and go to the refuge."

"Well, surely it's a good thing that she's out of harm's way?"

"Yes, but she's longing to get home – just as long as Vince doesn't

178

come near her. She's now got a non-molestation order on him, but she's terrified he'll break it and come after her."

"Well, in my opinion, it's a haunting and compelling work," Paul said in his slightly pedantic way. "Is it finished?"

"No, I'm having trouble with the last panel. It's not quite there yet. It's difficult making the transition from being blurry behind the glass/water barrier to sharp focus on this side. The sort of surface tension round the emerging parts."

"Well, I think it looks fascinating. The illusion of a transparent overlay in the foreground on the figure behind is pretty convincing on all three panels."

"So you really think it works?"

"Absolutely! And the rest of the stuff," he gestured towards the stack of canvases against the wall, "some great pieces. This life obviously suits you!"

He came up to her and looked searchingly into her face.

"There's something different about you, Kate. A sort of inner glow. What is it? Tell Uncle Paul!"

Kate laughed and gave him an affectionate hug.

"Must be the country air. And all the snow! Gets the nose glowing at any rate!"

Paul let it rest. But he knew there was a change in Kate. One day she would tell him who he was, the man who had lit this new fire in her eyes.

Chapter X

"Kate, love, are you up there?" Magda's voice echoed up the wooden steps that led to the studio.

Kate, immersed as she was in her work, was dragged back to the present. The painting she was working on was based on the spiral of an ammonite, which was unfurling from the inside back into the picture plane, the centre creating the illusion of receding into the far distance, becoming gradually more indistinct – an analogy of receding not only backwards into space, but into time as well; the physical manifestation of the fossil being a representation of a life lived in the dim distance of the Cretaceous.

She went to the door and, opening it, saw Magda climbing the stairs in her coat and with her bag over her arm.

"Hi Magda! Happy New Year," Kate exclaimed, pleased to see her. Then her expression clouded. "Is Annie alright?"

"Oh yes, she's fine. I've been cleaning at Tim's and I just came to tell you that Annie's coming home! She says that Vince has been told to leave the property and if he comes near her, it will count as a criminal offence. I saw him going off with a holdall in that little rat's van. He had a face like thunder!"

"That's great! But… what if he disregards the court order and comes after her?"

"That's what worries me. I think she should go where he can't find her. Start afresh somewhere else. But she's determined to come back here. Mike is going to change the locks on the front and back doors. Let's hope the court case comes up soon, and he's sent down for a while at least. Annie's been granted legal aid, and her solicitor is in the process of arranging the court case for assault."

"When is Annie coming home?"

"Tomorrow. Mike said he'd take me to pick her up."

"No, tell him not to worry. I'll go and get her. There won't be room for you as well though, Magda, I'm afraid."

"That's fine – I just thought I'd better go if Mike was going to get her."

"The only problem is car seats for the children. Has Annie got any?"

"No, they don't have a car, but I'm sure Tim will lend you ones the children have grown out of. I'm sure he still has Amy and Freddie's baby seat, which would do for Darren, and he has a spare booster seat that Becky can use."

"I'll ask him tonight when he comes home."

"Yes, do that. I'm sure he'll be only too pleased."

They arranged for Magda to phone the refuge to say that Kate would be picking up Annie at eleven, and Magda took her leave. Kate stood at the window of the studio and watched her disappearing down the lane, which, now the thaw had well and truly set in, was nearly free of snow, with water-filled potholes reflecting the sky.

She was glad for Annie's sake that she was coming home, but she could not help worrying about what Vince would do. She couldn't imagine that he would take kindly to being evicted from his home so that Annie could come back. She sighed and turned back to her painting, but her concentration had been broken, and the light was starting to go.

She had made good progress on this new painting since she had got back from London three days ago. The change had done her good. All the old crowd had been at Mimi's New Year party, and it was good to feel connected with them again. She had stayed on for a couple of days, to take in some exhibitions and revisit old haunts. She had seen Jake at the pub, but he had been with Lucinda, and had just given her a wave across the room.

She did not notice, though, how often his eyes had strayed in her direction during the evening, though Lucinda probably did.

Kate decided to call it a day, and after washing her brushes, put on her coat and went down the stairs, locking the outer door behind her. No one was around as she started off down the lane, and the windows of

Woodcote were dark in spite of the failing light. Gwen's car was not there, even though she had stayed on for the duration of the children's school holidays. She had nearly reached her cottage however, when Kate saw Gwen's blue Mini coming down the lane towards her. She had not seen them to speak to since Christmas, though she had dropped the thank you note through their front door on Boxing Day.

Now Gwen drew to a stop when she saw Kate standing by her gate.

"Hello, my dear!" she called, letting down the window. "We haven't seen you to wish you a Happy New Year. We saw the light in the studio but didn't want to disturb you."

Kate came up to the driver's window and smiled at Gwen and the children – Freddie in the passenger seat and Amy in the back.

"Happy New Year. And you wouldn't disturb me, it's nice to see you. Anyway, I wanted to arrange with the children when we would get back to the art lessons." She dipped her head and glanced in at the children again. "This Saturday? When does term start?"

Freddie groaned "On Tuesday, worse luck. But that's cool about the lesson on Saturday."

"Good, I'll see you then."

She turned to Gwen. "I also wanted to ask Tim if I could borrow a couple of child car seats. Tomorrow I have to bring home from the women's refuge the young woman Annie and her two children that I told you about."

Gwen glanced over her shoulder at the children. "Have you still got your baby car seat?"

Freddie nodded. "Yes, I think Daddy put it in the loft. Amy spilt Ribena all over it, but we cleaned it up."

"And there's a spare booster seat in the Discovery that Amy uses," Gwen said. "I'm sure Tim won't mind a bit. I'll get him to fetch the other seat down from the loft, and you can come over and pick them both up tomorrow."

Kate thanked her and Gwen put the car into gear, then exclaimed. "Oh, nearly forgot. The children have AT LAST done their thank you letters. I'll give them to you in the morning."

Kate laughed. "Bit of a drag, eh?" She winked at the children.

Amy chimed in: "I writ mine on the puppy notepaper Santa put in my stocking."

"Excellent! I'll look forward to reading it!"

She stepped back and Gwen put up the window and drove off.

The next morning, Kate drove up the lane to Woodcote and picked up the car seats from Gwen and a little wad of letters which Amy handed to her. As she got into the car again, Freddie came cycling down the lane in the crisp January sunshine, deliberately splashing into all the puddles, having been down as far as the main road. His jeans and trainers were splattered with mud and there were even splashes of mud on his face. He grinned at her as he came screeching to a stop by the gate. Kate smiled back and started the car. Turning round in the lane, she called goodbye to Freddie and to Gwen and Amy still standing at the front door and drove away to pick up Annie.

When she got to the refuge, Annie was waiting in the communal room with the children, her luggage beside her. Her eyes were shining with the anticipation of going home and she greeted Kate with an excited hug.

"Hello, Kate! It's ever so good of you to come and get us. I hope we can fit everything in."

"We'll manage. I've borrowed a couple of car seats for the children. I think Darren will fit into the baby one and there's a booster seat for Becky."

Somehow they got everything into the Mini, the pushchair stuffed into the tiny boot and the rest of the luggage crammed in round the children and Annie's feet in the front seat.

When they arrived at Annie's house, Magda, who had been looking out for them from her kitchen window, came hurrying out to greet them.

"Hello, Annie love. You look so well. I think you've put a little weight on to your bones!" She bent and gave the children a hug, slipping them a tube of Smarties each.

Kate and Magda hauled Annie's luggage out of the car, and they all crowded into Annie's house.

183

"I did my best to clean up after Vince left yesterday," Magda said, putting the holdall down and gesturing around her. "He left the place in a terrible state."

"Oh Mags! Thanks ever so!" Annie exclaimed, going into the kitchen. "It looks great. Oh it's so good to be home! And without Vince here!" She stopped, her smile fading, and looked nervously out of the window. "You don't think he'd have the nerve to come back here do you?"

"Well, if he does, he'll be breaking the restraining order. Thank goodness you applied for it at last."

"I was afraid to at first. What he would do to me. But the women at the refuge persuaded me. Lots of them have gone through the same thing." She paused and said ruefully; "Mind you, it *was* more difficult to get the order, because some weeks had gone by since he beat me up, but I had a really good solicitor. She's been great. She's told me about all my rights and stuff."

"Well, let's all have a nice cup of tea," Magda said, filling the kettle. "I've bought in some milk, bread, eggs and baked beans. Mike will take you to the shops later, when he comes back from work, while I mind the kiddies."

They sat round the kitchen table and chatted, Annie telling them some of the harrowing stories she had heard from the women at the refuge. Magda had been right. Annie's face had lost the pinched look it had had before. Her cheeks had a slight roundness to them and though still very thin, she looked much healthier. Kate realised that the face in the third panel of the triptych should reflect the change in Annie. The face which was emerging in the painting still had the haunted look of the old Annie.

"Annie, maybe now Vince is not around, you could come and sit for me again? I'm having trouble with the last panel."

Annie's face lit up. "Yes, I suppose I can now! Just let me know when. I'll give you my number." She paused. "I can't believe I can just phone who I want without worrying about what Vince will say!"

When she got back home, Kate sat down on a kitchen stool and read her letters. Two were from the children (the one from Amy in a pink envelope with Dalmatian puppies all over it), and the other two were from Gwen and Tim. She opened the one from Tim first.

Dear Kate
Just a note to thank you for the beautiful carving, and for helping my mother with the cooking. It was great that you could join us for Christmas Day, and not just because of your culinary skills. We all loved having you here. I hope the cottage wasn't too cold when you got in.
Love,
Tim

Tim's oblique reference to when they had parted at her door caused her to close her eyes, reliving those moments, before she read the other notes. Amy's informed her that her daddy had put her 'pitcher' up on the wall beside her bed, while Freddie wrote that he had scanned his picture of the stag beetle and put it on the desktop of his computer.

The rest of the week Kate spent first finishing the ammonite painting, then starting another based on the inside whorl of a nautilus shell. With both works, she had prepared the ground by creating a textured surface on the canvas with plaster-based filler and other collaged materials, aiming for bleached, muted, stone-like colours. Enjoying the way the textural ground took the paint, she became totally lost in the process, and by the time Saturday came, she felt she had put in a good week's work.

As arranged, the children came clattering up the stairs for their lesson on the Saturday morning, with Freddie clutching a canvas he had been given for Christmas by Gwen, eager to start on an oil painting. Amy, who had been given a book about mermaids, announced that she was going to make a painting of a mermaid queen, sitting on a throne under the sea. The session passed quickly, and they were all surprised when Gwen came up to cart them away for lunch. After admiring the children's efforts, she said briskly, "Now come on you two, say thank you to Kate and wash your hands. Toad-in-the-hole for lunch." She added over her shoulder to Kate, "If I didn't haul them off, they'd probably stay *ad infinitum*."

Later that afternoon, Kate downed tools and wrapping up against the wind, which was veering round to the north-east, she trudged off towards Zachary's cottage again, to tell him about Geoff's planned visit the following week. Geoff had called her that morning to confirm that he could come down on the Wednesday to see the rest of Zachary's work and to take back some more pieces.

She heard the *thwack* of Zachary's axe echoing from the clearing before she saw him splitting logs outside his cottage. The familiar tang of wood smoke scented the air and as she approached, a flock of rooks lifted off the treetops and flew away, cawing loudly. Zachary straightened and rested the axe head on the chopping block. He raised a calloused hand in greeting.

"Kate! You have a habit of materialising out of the woods like a sprite! How goes it?"

"Fine! Did you get my note?"

"I did. You didn't have to write, but thank you."

"I love the snail. He sits on the mantelpiece keeping sentinel with his eyes out on stalks!"

"I enjoyed the mince pies. Delicious!"

Kate made a face. "I think that's putting it a bit strongly, but it's sweet of you to say so!"

"Would you like some tea? I was just going to make a cup."

"No thanks, Zachary, I just came to tell you that Geoff said he could come down next Wednesday to have a look at your work if it's convenient to you."

"Really? He's coming all the way down here just to see my stuff?"

"Of course! He also wants to pay you for the pieces that were sold. Believe me he wouldn't come down if he didn't think it was worth it. He got a good price for your other pieces, and remember, he'll be taking his commission."

"Oh, I know that Kate. It's just that I can't believe a London gallery bloke would take the time to come down here to see my work. I'll have to give 'em a good dust down. Some of 'em have been sitting in the shed for years."

"He's hoping to take several pieces back with him, if that's okay with you, for putting out a few at a time in the galley. Then when it comes to the show, we can replenish the stock."

"Well, you'd better come by way of the main road, if he wants to take stuff back. There's a little turning just after the hairpin bend you come to, if you turn left out of Tuckers Lane. You follow the little unmade track till you come to the cottage. Come round the front and I'll show you."

He led Kate round the side of the house to the front of the cottage, which was almost obscured by ivy and by the thick bushes and trees which clustered round it. The front door looked as though it hadn't been used in ages. Zachary's ancient van was parked under an oak tree, covered in fallen leaves. The cottage and the van were almost invisible in the fading light behind all the vegetation.

They made their way back to the rear of the house, and Kate looked around the clearing. It was getting quite dark, the sky to the west a fading lightness where the sun had gone down, the bare trees standing black in silhouette against it.

"I suppose I'd better be getting back. I'll bring Geoff along next Wednesday – probably about twelvish."

"Thanks Kate. I'll be here. It really is good of you to go to all this trouble."

"It's no trouble. Your work deserves a wider audience! Bye for now."

Zachary looked around him at the gathering shadows. "Listen, hang on, you'd better let me walk you back."

"No, really, I'll be fine. I won't get lost!" Kate waved airily and, before Zachary could say any more, she was disappearing across the field into the shadows of the wood.

Before she emerged on to the main path, dark clouds had rolled up and obscured the remaining light in the sky. Kate suddenly wished she had let Zachary accompany her back. The wood was very dark, and she

187

could hardly make out the path. She felt a few drops of cold rain on her face, coming through the canopy of bare branches above her head as she stumbled along, sometimes tripping on exposed roots and stones.

Her gaze was fixed on the ground as she walked, so that she wouldn't stray off the path, but something made her glance up. She stopped dead, fear gripping at her throat and her heart thudding in her chest. A darker shadow loomed in front of her, barely three yards away, standing in the middle of the path. She heard a twig crack as the figure took a step towards her.

For a frozen moment, terror paralysed her, then she turned and started to run back along the path towards Zachary's cottage, a scream tearing from her throat before she was knocked to the ground from behind, her face hitting the trodden earth of the path with a thud. A hand clamped down over her mouth. The sour smell of stale beer, cigarette smoke and unwashed clothes filled her nostrils, the full weight of a bulky figure pinning her to the ground as she struggled on the muddy path. Roughly, she was pulled over onto her back, and the man sat astride her, one hand still over her face. With ever increasing panic, she felt him starting to tear at the buttons of her coat with his free hand and fumbling for the zip of her jeans. She tried to sink her teeth into the hand that was clamped over her mouth and nose, but her face was held in an iron grip. She could hardly breathe, and only muffled, strangled sounds escaped from her throat. All she could see was the dark bulk of the figure looming over her, its head enveloped in something black, like a balaclava, with a small opening for the eyes. As she fought to suck air into her lungs, her arms flailing, her thrashing feet churning up the muddy lane, she felt herself starting to lose consciousness, a darkness clouding her eyes. But then, all at once, the grip of the gloved hand over her mouth loosened. She heard a voice, seemingly a long way away, shouting her name. She took long, shuddering gasps of air as the weight of the man suddenly lifted. She felt him roll away from her and heard his heavy footsteps pounding away down the path.

As she lay sprawled on her back on the ground, she heard Zachary's voice urgently shouting her name, nearer now, and heard the thud of running footsteps coming towards her from the opposite direction to her attacker's, from Zachary's cottage. She rolled over on to her front and saw the light of a torch bobbing on the uneven ground and shining on to her face as Zachary ran up to her. He knelt down beside her and gathered her into his arms, holding her shaking body close against his chest as racking sobs of shock and reaction began to shudder through her.

For a while he just held her, stroking her hair, until her sobs began to lessen, and her body relaxed slightly. Then he said, "Kate, what happened? I went into the house to get a torch to see you home, and I was just coming to the path when I heard you scream."

"A man – he… he was standing in the path. I turned to run and he caught me and he…he put his hand over my f… face. I couldn't breathe. He was trying to undo my clothes. I think he was trying to… to..." Her voice trailed off and she buried her face in his shoulder again, smelling his wholesome scent of wood smoke and resin.

In the darkness, Zachary's lips tightened in fury at the brutality his sex was capable of. He longed to charge after the filthy bastard who had attacked this frail girl who clung to him, shaking like the sparrow he had found near his cottage that morning, having escaped the clutches of a kestrel. He longed to beat the living daylights out of him, but he knew he would be long gone, and he needed to look after Kate.

"We must get you back. You need some brandy or something."

He stood up and gently helped her to her feet, but when her knees buckled beneath her, he picked her up as though she were indeed as light as the sparrow and started walking down the path towards Tuckers Lane. As they emerged into the lane, he glanced towards the Babbidges' cottage.

"I don't think you should go home yet. But we must phone the police. Shall I take you to Bill and Lily's?"

Kate glanced towards the cottage. "Oh, I don't want to disturb them," she said, her voice still shaky. "It's okay, I'll be fine now, if you could just take me home. In fact, I'm sure I can walk now. I was just a bit in shock back there."

"I think you need to see a doctor. We ought to take you to A&E."

"No...no… I'm fine. I'm not hurt – well, not badly. It's just the shock".

189

"Well, we'll phone the police from your place. Have you got any brandy in the house?" As he spoke he continued carrying Kate down the lane, ignoring her assertion that she could walk.

They were passing Woodcote House when the headlights of a car rounded the bend, picking out the tall figure of Zachary carrying the bedraggled figure of Kate. Tim's Land Rover came to an abrupt stop in front of them.

Tim jumped out of the car, closely followed by Gwen and the children who had been in the car with him.

Zachary had stopped and at Kate's insistence, put her down on her feet, as Tim and the others hurried up to them.

"Kate! What's happened? Are you alright?" Tim's voice was harsh with concern.

Kate blinked and put her hand up to shield her eyes from the headlights streaming from the car.

It was Zachary who answered. "No, she's not alright. She was attacked in the wood on her way back from my cottage. I heard her scream. The bastard got away." He glanced at the children apologetically. "Sorry, kids, for swearing."

"My God!" Tim gasped. "Who was it? Did you see his face?" He looked at Kate, her eyes huge in her white, mud-streaked face, a trickle of blood coming from her nose, and his heart contracted with fear for her and the longing to take her in his arms and hold her close.

But it was Gwen who went to her, and putting her arm round Kate's shoulders, began to lead her gently towards the gate of Woodcote House.

"You poor darling. How terrifying! You must come in and let us have a look at you. You need a stiff brandy, and probably a trip to the hospital."

Tim, seeing Amy's frightened little face, bent and gave her a hug. "Don't worry sweetheart, Kate will be fine. Freddie, take Amy into the house while I put the car away." He turned to Zachary. "You go in as well. I won't be a minute."

Zachary nodded, and followed the children through the gate behind Kate and Gwen.

When Tim came into the house, he saw Kate's and Zachary's boots in the porch, and found everybody in the kitchen.

Gwen looked up from bending over Kate, who was sitting on a kitchen chair.

"She wouldn't go into the den. Said she was too muddy. Can you fetch her a brandy, Tim?"

He nodded and disappeared to the drinks cabinet in the dining room. Coming back to the kitchen he handed Kate the glass and turned to Amy and Freddie.

"Freddie, can you take Amy to the den? Put on the telly." When Amy protested, he said, "You can come back in a little while. Kate just needs to have a little rest."

Reluctantly, the children went out of the room and Tim, sitting down at the kitchen table beside Kate, put his hand gently on her arm.

"Can you tell us what happened?"

Falteringly, between sips of the fiery brandy, Kate told them, trying to marshal her thoughts as she spoke.

"I went to Zachary's cottage to tell him that Geoff was coming down to see his work, and when I was coming back, it was getting very dark, and I...I saw this dark figure on the path. I think he must have had a balaclava on his head or something. He just seemed to be a shadow. He...he started to come towards me, and I turned and started to run and I think I screamed. But he c...caught me and knocked me down and put his hand over my mouth...and I couldn't breathe. He started to... to tear at my clothes, my jeans..."

She stopped, the recounting of the incident re-awakened the terror she had felt as he tore at her clothes, the crushing weight of his heavy body and the hand over her mouth and nose preventing her from taking a breath. Tim's hand tightened on her arm, while his other hand balled into a fist as he fought not to let out an expletive.

Zachary interjected. "I said to Kate that I would walk her back home, and though she said there was no need and scuttled off, I went into the house to get a torch. If only I hadn't gone in for the torch, I would have been with her and the bastard would not have tried anything."

Kate looked up at him standing awkwardly a little apart, looking somewhat incongruous in the expensively appointed kitchen, with his greying hair pulled back in a long ponytail and the silver ring gleaming in his ear.

"Don't blame yourself." She said. "There was no cause to think anything like that would happen. Anyway, you got there in time to stop him from... from doing any more damage. You may well have saved my life. I couldn't breathe, and I was starting to lose consciousness when I heard you calling and the man ran off."

Tim got up. "I'm going to phone the police. Mother, could you make some tea or..." He looked at Zachary. "Would you like some brandy too, or something else?"

"Tea would be lovely! I don't drink, but I'm a tea addict!"

While Gwen bustled about making tea, Tim went to the telephone in the corner of the kitchen and phoned the police, giving a brief outline of what had happened to Kate. He put the phone down and came back to sit beside her.

"They're sending someone over – they should be here very shortly." He took her hand, noticing that it was still shaking.

"How are you feeling? Do you want some more brandy?"

"No thanks Tim, I'll get tipsy if I do." She managed a weak smile, then her face became serious again. "It's so horrible to think of someone like that lurking in that lovely wood. It just never occurred to me that it wouldn't be safe to walk home. And how on earth would they know there would be a woman walking back in the dark?"

Tim looked grim. "Unless they were following you." As soon as he saw the startled jerk of Kate's head, he seemed to half regret his words. But she needed to be warned not to go wandering about in the dark in future.

Gwen came to her with a steaming mug of tea. "You probably don't have sugar, but I read once that sweet tea helps with shock. I don't know whether it's true or not."

Kate smiled her thanks, while Gwen handed Zachary his own mug of tea.

192

Amy put her face round the kitchen door, and seeing Kate's smile, came tentatively into the room, followed by Freddie.

"Dad, she wanted to come and see Kate, she won't listen to me," he said, though in fact he looked quite glad to have the excuse to come into the kitchen.

Tim said "Okay, but when the police arrive you must go back to the den."

Freddie's eyes widened. "The police! They're coming here?"

"Yes, they'll be here soon. They've got a patrol car in the area."

Amy had gone up to Kate and putting out a small hand, touched her tangled hair while peering at her face.

"Granny," she said, looking across to where Gwen was sitting on the other side of the kitchen table, "Kate's nose has got blood. Shall we wash it?"

Tim interjected gently. "Not yet sweetheart, we'd better wait till the police have seen her."

Freddie, who had gone to the drawing room window to look out for the police car, came hurrying to the kitchen to announce that there were headlights coming up the lane. Tim got up and went to open the front door, just as the two police officers, a man and a woman, were getting out of the patrol car.

He raised a hand in greeting as they let themselves in the gate and came down the path to the front door.

"Mr. Crawford?" The youngish police officer extended his hand to shake Tim's. "I'm PC Mark Price, and this is PC Linda Miller," he said, turning to introduce his colleague.

Tim shook their hands and led them through to the kitchen. Telling the children to go back to the den, much to Freddie's disappointment, Tim took the police officers over to Kate. Gwen got up and getting a grateful "Yes please" from the officers to her suggestion of tea, went off to make it. The officers sat down on either side of Kate where she was sitting at the end of the table. It was the policewoman who asked Kate gently what had happened while Price took notes of her statement.

When Kate had finished outlining the sequence of events, Price turned to Zachary, who was still standing at the far end of the table. He cut an eccentric figure, which to someone who did not know him, could seem rather strange and different.

"And you heard her scream? How far away were you?" Something in his voice made Kate look at him sharply. Surely, no... surely they could not suspect Zachary? She looked at Zachary, and realised that he too had caught the note in the officer's voice. His face clouded.

"I was just coming to the path that Kate was on. I heard her scream and started running down towards where Kate was lying. I had a torch. I had gone back to get it when Kate started walking back after leaving my house. I was going to walk her back home. My torch picked out the back of someone running away down the path."

"What was he wearing?" The officer was jotting down notes as he spoke.

"Something dark. He was just a black shape."

"You didn't see his face at all?"

"No, and his head seemed to be covered with something black. There wasn't time to see properly."

"How far is your house from the path Kate was on?" Again the odd note was in Price's voice.

Zachary's jaw tightened slightly, but he answered evenly. "Not far, beyond a bit of a clearing off the main track."

Price turned to Tim. "We'd like to interview Miss Atkins alone please, if you could all just wait in another room.

Tim said, "Yes, of course, come on everyone, we'll go and wait in the den."

After they had gone out, Mark Price shut the door and came back to sit down beside Kate again. He nodded at his colleague, who asked, "How well do you know..." she reached over and looked at the notes that Price had been jotting down, "Zachary? Does he live alone?"

"I met him last October, but I feel I know him well already. Yes, he lives alone in a little cottage in the woods." She looked from one to the other of the police officers. "I hope you don't think... that Zachary... I would trust him with my life. Well – he saved my life!" Her voice became

194

agitated. "He would never... *never...*" she trailed off and tears of distress gleamed in her eyes.

The officers exchanged glances and the policewoman said, "Try not to get upset. We have to ask these questions."

Kate tried to look at the situation from the point of view of the police, who did not know Zachary. She had to admit that to unfamiliar eyes, his appearance and lifestyle set him apart somewhat. The fact that these things had never made her wary of him, that something in his eyes and demeanour made her feel completely safe with him, was hard to explain to anyone else.

"Anyway," she said firmly, "the man ran off in one direction, and Zachary came running up from the opposite direction. They could not possibly be the same person."

"Can you be certain? You said you were nearly losing consciousness?"

"Yes, I'm absolutely certain."

"How can you be?"

"Their smell."

"Their smell?"

"Yes. The man who attacked me – he smelt of cigarettes and beer and dirty clothes. Zachary smells of woodsmoke and resin and linseed oil. He works with wood."

"Have you had any sort of relationship with Zachary?" The policewoman, seeing Kate's bewildered look, put her hand on her arm. "As I said, we have to ask these things."

Kate shook her head vehemently. "No! He's a friend. A good friend."

The sergeant said, "Yet you have been close enough to him to know what he smells like."

Kate bridled. "You don't have to be in a relationship with someone to know their smell. And he held me to comfort me and carried me back here. Of course I would smell his scent."

The sergeant checked his notes. "What is his surname?"

"I... I don't know. He just signs his pieces Zachary."

"His pieces?"

"Yes, he sculpts wonderful animals out of wood. And," she added with a touch of pride, "he's just started selling his work at a London gallery." She stopped and looked again from one to the other of the officers. "Please believe me, he's a good and lovely man. He may look a bit strange, but he is so in tune with nature and the woods and the animals he carves. No-one who loves nature so much could ever do anything like...like that."

At last the officers seemed satisfied. They changed their tack, asking Kate where she lived and how long she had been living in the cottage. She outlined her situation since she had received the solicitor's letter informing her about her great aunt's inheritance, explaining how she was using the room above Tim's garage for a studio.

"Can you think of anyone who could have been following you? I don't think anyone would hang about in the cold and wet on the off-chance that someone would happen along." It was Linda Miller who spoke. "Have you met many people since coming here?"

"Not really. I know the Crawfords of course, and Lily and Bill Babbidge in the cottage at the end of this lane and Magda and her son Mike from the estate down the road. Mike fixed my car. He works in the garage in the village, and Magda cleans for Tim here. And there's Annie who lives next to Magda..." Suddenly, with a jolt of realisation, she knew with certainty who had attacked her. She exclaimed: "Vince!"

The policewoman looked at her sharply. "Vince? Who's Vince?"

"Annie's partner, Vince Dobbs. He's awful. He beats her up. In fact, the last time he beat her, Mike called the police and they took Vince away and put him in a cell for the night. It's the second time the police have been called apparently. I went round there and Magda and I were there with the policewoman who came round the next morning. You'll have the incident logged at the station. Annie at first refused to press charges, and they had to let Vince go. One of your officers took Annie and the children to the women's refuge, and just as they left, Vince came back in a very ugly mood. He was very aggressive to Magda and me."

"Is this... Annie... still at the refuge?"

196

"No, she came home today. And she's obtained a restraining order against him. Vince has had to leave the house and not come near her. I think he probably loathes my guts because Annie was sitting for me."

"Sitting for you?"

Kate explained how Annie had come and modelled for her painting and that Vince had found out and had beaten her up as a consequence.

The officers exchanged glances again, and Price, looking thoughtful, tapped his pen on his teeth.

"It's a possibility. I don't suppose you know where he's living now?" When Kate shook her head, he said: "Well, we'll find out. The thing will be getting proof that it was him who attacked you."

"Do you remember whether you scratched him or anything?" Linda Miller took Kate's hands and examined her nails, still muddy where she had scrabbled desperately on the ground.

Kate shook her head again. "I don't think so. He seemed to be covered from head to toe, and he had gloves on–I tried to bite his hand, but the gloves were too thick and he was pressing my face so hard."

"Well, we'll take your clothes for forensic examination. You'll have to come with us I'm afraid, to be checked out. We'll have to see if we can get any DNA and fibre samples. But we need to have a brief word with the others first." The sergeant got up and went to the door, opened it and called to Tim. "Can you come back in for a minute? Not the children."

While Tim, Gwen and Zachary were trooping back in, Price spoke into his radio briefly, then turned to the others, asking them if they had seen anyone wandering about in the lane or the woods. When he drew a blank, he said to Tim, "We're going to take Miss Atkins along to the SARC clinic - the Sexual Assault Referral Centre - for a medical examination. It looks as though the attack could have been attempted rape. Take samples from under her nails and so on. But first," he turned to Kate, "do you think you could take us to the spot where the attack took place? We need to cordon it off. The CSI people will be here shortly to make an initial sweep of the area." Kate nodded and stood up, a little shakily. Tim stepped forward to cup his hand under her muddy elbow.

The officer turned to Zachary. "Could you come along as well?"

197

"Yes, sure, but we'll need torches. I've got one here, but it's not very powerful."

"The CSI blokes will have powerful ones." Mark Price turned to Tim. "Can we bring Miss Atkins back here for the night? I don't think she should be alone."

"Yes, of course. We have another spare bedroom, and my mother is staying at the moment. She can help to look after her, and I'm not due back at work till Monday."

"Good. We'll have to keep her for a couple of hours or so."

Kate looked at Tim and Gwen. "I... I'm so sorry to disrupt your evening like this. I never meant to come and intrude. Zachary was going to take me back home and call the police from there. I'm sure I'll be perfectly okay at home tonight."

"Nonsense!" Gwen said emphatically. "Wouldn't hear of it!" She turned to the sergeant. "Do you really need Kate to go down that dark lane again now? Can't Zachary show you where it happened? Then Tim can take Kate to her house so that she can pack an overnight bag for him to bring back here, while I stay with the children."

Mark Price deliberated, then said, "Sorry, but I think it would be better if both Kate and Zachary came." To Kate he said, "When we've done that we'll take you to your house where you can get a change of clothes to take to the station. We'll need to borrow the ones you have on for forensic examination. And don't wash your face or hands or anything."

Kate looked at Zachary, then at the police officers. "Does Zachary need to come to the clinic, too?"

"Yes, we need to take samples of fibres from his clothes. Because he carried you back, there may be some cross-contamination with possible fibres from your attacker's clothes. We need to eliminate them from the evidence. Also, he needs to make a proper witness statement."

"Oh, I'm so sorry Zachary!" Kate exclaimed. "What a nuisance for you!"

Zachary put his long, lean arm around Kate's shoulders. "Kate, it's no big deal. I'd want to come anyway, to keep you company."

198

The trustful way in which Kate nestled into his enveloping arm and the easy friendship they seemed to have, dispelled any doubts Linda Miller might have had about Zachary. She went over and took Kate's arm.

"Well, we'd better go and see the site of the attack."

The four of them went out into the lane just as a police van drew up and two white-overalled men got out. After a brief word with the two police constables, they fetched some equipment from the van and Kate and Zachary led them and the police officers along the path to the spot where she had been attacked. In the raking torchlight, it was obvious there had been some sort of scuffle, as the muddy ground had been churned up. Kate and Zachary recounted the events again, describing in which direction the attacker had run off and where Zachary's cottage was, after which the officers suggested that Kate and Zachary went back so that Kate could go to her cottage and pack an overnight bag, while they and the crime scene investigators secured the attack site.

"Just make sure someone accompanies her," Linda Miller warned.

When they got back to Woodcote, Tim was standing outside waiting for them.

"I'm just going to pop back home to pack a bag for the night," Kate said to him, at which he immediately responded, "I'll come with you. Zachary, you go into the house for a minute, have some more tea."

"No need, I'll just wait out here," Zachary said, sitting down on Tim's low garden wall.

Kate and Tim made their way down the lane to Kate's cottage. While they walked, Kate voiced her conviction that it was Vince who had attacked her.

"He has every cause to hate my guts. He really resented me asking Annie to sit for me, and that sparked him off into beating her up which led to him being served a non-molestation order. He's a violent bully."

Tim glanced at her dim profile in the dark lane. "I wish you hadn't got involved with such a nasty piece of work, Kate."

"At least Annie's had some respite from him."

They had reached the cottage and Kate fished her keys out of her pocket and opened the front door.

Inside, the cottage felt cold and Kate gave a shiver as she said; "Sit down for a moment, Tim. I'll just throw some stuff into a bag. Won't be a sec." She went upstairs, and turning to go into her bedroom, was struck by a strong smell of lavender which seemed to be coming from the open door of the second bedroom. She went in, but all was as she had left it.

Tim, standing by the window, hearing Kate moving around upstairs, gazed out into the blackness of the night. Was there someone stalking Kate? Was it Vince? But the attack seemed to have another element to it, rather than just revenge and bitterness. Kate had said that he had started to fumble at her jeans. Had he intended to rape her? The police evidently thought so. Not for the first time he mentally thanked Zachary for coming to her rescue. His mind recoiled from what the outcome could have been.

Soon, Kate came back down again, clutching a carrier bag of clothes in one hand and a small holdall in the other.

"I think I've got everything. Are you sure you don't mind me staying the night at your house?"

"Mind! I insist on it!" He walked over to her and looked down at her dirty, bloodstained face.

She turned her head away. "Don't look at me. I'm all filthy. They won't let me wash!"

Gently, he turned her face back towards him. "You could never look anything but beautiful, Kate," he said softly. Their eyes met and locked. Kate felt her heart pounding and felt sure he could hear it.

A rap on the door brought them to their senses. Kate gave a start and hurried to the door. It was Mark Price. The squad car stood in the lane, its headlights shafting out into the darkness.

"Ready?" Price asked. "Hop in the car then."

Kate let Tim go out first, then switched off the sitting room light and stepping out, locked the front door.

"Do you mind taking my overnight bag back to your house?" she asked, handing it to him.

"Of course. Bye Kate and good luck. See you later."

Kate followed Price and got into the back seat of the car beside Zachary, where the police officers had spread anti-contamination sheets.

Tim stood in the lane and watched as the car disappeared round the bend. Then he turned and walked back to his house, his mind in turmoil. Kate had looked so helpless, so woebegone, with a dark, purplish bruise blooming on her cheekbone, the dried blood coming from her nose and the mud streaking her face. Watching her being taken away, unable to do anything more to help, renewed his fury towards the brute who had come so close to raping or even killing this fragile young woman. A young woman, he now realised fully, that he was hopelessly in love with.

When they reached the SARC, Kate was led into a room which had had some attempt to make it comfortable and unintimidating. There were easy chairs scattered about and a TV set, but the next two hours were confusing and exhausting for Kate. Wrung out by the terror of the attack, battered and bruised physically, and emotionally charged by the brief closeness she had experienced with Tim, she just wanted to have a hot bath and go to sleep in a safe warm bed. But she had to go through a thorough medical check-up and forensic examination after stripping down to her underwear. Since a sexual attack had not taken place, she was spared the kind of examinations which that would have entailed, but by the time her injuries had been photographed, swabs had been taken from under her nails and from her face and she had gone through a video-recorded police interview, she was ready to drop. At last she was allowed to wash her hands and put on the change of clothes she had brought.

She was offered counselling, but declined it, her natural resilience coming to the fore. However, she was told that she would be contacted by a witness care officer if someone were to be charged with the attack, who would be her point of contact if the case came to trial.

Finally she was led out to where Zachary was waiting for her. He had meanwhile given a statement of his own version of events and had had some samples taken of his hair and fibres from his clothes, so that if the same sort were found on Kate's clothes, they would know they were not

201

those of her attacker. That had not taken as long as Kate's procedures, and though he had been waiting for quite some time, he had the rare ability of being able to live in the moment and seemed quite relaxed.

He got up when Kate came towards him, noticing with concern how pinched with tiredness her face was.

"Zachary! Have you been waiting ages?" Kate said anxiously.

"Never mind about me. It's you I'm worried about." He looked at the policewoman who had accompanied her out.

"I think we need to get her back. She looks whacked."

"Yes, I've arranged for a car." She looked out of the glass door. "Here it is now." She ushered them out to the car and gave a wave to Kate as it pulled away.

On the journey back to Tim's house, Kate sat with her head back against the seat of the car, her eyes closed. Zachary sat beside her, occasionally glancing at her, wondering if she was asleep. But Kate's mind was still spinning with the events of the past few hours and the thoughts that kept crowding into her head. What would she do now? How could she go walking back to her cottage from the studio in the evenings in the dark? Would her attacker strike again? Would he be lurking in the hedge that bordered the lane? Hiding behind the trunk of a poplar? Crouching in the ditch?

Her conviction that it was Vince who had attacked her was still strong. Would he try anything similar so near to Tim's house and the Babbidges' cottage? She didn't know. She would worry about it in the morning. Right now, she couldn't wait to soak in a deep, hot bath.

When the police car pulled up outside Woodcote House, it was coming up to ten o'clock. Kate opened her eyes and gave Zachary a slightly tremulous smile that went to his heart.

He helped her out of the car and as it turned in the lane and pulled away, they both waved their thanks and walked down the path to Tim's front door. It opened just as they reached it, and Binky's familiar barking greeted them. Tim stood at the door, silhouetted by the porch light.

"Come in. You too, Zachary. You must both be in need of sustenance."

"I'll not stay, thank you, Mr Crawford. I'll be getting on home," Zachary said, taking his torch out of his pocket as he spoke.

"Do call me Tim. But Zachary, you must be hungry. Mother's made a casserole."

"Good of you, but I've got some soup at home. Thank you all the same." He turned to go, but Kate put her hand on his arm.

"Zachary, how can I thank you enough for saving me today? Without you…" she shook her head as words failed her. She stood on tiptoe to give him a kiss on the cheek. "I'll see you soon. Remember, Geoff is coming down next week."

Zachary grinned at her. "I remember! Goodnight Kate. Now go and try and get a good night's sleep." He nodded at Tim and with a last wink at Kate, he was gone into the darkness of the cold January night.

Gwen was waiting for Kate in the hall and immediately took her up the stairs to her room so that she could unpack her little bag and go and have a bath.

"I've put out a dressing gown for you," she said. "It belonged to Claire, but Tim doesn't mind. When you've had a bath, come down and have something to eat. You must be starving. There's a bathroom just next to this room. It's the one I use. Tim has his own and the kids have their own one too. They've gone to bed." She bustled off, and Kate lost no time in running a hot bath. She sank into it gratefully, leaning back and letting the hot water ease her exhausted, bruised body. She tentatively prodded the large bruises that were appearing on her arms, and when she washed her face, the graze on her chin and the bruise on her cheekbone stung with the soap. But it felt so good to be clean again.

Later, in pyjamas and Claire's fluffy blue dressing gown, she went downstairs, and found Tim and Gwen in the kitchen, drinking coffee and talking quietly at the kitchen table. Gwen immediately jumped up and made her sit down, while she clattered about putting out some supper for her. Tim looked at Kate as she sat there in Claire's dressing gown. She had washed her hair, which was combed away from her face and hung damply down her back. The angry bruise stood out on her cheek and there were grazes on the bridge of her nose and on her chin. He went to a drawer in the dresser and took out a tube of antiseptic cream.

"You'd better put this on those grazes on your face," he said, handing her the tube.

Kate smiled her thanks as Gwen brought a steaming plate of chicken casserole and put it down in front of her.

Though she had not had anything to eat for several hours, except some coffee and a biscuit in the police station, Kate did not feel very hungry, but did her best to eat as much as she could. Gwen's sharp eyes soon spotted that she was struggling, and said briskly, "I think you ought to go up to bed, my dear, before you keel over. You don't need to finish that. Binky will polish it off for you!"

Kate looked at her gratefully. "I think I will go up now. Thank you, it was delicious." She looked at Tim. "Thank you again for giving me a room for the night. I must admit, I would have been a bit nervous on my own. I'll be fine tomorrow."

"You can stay as long as you want," Tim said, looking at her with concern in his eyes. "I mean it, really."

"Oh no, honestly, I wouldn't dream of it. I'll be perfectly alright." She turned to Gwen and gave her an impulsive hug. "Goodnight, and thanks for supper. You are all so kind."

Gwen hugged her back, and suddenly, without warning, Kate's eyes welled, and the tears which she had held in check all evening flowed freely as sobs of reaction shook her body. Gwen kept holding her, looking over Kate's shaking shoulder at Tim who stood helplessly by.

"Let it out my dear, you've been so brave," Gwen said, patting Kate's back as she would a small child.

She looked at Tim. "I think she should have another stiff brandy. Help her sleep. Come on into the sitting room. There's a nice fire, and your hair is still damp. You need to dry it before you go to bed."

Still with her arm round Kate, she led her into the sitting room and settled her on a sofa. She picked up the poker and vigorously stirred the fire into new life, throwing on another log, which immediately flared up brightly. Then she sat beside Kate, occasionally patting her arm soothingly.

Gradually Kate's sobs subsided. Gwen handed her a tissue and she blew her nose and dabbed her eyes.

"Sorry about that. I didn't see it coming," she said ruefully, managing a watery smile. Tim returned with a glass of brandy which he handed to her.

"Get that down you," he said. "We'll join you, I think." He went and got another two glasses and they sat sipping while the log crackled in the grate. Kate told them what had transpired at the police station.

"If they find any forensic evidence, they'll probably take Vince in for questioning. I know it has to be done, but it's going to make him even more vengeful against me," Kate said with a grimace.

"Well, if they find any incriminating evidence against him, he'll only get bail if there are conditions," Tim said. "They'll order him not to come anywhere near you."

"He's already got a non-molestation order against him, forbidding him from going near Annie. I'm worried about him breaking that and going after Annie as well." It was hard to believe it was only that morning that Annie had come home. It had been a long, harrowing and exhausting day.

"Well, let's hope it won't be too long before they find the culprit, whether it was Vince or whoever it was, and he's brought to justice," Gwen said grimly. "It's horrible to think of someone like that prowling around here, lurking in the woods."

"Oh God, if it weren't for me, you wouldn't have to worry about anything like that!" Kate said wretchedly, tears starting to her eyes again.

Gwen clapped her hand to her head. "Me and my big mouth! Please don't blame yourself. Anyway it's not us who is in danger, but you. Now I think you ought to go to bed, your hair seems to be dry now." She put her glass down and stood up.

"Yes, I think the brandy will help me sleep. I feel a bit tipsy actually," Kate said, getting up off the sofa.

"I'll come up with you. I think I'll be off to bed as well," Gwen said. "'Night, Tim."

Kate turned to Tim, who had also got up and was standing with his

205

back to the fire.

"Good night, Tim, and thank you again."

"Goodnight, Kate, I hope you sleep well. No nightmares." He looked at her bruised face. "You say they gave you a medical check at the SARC clinic?"

"Yes, very thorough. It's just bruises, nothing broken."

"Well, don't forget to put on that antiseptic cream." He touched her face gently.

When she had gone up with Gwen, Tim stood gazing into the fire, a crease of worry between his eyes as he thought about the implications of Kate's attacker still being at large. Suppose they never found out who it was?

Kate, snuggled down among soft white sheets, hugging the hot water bottle that Gwen had slipped into her bed, and looking towards the dim outline of the window, realised that this must be the room at which she had seen the face of Claire on that first October evening when she had come down to view the cottage.

She drifted off into an exhausted sleep, the brandy helping to relax her body. In the early hours of the morning, whether dreaming or half awake, she felt a presence in the room. Opening her eyes, she looked towards the window again. It was very dark, and the window was barely visible. Was she dreaming, or was there a slender figure standing there, the pale oval of a face turned towards her?

She felt no fear, and soon she slipped back into dreamless sleep again.

Chapter XI

When Kate woke the next morning, the sun was streaming in through the window and falling across the floor of the bedroom. The dreamlike experience of the night before, when she had seemed to sense the presence of someone in the room seemed to be just that – a dream. She sat up, feeling rather stiff and touching her face gingerly. The smell of coffee and bacon wafting under the old latched door of the bedroom made her feel ravenously hungry.

She got up and went to the bathroom to wash. The face that looked back at her from the bathroom mirror startled her a little. The bruise on her cheekbone had darkened to a purplish blue, she had a black eye, and the grazes on her chin and the bridge of her nose looked as sore as they felt. She dressed quickly, noticing that it was nearly nine o'clock, and went downstairs.

Everyone was in the kitchen, and when Kate appeared, there was a collective gasp as they took in her appearance. Amy rushed over to her and gazed up at her face.

"Kate! Does your face hurt a lot? I bet it does! When I fell off the swing and it banged my face, it really hurt."

Kate smiled. "It's not too bad. I expect it'll get better soon."

Tim came over to her. "How are you feeling? Did you sleep okay?"

"Like a log actually. I suppose I was quite tired."

Gwen looked at her with concern. "Are you sure you don't want to go to the doctor's or to A&E?"

"No, really, I'm fine. It looks worse than it is."

"Well, come and sit down and have some breakfast. There's some coffee in the pot."

Kate went over and sat down at the table. Freddie was standing beside it, a taut, anxious expression on his face. He looked intently at Kate. In the months after his mother had been killed in the car crash, the image of her beloved face would come unbidden into his mind's eye, and always, there had been a bruise on her cheek, similar to the one on Kate's. The memory shook him, but he said as normally as he could; "Would you like some cereal? There's muesli, Rice Krispies, Weetabix or cornflakes."

Kate chose muesli, and then Gwen brought her a plate of bacon and eggs. Tim kept refilling her coffee cup, and Amy and Freddie hovered around her, offering her orange juice, toast, butter and marmalade.

Later, helping to clear up, she asked if she should strip her bed.

"Leave it, Kate, I'll see to it," Gwen said. "Or Magda's coming tomorrow, she could sort it out."

Kate did not like to leave it but felt that she should now get out of their hair and go home.

"You don't need to go, Kate." Tim said. "Stay as long as you like."

"No, Tim, I've imposed on you long enough. I'll slope off home."

She went upstairs and got her things together. When she came back down, there was a farewell committee waiting for her in the hall. Thanking them again, she turned to go.

"I'll walk you back," Tim said firmly, taking her bag. He ignored her protestations. "No arguments."

The children insisted on coming too, and Binky, not to be left behind, came bounding out of the door, nearly knocking Gwen over. As they emerged into the lane, a police patrol car came around the bend and pulled up beside the house and Kate could see the same two officers that had come round the night before. Both officers got out of the car, and Linda Miller, eyeing Kate's face, exclaimed; "Gosh, that's quite a shiner! How are you this morning?"

"Better, thanks to these lovely people and their TLC."

"Good. We're just going to have another look at the site of the attack. Do you feel you can come along with us for a short while to have a look at it in daylight?"

Kate glanced at Tim, who quickly said; "We'll go along and tell Mr and Mrs B. what's happened and wait there till you come back."

"OK, see you in a minute," Kate said to Tim then turned to the police officers who led the way into the wood. When they reached the site of the attack, she saw that some red and white tape had been strung across the path. It was easier to see the churned-up mud in daylight, though there had been a frost in the night and the ground was still frozen. In daylight it was possible to see at least one clear tread mark from a large boot.

"The CSI people will be along again shortly," Price said. "They'll check this area thoroughly in daylight. Is there anything else you can remember about the attack?"

Kate shook her head. "It's all a bit of a blur, I'm afraid."

Miller patted her arm. "Never mind. But if you think of anything, just let us know. A Witness Care Officer will be contacting you soon, and you can always tell her anything that occurs to you. Now we'd better be getting back."

Meanwhile Tim and the children had walked across to the Babbidges' cottage. Lily had seen the police car and had already opened the door, having called to her husband in alarm. She was horrified when she heard about the attack on Kate. Her quick mind immediately came to the same conclusion as Kate had.

"I bet it's that Vince!" she said, her usually cheerful face grim. "He's probably got it in for Kate even though it's his awful temper which has caused him to have to move out of his house."

"Yes, Kate thinks the same thing. Though I think there may be another element to it as well." He glanced at the children who were stroking Nutty, the Babbidges' ginger cat who kept a weather eye open for Binky ranging about in the lane.

He said in a low voice: "He was starting to rip at her clothes."

The Babbidges looked at each other in renewed horror, and Bill immediately said, "But the girl is not safe! He could try it again at any time!"

"I know! It's very worrying. We'll have to work something out."

"I saw Kate going off with the police into the wood," Lily said, glancing over at the police car.

Tim nodded. "Yes, they've gone to look at the place where it happened."

209

"To think all that was going on and we didn't realise!" Lily exclaimed. "We probably had the telly on in the living room at the back."

When Kate returned, she found Tim, the children and the Babbidges still standing at the door of the Babbidges' cottage, Tim sipping at a mug of coffee and Lily and Bill with coats pulled round their shoulders. Tim had declined Lily's invitation to go inside, saying they all had muddy boots and it would be too much of a hassle to take them off.

Clucking with concern at the state of Kate's face, Lily hurried off to get some arnica.

"This'll help dear. Why don't you come in? Tim says they're too muddy, but it doesn't matter."

Kate looked at the immaculate state of the carpet inside Lily's front door.

"No, thank you Mrs B. I must go home – get the fire lit. It's turning colder again."

The police officers said they wanted to question the Babbidges, in case they had heard or seen anything, so Kate and the others left them there and walked away down the lane, with Tim still carrying Kate's overnight bag. Before they reached Kate's cottage, the police car passed them, having discovered that Bill and Lily had not noticed anything unusual the night before.

Freddie and Amy had run ahead, and as they walked, Tim turned to Kate and said seriously, "What are you going to do about going back to your cottage in the evenings from the studio in the dark? I don't think you should be doing that, at least until the evenings get lighter, or they catch the culprit."

"I know, that's worrying me too," Kate said, glancing at him. "I don't know whether he would try anything so close to your house, but I'd be a bit nervous, I have to say."

"Either you would have to go home before it got dark, which is probably about four or five o'clock, at the moment, or you would have to wait till I get home about seven. Then I could walk you back."

"No Tim, I wouldn't dream of imposing on you like that."

"It's not negotiable, Kate. While the evenings are still dark, or until they've caught your attacker, there is no way you are going to wander about in the dark on your own. Even if you drove up, you would still have to get from the car to your front door."

They had reached her gate and Kate stopped and looked at Tim thoughtfully.

"Well, I've been thinking about what I said to you about the children waiting with me till you come back from London, so that Mrs B. can go home after she's given them their supper. Maybe we can do a reciprocal thing. I look after the children in the studio and you walk me back when you come home."

Tim's eyes lit up. "Well, that sounds an excellent plan, although I think you may have picked the short straw, looking after these two!" he said with a grin at Freddie and Amy, who were standing and listening to their conversation at the gate of Lavender Cottage.

"Not at all. They can do their homework, or they can sit and draw or something. Or if they wanted to watch TV, I could come and take over from Mrs B. and wait in the house with them."

"Are you going to be working in the studio today?" Tim asked.

"No, I don't think so. It's a nice day, I might do a bit of gardening. This front garden is so overgrown."

"Well, don't overdo it. A bit of R&R is what you need."

Kate smiled. "Gardening is very therapeutic! She looked up at him and smiled. "Thanks again, see you soon." Before she turned away, she heard the sound of a car, and Elaine's red Volvo came into view.

Seeing the little group clustered round Kate's garden gate, Elaine's first reaction was annoyance, followed by a stab of jealousy. Kate was standing close to Tim, her head thrown back, smiling at him, while the children stood nearby. It seemed an intimate little family group, with Kate an integral part of it. Duncan, beside her on the front passenger seat, exclaimed, "There's Freddie" and, as Elaine stopped the car, he undid his seat belt and jumped out, going up to Freddie to show him the new iPhone he had got for his birthday shortly after Christmas. Elaine arranged her face into a chilly smile, and got out more slowly, pulling her coat around her against the cold air. She looked at Tim and then at Kate. She was startled when she saw the bruising on Kate's face, and gasped involuntarily.

"What's happened to *you*? You look as though you've had six rounds with Mike Tyson!"

Tim responded to her rather crass attempt at jocularity with a serious expression on his face. "Kate was attacked in the woods last night. Thank God Zachary, who lives nearby, came along before too much damage was done."

"Attacked? Who by?"

"I don't know for sure, it was dark. But I've got a good idea who it was," Kate said.

Elaine looked from Tim to Kate and back again. "Have you told the police?"

"Yes. Look, come along to the house. I'll explain. It's cold standing about here. Was Duncan coming over to play with Freddie today?"

"Yes, don't you remember? Duncan was going to come for the day before the holidays finish. They're back to school on Tuesday."

"Oh, yes, sorry, I'd forgotten. And I think a little friend was going to come to play with Amy. With all that happened last night, it slipped my mind. I better go back and warn my mother! Come on kids. Binky!" He whistled to the dog, who scampered up, muddy-pawed.

"Bye Kate," he said, handing her the overnight bag, then turned to Elaine. "Are you coming in, or are you going straight off?"

"I'll come in for a quick coffee. I have to come down the lane to turn anyway."

The children said goodbye to Kate, and the two boys ran off, followed by Amy and Tim. Kate was left standing with Elaine.

"Did you stay overnight at Tim's then?" she said with studied casualness, glancing at the holdall in Kate's hand.

"Yes. Gwen and Tim insisted on it, though I didn't like to impose."

"Gwen's a darling, isn't she? Probably told Tim you should stay

212

after your experience. She's a bit ditzy though. She probably isn't expecting Duncan for lunch. Oh well, I don't suppose he'll starve. He's like one of the family anyway. He and Freddie will raid the fridge, no doubt."

She went back to her car and drove off towards Woodcote. Her face was impassive, but inside she was churning with the knowledge that Kate had stayed at Tim's house overnight and probably had Gwen and Tim dancing attendance on her, all solicitous and worried. What was the stupid woman doing wandering in the woods in the dark anyway? Asking for trouble. And who the hell was Zachary?

Her irritation only increased as she was having a coffee with Gwen who gave her an account of the previous evening's events. Gwen's affection for Kate and her worries about her safety were obvious as she spoke. But it was when Tim came into the kitchen and joined in the conversation, that her resentment against Kate really took hold.

"I told her she shouldn't be walking back from the studio in the dark in the evenings," Tim said, and Elaine was quick to pick up the concern in his voice as he continued, "I insisted that the children and I will accompany her home, and Kate immediately said that in return she would look after the children after Lily has given them their supper, before I get back from work." Unaware that his words had nearly made Elaine choke on her coffee, he wandered off to his study.

Aware of Gwen's curious look, Elaine struggled to compose herself. So, Tim had appointed himself as guardian to the poor little damsel in distress. And Kate in her turn was making herself indispensable to Tim by babysitting his children. What was wrong with the set-up they had had before, when Mrs B. had stayed with the children till Tim got home? After all, she was paid for her housekeeping and childminding. She wished that it had occurred to her to offer to stay with the children when she brought them back in the evening. She would have been able to see Tim every day. But he had seemed to have a good arrangement going with Lily Babbidge and having to play nursemaid to Freddie and Amy on a daily basis would have been restricting. Doing the school run made her indispensable to Tim without it being too onerous a task. She had been

213

glad that Tim had decided against employing a nanny, who would have done the school run instead of her.

"Well, I suppose it's the least our little artist could do, considering she's using Tim's garage room as a studio," she said, putting down her cup on the kitchen table and standing up.

Gwen did not miss the hint of sarcasm in Elaine's voice. "I think the arrangement is mutually beneficial," Gwen said. "I do worry about how Tim manages."

Elaine picked up her bag. "I think I do *my* bit," she said. "Coming and getting the children in the morning and bringing them back after school."

"Oh, of course, my dear, I don't know what Tim would do without you," Gwen said soothingly. It was obvious that Elaine was unhappy with the new arrangement.

On her way out, Elaine put her head round the door of Tim's study, where he was sitting at his desk.

"Tim darling, I'm off now." She went over to him and put her hand on his shoulder. "What about going out to dinner before your mother goes back? That way we won't need a babysitter. How about tonight? Do you think Gwen could look after Duncan as well?"

Tim swivelled in his chair and looked up at her. She was, as usual, looking very attractive and beautifully groomed, and her scent wafted over him as she bent to kiss him.

"Er... yes, if you like. Where do you want to go?"

"Good! I've discovered a lovely place out towards Dorking. I'll book a table and pick you up around seven thirty. Then you'll be able to drink more than just a glass." She bent and kissed him again, on the lips, lingering over it and running her hand through his hair as she did so.

Freddie, passing the study door with Duncan, looked in and saw the little tableau. He felt the familiar knot of worry and dread that he always felt when he saw Elaine showing affection to his father. How could he let her kiss him like that? Duncan, following behind him, also saw his mother with Tim. In contrast, his heart lightened. Anything that brought the two families closer was fine by him. He loved the rather chaotic atmosphere of Woodcote, with Binky padding about, getting under everyone's feet, Socrates whizzing away on his wheel, Gwen clattering in the kitchen, or Mrs B's comfortable motherliness, coats piled on the newel post of the banisters, books and toys lying around. So different from the immaculate order of his own house, with exquisitely arranged flowers in the hall and drawing room and not a thing out of place in the elegant kitchen. He stole a look at Freddie, but his face was turned away.

Later that evening, sitting in the restaurant together, they both felt a certain constraint in their conversation. Each knew they could not tell the other what they were really feeling. Tim needed Elaine's help and must keep her sweet, while trying to hide from her his attraction to Kate. Elaine, deeply in love with Tim, was hungry for commitment from him.

Looking at Tim across the table, Elaine thought he seemed quite distracted. She had longed to be alone with him for a while. New Year's Eve had been fine, but she would have preferred an intimate dinner with Tim rather than to have had everyone at her house, with the children prattling on and Gwen putting things away in all the wrong places. But now that she had him to herself, he did not seem to be giving her his whole attention. Was he worrying about that wretched little artist? She was careful not to introduce the subject of Kate and her ordeal the night before. She did not want Tim's thoughts to dwell on Kate, and instead put forward the idea of Tim and the children joining Duncan and herself on a holiday in Tuscany in the summer.

"We could get a villa with a pool and have a lovely relaxing time," she said, taking a sip of her wine, and giving Tim a searching look from under her lashes. Though she spoke in a casual manner, as though she had only just thought of the idea, the reality was that she had been mulling over the plan for months and trawling the internet for places to stay. To be in such close proximity to Tim, day and night, would surely mesh the two families together like nothing else. They would be like a couple, and they would employ a cook, so that she would always be relaxed and able to give Tim her full attention. That's what men wanted wasn't it? That's

215

why Giles had gone off with that mousey secretary of his – because she pandered to his every need and made him feel that he was God's gift.

Tim looked at her. The low lighting softened her face and her hair gleamed gold in the light of the candle on the table. She looked relaxed, but there was a watchful look in her eyes, to see how he would react, and one hand fiddled restlessly with a bread roll on her side plate.

"Sounds idyllic," Tim said carefully. "But would there be enough for the children to do? And Amy may feel left out with no little friend to play with."

"Well, I did think of that. We could ask the Hunters to join us. You know, Chloe and Phil. They have a little girl about Amy's age. You met them at my house at that dinner party. You got on well with Phil, setting the world to rights."

Tim felt trapped. He didn't want to commit himself to a house party in Tuscany. Elaine was pushing things. He could feel himself being sucked into a situation which he did not want and from which it might be difficult to extricate himself. He stalled.

"I'm not sure what's happening at work. I'll have to give it some thought. And the children usually go to stay with Claire's parents for a couple of weeks in the summer holidays, and another two weeks with my mother."

"Well, we can work round that." Elaine reigned herself in, sensing Tim's reluctance to commit himself. Did it have anything to do with the little red-haired Bohemian? She forced herself to lean back in her chair, giving a slight shrug of her shoulders. "Give it some thought. You ought to have a break. You haven't been on a proper holiday since Claire..." she stopped and knew that it had been the wrong thing to say. Tim gazed past her, his eyes unfocused.

"We used to go camping in the Hebrides, when Claire was here, even when the children were very small. They loved playing on the beach in the rock pools, in all weathers."

Elaine suppressed a shudder. Camping! In the Hebrides! "It sounds very cold."

"It's certainly a far cry from Tuscany, but we loved it."

Elaine decided to change the subject. "Are you back to work on Monday?"

"Yes, I took a couple of weeks off over Christmas and the New Year. Back to the old routine on Monday."

"Well, don't worry about the children, I'll do the school run as usual."

"Thank you, Elaine, you're a lifesaver." Tim patted her hand as it lay on the table next to her plate. Despite Elaine's cool exterior, Tim could sense an undercurrent of anguish which she could not altogether hide, and he was beginning to realise that it was due to the arrival of Kate in his life. He also knew he was as much to blame as Elaine was, for Elaine to feel that they were an item. Elaine had come to his rescue when he had been at his wits' end as to how he was going to cope in the months after Claire had been killed. His mother and Claire's parents had shared the care of the children between them, staying for weeks at a time, taking them to school, having them to stay in the holidays. But they could not look after them indefinitely. The two au pairs he had employed had not worked out, and anyway, having someone else living in the house did not feel quite right at that time. Then Magda, who was already working at Woodcote while Claire had been alive, had mentioned that Lily Babbidge could take on the role of housekeeper and childminder. Not long after, Elaine had appeared on the scene.

She had spotted Tim, standing a little apart from all the parents waiting for their children to emerge from the school at going home time. He had looked lost and somehow haunted, that quiff at the back of his head sticking up endearingly, and something stirred in her cold, parched heart. A heart that had been badly damaged by Giles's betrayal. She had felt a connection with Tim, discovering from Duncan that he was his friend Freddie's father, who had lost his wife, and one day she had gone up to him and introduced herself. By the time Duncan, Amy and Freddie emerged, she had learned more about Tim's situation. Though she was not a naturally empathetic person, she sensed the effort that Tim was putting into holding himself together, and it had a profound effect on her. The heartbreakingly cheerful smile with which he greeted his children, and the look of intense gratitude he had given her when she had, unusually for her, there and then impulsively offered to take the children to and from school every day, only served to heighten her fascination with this man. It was not many weeks before she found herself falling deeply in love with Tim. She had never felt this way about Giles, and the intensity of her feelings took her completely by surprise.

Tim, for his part, bereft, lonely, coping with his job in the City, found himself being drawn into a relationship which he did not feel ready for, but which he felt powerless to resist without alienating Elaine. Her willingness to do the school run had taken a weight off his mind.

Elaine covered his hand with her other one. "Tim, I don't want just to be a 'lifesaver'. I want to be more than that to you."

Tim met her gaze and knew what she wanted him to say. His feelings for Elaine were not, he knew, what she wished them to be. The times they had slept together had always been at her instigation. She always made sure that the children were not around so that he would not have an excuse to spoil her plans to stay the night. She had a habit of interrogating Lily Babbidge as to when they would be going to stay with their grandparents, and always tried to arrange that Duncan would be with his father at the same time.

"What can be more important than to be a lifesaver?" Tim said emphatically, and Elaine was about to retort, "You know what I mean, Tim," when the waiter defused the moment by coming to their table to ask if they had finished their main course. Tim gave Elaine's hand a squeeze and slipped his away to pick up his wine glass. She bit back the words and matched his smile with hers, realising that to press the issue would be counterproductive. But if she could only get him to commit to the holiday in Tuscany...

*

Kate had spent the morning and the early part of the afternoon tidying up the garden. She started in the front garden, clearing the soggy drifts of poplar leaves which had lain there since the autumn. The

218

flowerbeds which bordered the path were greatly overgrown, but carefully cutting back the dead stalks of weeds and flowers which grew between the lavender bushes, she saw the green tips of snowdrops pushing through the earth. The pale winter sun slanted through the hedgerow trees on the other side of the lane and she could hear the breeze hissing through the bare branches of the poplars high overhead. It was very quiet and peaceful, and the physical exercise combined with the cold fresh air helped to mitigate the effects of the traumatic experience of the night before. Occasionally, she did look up and down the lane to see if anyone was there, but she did not really think her attacker would try anything in broad daylight.

Having got the tiny front garden looking tidier, she started on the back, but it was not long before the sun started going down, turning the clear sky pink, and gradually the cold started to seep through her clothes. She had been absorbed in her work and suddenly became aware that the shadows were starting to gather. Filling her arms with logs from her store, she went in the back door and closed and locked it. She took off her boots and padded into the sitting room to light the fire. When she had got it blazing she went and examined the windows. How easy was it for someone to break one of the little leaded panes and open the latch? Was anyone out there, in the field beyond the poplars, staring in? She wished she had thought to bring some wire in from the shed to twist round the window fastenings, but it was now nearly dark, and she felt nervous of venturing outside.

She shivered and for the first time since she had moved into the cottage, she closed the curtains of the sitting room. But she could not relax. What if he broke the window and put his hand through and opened the catch? It would be a squeeze, but he could clamber in through the little window. How could she go to sleep that night worrying that he would break in? If she had some wire she could twist it around the catch securely and it would at least make it more difficult to open the window. She knew there was some wire hanging from a nail in the shed and decided to risk going out to get it.

First, she went upstairs and without turning on the light, peered out into the darkness through her bedroom window. She could make out the hedge beside the cottage and the trunks of the poplars looming in the field beyond the ditch. Nothing stirred, but what was that shadow beside one of the trees? She stared at it for a long time before deciding it was too still to be a person. Looking out of the small window of the second bedroom, she scanned what she could see of the front garden and the lane beyond. Reasonably satisfied that there was no-one there, she made her decision. Going down to the back door, she pulled on her boots, and searching in the kitchen drawers, found a rolling pin which had belonged to Amelia. Clutching it in one hand, she quietly opened the door and looked out. The air was cold and crisp, and a frost was starting to settle on the grass as she cautiously slipped out of the door and went quickly down the shaggy lawn to the shed. There was no electricity in the shed, but she would not have turned a light on anyway. Negotiating the gardening tools leaning against the wall, she felt along the wall till her hand touched the looped bundle of wire hanging on a nail. She lifted it off and turned back to the door. Her heart lurched in fear as a shadow moved past the door. But it was the wrong shape. A second, smaller shape followed the first, and with a shudder of relief, Kate realised that it was a deer and her fawn which had passed by the shed door. Quietly, she went to the door and watched as the pair stepped delicately through the grass to the far end of the garden. The doe leapt the ditch easily and turned to watch as her fawn negotiated it more carefully. Kate was so enchanted that for a moment she forgot her fear and watched as the beautiful creatures disappeared into the night. Then she gently shut the shed door and made her way back to the cottage.

It was only after she had locked the door again and heaved a sigh of relief that an awful thought struck her. Suppose someone had slipped into the house while she was in the shed? But if that had been the case, the two deer would have been spooked and would have been running from the direction of the cottage rather than walking slowly. Nevertheless, she looked carefully at the floor to see if there was any evidence of muddy footprints. All was as she had left it, but she still made a tour of the cottage, feeling a little ridiculous as she looked in the wardrobe and behind doors.

After she had secured the windows of the sitting room and kitchen as best she could, she felt a little safer. She made herself a warming bowl of porridge and sat eating it curled up by the fire in the old armchair, staring into the fire, lost in her thoughts.

Elaine, driving Tim back after their dinner at the restaurant, did not fail to notice how Tim turned to look towards Kate's cottage as they went by. It was in darkness apart from the dim rectangle of light coming through the drawn curtains of the sitting room.

What Elaine could not know was the way Tim strained his eyes to search beyond the beam of the headlights for any sign of a shadowy figure in the moonlit lane.

*

The ringtone of Gerry Rafferty's *Baker Street* emanated from Kate's mobile, and when she answered, a woman's voice inquired:

"Kate Atkins?"

"Yes, speaking."

"Hello, this is Linda Miller from Surrey Police."

"Oh yes, hello."

"How are you today?"

"Getting better all the time thanks."

"Well, I'm just calling to fill you in on what's been happening. We received information about Dobbs's whereabouts, and he has been arrested and interviewed. He was very uncooperative and denied everything."

"Now there's a surprise!" Kate said with heavy irony.

Miller continued. "He failed to give an adequate alibi as to his whereabouts at the time of the attack. As a matter of routine, his DNA samples were taken, and since it is relevant to the investigation, they have been sent for analysis. We also sent some of his clothing for forensic examination, including a coat which was covered in mud. We'll let you know when the results come in, but meanwhile, we have had to release Dobbs under police bail, I'm afraid."

Kate's heart sank. "So he's still at large!" It was more of a statement than a question.

"Yes, he's been released under conditions, including not to come anywhere near you. But you must still take care not to go out alone after dark, or even in daylight in the woods or anywhere lonely."

"Yes, I'll be careful. I must admit, it's made me a bit nervous. I keep imagining him lurking behind every tree."

"Quite understandable. The psychological effects of something like that are sometimes much more difficult to get over than the physical ones. Are you sure you don't want counselling?"

"I'm sure. I tend to think mulling over something prevents you moving on."

"Well, if you change your mind, let your Witness Care Officer know. Her name is Lynn Keswick. I'll give you her number, and you can phone her if Dobbs contacts you or intimidates you in any way."

Miller gave Kate the number and no sooner had she rung off than there was a knock on the door.

Opening it, she was pleased to see the tall form of Zachary standing there. He gave a low whistle when he saw her face.

"Zachary! Good to see you! Come in." She stood back and Zachary, dipping his head to get under the doorway, stepped down into the room, bringing a waft of cold air with him. Kate shut the door and turned to face him. He put a calloused hand on her shoulder.

"You sure have a spectacular black eye!" he said, his tone light, but with concern in his eyes.

"I know, I wish it would go away. It's most embarrassing!"

"I didn't come yesterday, because I thought you might still be at Tim's, or just wanting to be quiet. But I was worried about you last night if you were here and on your own."

"I was here, and I *was* a bit nervous of someone breaking the window and undoing the catch, so I wired them up. It might have been a deterrent."

Zachary went over to the window and examined Kate's efforts at securing the window.

"Hmm…what you need are proper window locks. I'll go and get

222

you some and fit 'em for you. What about the kitchen?" He went through to the kitchen and had a look at the window there.

"I'll nip back and get the van and go and get you some locks."

Kate was torn between not wanting to give him the trouble and her fearfulness at the thought of someone breaking in. She decided that Zachary would do it anyway, so she said, "That's very good of you! Have a cup of coffee first."

"I'll have one when I come back. I won't feel happy till I've fitted them locks."

As Zachary opened the front door, they saw Magda coming down the path. She looked surprised to see Zachary, but her expression was shocked when she saw the bruising on Kate's face.

"Kate! My God! What has that beast done to you? Tim told me all about it – I've just been there cleaning. Do you think it was Vince?"

"Yes, I do. Don't you think it could be him?"

"It's just the sort of thing he would do!" Magda's expression was eloquent.

"Magda, do you know Zachary? He's the one who came to my rescue."

Magda shook Zachary's proffered hand. "No, we've never met. Funny that, you living so close and all. Tim told me you live in the woods past Lily and Bill's." She took in Zachary's lean, weather-beaten face, the ring in his ear, the hair scraped back into a ponytail, and noticing also the kindly expression in his eyes, immediately decided that he was a 'good 'un'. She gave him a grim smile.

"Thank the good Lord you got to Kate before too much damage was done."

"I only wish I'd got there sooner. If I'd caught the bastard..." Zachary's hands bunched into fists, his voice tailing off.

Magda gave a grimace. "Well, you look tough, but if it *was* Vince, he would have given you a run for your money. He's a right bruiser."

"I'd like to have had a go at him anyway." He turned to Kate. "I'd better go if I'm going to get them window locks. See you later." He nodded to Magda and strode off. Magda, looking after him said

223

approvingly; "He seems nice. How do you know him?"

Kate explained how she had met him and told her about his carvings.

"He's started selling his work in a London gallery!" she said with satisfaction. "And he's going to be part of our exhibition in the summer."

"Well, well – he must be good. Though I bet he's got you to thank for being able to sell his work in London!" Magda's face grew serious again. "But Kate, getting back to what happened to you. It seems to me you're in real danger. I was worried enough about Annie, but at least she lives on the estate with lots of people around. You're a bit isolated here in this cottage."

"I'll be careful not to go out alone after dark. And Zachary is going to fit window locks for me. I think I'll be okay."

Magda declined Kate's offer of coffee, saying she had to go and clean for old Mrs Campbell.

"Oh, give her my love. Tell her I'll come and visit her again soon if I may."

"I will. She'll like that. She doesn't get many visitors. Now I must be getting on. You take care, for heaven's sake." Magda, tutting again at the state of Kate's face, hurried off, giving Kate a wave over the hedge as she went.

The rest of the day saw a succession of visitors to Lavender Cottage, and Kate abandoned any idea of getting some painting done. First of all, Tim and the children called in on their way to the supermarket to see if Kate wanted anything, for which she was very grateful, not wanting to go out with her face in the state it was. She gave them a list of things she needed and no sooner had they gone than Lily and Bill Babbidge knocked on her door, asking how she was. While Kate and Lily sat chatting over a mug of tea, Bill busied himself putting a new hinge on Kate's garden gate. The Babbidges were still there when Zachary returned and both he and Bill got to work fitting the window locks to Kate's downstairs windows, and a chain for the front door which he had also bought. In the middle of all this, Tim returned with the children and the little sitting room was suddenly crowded with people. Kate felt

224

overwhelmed by the way they were all rallying round and going into the kitchen to make some more tea, had to swallow the lump which had come to her throat.

Tim had seen the unshed tears shining in her eyes and followed her into the kitchen. He caught her hastily wiping her eyes with the back of her hand and was not fooled by the bright smile she gave him. "I was worried about you last night," he said. I'm so glad Zachary went and got those locks. I should have thought of it myself."

"Look, you've done enough for me already. And thanks for doing my shopping. Tell me how much I owe you."

Tim reluctantly fished out the receipt and as soon as Kate had made another pot of tea, she went and got the money to pay him. She also asked Zachary how much the locks had cost.

"I'll have to get some money tomorrow, I don't think I'll have enough on me."

"I don't want any money, consider it your commission for finding an outlet for my carvings," Zachary said firmly. He put up his hand at Kate's protestations. "I mean it, Kate. Please let me do this."

Kate realised that nothing she said would change his mind and felt that it would seriously offend him if she continued to try to pay him. So she conceded defeat and gave him a grateful smile.

By the time the locks were fitted, it was growing dark outside and when Tim opened the front door to go home where Gwen was waiting, it was starting to snow.

He turned to Kate who had come to the door with him. "Mother asked me to say goodbye, in case she doesn't see you. She's off tomorrow."

"Oh, what time is she going?"

"About eleven or so I think."

"Well, I'll be coming up to the studio, so I'll probably see her to say goodbye."

"She's sure to have left things all over the house, so no doubt there'll be two or three false starts before she finally gets away." He turned to Bill and Lily.

225

"It's snowing quite heavily, why don't you hop in the car? I'll take you down the lane. We can fit you in too Zachary, if you want."

The Babbidges readily agreed, but Zachary said he liked walking in snow, and after they had all left, Kate was alone once more. She stood at the door as the headlights of Tim's car bounced away down the lane and Zachary's tall form disappeared into the curtain of falling snow. Then she went inside and shut the door. She felt much more secure with the window locks fitted and sat staring into the fire, glad that she had brought in a good supply of logs and coal and would not have to go outside in the dark to replenish them.

Outside, the snow continued to fall for another hour or so, then the clouds drifted away, revealing a clear, starry sky. The temperature dropped and not a breath of wind stirred the branches of the poplars. A lopsided moon rose above the trees and bathed the snowy countryside in a cold light.

Kate felt her eyes closing, but suddenly a sound impinged on her consciousness. She was instantly wide awake, her heart pounding. It was a faint crunching or rustling sound coming from outside. Was someone out there, walking round the house in the frozen snow? She sat very still, listening, but the sound did not come again.

The next morning Kate walked around the outside of the cottage, to see if there were any footprints in the snow, but found only the tracks of what must have been deer, leading from the field beside the cottage and through the fallen-down fence – perhaps the same pair which had passed by the night before, and another set of tracks that could have been a fox. She breathed a sigh of relief, and feeling much more optimistic, decided to go to the studio and do some work. It was a sparkling day, and the light would be excellent. She was also hoping to be in time to say goodbye to Gwen.

As she was locking the front door however, she heard voices in the lane and turning, saw Annie struggling through the snow with Darren in the pushchair and Becky stomping along beside them on her sturdy little legs.

"Annie!" Kate called, going up the path towards them. "Lovely to see you. Hello Becky. Hello Darren."

Annie's hand flew to her mouth when she saw Kate's face. "Oh my God!" she gasped. "That certainly looks like Vince's work! Magda told me what happened. I can't believe he's started on you now!"

"It's getting better," Kate said. "It looks worse than it is. It's not as bad as what he did to you last time. Most of this happened when he knocked me to the ground. That's if it *was* Vince."

"Well, it looks pretty bad to me. And I bet it was him. I've been afraid of him having a go at me; I never guessed he would come after you." She stopped and looked at Kate in her coat. "But you're obviously going out. I wanted to come and see how you were. I should have phoned first."

"I'm only going to the studio. Why don't you come along? You haven't seen it yet, have you? You could see how the triptych has progressed."

Annie readily agreed, and they began walking up the lane, keeping to the tracks in the snow left earlier on by the post van and the milk cart. Rounding the bend, they saw Tim and the children helping Gwen to load up her car. Glad she had not missed saying goodbye to Gwen, Kate went up to her and gave her a goodbye hug.

"I was going to call in on you on my way past to say goodbye," Gwen said affectionately. "Thanks for all your help on Christmas Day. I think we made a good team!"

"We did! It was fun!" Kate stepped back to introduce Annie to the family, and when Gwen realised who Annie was, she looked at her searchingly.

"Do you think it was Vince who attacked Kate?"

"I bet it was," Annie replied grimly. She turned to Kate. "I haven't told you yet, but that rat-faced friend of Vince's came round the other day to get some of Vince's things, and he said Vince was that angry with me for getting a restraining order against him and with you for giving me 'ideas'."

Tim interjected. "I think you should tell the police that," he said seriously.

"I'll mention it to them next time they contact me," Kate said, then added, "I'm just going to take Annie and the kids up to the studio, we won't keep you standing about in the cold. Goodbye Gwen, have a safe journey back to Dorset. I hope the roads are clear."

"The postman said the roads are fine, there was only about two or three inches of snow." She looked at Kate worriedly. "I'm more concerned about you. Take care my dear, won't you?"

Kate assured her that she would and with a last wave, she took Annie up to the studio.

"Ooh Kate! It's lovely! So bright, and it feels nice and warm." Annie's eyes fell on the three canvases of the triptych leaning against the wall.

"Blimey! I can't believe that's me! The last one really looks like me. Is it finished?"

"No, I want to change it a bit. It's too dark. I need each canvas to have a lighter overall tone than the one before, so I have some more work to do on them."

They heard a chorus of goodbyes coming from outside and, going to the window, they saw Tim and the children waving as Gwen's blue Mini started off down the snowy lane.

Annie stole a look at Kate's face as she watched Tim shooing his children and the dog back into the warmth of the house.

She's in love with him, she thought with conviction.

Chapter XII

By the time Geoff Banks came down the following week, Kate's face was looking better. She had been troubled by a series of flashbacks since the evening of the attack, but tried to push the whole episode to the back of her mind and immerse herself in her work. Freddie and Amy went back to school on the Tuesday and had usually been picked up by Elaine by the time Kate got to the studio in the mornings. When they arrived back in the evening, Kate would see Elaine decant them from the car before driving off, and Lily Babbidge waiting at the door of Woodcote to let them in. Then after their tea, they clattered up the wooden steps to the studio, allowing Lily to go home to give Bill his supper.

Kate had to admit that at first it was hard to concentrate with Amy prattling away in spite of Freddie's attempts to keep her quiet, but she soon got used to it, and enjoyed their company. When Tim came home in the evening, they would all - including the dog - walk down to her cottage together. Amy always insisted on walking between her father and Kate, holding their hands, and Kate came to look forward to these little walks in the wintry darkness, with Tim so near, Amy's little hand in hers, and Freddie leading the way with Binky as lookouts for suspicious characters.

The day Geoff was due to come down, Kate did not go straight to the studio, but waited for Geoff to arrive. When he saw her, his eyes widened in consternation. Though the bruises had faded to a certain extent, she still had the remains of a black eye and the graze on her chin was still in evidence. He tilted her face up to examine it.

"You look as though you've been in the wars! What happened?"

Kate stepped back. "Come in and have a coffee, and I'll tell you. Did you find the way alright?"

"Yes, I just put on the sat nav." He looked around the small sitting room. "Nice cottage, by the way. Now, what *did* happen to you?"

While Kate was giving Geoff a brief account of the attack, his face grew steadily more horrified.

"You could have been murdered!" he exclaimed. "Presumably you called the police?"

Kate went on to tell Geoff about her visit to the police SARC facility and the ongoing investigation. But she was impatient to take him to see Zachary, and soon hustled him out of the door.

"Do you mind if we walk there? Then we can go back later by the road with the car to pick up his stuff. I want to show you the studio on the way back."

They walked down the lane, Kate pointing out the studio above Tim's garage as they went past, and entered the wooded path at the end. As they came up to the spot where she had been attacked, Kate noted that the tape had been taken away. She stopped, and in response to Geoff's enquiring look, said: "This is about where Vince – if it was Vince - knocked me down and..." She stopped, as a shudder shook her body. Geoff put his arm round her shoulders.

"Try not to think about it," he said, hurrying her past. Kate nodded and gave him a tight-lipped smile, trying to focus on the imminent meeting of Zachary and Geoff.

As they turned into the clearing in front of Zachary's house, Kate watched Geoff's face as he took in the scene. She had wanted to bring Geoff the back way so that he could see the clearing first, rather than driving round by the road. There was still some snow on the ground, and the carved animals dotted around stood out dark against the whiteness, some with a light covering of snow still on their backs. He grinned in delight.

"It's magical!" he said. "All my instincts say that they should not be out here getting weather damage, but actually the weathering adds another dimension. Of course, they won't last as long."

The door of the cottage opened and Zachary emerged. Kate saw that he had tried to smarten himself up and had on a fairly new looking polo neck pullover and dark blue trousers. He came up to them, smiled at Kate, and extended his hand to Geoff, who shook it and said, "Good to meet you, Zachary. Kate's told me all about you. I love your work. I've sold the pieces Kate brought up, and I've got some money to give you. I'm looking forward to seeing some more, and I want to take more pieces away today."

"Come in and have a cup o' tea first," Zachary said, a little diffidently.

"Maybe later, I've just had a coffee with Kate. Can we see your stuff first?"

"Okay, they're all in the shed yonder."

He led them to the shed and, opening the door, stepped aside so that Geoff could go in. As Kate passed Zachary, he looked searchingly into her face.

"Looking more like yourself, I'm pleased to see," he said.

Kate smiled, then her grin broadened as she saw the expression on Geoff's face as he took in the wealth of carvings which filled the shed.

"Good God! You've got enough here for a full-sized exhibition on your own! And the quality! Every one a gem. I love the way that some are angular and more rough-hewn and some smooth and highly polished, depending on the creature." He inched his way into the shed, stepping carefully around the carvings, some of which were covered in dust, running his hand over them or picking them up and turning them round in his hands.

Eventually, he said; "Look, I'll just take about eight or ten pieces today, I haven't got space for any more at the moment. But when Kate and the others are staging their exhibition, you can choose some more to bring up. Kate will be able to tell you how much space you'll have when she comes up nearer the time."

Geoff spent the next twenty minutes choosing smallish pieces which he passed out to Zachary and Kate, who took them into the house for collection later.

Thoroughly chilled by this time, they went inside and sat by Zachary's fire with mugs of tea, or rather Kate did, while Geoff prowled around examining Zachary's wooden furniture, bowls and other artefacts which filled the room.

"Where do you get all the wood from?" Geoff asked, mesmerised.

231

"Foraging mostly. Sometimes I go down to the coast to find driftwood, but mostly I forage in the woods all round Surrey. Fallen trees and branches, root balls. This here bowl I made from the top of a fallen pollarded willow. See all the knotty bits, with little gaps and holes."

Geoff picked the bowl up, running his hands over its silky surface. "Bloody marvellous. I'd like this one myself. Can I buy it?"

Zachary's brow wrinkled. "Yeah, if you like. No idea what to charge you though."

"I'll give you a hundred quid. Or more?"

Zachary raised a hand in protest. "A hundred is more than enough, if you're sure."

Geoff took out his wallet and counted out a substantial sum for the bowl and the sculptures he had sold in his gallery.

"Are you sure about all this?" Zachary said, looking at the wad of notes in his hand. Kate wondered affectionately if it was more cash than he had seen in his life.

Geoff looked across at Kate. "What are we going to do with him?" he said in mock despair.

Kate grinned. "He's incorrigible. He'll *give* his work away at the drop of a hat."

"Well, if people are prepared to pay good money for your work, don't feel awkward about it," Geoff said, turning back to Zachary. "And don't forget, I've deducted my commission for selling the pieces, so we've both done well out of it."

Zachary looked again at the money in his hand.

"Reckon I can afford a new set of carving tools now," he said with a gleam in his eye, "and maybe a new chainsaw."

Later, walking back with Kate, Geoff stopped and looked back at Zachary's cottage nestled in the trees on the other side of the clearing, a coil of smoke rising from the chimney.

"That scene would have looked very similar two hundred years ago," he said. "No TV aerial or satellite dish, and the man himself seems to be from a different age. His disengagement from modern life is what makes

232

him who he is. We shouldn't attempt to make him more street-wise, but try to look after his interests for him."

"I agree. He's very naïve in some ways, but I think it's wonderful that people like him still exist in this country. Unworldly people who truly seem to be in tune with nature."

They walked on, and when they came to Tim's garage, Kate took Geoff up to the studio. He gave an appreciative whistle when he walked in. The wintry sun streamed in, and the north-facing windows framed the poplars on the other side of the lane.

"Great place to work!" Geoff exclaimed. "You struck lucky here!" He walked up to the painting based on the spiral of a nautilus shell which was on the easel. "Hmm... I like this. Lovely washed out colour, and this chalky, textured effect – looks like stone."

Kate was gratified. "Yes, that's the effect I was trying to achieve. I'm going to do a series of them. I'll have to get some more canvases made up."

Geoff turned his attention to the other canvases stacked against the wall, especially the triptych of Annie.

"I still have work to do on those," Kate said. "There are not enough hours in the day."

"Better that than running out of ideas," Geoff said, then added thoughtfully: "Although, some may say you're dodging about a bit, jumping from theme to theme, engaging on too many things at once."

"I know, but I can't help it. All these ideas keep coming into my head, and I have to get them down. I can't seem to work like some people, who focus on one idea and develop it and develop it until they've wrung the last drop of juice out of it."

"Well, you must be true to yourself, and do what your heart and mind dictate. I wouldn't want to change you, just as I wouldn't want to change Zachary. You carry on as you are. I think it's going to be a great show. You girls - your work is all so different from one another's. It'll certainly make for variety. And now, how about a spot of lunch? Is there a pub around here?"

After Geoff had bought Kate lunch at The Jolly Farmer, they drove round to the front of Zachary's cottage via a small track that led off the main road. Zachary helped them put the carvings into the boot of Geoff's car, wrapped in bubble wrap which Geoff had brought down with him. Dropping Kate back at the studio, Geoff left to drive back to London, and Kate managed to put in a couple of hours work before the children came up to the studio to wait with her till their father returned from London.

She had been gratified by Geoff's enthusiastic reaction to the quantity and quality of Zachary's pieces, and also at the encouraging comments he had made about her own work.

Two days later, an indignant Mimi phoned her.

"Kate! Grace has just rung me. She said Geoff was round at her parents' for dinner last night and he told them that you'd been attacked! Why the hell haven't you told us? Are you all right? Geoff said you think you know who did it. Who was it? Were you badly hurt?"

When Kate could get a word in through the barrage of questions, she said, rather lamely, "I was going to tell you soon. I haven't really wanted to think about it."

"We're coming down to see you, I don't care what you say. Grace, Bea and I, and I bet Paul will want to come when I tell him."

Kate was touched by Mimi's concern, and couldn't deny that it would be good to see her friends. At the same time though, she didn't know whether she could face going through the whole experience again, since she would have to tell them all about what happened. But she said as brightly as she could,

"You don't need to come down, I'm fine now, but it *would* be great to see you guys."

"Can we come tomorrow, and Paul too if he can make it? It's a good thing Grace's mother is Geoff's sister, otherwise we may not have known for ages."

"Not to mention that without that connection, I doubt if we would have got our own show so soon after leaving Camberwell."

"Yeah, it's good to have friends in high places!" Mimi's voice grew serious again. "But tell me honestly, Kate, are you all right? Geoff says

234

this man is out on bail. What if he comes after you again?"

"I'm being careful. Not going for walks on my own in the countryside and stuff. And his bail conditions forbid him coming near me. He's also got a non-molestation order preventing him going near his former partner Annie, who he beat up before Christmas."

"He sounds like a *charming* character," Mimi said with a snort. "Anyway, you can tell us everything when we come. So is it okay if we come tomorrow?"

"Yes, great. See you then."

Kate did not go to the studio the next morning, and her friends arrived about eleven, crammed into Mimi's car, and Kate was immediately inundated with questions, cries of concern when they saw the still visible damage to her face, and much hugging from the three girls. Paul first held her at arm's length, looking into her face with his hands on her shoulders, then he enveloped her gently in his arms.

"You need a bodyguard," he said quietly. "Perhaps you should get a dog."

"Or come back to live in London. This countryside living seems more dangerous than town!" Mimi said caustically.

Bea folded her arms and looked at Kate with a grim smile. "Or I could get some of my biker friends to do him over. Give him a taste of his own medicine." Kate knew that she was not entirely joking.

"I can't bear to think what could have happened to you!" Grace said, in her cut-glass accent. "I mean, what did happen was bad enough. Come on, tell us about it."

So with her friends sprawled in front of the fire sipping at mugs of coffee, Kate recounted the story of the attack, and allowed herself to be questioned on every little detail. Then she called a halt, and suggested they go to the pub for a snack lunch. Once they were ensconced at a table near the bar, she demanded to know what her friends had been up to. They proceeded to fill her in on all of the gossip, including the fact that Jake was still to be seen out and about with the beautiful Lucinda, and was inundated with commissions for work.

As they sat chatting, the door opened and Mike walked in, still in his mechanic's overalls. Mimi's sharp eyes spotted him before he saw them, and with a delighted squeal, she leapt up and accosted him at the bar where he was ordering a pint. He looked equally pleased to see her, and readily agreed to join them at their table, removing his greasy overalls before sitting down on the banquette next to Mimi. A somewhat raucous hour followed, with Dave, Mike's friend that he had brought to the housewarming party, and who was serving behind the bar, joining in the conversation from time to time. Apart from them, the pub was empty except for a couple of elderly men at the far end of the room.

Mike had just stood up, saying he had to get back to the garage, when the door opened again and a man walked into the pub. He had on an old sweatshirt with the hood pulled over his head. Behind him in the doorway was a scrawny little man with a thin face and straggly greying hair. Kate saw Mike stiffen as he looked towards the figures, who stood just inside the open door regarding them. She followed Mike's gaze and felt the blood drain from her face and her heart started thudding in her chest. *Vince.* He looked directly at her, and the malevolence in his eyes shook her to the core. She heard Mike saying grimly under his breath, "How he's got the bare-faced cheek to come in here…"

The others fell silent as they looked from Kate to Mike and then to the bulky figure of Vince and his companion, an unspoken question on all their faces. Vince's gaze left Kate and he walked towards the bar.

Before he could speak, Dave, his hands resting on the bar, said in a clear, steady voice: "You're not welcome here, Dobbs. I must ask you to leave."

Vince pushed the hood off his closely shaven head.

"You can't refuse to serve me," he said menacingly.

"Yes I can," Dave replied calmly. "This is a free house, owned by my dad. It's up to us who we serve and who we don't."

Mike unhurriedly strolled up to where Vince was standing, his hands in his pockets. He stood looking at Vince and, without taking his eyes off him, said over his shoulder to Dave, "Want me to help him out of the door, Dave?"

Though not particularly tall, Mike's body gave the impression of wiry strength and power. His black belt in karate gave him the confidence and self-knowledge that he could easily get the better of Vince, with his beer belly and lack of fitness. Vince clearly knew this and decided not to press the issue. He turned to his friend, who had hung back near the door.

"Come on, Reg, we wouldn't give this dump our custom anyway," he sneered. At the door he stopped and turned back to face the table where Kate was sitting, white-faced and shaking. His lip curled in a mocking smile as his hard stare bored into her again. Then, with Reg scurrying after him, he was out of the door, which swung shut after them with a bang.

There was a collective letting out of breath round the table, and Paul said quietly, "Was that…?"

Kate nodded wordlessly and felt Paul's arm go around her shoulders, giving her a comforting squeeze.

Mimi gave a small shriek. "Oh my God! I can't believe he's allowed to roam around freely after what he's done! To be able to come face to face with you!"

"There's no proof yet that it was him who attacked me," Kate said, her voice still shaky. "He's innocent until proved guilty." She looked across at Mike, who was still standing at the bar. "Thanks Mike, and you too, Dave."

Dave grinned. "No problem, I'm not having that thug in this pub."

Mike came over to Kate, and taking out a pen, scribbled a number on a paper napkin. "Here's my mobile number, Kate. If ever you need help, just ring me. Now I'd better be off." He said goodbye to the others, paying special attention to Mimi, picked up his overalls and strode out of the door, waving to Dave as he went.

When they got back from the pub, Kate took her friends along to see the studio, which met with a chorus of approval. Bea was envious, since for her workshop she had to share a freezing disused warehouse with several other art school graduates, and the size of her light boxes meant that she was always short of space. Mimi's crazy soft sculptures also took up a lot of room, but she had the use of her parents' garage, which she used as a workshop and her old bedroom at their house, which was filled with completed pieces. Grace, who still lived with her well-off and indulgent parents in their big house in Richmond, had a purpose-built studio in their garden, where she had plenty of room to work on her large tapestries, and Paul, thanks to his burgeoning career, had been able to move into a bigger flat, where he had set up a light and airy photographic studio.

It was not long before they pounced on Kate's canvases stacked against the wall, and the next half hour was spent in animated commentary as they examined each in turn.

Later, Mimi, perching on the table which Freddie and Amy used to do their art, gave Kate a sly look.

"So this studio is courtesy of your City slicker! Do you rent it from him?"

"No, I give his children art lessons in lieu," Kate replied. "And now I also look after them when they are waiting for their father to come home."

"He's a widower, isn't he?"

"Yes, his wife was killed in a car crash two years ago."

"How awful!" Grace exclaimed. "How old are the children?"

"Freddie's ten and Amy's six."

"Poor little mites!" Grace said, her large blue eyes filling with tears. "And it must be difficult for their father. Has he not got a nanny or an au pair?"

"No, they had one or two unfortunate experiences with au pairs and decided to manage without for the moment. A lovely lady from that cottage over there acts as a sort of housekeeper for them." She pointed towards the Babbidges' cottage, which could be seen at the end of the lane.

"He seemed really sweet when we met him at your house last time we were down," Grace said. "And it's good of him to let you use this as your studio."

"Yeah, and he's a bit gorgeous as well," Mimi couldn't help adding. "I suppose there are compensations for burying yourself out in the

238

country." She gave Paul an exaggerated wink.

Kate rolled her eyes. "He's got a girlfriend, Mimi," she said, a slight edge to her voice. "She takes the children to school in the morning and brings them back in the evening. Her son goes to the same school."

Bea, who had been watching Kate, noticed her discomfiture and changed the subject. "When are you coming up to London, Kate? There are a couple of good exhibitions on and I think we all ought to go and look at Geoff's gallery to sort out what's going to go where. I need to plan out my space."

"I went over there the other day," Grace interjected. "It looks great – much more space. It's just about ready now. He's got a show starting in a couple of weeks. Some sculptor I've never heard of."

"Well, maybe I'll come up when that starts, then we can see it with work installed. It'll give more of a sense of scale," suggested Kate.

Paul looked at his watch. "I think we should be starting back before too long. I've got to get some work finished before tomorrow."

"Well, come back to the house for a coffee before you go," Kate said, looking at her own watch. She would have to be back in the studio for the children later on. She followed them out of the door, locking it behind her, and they tramped back to Lavender Cottage as the short January day started to fade.

Before they left, Kate saw Bea go up the stairs to the door of the second bedroom, and stand there, peering inside. The room was nearly dark, the only light coming from the last gleam of daylight in the western sky filtering in from the window. Bea walked slowly into the room and faced the cupboard which was set into the wall at the far end. Kate followed her up and tried to get her attention, but she looked lost, faraway. She didn't answer, but said, almost to herself: "There's something... something..."

Kate put her hand on Bea's shoulder. "I know, I've felt it too. I feel as though someone is watching me when I'm in here. And sometimes the wind makes a strange sound in the chimney. It sounds like sobbing."

"Yes, there's a sadness. A feeling of loss."

Mimi's voice called up the stairs. "Come on Bea, gotta go."

Bea turned, and walked thoughtfully down the stairs.

In the weeks that followed, in spite of the attack in the woods, Kate felt a renewed burst of creativity, and though she was not aware of it, the terrifying experience had imbued her painting style with a new energy, almost a recklessness, which lifted her work to another level. She painted all day in a highly focused, almost frenzied way, which was quite exhausting, and she would fall into bed early at night. She usually drifted instantly into a deep sleep, only to wake in the early hours, and find it difficult to get back to sleep, her mind churning with ideas for her work, or dozed fitfully, troubled by flashbacks of the attack. Sometimes, in the dark watches of the night, the wind would make the sobbing noise in the chimney. Somehow the unearthly sound did not frighten her, but filled her with an inexplicable sadness.

When Lynn Keswick, her Witness Care officer, phoned her, Kate was in the studio and the ringtone jolted her out of her absorption in the painting she was working on.

"I'm calling to inform you of the results of the forensic tests on Dobbs' clothes," Lynn said. "They've found fibres matching those of your duffle coat, and also some of your DNA from your saliva, on his glove. They also matched one of the footprints in the mud on the scene of the attack with the tread pattern on his boots."

Kate gasped. "I knew it! I knew it *was* him! So has he been charged?"

"I was coming to that. Yes, because you sustained severe bruising, he's been charged by the Crown Prosecution Service with ABH – actual bodily harm. The original charge of attempted rape has been downgraded by the CPS due to lack of evidence. Dobbs will be brought before the magistrates' court next Tuesday. If he pleads not guilty, you'll have to go to court to testify when the trial comes up. But the trial will take months to come to court."

"But he'll be in custody till at least Tuesday?"

"No, I'm afraid not. We have had to let him out on bail with conditions again, with orders to attend the magistrates' Court on Tuesday."

"Pity, I was hoping to go for a walk to get some fresh air and exercise, but if he's still at large, I can't do that."

"No, I wouldn't advise it, not by yourself."

Something Paul had said struck Kate. "What if I had a dog with me?" Maybe she could take Binky for a walk, and he could act as her bodyguard.

Lynn paused, then said, "Well, if it was a good-sized dog, capable of going for anyone who attacked you…"

Kate interposed. "It's a golden Lab. Very fit and lively."

"Is he yours?"

"No, but we're firm friends. He's my neighbour's dog."

"Well, I suppose if you went out in daylight it would be okay."

Kate felt a renewed surge of anger that she should be constrained by fear of what Vince would do. It was one thing to go out in the car, or walk along the road in daylight, but she realised that if she wanted to go across the fields or on the common, she shouldn't do so alone. She would ask Tim if she could borrow Binky occasionally as protection and give him some exercise at the same time.

After Lynn had rung off, Kate, her concentration broken, walked over to the window and looked out. The cold spell had given way to milder weather and it was one of those soft, late January days, where the colours of the countryside with the muted purples and dun browns of the hedgerows merged into the blue of distant fields and low hills. She marvelled that even in densely populated south-east England, you could still get vistas like this, where there was not much sign of human habitation. It looked so peaceful that it was hard to imagine a violent thug like Vince could be out there waiting to pounce on her again.

From her vantage point, she could just make out the chimney of her cottage through the trunks of the poplars beyond the bend in the lane. It seemed silly that once it was dark, she should have to be accompanied back home for such a short distance, but she had to admit that when she had hurried back to the studio in the twilight the day her friends had come down to see her, she had felt a frisson of fear. She doubted that Vince would try anything so close to Woodcote House, but she knew it was not

241

worth taking the risk once it was dark. Her worries about Tim having to go to the trouble of walking her home each evening were mitigated by the fact that she was helping him out by looking after the children till he came home each night, while enabling Mrs B. to get home earlier.

The forensic results - which to Kate's mind proved without doubt that Vince was her attacker - both relieved and unsettled her at the same time. Still standing at the window and looking over again at the chimney of her cottage, she remembered that she needed to collect some twigs for kindling in order to light the fire that evening. It was still only early afternoon, and she would have time to collect some sticks and still be back before dark.

She pulled on her coat, locked the door and started walking back towards her cottage, jumping the ditch occasionally to gather fallen twigs and small branches. Her arms full, she walked briskly to her door and after fumbling for her keys in her pocket, let herself in. As she negotiated the entrance, loaded as she was with sticks, she heard a clatter and realised that one of the long twigs had knocked a picture off the wall. Shutting the door with her foot, she dumped the kindling on the hearth and went to pick up the picture. It was the little framed one of what looked like a Victorian Valentine card. It had landed on the thick doormat and though the frame had come apart, the glass had not broken. The thin wood which had been backing the card had come away from the frame and the card had fallen out. Picking up the pieces she took them to the table by the window. Still in her coat, she sat down at the table and picked up the card. Stuck to the thick paper was a delicate, yellowing piece of lace in the shape of a heart, with a lacy frill around the edge and a faded red paper rose fixed to the centre. Below, written in copperplate, were the words *With Love and Devotion.* When Kate opened the card, two yellowed newspaper cuttings fell out. She picked up one of them and carefully unfolded it. The cutting included a section of the top of the page, showing the date of Monday 13th June 1864. As she read the article, tears started to her eyes.

MELANCHOLY SUICIDE OF A YOUNG LADY
On Saturday last, an inquest was held at the Dog and Bell

242

Inn at Hamshall before Joseph Blackburn Esq., Coroner for the liberties of Hamshall and Weyford on the body of Susan Gatling, a young woman of seventeen years of age, whose body had the same morning been taken from the river near the mill of Messers Johns at Hamshall Green.

Hers is indeed an unhappy story. Her widowed mother, with whom she had lived at Lavender Cottage, Tuckers Lane, passed away some few weeks previously, and Susan had lived alone since that time. However, it is understood that as her home was a cottage tied to the Estate of Woodcote House, after the death of her mother who worked in the dairy of Woodcote Farm, she was due to be evicted in the near future, by order of Charles Locksley of Woodcote House.

From the evidence adduced, it appears that the deceased was seen wandering by the river two days previously, seemingly in extreme distress of mind. The following morning, her cousin, Elizabeth Carter, having not seen Susan at Weyford Fair where she used to sell lavender, went to visit her at her residence. She found the front door open, but could find no trace of Susan. All enquiries respecting her leading to no result, a search was carried out and her bonnet and shawl were found on the riverbank. Due to her previous despondency of mind, her relatives began to fear the worst, and the river was dragged. After several attempts, the body of Susan Gatling was brought to the surface from a deep hole and conveyed to the Dog and Bell, Hamshall. An inquest was held upon the body before Mr Blackburn on the same day. There were no marks whatsoever of violence on the body, but it was discovered that she had recently given birth to a child. There is not the slightest reason to doubt that the unhappy girl had thrown away her own life in a moment of aberration of intellect.

The verdict was returned as "Found Drowned."

243

Kate sat staring at the fragile newspaper clipping. Blinking away the tears that misted her vision, she re-read the article, then picked up the second cutting. This was much shorter and was a clipping from the Deaths column of a newspaper.

3rd May 1864, Edwin Locksley, beloved younger son of Mr and Mrs Charles Locksley of Woodcote House, Hamshall Green. Edwin was killed in Africa where he was fighting with his regiment against the Ashanti in the war against that people. He was buried in Africa.

Looking at the card again, she saw that the inside was blank except for the initials *EL* written in faded brownish ink at the bottom.

Questions and speculations crowded into Kate's mind. Who was EL? Was he the Edwin Locksley mentioned in the newspaper clipping? If so, could he have been the father of Susan's child? Susan had lived in this very cottage, a stone's throw from Woodcote House. They would surely have come across each other. Had they had a love affair and had Susan become pregnant by him? Then, when she heard of his death, and found that she was due to be evicted by Edwin's father, had she taken her own life in her "extreme distress of mind?" The cutting had mentioned that she had recently given birth. What had become of the baby?

Kate gazed unseeingly out of the window, the Valentine card still in her hand. She pictured the young girl wandering by the river, distraught at the death of her lover, her mother and possibly her baby, and facing eviction from her home. In her mind's eye, she saw her tearing off her bonnet and shawl and throwing herself into the river. She looked again at the card. Why was it hanging on the wall more than a hundred and fifty years later? She fingered the broken frame. It was a plain unvarnished wooden one. The thin backing piece of wood had been attached to the frame with little soft metal flaps, which could be bent back to remove the picture. Kate suspected that it was not as old as the card and newspaper clippings, but she could not be sure. Who had put the clippings in the card, framed it and hung it up? It could not have been Susan herself, because it contained the account of her own death. Suddenly, a startling thought occurred to her. By extraordinary coincidence, today was 14th February. The day she had knocked the framed Valentine down and discovered the contents, was Valentine's Day!

Her mind went back to Susan. Where had she been buried? Did they not refuse to bury suicides in consecrated ground? Kate resolved to go to the churchyard in the village the next day to see if she could find any trace of a grave with Susan Gatling's name on it.

But now it was getting late, and the overcast sky would make the evening draw in even earlier. Not for the first time, she felt a wave of resentment towards Vince, for causing her to have to worry about being outside alone in the dark. She gathered the pieces of the frame together, and putting the cuttings back in the card, she left them on the table, meaning to mend the frame later. Letting herself out, she locked the front door after her.

Elaine, bringing Freddie and Amy back from school, saw Kate walking back along the lane to the studio. Amy sang out, "There's Kate!" and lowered her window to call to her. Kate turned and waved, bending down to give Amy a smile as they passed. Elaine, barely acknowledging Kate, did not slow down, but continued on towards Woodcote House.

Freddie said: "She shouldn't be walking along by herself. It's getting dark."

Elaine glanced at him over her shoulder to where he sat in the back seat.

"Oh, I think she'll be perfectly safe!"

"No, Daddy says it's *not* safe. We always walk her back to her house with Daddy when he comes home."

Amy butted in, "In case the bad man hurts her again."

Elaine felt as though an icy hand had gripped at her heart. In spite of Tim telling her about the arrangement, she had hoped it had not been put into practice. Every night! Every night Tim was walking Kate back in the dark, being her heroic protector, in the unlikely event that she would be attacked again.

245

"Surely that's a bit over the top!" she said, as she drew up outside Woodcote. "He's hardly likely to attack her here."

"That's what Kate said, but Daddy said she shouldn't take the risk." Freddie, young as he was, sensed that Elaine was far from happy with the arrangement. Saying goodbye to Duncan sitting in the front, Freddie said a dutiful thank you to Elaine and got out of the car, followed by Amy.

As Elaine turned the car and drove off, Kate came up to the children and stopped. "Had a good day at school?" she asked.

"It was okay," Freddie answered, putting down his schoolbag and undoing his tie. "Double maths and a science test and stuff like that."

"We had art and we had to do a picture of sunflowers, like Van Gogh," Amy piped up, just as Lily opened the front door and waved to the little group by the gate.

Kate waved back and said to the children, "Well, I'll see you later." She looked at Amy. "Maybe you could show me your painting when you bring it home."

"Yes, and can we put it up on the wall in the studio? Miss Long said it was very good."

"I'm sure it's brilliant. See you."

The children made their way into the house, while Kate walked round the side of the garage and let herself in. As she went into the studio at the top of the stairs, her eye was caught by the painting of the middle panel of the triptych, the one of Annie's face up against the wavy glass, which was leaning against the wall. She looked suddenly like a drowning woman, just below the surface of the water, and her thoughts immediately returned to poor Susan Gatling, drowning alone and in despair in the murky depths of the river.

*

A cheerful voice calling out "Good morning!" cut into Kate's thoughts as she wandered among the grey, lichen covered gravestones of the churchyard. Looking in the direction of the greeting, she saw the sprightly figure of the vicar approaching around the side of a graceful marble angel standing guard over a rather grand tombstone.

"Good morning," she called back, and waited for him to come up to her.

He held out his hand and shook hers, tilting his head to one side like a bird. "We've met before, haven't we? Ah yes, you live in Amelia's cottage, I remember now. How are you getting on?"

"Fine thanks, Reverend." Kate decided not to mention Vince's attack. She wanted to talk to him about Susan Gatling.

"I'm glad I bumped into you. I'm trying to find out about the death of a young woman in 1864. A suicide, I think." She pulled a folder from her shoulder bag and took out the Valentine card. Could you please take a look at this? Careful, there are a couple of newspaper cuttings inside."

Intrigued, George Blackwell adjusted his spectacles on his nose and, taking the card from her, he opened it. First he scanned the inside, noting the faded initials EL, then he carefully unfolded the fragile cuttings and read them through, his cheerful face growing solemn as he did so. When he had finished, he folded them again, replaced them in the card and handed them back to Kate.

"A tragic story indeed," he said, a suspicion of tears in his pale blue eyes. "Poor child, she must have been in such distress. I wonder what happened to the baby."

"That's what I was wondering. I was hoping that maybe you would have some parish records going back to 1864 that might shed light on where Susan was buried, and if there was any record of her baby."

"Where did you come across this?"

Kate explained how it had been hanging in the cottage and how she had knocked it off the wall.

"Hmm... a whole possible scenario seems to be here. The son of the landowner has a dalliance with the daughter of a farm worker, gets her pregnant, then gets killed. The poor girl is about to be evicted and, what with losing her mother so recently, takes her own life in despair. Tragic."

"Yes, that's how it looks to me. But why was the card framed and still hanging in the cottage nearly a hundred and fifty years later, with the

247

cuttings inside?"

"Amelia may have known. If only we could ask her. But the next best thing would be to ask Lydia Campbell. I think you've met her, haven't you? Amelia may have mentioned something to her. They were great friends. But first let's have a look at the parish records. They go back to 1837 I believe. You're lucky; most parishes no longer keep the records on site. You would normally have to go to the Parish Records Office or look online. But for some reason, we've hung on to ours."

As they walked along the path between the gravestones, Kate said: "Would Susan have been refused burial in the churchyard because she committed suicide?"

"Not necessarily. By the mid-nineteenth century, the Church was much less strict about that sort of thing. Often suspected suicides were given the benefit of the doubt that their deaths may have been an accident. Especially drownings."

The vicar led Kate round to the back of the church, to a small, separate building. Unlocking the door, he took her through an office containing two desks, a couple of computers, various office equipment and shelves of files, to a smaller room, lined with glass-fronted bookshelves. Opening the deepest one, he peered at the hefty old ledgers inside.

"Aha, here we are," he said, pulling out one of them. "1850 – 1870. This'll be the one. If she's anywhere, she'll be here."

He carried the book to a table by the window and started leafing through it. Kate went and stood beside him, eagerly scanning the names written in beautiful copperplate handwriting.

"1860, 1862," the vicar muttered, continuing to turn the pages. "Ah! 1864!" He ran his finger down the page, scanning the names.

Suddenly, Kate's searching gaze fell on a name which quickened her pulse and she pointed it out: *3rd May 1864. 'Edwin Charles Locksley, (M) of Woodcote House, Hamshall Green. Killed in action in Africa. Buried in Africa.*

The vicar gave a grunt of satisfaction. "Well spotted! Now, where's poor Susan?"

They found her just a few names below that of Edwin. The entry

248

was very short. *11ᵗʰJune, 1864. Susan Gatling, (W) aged 17. Drowned.*

They turned and looked at each other, and for a moment the poignancy of those few stark words caused a silence between them. Then Kate re-read the entry, written all that time ago, and thought of the heartbreak behind the dispassionate recording of a life ended before it was even half lived. She wondered again about the infant Susan had given birth to. She voiced her thoughts, and she and the vicar both searched the previous entries again and also subsequent ones, but there was nothing that could have been Susan's baby.

"I wonder what happened to the poor mite," the vicar said, closing the book, which let out a little puff of dust as he did so. "Of course, it would have been quite a stigma for her to have given birth out of wedlock, and with her mother dead or dying, she may have had the baby all on her own, poor thing, and the child may have died, perhaps a stillbirth. Susan may have just buried it in the garden or something."

Kate's eyes flashed. "Same old story," she said grimly. "The woman has to suffer the consequences while the man gets off scot-free."

"Well, he didn't quite get off scot-free!" George Blackwood said wryly. "He was killed, remember?"

"That's true, but that had nothing to do with his affair with Susan."

"I wouldn't be too sure about that. I'm willing to bet that his father packed his younger son off to the wars to get him away from his dalliance with the dairy maid's daughter. Who knows, his son may have genuinely loved Susan. He sent her a Valentine's card after all. The EL on the Valentine's card probably stands for Edwin Locksley."

"Yes, I'm sure it must be."

"A pair of star-crossed lovers, very sad. Very sad indeed." The vicar's kindly face was serious and he patted her hand sympathetically. "It must be especially affecting for you, living as you do in the house Susan also lived in."

"Yes, I keep thinking about her state of mind," Kate murmured. Then, bringing her mind back to the present, she said gratefully, "Well, thank you so much for letting me see the book. I'm going to have another prowl round to see if I can find Susan's gravestone. Edwin's won't be here, since he was buried in Africa, according to the cutting."

As he saw her out, the vicar said, "Don't be surprised if you don't find Susan's grave. Many of the headstones from the eighteen hundreds are very weathered. A lot of the inscriptions are indecipherable. Anyway, for Susan, I doubt if there would have been money for a headstone. There is an area over there," he said pointing, "where there are no gravestones, just mounds of earth where a wooden cross may have been at one time. And I believe there is an area just outside the wall which was probably used for criminals and suicides. Rather overgrown now I'm afraid." He gestured off to the right, beyond some old yew trees, where a stone wall formed a boundary to the churchyard.

Kate hesitated, then said, "Sorry to take up any more of your time, but I was wondering if you can remember where my great aunt Amelia is buried. My father came to the funeral, but I couldn't because I had an exam on that day."

"Yes, indeed. If I recall, she's just over there, near that patch of snowdrops. Old Mrs Campbell told me that Amelia bought the plot of land next to the grave of her fiancé way back in 1944, long before my time, so that she could be buried next to him when her time came. Perhaps she was the one who planted those snowdrops on his grave."

He led her between the graves, some marked with granite boundaries, with both of them taking care not to step on the graves. When they reached Amelia Hopkirk's headstone, the vicar patted her arm and said gently, "I'll leave you to your thoughts, my dear."

Kate shook his hand gratefully. "Thank you so much for your time."

"Not at all. Pleased to have been of help. Goodbye." He turned and picked his way back through the graves and disappeared round the side of the church.

Kate turned back to her great aunt's plain, granite headstone, which looked very new compared to the weathered ones all around, and read the inscription. It said simply:

Amelia Jane Hopkirk, Died 12th August 2017, RIP

There was no *In Loving Memory* because she had not had any close family to remember her lovingly. Kate wished she had followed up the conversation she had had with Amelia at her mother's funeral and gone to visit her sometimes. It was a regret that she had felt ever since she had heard that Lavender Cottage had been left to her. And now it was too late.

She turned to the grave beside Amelia's. Though covered in lichen, it was obviously an expensive stone, with a carved border and the lettering picked out in black. It read:

In loving memory of our hero son James Lawrence Lovell who gave his life for his country 20th February 1943 aged 25 years.

Kate's throat ached with sadness as she stood looking from one headstone to the other. Edward's grave was covered in a drift of snowdrops, but the granite surround of her great aunt's grave contained nothing but grass. On impulse, Kate took her house key from her pocket, and using it to loosen the turf around a little cluster of snowdrops on James Lovell's grave, she gently lifted them out, managing to keep the bulbs intact. Then she made a hole in the turf on Amelia's grave and planted the little corms in the damp earth, patting them down firmly. With luck, they would proliferate, and one day her grave may be covered in snowdrops too.

With a last look at the two graves, Kate made her way in the direction that the vicar had pointed in when discussing Susan's grave, looking at the headstones on either side as she went, deciphering the weathered inscriptions. Some were heart-breaking. A small marble cherub knelt at the head of a tiny grave, whose granite headstone read:

Jesus called little children unto him.

Jennifer Sorrell. Fell asleep 20th December 1921, aged 2yrs 6 months.

Another headstone in the shape of a cross bore the inscription:

Mary Harlowe, 28 yrs, and Peter Harlowe, stillborn.

Died 25th August 1906.

Beloved wife and son of Robert Harlowe.

Safe in the arms of Jesus.

What a huge weight of grief was encapsulated in such few words.

Wandering among the headstones, reading the inscriptions, Kate's eyes were often wet with tears, as she thought of the ones that were left behind. Husbands and wives, buried in the same grave, but many years apart, not unlike Amelia and her James. She thought of the long, lonely years they had endured until they could fulfil the often-repeated phrase, 'Till we meet again'.

While the inscriptions were immeasurably sad, a pervading feeling of peace and solace seeped into her. It was very quiet. The day was cold but the wintry sun sifted through the towering oaks at the edge of the churchyard, throwing shadows from the trees among the overgrown dry grasses around the gravestones, and warming her back. To the left of the church, shaded by a cluster of yews, the headstones seemed to be bigger and much older. Some were half-buried in the earth, others lifted up by the roots of the trees and standing at crazy angles, while others had fallen over altogether. Kate walked among them, trying to make out their inscriptions, but many of them were totally obliterated by weathering and lichen. As she approached the low stone wall surrounding the churchyard, sure enough, she came across the unmarked mounds of earth, which obviously belonged to those too poor to afford a gravestone. Was one of them Susan's? She looked over the wall and tried to make out if there were similar mounds amongst the tangle of ivy which matted the ground and grew up the trunks of the trees. In the summer, the mass of nettles would have made it impossible, but she thought she could see vague rectangular mounds under the covering of ground ivy.

Kate turned away and started making her way back through the churchyard, suddenly aware that she was quite isolated under the trees. Not that she really thought that Vince would try anything here, but she could not help a searching backward glance into the dappled shade of the wood beyond the churchyard.

After another half hour of examining the inscriptions on the gravestones without finding Susan's grave, Kate let herself out of the lych gate, and on impulse, instead of getting into her car, she walked past it and turned into the gate of old Mrs Campbell's house. There was no sign of the ancient gardener as Kate went up to the door and rang the bell. As was

252

the case the first time, there was a long wait before the door opened a crack and the same bright, beady eye peered out at her. As soon as she saw who it was, Lydia Campbell opened the door wider, her face breaking into a smile as she put out a hand and drew Kate into the house.

"My dear! How lovely to see you again! Come in, I was just going to have some elevenses. You can join me."

Her delighted reaction made Kate feel guilty that it had been so long since her first visit. She followed the old lady through the gloomy hall to the kitchen, where a kettle was singing on the hob. Kate busied herself making the tea, while Lydia went over to the dresser, her stick tapping on the tiled floor, and got out a tin of biscuits.

"Why don't we go through into the drawing room, dear? There's a bit of sun coming in there. There's a tray on the dresser."

Kate put the two cups of tea and the tin of biscuits on the tray and slung her bag over her shoulder. Led by the frail little figure in her long, grey cardigan, she carried the tray into a large, sunlit room which overlooked the back garden. Lydia headed for an armchair by a French window, which was obviously where she habitually sat. On a small table next to the chair were a newspaper, open at the crossword, a pair of spectacles, a dictionary and the remote control for the TV which was positioned opposite the chair. A bag of knitting sat on the floor and one bar of an electric heater warmed the area by the armchair.

"This is a nice sunny spot," Kate said, looking round for somewhere to put the tray. Spotting another occasional table nearby, she put the tray down and, after Lydia had settled herself comfortably in her chair, handed her a cup of tea.

"Pull that chair closer, dear, that's better. Help yourself to a biscuit. I'll have one as well."

Kate passed her the biscuits and took one herself. As before, it was slightly stale, but Lydia didn't seem to notice.

"How have you been keeping, Mrs Campbell? I've been meaning to come and see you for ages."

"Oh, I'm fine. Though I'll be glad when the weather gets warmer. Nice today though. There's a bit of warmth in the sun. Maybe spring is

253

on its way."

"Well, it's still only February. We could still have another cold snap."

"I suppose so," sighed the old lady. "My poor sparrows and tits and robins didn't like all that snow at all. I put out food for them, but those horrid crows and magpies came and snaffled most of it. I sit here and watch them, and no matter how often I shoo them away, they always come back. Those pesky grey squirrels, too."

"A couple of deer came into my garden a little while ago. A mother and fawn. They were beautiful."

"Beautiful, yes, but they eat everything in sight. Luckily they don't come into my garden much."

Kate picked up her bag and took out the envelope containing the Valentine card. Taking the card out of the envelope, she said, "Mrs Campbell, it's lovely to see you anyway, but I also wanted to ask you whether my great aunt ever mentioned this Valentine card to you. It was hanging up in the cottage when I came to live in it, and I accidentally knocked it off the wall yesterday. There were two old newspaper clippings inside."

Lydia pushed the clutter on her table to one side and putting her cup down, she picked up her reading glasses. Kate handed her the card and, just as the vicar had done, she first looked at the inscription inside, then read through the two clippings. When she had finished she folded them and put them back in the card. She sat looking at the front of the card for a while in silence. Then she peered at Kate over the top of her glasses.

"I've seen this before," she said, gently touching the edge of the lace heart with an arthritic finger. "Amelia had it up on her wall. I remember asking her about it. She said she found it under a floorboard in one of the bedrooms when she was trying to locate a mouse which was scratching under the floor. The cutting about Edwin's death was inside. As for this other cutting, she found that long before, when she first moved into the cottage. It was under some oilcloth which was lining a shelf in a cupboard. I remember it clearly, because she had just found it the day before I went to visit her one day. She had been spring cleaning and had

254

taken the oilcloth off the shelf, and the cutting fell out. It affected her greatly, just as it seems to have affected you. After all, you both lived or live there." Her words echoed those of the vicar.

The old lady paused, looking at Kate thoughtfully. Then she said, "There's something else. Amelia said that on the evening of the day she found the cutting, she saw the figure of a young woman standing at the door of a cupboard in one of the bedrooms. She had her hands over her face and seemed to be crying. Then she just walked into the wall and disappeared."

Lydia looked down at the card again. "When Amelia found this card, years later, she immediately connected it with the newspaper cutting of Susan's death, even though her name is nowhere on the card. I must admit it does seem to be of the same era. I remember her telling me that she was going to frame it and hang it up on the wall in remembrance of Susan. She was convinced it was Susan she had seen that day." She looked up from the card and her thoughtful expression changed to concern when she saw the pallor of Kate's face.

"Oh, my dear, I hope I haven't frightened you with talk of ghosts. Amelia said that she didn't have any feeling of malevolence from the figure, just terrible sadness."

Kate, who had been sitting transfixed since Lydia had told her about the figure that her great aunt had seen, gave herself a mental shake and said, in as normal a tone as she could muster, "It's just that though I've never seen anything, I've often heard sounds like sobbing, which I put down to the wind in the chimney. I also get a scent of lavender coming from somewhere at random times. And a friend of mine seemed rather disturbed when she went into the little bedroom and was staring at the corner of the room where there is a cupboard built into the wall." She stopped and got up to stand staring out of the French window. Something had struck her forcibly, and she turned to Lydia again. "It's strange, there always seems to be some connection between the big house down the lane, Woodcote House, and Lavender Cottage. First it was Susan Gatling and Edwin Locksley, then Amelia and her fiancé James, and now…" she stopped herself abruptly, and turned back to the window.

255

Lydia Campbell did not press her to continue. She had seen the colour rise to Kate's pale cheeks, and, knowing that the owner of Woodcote was a widower, she at once wondered if Kate had fallen for Tim Crawford. *I can certainly see why he could have fallen for Kate*, she thought as she watched the young woman standing at the window, slender as a wand, with the sun glinting on her fabulous hair. She recalled that Magda had let one or two hints drop when she came to clean once a week. Lydia was lonely, and looked forward to pumping Magda about any snippets of gossip from the village. Consequently, Lydia also knew about Elaine and how she was obviously determined to claim Tim for herself. Would history repeat itself again and result in a third doomed love affair between the occupants of the two houses?

Chapter XIII

As February went on and the days lengthened a little more each day, Kate thought about the idea of taking Binky out for occasional walks and mentioned it to Tim when he and the children were accompanying her back to her cottage one evening.

"I think that's an excellent idea," Tim said. "It would do him the world of good to have some proper walks during the week, instead of the mini ones he gets before I go to London and these little strolls in the evening. And I'm sure he would go for anyone who attacked you. I think you would be quite safe if you had Binky with you, but all the same, I wouldn't go too far off the beaten track."

"I thought I would explore that stretch of common land on the other side of the road, and maybe sometimes walk along the towpath by the river."

"Yes, we sometimes do that river walk. In fact…" he stopped and turned to her, his face brightening, "Why don't we all go for a walk along the river on Saturday and stop for lunch at the Lock Inn? My treat. Then I can show you how to get to the river via the footpath, and also give you and Binky a chance to interact, so that he can have the experience of you being in charge of him. That way, he would be more likely to leap to your defence if anything should happen."

The children chorused their approval of the plan, and it was agreed that they would set out for their walk after Freddie and Amy's art lesson on the following Saturday.

As they were walking back after leaving Kate at her front door, Freddie, who had gone ahead, turned back to walk beside his father.

"Dad, you won't mention the walk to Duncan's mum, will you?" he said anxiously. "She'd probably decide to come as well and I don't want her to."

"No, I don't either," Amy piped up, hanging on Tim's arm. "I just

257

want Kate and us."

Tim smiled. He just wanted Kate and us too.

*

Saturday dawned grey and drizzly, but by midday the rain had stopped, and the clouds were thinning, showing "enough blue sky to make a pocket handkerchief," as Kate's grandfather had been fond of saying. By the time they started out on their walk, the sun was struggling to break through, and wrapping up against the brisk westerly wind, they set off. Led by Freddie, they entered the wood to the left of Tim's property and followed a footpath leading among the trees until they came out on to the edge of a large field planted with winter wheat.

"All this land used to belong to Woodcote, apparently," Tim said, with a sweeping gesture at the fields which lay behind his house. "Woodcote was a farm up until the turn of the 20th century."

Kate glanced at him and said; "I know. I discovered that when I was investigating something I found in the cottage."

"Oh? What did you find?" Tim said, intrigued.

"I'll tell you over lunch," Kate said. "It's very sad actually."

Tim had to contain his curiosity and they continued in single file along the footpath which skirted the field and, crossing a road, re-joined the path as it sloped downhill until it met the river. Turning right, they started off along the towpath with the river on their left and changing vistas of fields and wooded areas to their right as they walked along. The children went on ahead, peering into the river to catch glimpses of fish in the shadows of the riverbank. Occasionally, they passed little groups of ducks, quacking softly to each other, or a pair of swans gliding along imperiously.

"We'll be coming to a lock soon," Tim said, getting Binky's lead out of his pocket. "I'll put this on Binky, and I think it would be a good idea if you were to hold it and be in charge of him, so that he can get used to you being in control," he continued, attaching the lead on to Binky's collar. "There are usually people and dogs hanging about the lock, and

258

there is sometimes the odd scuffle with other dogs."

Kate took the lead from Tim, and with Binky walking to heel, they approached the lock. A narrowboat was in the process of passing through the lock, and a small group of people was standing around watching the proceedings. Two or three dogs were with them and Kate kept Binky close to her side as they watched the narrowboat slowly sinking down as the water gushed through the sluices. Freddie and Amy watched fascinated as the water in the lock reached the lower level and the boat owner opened the gates, allowing the woman on the boat to guide it out of the lock.

The sun glinted on the water, causing intense spangles of light which reflected on the wet, black gates of the lock. A dog barked, the wind gusted through the overhanging branches of a willow which leaned over the water. Everything seemed infused with colour and light. The horror of Vince's attack on her and the subsequent weeks of anxiety and constraint seemed to fall away, and suddenly Kate felt a surge of elation and what she could only describe as pure joy. And it had everything to do with the fact that she was with this family, with this man, on this lovely day. Kate looked at the children still watching as the boat owner closed the lock gates, and jumped back on to his boat. She stole a look at Tim, and found him watching her, an unfathomable expression on his face. He opened his mouth to speak, but at that moment, Binky darted forward, nearly pulling the lead out of Kate's hand, and she found herself being dragged towards a large Dalmatian which had come bounding along the towpath towards the lock.

Luckily, both dogs were wagging their tails and after exchanging pleasantries with the Dalmatian's owner, they continued on their walk, Kate keeping a rather reluctant Binky on the lead as they came to a road and crossed over a little humpback bridge to get to a riverside pub where Tim announced they would have lunch.

In spite of the sun, it was a bit too cold and windy to sit outside, but they managed to get a window table, and sat looking out at the river, the people walking past and the ducks congregating near the pub's little landing stage, hoping for scraps of bread.

The young waiter who came to get their order also brought some

259

worksheets of river wildlife and some crayons for the children. Freddie was soon immersed in reading about the different varieties of fish and insects to be found in and around the river, while Amy set about colouring in the line drawings of chub, perch, roach and the like, in a startling array of colours and patterns.

When the wine and the drinks for the children arrived, they all clinked glasses together with a chorus of "Cheers", then Tim leaning back in his chair, said to Kate, "What were you saying about something sad you found in the cottage?"

Kate took a sip of her wine. "It's a newspaper cutting. Two actually, which were tucked in behind a picture on the wall." She went on to explain about the Valentine card and how she had found the cuttings, and her subsequent visit to the church.

"I also went and had another chat with old Mrs Campbell, who knew my great aunt. I had already met her when I first came down here, and this time she told me that Amelia, my great aunt, had found the Valentine card under the floorboards and the cutting about Susan Gatling under some oilcloth in a cupboard. She put two and two together and realised that the EL probably referred to Edwin Locksley, so she put the two clippings in the card and framed it as a sort of memento of poor Susan."

"It is a sad story," Tim said. "I'd like to see the cuttings sometime, if I may."

"Of course. I'll show you when we get back if you like. Come back for a cup of tea. The cutting about Susan mentions a mill and a deep hole where they found Susan's body. Do you know of anywhere round here like that? I've been keeping my eyes peeled as we were walking, but I didn't see anything that could have been a mill. It couldn't have been too far from Susan's home."

"There were lots of mills along the river in the nineteenth century. Some probably burnt down, with all the sparks flying from machinery. Actually, I think there is a converted mill downstream from where we joined the river."

Kate took another sip of her wine. She gazed out at the river. "I

260

think Amelia felt a particular empathy with Susan. After all, she herself, who also lived in Lavender Cottage, was engaged to be married to the son of the owner of Woodcote House." Suddenly, Kate realised what she was saying and the unspoken implication that history could be repeated again with Tim and herself caused her to stop speaking abruptly. She sipped at her wine again and leaned over to look at Amy's colouring efforts.

The same thought seemed to have struck Tim forcibly, and he too made a show of being very interested in Amy's brightly coloured fish.

Freddie looked up from his wordsearch on river fauna. "Amy, that's supposed to be a brown trout. Why have you coloured it purple, orange and green?"

"'Cause it's pretty," Amy retorted, jutting out her bottom lip determinedly.

"Maybe it could be a rainbow trout," Tim said placatingly, which seemed to please Amy. Freddie shrugged and went on with his word search.

"Aha! Damsel fly!" he exclaimed. "Been looking for that!"

*

After lunch, they walked back the way they had come, but went a short distance past the footpath from which they had joined the river earlier, to where the river widened somewhat then narrowed again. Just beyond was a large, rectangular building on the other side of the river which Tim pointed out as being a converted mill.

Kate exclaimed: "This could be the place! Oh God! I wonder if this is where she jumped in!"

"Could be, couldn't it?" Tim said. He put his hand on her shoulder and gave it a comforting squeeze.

"It looks deep here," Freddie said, looking down into the water. "But wouldn't she have floated? You said the newspaper article said they dragged the river and brought her out of a deep pool."

Kate and Tim looked at each other. Neither had realised that Freddie had been listening to every word they had said when discussing

261

the tragedy.

"Maybe her clothes and the current dragged her down," Tim said. Then, looking down at Amy's solemn little face he said brightly, "Come on, chaps! I think it's time we headed back. Lead the way Fred. Call Binky to heel, Kate."

The sun was a big, red ball sinking behind the trees and though the wind had dropped, the air was growing chill as they tramped back, leaving the river behind them and re-joining the footpath that ran along the field behind Woodcote. Sparrows twittered and fluttered about in the hedgerow before settling down for the night, and a flock of rooks, cawing stridently, flew overhead, heading back to their rookery.

Tim, bringing up the rear, remembered the times he had walked here with Claire, with Amy either ensconced in the child carrier on his back, or when she was older, trudging along, trying to keep up with Freddie, who even then would be on the lookout for caterpillars or beetles. And he remembered the times after Claire had died, walking with her absence, his heart aching for his children and for his own loss. And now, as they walked in single file, strung out along the narrow footpath, here was Kate, her bright hair tousled by the wind, striding along with them, the dog at her side. He noticed how her hand reached out to pat Binky on the head from time to time. How Amy frequently turned to her to tell her something. He felt again as though a hollow loneliness inside him was filling up, that a balm was being applied to the grief that for two years had been so raw. It was a feeling he had never had when he was with Elaine.

Tim's heart told him that Kate returned his feelings, but a voice in his head continued to refute this, insisting that she would feel he was too old for her, that she and Jake still had a thing going between them, that it would not be fair on Kate to expect her to take on a widower and his young family when she herself was still so young.

This mindset was reinforced when they emerged again into Tuckers Lane, and after passing Woodcote, rounded the bend and Kate's cottage came into view. Parked outside the gate was a big, blue van. Kate gave a small exclamation of what Tim wanted to think was annoyance. "Jake!"

"Looks like you've got company," Tim said, trying to keep the

262

disappointment out of his voice. "Look, we won't come in now. I'll see those cuttings and cadge a cup of tea off you another time."

Kate looked quickly at him. "Sorry about this. I wasn't expecting him. Why don't you come in anyway?"

"I won't Kate, but next time definitely. Oh, by the way, the kids are going to Claire's parents in Colchester for half term next week, and I'm going to pick them up again on Saturday, which means they'll miss their lesson with you, I'm afraid. I'm taking them and Binky over tomorrow and I'll be staying overnight. Will you be working in the studio? You don't usually on a Sunday, but if you do, don't leave it till after dark before you go home."

"I won't, don't worry," Kate answered, giving Binky's lead back to Tim, which she had unfastened after they left the river. They were approaching her gate and Jake's van, and as she spoke, the driver's door opened, and Jake stepped out. Tim was struck again how extraordinarily good looking the fellow was. His unruly, blond hair framed his lean, high-cheekboned face, the stubble of beard only adding to the overall rakish effect. He stood there, leaning his lanky frame lazily against the van, a cigarette dangling from his fingers.

Kate looked from Jake to Tim, but what she saw was the contrast between the arrogant nonchalance of the one and the heart-piercing expression of quiet strength mingled with diffidence in the eyes of the other. She wanted to blurt out to Tim: "We're not together! It's not him I want!" But instead gave Jake a wave, and turned to Tim, who had also raised a hand in greeting to Jake.

"Thanks for a lovely walk and lunch and dog-training exercises!"

"Thanks for coming! See you soon." He turned to the children. "Come on, you two. Home James, and don't spare the horses!"

Amy reached up and gave Kate a kiss on the cheek and, with a grin from Freddie, the two children turned and started back, followed by Binky. Tim seemed to hesitate for a moment and Kate thought he was about to kiss her too, but he turned away with a smile and followed the children up the lane.

Jake, for his part, had watched as the little group approached and had got a sense of how Kate seemed to be an integral part of the family. Nor did he miss the look which had passed between Kate and Tim as they parted, like a hunger to drink in the other's presence, mixed with reticence on both sides. It was a look which said that they were not yet lovers, but Jake felt an unfamiliar twinge of jealous anxiety, because it looked very much like a look of love.

He stepped towards Kate as she came up to him. He tilted her face up to him and looked at her searchingly. The bruising had gone from her eye, but a faint trace of the graze on her chin still remained. Jake, not for the first time, felt angry with himself for letting this lovely creature slip through his fingers. He had side-lined her in his single-minded determination to make it in the art world, and this included his involvement with Lucinda, with her money and generous nature.

"I saw Mimi in the pub and she told me about how you were attacked! So I came down to see how you were," he said, wrapping his arms around her and pulling her to him.

Tim, about to round the bend in the lane, looked back over his shoulder. Seeing Kate in Jake's arms, while not surprising him, was like a blow to his solar plexus. He did not however see how quickly Kate pulled away from Jake.

"I'm fine now," Kate said brightly, hoping Tim had not seen Jake's hug. Glancing down the lane, she was relieved to see that Tim had disappeared from sight. "Come in, I'll tell you about it. Have you been waiting here long?"

"About half an hour. I walked down to your studio to see if you were there, but obviously you weren't, so I thought I'd better just wait till you got back. I texted you, but there was no reply."

"Oh, sorry! I forgot to take my phone. We went for a walk by the river."

Kate led the way into the cottage and busied herself making some tea and lighting the fire. Then, curled up in the armchair, facing Jake sprawled on the sofa, she gave him a brief account of Vince's assault. Jake let her finish, then plied her with questions. Kate had not wanted to relive the experience, and changed the subject as soon as she could, asking

Jake about his work. True to form, he was soon in full flow.

"You know the *Why Are You Here?* piece you saw under construction when you came up that time?"

"You mean the one with the door and the eyes behind the keyholes?"

"Yes, that's the one. Well, it's finished, and a dealer from New York has already bought it."

"Wow! That's fantastic! And what about the rain installation?"

"Well, use its proper title, you thought of it after all. *The Quality of Mercy*. That's just about ready. Straker's buying it. When it's installed, you must come and see it. I'm quite excited about it. I hope it lives up to my image of how I want it to look. And I've started on that piece about brain synapses – *Cogito ergo sum*. I've decided to wall mount it. That's going to be interactive as well. I've got to work out how the viewer can influence where the lights come on in the synapses."

"It looks like your work is evolving to be all about either the viewer influencing what happens in the sculptures, or interacting with them in other ways," Kate said.

"Exactly. With the pods, it was movement among them which caused them to open. *Why Are You Here?* engages the viewer personally, asking them questions. The rain installation allows you to walk into it so that you are surrounded by the music and the hanging globes, and the synapses piece will also be able to be controlled by the viewer, probably by movement sensors again."

"All these pieces must cost a fortune to make. How on earth are you funding it all?" Kate said, finding it difficult to believe that Lucinda, wealthy though she was, could be bankrolling Jake for the sums he must be spending on his work.

"Well, when I sell one piece, I use most of the money to fund the next one mainly. So there's not much left over to live on. Still, dealers are prepared to pay more for my work these days. I'm hoping to exhibit at Frieze this year. There's a gallery that's interested. That should get me on the international stage."

"Wow, you *are* going up in the world, Jake! You'll be as famous as

Damien Hirst before we know it!"

"Yeah! I could do with his dosh!" Jake said wryly, then, glancing out at the darkness beyond the window, he said, "you mentioned that the bloke who attacked you had a restraining order not to come near you. Aren't you nervous that he'll break it and come after you again?"

"I wouldn't put it past him. Did Mimi tell you he came into the pub when we were all in there and gave me a horrible look?"

"Yes she did. Kate, I don't like the sound of this. He could break into this cottage one night and attack you again. Or jump you when you're out somewhere."

Kate told him about the window locks, how she did not go out after dark, and how she had arranged to take Binky if she wanted to go for a walk. When she mentioned the fact that Tim and the children accompanied her home from the studio in the evenings, Jake remarked with some acerbity: "Quite the knight in shining armour, isn't he?"

"He's just being neighbourly!" Kate said, a little too lightly.

Jake noticed the colour that had come into Kate's cheeks. She's falling for this guy he thought, then decided to dismiss the thought, telling himself that she was just lonely and was fastening on to the nearest sympathetic man for comfort and reassurance after her ordeal. He had never come across a girl who was immune to his own charisma and good looks. He would win Kate back, but he would do so when he no longer had a use for Lucinda and her money. This last thought made him feel guilty. Lucinda was a sweet girl, very generous with her money, and she was deeply in love with him.

But she wasn't Kate.

"Mind if I crash here for the night?" Jake said, adding quickly, "I'll sleep on the sofa, don't worry. Then we can go over to your studio in the morning and you can show me what you've been doing."

"Okay, if you like," Kate said, feeling that it would be churlish to tell him to leave when he had come all the way down to see how she was. And it would be good to have one night when she did not go to bed with one ear cocked to listen for anyone trying to break in.

"I've got a bottle of wine in the van. I'll just go and get it." Jake got up and went outside, returning with a bottle of Rioja. Kate dug out a corkscrew and Jake poured them both a glass. He stood leaning against the door jamb of the tiny kitchen, while Kate rustled up a couple of cheese omelettes. They ate sitting on the sofa by the fire, with their plates on their knees. Not for the first time, Kate imagined Susan Gatling sitting by this same fire, knowing she was carrying a child, and in despair, not knowing what to do.

She found herself telling Jake about the Valentine card and the newspaper cuttings, and from that, the wine loosening her tongue somewhat, went on to mention how Amelia had been engaged to the son of the owner of Woodcote, who had been killed in the war. Though he remarked on the coincidence of the tragic circumstances of the two disparate couples, all those years apart, Kate was relieved that Jake did not make the connection that Tim had seen immediately - that the same sort of connection between the two houses may be playing itself out again, here and now, with Kate and Tim.

They talked on, until Kate, feeling the effects of the wine and the fresh air of her walk earlier, stretched and got up. "I'm for bed. I'll get you a blanket, and if you occasionally chuck a log on the fire, you shouldn't be cold."

That night, for the first time in the cottage since the attack, Kate slept soundly, knowing she was not alone in the house if Vince should try to break in.

Tim on the other hand, slept fitfully, wondering if Jake was spending the night with Kate. His fears were confirmed when Freddie, having gone for a ride on his bike up the lane next morning, reported to his father that Jake's blue van was still parked outside her cottage. The full possible implications of this fact escaped Freddie, but it disturbed him nevertheless, especially when he saw the quickly disguised look of dismay on his father's face when he told him.

Tim was getting the children into the car to drive them to Claire's parents in Colchester, when Kate and Jake came up to them on their way to the studio. Kate noticed that Tim looked rather hassled, as he stuffed wellington boots, holdalls and anoraks into the boot. He greeted her and Jake with a distracted grin.

"God knows how many vital things are going to be left behind!" he said. Then he clapped a hand to his head. "Toothbrushes! Freddie, Amy, have you put your toothbrushes into your bags?"

"Whoops! No! We were waiting till we brushed our teeth after breakfast," Freddie said, clapping his hand to his head, using the same gesture as his father.

"And *have* you brushed them?"

"Er, no!"

"Well, go and do it now, and put both toothbrushes into that blue wash bag and bring it out here. Chop, chop!"

The children ran off, with Binky not knowing whether to follow them or to wait by the car in case he was left behind. In the end, he decided to stay.

"I don't know how Claire did it! I always manage to leave something behind. And the kids seem to take half the house with them. Amy seems to need a vast array of teddies and other creatures, while Fred stuffs the car with books, iPads and goodness knows what else."

Kate laughed, and peered into the car. Sure enough, surrounding Amy's car seat was a conglomeration of teddies, pandas, dolls and gadgets with wires snaking from them, not to mention bottles of water, packets of crisps and a bag of apples.

"They're only going for five days! You'd think it was a month." Tim straightened up from packing the boot, and said more seriously to Kate, "Don't forget, no wandering home in the dark. I'll be back tomorrow night."

"Yessir!" Kate said, giving a mock salute. "Well, have a safe journey." She turned to go, followed by Jake who had been standing a little apart, watching proceedings. Calling goodbye to the children, who came running back out of the house with the wash bag, and various other items they felt they had to take, she led Jake round to the side of the garage and took him up to the studio. With a heavy heart, Tim watched them go.

Jake left later that morning. He let slip that Lucinda had been at her parents' house over the weekend and was due back that evening. Kate was not surprised, as she had suspected that it was something like that which had made Jake think he had the time to come down to see her. Still, she did appreciate the fact that he had done so, even while worrying what Tim would think about her relationship with Jake.

After Jake had left, she found herself at a loose end. She normally tried to do some gardening on a Sunday, but it was starting to rain, so she decided to go to the studio to put in a few hours' work. Jake had seemed very interested in what she had done lately, and some of his observations and suggestions rang true, opening up more possibilities. She was soon deeply involved in her work, unaware of the passage of time. It had been a gloomy day and she had turned on the lights when she went up to the studio, even though she preferred working by natural light. Consequently, she did not notice that the light was fading outside, and was startled to see that it was nearly dark when she finally looked out of the windows.

She went to the window and could just about make out the lane and the dark bulk of Woodcote on the right. Walking to the opposite window, she saw the comforting light coming from the Babbidges' kitchen window further down the lane, and considered nipping across to ask if Bill would accompany her home. Their cottage was much nearer to Woodcote than her own, and she was sure she would be safe going over there.

Almost immediately, she dismissed the thought. She knew Bill would be only too pleased to walk her back, but she did not like to disturb them when they would be settling down for the evening. The wind was getting up and blew a spattering of rain against the window. She didn't want to drag him out on a wet and windy night. She cursed herself for not keeping an eye on the time. If only Zachary had a phone. Kate knew she could ask him to come over, but he did not even have a mobile.

Suddenly, she realised that the studio must be a blazing beacon with all the lights on and that anyone watching would see her moving about there. Added to that, Woodcote was in darkness, making it obvious that

269

there was no-one at home. A feeling of dread settled in the pit of her stomach and she hurriedly switched off the lights. Going back to the windows, she waited for her eyes to get accustomed to the dark and scanned the area around the studio. It was not quite as dark as it had seemed when the lights were on, though it was dark enough. But surely Vince was not lurking around on the off chance that she would be walking home on her own. She told herself he had other fish to fry and was highly unlikely to be waiting to pounce on her. She was just being paranoid.

Grabbing her keys, she felt her way down the stairs and, taking a deep breath, let herself out of the outer door and started walking briskly down towards her cottage, pulling up the hood of her duffle coat against the rain. Rounding the bend, she made out the shape of the cottage with the Mini parked outside and the dim shapes of the poplars beyond.

And then she stopped dead.

A figure was approaching her in the lane, barely distinguishable from the darkness around it. Immediately, her mind lurched back to the attack in the woods, when she had seen the figure of Vince standing and blocking her way. The figure was still a little way from the cottage and Kate, her heart thudding in her chest, broke into a run. If she could reach her door first...

Pulling her keys out of her pocket, she turned into her gate and dashed down the brick path to her front door, slipping slightly on the mossy surface. Sobbing with fear, she fumbled with the keys, feeling for the keyhole. And then she dropped the keys. Bending down, she grabbed them with shaking hands. Through her panic she heard footsteps coming up behind her.

"Kate!" The voice was close behind her, and it cut through her panic like a bolt of lightning. Zachary's voice! She turned and flung herself at his chest, shaking, and trying to control her sobs of relief. Just as he had done after Vince's attack, Zachary held her close, murmuring soothing words and giving her little comforting pats on the back.

"Come on, let's get you inside. I'm so sorry I frightened you," Zachary said, taking the keys from Kate and opening the door. Switching on the light and shutting the door, he led her to the sofa, taking off her wet coat and making her sit down. Quickly and efficiently he cleared the cold ashes from the grate and lit the fire. Then he went into the kitchen and made some tea. Handing Kate one of the steaming mugs, he sat down opposite her cradling his own mug, and looked at her quizzically.

"Did you think I was Vince? And what were you doing walking home in the dark by yourself?"

Kate answered his second question first. "I was painting and I didn't realise it was nearly dark. Tim and the kids are away, and I meant to go home while it was still light. I didn't think Vince would be loitering about on the off chance. Then I saw you. I should have realised you were too tall to be Vince, but it's dark and I panicked. I certainly didn't expect to see *you* coming up the lane."

"I've just been to see old Sam who lives down the road. Age of ninety-nine. He was a great friend of my dad." He took a sip of his tea. "I don't blame you for panicking, after what happened to you in the wood. But why didn't you ask Bill Babbidge to walk back with you?"

"I didn't like to. It's cold and rainy. If he became ill because of me, I would never forgive myself."

Zachary looked grim. "That settles it, I'm going to get myself a mobile phone. If I'd had one, you could have called me to walk you back."

"Oh, don't get one on my account, but it would be good to be able to phone you about the exhibition or anything like that," Kate smiled, feeling much better now, in Zachary's strong, calming presence. "Not that I would want to drag you kicking and screaming into the twenty-first century or anything!"

Kate went on to tell Zachary about borrowing Binky to accompany her on walks, but while Zachary thought it would be a good thing to have Binky with her, he was not convinced that it would guarantee her complete safety.

"You say Dobbs is a heavy-set man. It's possible he could overpower the dog – knock him over the head or something. I wouldn't go into lonely places – dog or no dog."

Kate sighed. "It's so restricting. I wonder when his trial will come

271

up. Could be months. I suppose I could drive somewhere, like down to Dorset where I used to live, and get a breath of sea air. I wouldn't have to worry about Vince lurking about there."

"I sometimes go down to the coast to look for driftwood," Zachary said. "Maybe you could come along sometime, take a break from the painting."

Kate's eyes lit up. "That would be great. I've been wanting to go and take pictures of pebbles and waves and stuff like that."

"I'll let you know when I'm going, shall I?"

"Yes, I'd like that"

Zachary got up. "Well, I'd better be getting along. You going to be alright?"

"Yes, I'm fine. Sorry for freaking out like that."

"Not surprising. Dobbs' attack must've had more of an effect on you than you realise."

When Zachary had gone, Kate drew the curtains across the window. Before the attack, she had never bothered to draw them, but now she could not help wondering if Vince was somewhere out there in the dark, spying on her. She went back to the fire and, curling up on the sofa, sat staring into the flames, still feeling a bit shaken. She would be glad when Tim got back from Colchester, and he could go back to walking her home.

But she had reckoned without Elaine.

*

Tim had driven back from Colchester early on Monday morning, and leaving the car at the station, had taken the train straight to London. Arriving back that evening, he drove home, looking forward to walking back alone with Kate to her cottage. His worry that Jake would still be there was dissipated when there was no sign of his van in the lane. But his relief was dashed when he rounded the bend and saw Elaine's red Volvo parked outside his house. The kids must have mentioned they were going to be away this week and she had probably farmed out Duncan to his father for half-term. Looking over to the studio above the garage, he saw

272

Kate painting near the window. She turned her head to look at Tim's headlights coming up the lane and raised her brush in greeting. He waved back, even though he knew she couldn't see him in the darkness and drew level with Elaine's car. She was still sitting in the driver's seat and lowered her window. He did the same to the passenger window of his car.

"Tim!" she called. "I've been waiting for you. I'm freezing! I was just about to let myself into the house with my key."

Tim tried to keep the irritation out of his voice. "Hang on, I'll just park the car. Be with you in a moment."

Tim parked, got out his briefcase and overnight bag and walked over to where Elaine was emerging from her car. She put her arms around his neck and kissed him lingeringly.

"Tim darling! I've been so looking forward to half term. We haven't had a chance to be alone for ages. Duncan is with Giles and his wench this week, so we can be together every night. I could have supper ready for you when you come home. Give Mrs B. the week off. And maybe we could go out somewhere one evening."

Tim groaned inwardly. The prospect of being alone with Kate was receding fast. He had even thought he might take her out to dinner one night. He disentangled himself from Elaine's enveloping arms.

"I've already given Mrs B. the week off. But there's no need to cook for me. I'm quite happy to do myself an egg or something in the evening. Anyway, you'd better come in, Elaine. It's a bit chilly out here." He led the way to the front door and unlocked it.

Elaine slipped her coat off in the hall and resumed the conversation. "Oh, but I *want* to cook for you. It's no trouble. We can have some cosy evenings, just the two of us."

"Do you mind if we give it a miss for tonight? I was up at five thirty, and it's been a bit of a hectic day. I think I'm for an early night."

She gave him a suggestive sideways look. "An early night sounds good to me!" She came up to him and slipped her hands under his jacket and round his waist. "You're not really going to send me packing, are you? Out into the cold, dark night to my lonely bed?" She pressed her body against his, seeking out his lips hungrily with her own. Against his

273

will, he felt his own body responding and he returned her kiss. Elaine felt the response, but her glow of triumph would have been short-lived if she could have heard the name that was repeating itself in Tim's head over and over again. *Kate, Kate, Kate.*

Elaine broke away from Tim and taking off his suit jacket, pulled him towards the drawing room. She flicked on the light and kissing him again, her hands in his hair, murmured, "Come and sit down. I'll pour you a drink."

"Hang on, Elaine. I must walk Kate home first." As he spoke, through the window he saw the light of a torch bobbing past beyond the gate. He turned abruptly away from Elaine and almost ran from the room. Wrenching open the front door, he dashed up the path calling, "Kate! Wait! I was just coming up to get you!"

Kate stopped, and waited till he came up to her, the torch hanging from her hand forming a pool of light on the ground. She was glad of the darkness which hopefully would hide the anguish she felt after seeing Tim in Elaine's arms, her lips on his, as she walked past the drawing room window. She had seen Elaine's car stop in front of Tim's house, and then, ten minutes later, Tim's headlights coming down the lane. She had heard the clunks as Tim shut the car door and the boot and the electronic sound of the door lock. She had willed herself not to look out of the window again, but heard Elaine's car door shut and then a pause before the front door banged shut. She had wondered if Tim would come up to walk her home, but then thought that Elaine would be far from pleased if he did. She decided to risk it and go home on her own. Now he stood there in front of her in his shirt sleeves in the chilly February night.

"Why didn't you wait for me?" Tim said reproachfully, putting his hand out to touch her arm.

Kate forced herself to reply lightly. "I saw that Elaine was here, and I didn't want to disturb you."

"I didn't know she was coming, but I said I would take you home. You should have waited."

"Tim, I'm sure it would have been alright," Kate said, and she meant it. Somehow the scare she had had the previous night, which had

274

ended well, had defused her anxieties to a large extent.

Tim, however, was having none of it. "It's not alright."

From the look on Kate's face, he knew she could hear the anger in his voice. Mostly he was angry with Elaine, and at himself. Why hadn't he gone straight up to the studio? Why did Elaine have to come over, and then kiss him in full view from the lane? Kate must have seen them and be more convinced than ever that he and Elaine were an item.

Kate for her part thought back to Tim's expression when he had seen Jake at the cottage, and how he would have drawn his own conclusions about her relationship with him. Maybe that was contributing to consolidating *his* relationship with Elaine. She wished she knew how deep his involvement with Elaine was.

Almost roughly, Tim linked his arm into Kate's and they walked at a brisk pace towards Kate's cottage. As they approached her gate, Tim slowed down and broke the silence.

"Promise me you'll wait for me next time, Elaine or no Elaine."

"Okay, I promise - at least until the clocks go forward and it's lighter in the evenings."

Tim had to be content with that and they turned into Kate's gate. At her door, he took her hand in his, peering at her in the darkness.

"Sorry I was angry. It's just that I... we... don't want anything to happen to you."

Kate smiled. "I know, and I'm very grateful to have a guardian angel like you." She unlocked the door and went in. "Goodnight, and thanks Tim."

The door closed and Tim turned away.

After Tim had rushed out of the house, Elaine stood rigid in the middle of the room, her fists clenched, an expression of fury mingled with humiliation on her face. Why was it so damned important to walk the wretched girl back? Why did Tim have to go rushing off like that in his shirtsleeves, leaving her looking like a fool? Nobody was going to attack that girl this close to people. What a fuss about nothing! The little minx probably exaggerated the attack to gain Tim's sympathy, the damsel in distress. And now Tim was playing the gallant protector. Her mind conjured up a vision of them walking along together in the dark. Would he kiss her goodnight? What was going on there? Was Tim two-timing her with Kate? Men! As soon as a woman shows an interest in them, they get flattered and seduced. Look at Giles with that devious secretary of his playing the ingénue, bringing him coffee, listening to his problems and wriggling her way into his affections. Next thing you know, he's sleeping with her. The humiliation she had felt far outweighed any anguish she might have felt at the loss of the man.

But with Tim, it was different. Yes, she felt pushed aside when he rushed off, but her fury was soon replaced by a physical pain which she could only think of as heartache. She couldn't lose him. He was the love of her life. Forcing herself to relax, she went to the kitchen and started to prepare some supper, the ingredients for which she had brought with her. With some food and wine inside him, Tim would relax, surely, and she would make him forget about Kate, at least for this evening. He couldn't object to her staying over after cooking his supper.

When Tim returned, the aroma of garlic and wine and sizzling mushrooms was wafting out of the kitchen. Elaine greeted him with a glass of wine and a welcoming smile. Studiously avoiding any mention of Kate, she solicitously touched his cold cheek.

"You must be frozen. You go up and change and I'll finish getting the supper."

Tim looked at her. On the face of it she seemed at ease, but there was a hint of desperation in her eyes which made him more sympathetic to her than any seduction techniques she might employ. Yet more than anything, if he couldn't be with Kate, he wanted to be alone tonight and relax after a long day, but he didn't have the heart to ask Elaine to leave. Anyway, who was he kidding? Jake had spent the night with Kate at the weekend. And how could she not want to be with him? He was an artist like she was, nearly her own age, and devastatingly good looking. How could she *not* be in love with him? He went upstairs, changed and washed, and when he came down, Elaine had the table in the kitchen laid for two, and was putting out a supper of steak with a mushroom and wine sauce.

276

Tim found he was hungry, having had little to eat since his early breakfast, but Elaine barely touched her food, watching with satisfaction as he did justice to his steak. Afterwards, she shooed him out of the kitchen while she cleared up. He went into the family room where Socrates was rustling about in the bedding in his cage. He sat down on the sofa and leaned his head back, his legs stretched out in front of him. When Elaine came into the room a little later, he was fast asleep.

She stood looking at him for a long moment. So much for her plans for a romantic evening together. But at least she was here with him. If she hadn't been, would Kate have invited him into her cottage when he took her home? And if so, who knows what would have happened? She was determined that there would not be an opportunity for the two of them to be alone any longer than the time it took for Tim to walk Kate home. Even that was too long, but she had to resign herself to it. She would make sure that she was here every evening until the children got back.

She sat down beside Tim and kissed him. He stirred and murmured a word which sounded very much like "Kate."

Instantly, a stab of fury, mingled with pain and despair pierced Elaine's heart. She wanted to slap his face, wanted to scream "I'm not Kate! You don't love *her*. It's *me* you need. It's *me* you want. Look at all the things I've done for you! For your children!" But she bit her lip. She would pretend she hadn't heard him.

She gently shook his shoulder and he opened his eyes groggily. For an instant, he looked at her uncomprehendingly, then his eyes focussed and he sat up, rubbing a hand over his face. "Uh…Sorry, must've dropped off."

"You're exhausted, darling. Come on, let's go to bed."

But by the time Elaine came to his bedroom after making herself fragrant and artfully tousling her hair in the guest bathroom, he had already had a shower and was stretched out in the bed, fast asleep again. Elaine had to admit defeat. She slipped into bed beside him, but sleep did not come till the early hours. In her mind, she kept hearing the name that Tim had uttered in his sleep.

In the morning, he was up before six and out of the door by half past, giving her a quick kiss on the cheek, and a reminder to lock up before she left.

Elaine sat on the edge of the bed, her stomach churning with the humiliation of being treated so casually. The intimate evening she had planned so carefully the night before had fizzled out, with Tim dropping off to sleep as though she wasn't even there. And she laid the blame squarely with Kate. Her mind roiling with bitter thoughts, she dressed and hurried out of the house. She would make sure that tonight would be different. For a start, she would accompany Tim when he took Kate home, and with that out of the way, they could settle down to the rest of the evening together.

That evening she made sure that she was at Tim's house before he got back. She started cooking, all the while listening for his car, and because she couldn't see the lane from the kitchen, she kept going to the drawing room window to check whether he had arrived yet. As soon as she saw the headlights of his car, she hurried to the door, opened it and saw him starting to head for the studio. She called to him, "Hi Tim! Hang on, I'll come with you down the lane, keep you company on the way back."

Tim stopped, his jaw tensed in exasperation. He called back, "No Elaine, it's muddy and cold. I won't be a minute. You go back in." He gave her a quick wave and disappeared through the studio door. There was nothing Elaine could do but go back inside. She would not demean herself by running out to walk with them when Tim had brushed her off like that. She went into the darkened dining room and watched as, a few minutes later, Tim and Kate walked past the house. She couldn't see them properly, but they seemed to be walking very close together. Again she imagined a scenario with Tim kissing Kate goodnight in the darkness. Tears stung her eyes, but she blinked them back angrily, not wanting to smudge the mascara she had applied so carefully earlier.

When Tim got back, she didn't go into the hall to meet him, but stayed in the kitchen, cooking, and telling herself to play it cool. Tim greeted her with a kiss on the cheek, and in spite of her annoyance and jealousy, the thought came to Elaine that it was as though they were a

278

married couple. The little glow of pleasure the thought gave her dissipated however, when Tim, taking a sip from the glass of wine she handed him, said: "Elaine, as I said before, there's really no need to cook supper for me every night. And I won't be much company tonight. I have some work to do, I'm afraid."

Elaine put her arms around him. "Oh darling, do you have to? What's so important that you have to do it tonight?"

On the pretext of taking off his tie, Tim disentangled himself from her. "Important meeting in the morning." He put his wine down. "And I mustn't drink too much of this either. I'll have to focus."

When Tim was still working in his study at eleven thirty, Elaine had once again to accept the situation and went up to bed on her own. Was he trying to avoid her? He had seemed quiet and distant at supper, and she had had to repeat herself more than once because he hadn't heard her. She had tried to introduce the subject of the holiday in Tuscany again, but he had once again fobbed her off.

In his study, Tim sat staring unseeingly at his computer screen. All he could think of was the brief moment when Kate had opened her front door and turned to say goodnight to him. He had longed to take her in his arms, but in the darkness he could not make out her expression. The moment passed and Kate had turned away. He switched off his computer and went upstairs, wishing it was Kate who was sleeping in his bed.

Chapter XIV

Hearing the sound of a car coming up the lane, Kate looked out of the studio window and saw Elaine's red Volvo drawing up beside the garage below. She wondered what Elaine was doing here at eleven in the morning, and was even more mystified when she saw her walking towards the door at the bottom of the studio steps. Surely she was not paying her a social call! Seconds later, footsteps sounded hollowly on the wooden stairs. The door opened and Elaine stood in the doorway. As usual she was immaculately turned out. Designer jeans, soft, tan leather jacket and high-heeled boots. She had a brittle smile on her face as she stepped into the room.

"Oh, hello!" Kate said, stepping away from her easel and wiping her brush on a rag.

"Hello," Elaine said in her turn, walking across to the window and staring out. "I just wanted to have a word. I..." She stopped and turned to face Kate. "There's no point in beating about the bush. I just want to ask you if there's anything going on between you and Tim."

Kate stared at her, her lips parted in surprise, the suddenness of the question causing her heart to hammer in her chest. "Anything going on? What do you mean?"

"Oh, don't pretend you don't know what I'm talking about. Have you and he... Has he made a move on you? Or more to the point, have you made a move on him?"

Anger rose in Kate. She took a step towards Elaine, then stopped. "No, of course I haven't *made a move* on him, as you put it."

"And what about him? Has he...?"

"No, he hasn't. Not that it has anything to do with you if he had."

"Oh, but it has everything to do with me! He and I, we're... we're together. I love him and I know he loves me, or at least he seemed to before *you* came along, insinuating yourself into the family, and he... he rushes around giving you the use of a studio and guarding you from non-existent dangers like a knight in shining bloody armour!"

An angry response died on Kate's lips when she realised that Elaine's eyes held a look akin to desperation.

"Elaine," Kate said, taking another step towards the other woman. But Elaine backed away.

"Don't come near me. You've ruined everything. Why don't you just leave and go back to London or wherever you came from and leave us alone? You've got your blond Adonis of a boyfriend. Why don't you go and live with him?"

Kate, white as a sheet, stood staring at the woman standing in front of her, her shock and anger at Elaine's verbal onslaught warring with her tendency to see things from the other person's point of view. Though she thoroughly disliked her, she couldn't help putting herself in Elaine's place. Given the way she felt about Tim, she knew she would be as desolate as Elaine looked now, if she suspected that he had transferred his affections to someone else. With a lurch of her heart, she remembered the previous evening when she had thought that Tim was about to kiss her, and how she had longed for him to do so. In spite of herself, she knew Elaine was right to resent her, and if Tim had kissed her, she would not have pushed him away. How could she, Kate, live with herself if she knew she was destroying Elaine's dreams?

But what could she do? She had not encouraged Tim in any way, she was sure. And this was her home now. Was she supposed to give up the studio, sell the cottage and move back to London? If not, and the thought of doing so filled her with despair, how could she avoid seeing Tim? She was teaching his children, who seemed to like being with her. And she in turn had grown very fond of them. Her furious response to Elaine, that she had a right to live where she chose, died on her lips and instead she said as calmly as she could, "Elaine, there is nothing 'going on' between Tim and me. He is just being neighbourly, offering to see me home in the evenings, because of what happened. It...it was very frightening, you know, the attack. And violent. If Zachary had not come along..." She paused. "The evenings are getting lighter, and the clocks will be going forward soon,

281

then there'll be no need for Tim and the kids to walk me back."

Elaine cut in. "Thank God for that. It must be a bit of a chore for the poor man, after a long day in London. But it's not just that. I just wanted to tell you to back off. Tim and I are lovers. He needs a woman, and that woman is me, not you."

"Don't worry, I don't have any intention of 'making a move' on Tim. As you say, I've got Jake."

Kate did not know quite why she added the last remark, except perhaps to calm Elaine's fears, and get her to leave. The whole conversation was deeply upsetting and she just wanted it to end.

Elaine drew herself up and visibly took a grip on her emotions, though her voice shook slightly as she spoke. "Good. Then there's nothing more to discuss. Goodbye." She turned on her heel and without a backward glance, went back down the stairs.

Kate watched the car turn in the lane and disappear round the bend. She let out a long breath and sat down shakily in the old armchair. It had come as a shock to see the self-contained Elaine losing control like that. And to realise the full extent of Elaine's feelings for Tim. In spite of herself, she felt responsible for the other woman's misery. The fact that she, Kate, was also in love with Tim, did not make her feel entitled to destroy another person's happiness. It was all too much to think about. She needed to get away for a while. She made a decision: she would go and see her father. It was his birthday in a few days' time, and since she had not made it up to Yorkshire for Christmas, now would be a good time to go. She had been working flat out and needed a break. And she needed to think.

Her thoughts were interrupted by Zachary's voice calling up the stairs, and she got up to greet him as he made his way up. With a broad smile on his face, he held a mobile phone aloft as he came into the room.

"Just been into town and got myself a mobile phone at last!" he said, showing it to Kate. "The bloke in the shop showed me how to work it. I hope I can remember."

Kate, covering her dismay at Elaine's outburst as best she could, smiled back at Zachary.

282

"Excellent! Tell you what, ring my mobile now." She scribbled her number on a piece of paper and handed it to Zachary, who painstakingly tapped the number onto his phone. Almost immediately, the saxophone solo from Baker Street rang out, and Kate picked up her phone.

"Hello. How may I help you?"

"Ah, hello! Be that the world-famous artist Kate Atkins?"

Kate laughed. "Oh, that sounds like the internationally famous wood sculptor Zachary..." she stopped. "I still don't know your surname!"

"Hills," Zachary said, then looked down at his phone. "Do I press this to end the call?" he said, indicating a button.

"Yes, that's right. Now, do you know how to text and leave messages?"

For the next twenty minutes or so, Kate got Zachary used to the functions on his phone. Then Kate said, "Zachary, can I ask you to walk me back later? Tim said he would, but Elaine is not at all happy about it, because the children are away, and she thinks I'm going to pounce on Tim."

"Who is Elaine?"

Kate explained who Elaine was, and their recent confrontation came pouring out.

Zachary noticed her agitation as she spoke, and gave her a searching look. Her show of light-heartedness just now had not disguised the pallor of her face and the way her hands shook slightly. The encounter with Elaine had clearly upset her. And he had a shrewd notion that it was because she was in love with Tim herself. He refrained from saying anything to that effect, confining himself to muttering, "Bit of a cheek, if you ask me. He's not her property. But of course I'll walk you back."

"Thanks. It's only for tonight. I'm going up to see my father in Yorkshire for a few days tomorrow."

Zachary promised to return later and clumped back down the stairs. As he emerged onto the lane, Kate saw from the window that Magda was coming out through Woodcote's garden gate after her cleaning session. She saw Zachary raise a hand in greeting and they stood talking for a while. Kate noticed how good they looked together, and how easy they seemed in each other's company, even though they hardly knew each other. Into the turmoil that Elaine had caused in her mind, stole the warming thought, "Wouldn't it be nice if Zachary and Magda...?"

When Tim arrived back that evening, he groaned when he saw Elaine's car once again parked outside his house. She was obviously inside, because the lights were on in the house. He decided to go straight up to the studio to take Kate home. But when he went up the studio steps, he was dismayed to see Zachary standing just inside the door. Kate was putting on her coat. Tim managed a nod of greeting to Zachary.

"Tim!" Kate said. "I was waiting till you came back to say that there's no need for you to walk me back. Zachary said he would." She glanced towards the window. "I see Elaine is here, so she'll probably be expecting you home."

Tim's expression was one of disappointment mingled with bafflement.

"But Kate, it's got nothing to do with Elaine. I didn't ask her to come over you know."

Kate took a step towards Tim. "I think she would prefer it if you didn't take me back. And since Zachary's here..."

"I don't care what she would prefer. Has she said anything to you?"

"It doesn't matter Tim," Kate said, avoiding answering him, and carrying on hurriedly, "and I'll be going up to Yorkshire tomorrow to see my dad for his birthday, so there's no need for any guard duty for the rest of the week. I probably won't be back till Sunday. But the children won't be here for their lesson on Saturday anyway, will they?"

Tim, taking in the information that he would not be seeing Kate alone as he had been anticipating all day, struggled to answer lightly. "No, I'm going across to get them on Saturday, and we won't be back till evening."

"So that works out well," Kate said briskly, successfully keeping a tremor out of her voice. "I just thought since I didn't see Dad for Christmas, I should make the effort to go up for his birthday."

There was nothing Tim could do except wish her a safe journey and go back down the stairs. Kate and Zachary followed a moment later. Getting his briefcase out of the car, Tim watched as they disappeared into the darkness. Something had happened. He was willing to bet that Elaine had confronted Kate that day, telling her to back off. Kate's whole demeanour had changed. She seemed rather brittle and had avoided eye contact with him. Fury rose in him towards Elaine. Maybe it was time he tried again with an au pair or a full-time nanny who would take the children to school. Then he would be able to dispense with Elaine doing the school run. But then he thought of having to tell Lily Babbidge that he would no longer need her, and he had a feeling that she relied on the extra money she earned looking after Freddie and Amy.

As he stood there, his mind churning, the front door opened, and Elaine looked out.

"Tim, what are you doing out there?" She looked up towards the studio, and seeing that the lights were off, added, "Have you done your escort duties?"

Tim bit back a sharp retort, and opening the gate went down the path to the house and shut the door. He would have to work out what to do.

*

Leaving the motorway, Kate joined the A64, driving through a landscape of rolling hills, villages with their church towers, and a patchwork of fields dotted with coppices and occasional groves of poplars and willows beside the road, their still bare branches already flushed with the rising sap of the approaching spring.

Turning left towards Scarborough, she drove on into the wolds of North Yorkshire, a countryside of wide-open fields and big skies of sweeping clouds, with blue hills in the distance.

Although he had been writing about Shropshire, a snippet of an A.E. Housman poem came into her mind.

Into my heart an air that kills

From yon far country blows
What are those blue remembered hills,
What spires, what farms are those?
That is the land of lost content.
I see it shining plain,
The happy highways where I went
And cannot come again.

The land of lost content. The line made her heart ache anew. How could she know whether she would be doing the best thing for Tim if she tried to stifle her burgeoning feelings for him? How could she know whether he felt the same about her? Was it wishful thinking which made her feel that he did? Perhaps he did love Elaine. She was a very attractive woman. Otherwise why would he tolerate her staying overnight with him? But what about the children, for whom she had grown to care deeply and who she believed were fond of her? How could she continue to have so much contact with them and yet avoid contact with Tim? And the more she saw Tim, the deeper her feelings for him became.

But Elaine's distress when she had confronted Kate had been so intense and so genuine. Kate felt, in all conscience, that she could not think of taking Tim away from her. Kate believed that in her way, Elaine was genuinely in love with Tim.

Her state of mind was so fragile that a floral tribute beside the road, the evidence of a road accident fatality, made tears well in her eyes, and her vision blurred. Blinking them away, she concentrated on the road ahead.

Coming into Scarborough, she drove nearly as far as the bay, then turned right, up the hill, past imposing houses and hotels, towards the tall town houses on the South Cliff where her father and Doreen lived.

Kate found a place to park on a side road and walked back to the Esplanade, carrying her holdall. Reaching her father's house, she climbed the steps to the front door. Doreen greeted her warmly, giving her a jasmine-scented hug before ushering her into the house.

"Your dad's up in his study, dear. He's got a student in with him for

286

a lesson at the moment. He's been doing quite a lot of tutoring over half term."

"That's good. But I hope he's also getting some R&R. Before he knows it, he'll be back to school and he'll be in the thick of it again."

Kate remembered to take off her shoes inside the front door. "I'll take my bag up to my room, shall I? I'll see dad later."

"Yes, you go on up, I've got your bed all aired. Then come down for a nice cup of tea. You can tell me all your news."

Kate climbed to the top of the stairs to her attic bedroom, dumped her bags on the bed and, going to the window, opened it and breathed in the smell of the sea. From up here at the top of the house, she could see the curve of the shoreline to the north, where lights were beginning to come on along the seafront. Tim seemed a very long way away.

When she went down again, her father was seeing the student out of the door. He turned and his thin, ascetic face broke into a smile when he saw her.

"Kate, my lovely!" He opened his arms and she went into them, her face resting on the rough tweed of his jacket. There was something in the way she clung to him that gave him a twinge of concern. He held her away from him and searched her face.

"How are you, my dear? You look a little pale." He did not add that there seemed to be a sadness in her eyes that he had last seen when her mother had died.

"Oh, I'm fine, dad. Just been working very hard. How are *you*?"

"Never better. We missed you at Christmas though." He tucked her hand under his arm and drew her into the kitchen, where Doreen was pouring out tea. "Come and tell us what you've been up to."

They sat talking at the kitchen table, Kate telling them how her work was progressing for the upcoming exhibition. She refrained from mentioning Vince's attack, not wanting to alarm her father.

The next morning dawned grey and chilly. Big, dark clouds threatening rain were building up from the west, sliding swiftly across the sky and out to sea. The offshore wind took the white foam off the tops of the breaking waves and blew it backwards out to a sea covered with white

287

horses.

After breakfast, with her father ensconced in his study again, Kate felt restless and in need of physical exercise. She stuck her head round the door of the kitchen where Doreen was peeling potatoes.

"I'm going for a walk, Doreen, unless there's anything I can do. Do you want me to go to the shops for you?"

"No dear, you go ahead. But I do think you're mad. It looks as though it's going to pour any minute."

"Oh, I don't mind. I like it like this. See you later."

By the front door, Kate pulled on the wellington boots she always kept at her father's house, and putting on an old raincoat of his, she let herself out of the front door and made her way to one of the paths which zigzagged down the South Cliff till she got to the beach. Shunning the north end of the bay with its tourists and amusement arcades, she turned to her right and began walking south along the wide, sandy beach. The tide was well out, leaving exposed the occasional flat areas of rock, gleaming wetly in the sand.

There were few people about, but one hardy soul in a wetsuit was attempting to windsurf into the teeth of the wind. An elderly woman with her dog passed her, walking the other way. She called a brisk "Good morning" to Kate as she went by.

Keeping to the edge of the water, the waves lapping at her boots, Kate walked on round the wide sweep of the bay, lost in her thoughts. Reaching an area of tumbled rocks, she cut back to the top of the beach and continued beyond the end of the promenade along a grassy path. Here she was completely alone. She sat with her legs over the edge of the slope down to the rocks and, shutting her eyes, let the sound of the surf, the screaming of gulls and the wind in the grasses wash over her.

What was she to do? What was the right thing to do? Should she give up her own chance of happiness to make way for Elaine? She didn't know. All she knew was that the prospect of renouncing Tim, and the children, was almost more than she could bear.

After a while, she got up and made her way back along the top of the beach until she reached the steps leading up to a café perched a little way up the cliff. She climbed the steps, and going in to the café, bought a coffee and sat at a table by the window, staring out to sea. What would she do if Tim 'made a move' on her, as Elaine had rather crassly put it? Would she be able to back off and give him to understand that she did not want him, when every fibre of her being longed to be with him? Then the image of Elaine's stricken face would come into her head and her mind baulked at the thought of being the cause of so much pain to anyone.

Her coffee finished, she left the café and began to make her way back up the South Cliff, coming to a grassy area where a number of benches had been placed, each with a plaque in memory of loved ones who had delighted in the view from this spot. She had read these plaques before and they always brought a lump to her throat. She sat for a while on one of the benches and took in the view; the wide sweep of the bay to the harbour and lighthouse to the north, with the castle perched on its high crag above the town, and to the south, the curve of sandy beach ending in rocky coastline away towards Flamborough Head.

Realising that Doreen would be expecting her back for lunch, Kate carried on up the winding paths which divided and went along different routes through the gardens and woods, the sea with its attendant roar always evident far below beyond the trees.

Over the next few days, Kate felt herself beginning to relax. Even though she desperately missed seeing him, the physical distance she had put between herself and Tim gave her space to think. But it was the fact that she was where Vince could not reach her that caused the tension to leach out of her body and mind. She had not realised how much she had been metaphorically and physically looking over her shoulder in case he should attack her again.

On the Friday it was her father's birthday, and the three of them drove out into the country, taking a wide sweep across the moors, which Kate knew in summer would be purple with heather as far as the eye could see. Even now, in late February, the colours were beautiful, both on the moor and in the clouds billowing across the huge, duck egg blue sky. Dropping down into a little green valley, they stopped at a pub for lunch, electing to sit in a sunny spot outside, since the weather had turned very mild.

Under her father's gentle questioning, Kate described the cottage in more detail, the poplar trees which gave her such joy, and how she had come to have the use of a studio to paint in.

When she mentioned Tim, Charles Atkins noticed a subtle change in the tone of his daughter's voice; an undercurrent of emotion overlaid by a controlled casualness. He knew instantly that this Tim was someone special to Kate and from then on he watched her carefully but covertly whenever Tim's name came up.

Doreen, who was oblivious to any discomfort on Kate's part when talking about Tim, plied her with questions, clucking with distress at the tragedy of his wife's death and the plight of the two children left motherless. Charles noted the genuine affection Kate seemed to have for the children and how they seemed to have become an important part of her life. But it was when Doreen asked about how Tim managed to get them to school and back and still work in London that the full situation began to reveal itself to her father. The slight tremor in her voice when Kate explained about Elaine doing the school run spoke volumes. So, there was another woman on the scene. He gave an inward sigh. Here was a situation which could result in heartache for his daughter. He decided to change the subject.

"But tell us more about your exhibition. You haven't told us the date yet."

Kate shot him a grateful glance, glad to talk about something else.

"The date's been put back to the second of June. At least it gives us more time."

"Is that a Saturday?"

"Yes, the preview party will be in the evening."

"In that case, we can take the train down and come straight there."

Kate looked delighted. "You'll come down for it?"

Her father looked at her quizzically. "Do you think we would miss something like that?"

"It's an awfully long way to come, but it would be great if you

290

could."

"Come to think of it, it's probably half term the following week, so that makes it easier."

"You could come back home with me and stay the night at the cottage."

Doreen interjected: "Ooh, yes, I'm dying to see your house. It sounds so sweet!"

"But won't you be wanting to go out with your friends afterwards, perhaps stay up in London?" Charles looked anxious. "We don't want to cramp your style."

"Dad, believe me, we'll probably all be knackered by then, after putting up the work beforehand. All I'll want to do will be to go home."

"That's settled then!" Charles said with satisfaction.

*

The journey back down from Yorkshire was uneventful. When Kate pulled up in the lane outside her gate it was past eleven at night. The cottage was wrapped in darkness, dwarfed by the poplars towering overhead. She switched off the engine and let her eyes adjust to the darkness, peering out of the car windows before opening the door. Quickly going round to the boot and getting out her holdall, she hurried to the front door. Once inside, she breathed a sigh of relief. It had been good to have felt completely safe when she had been at her father's house. Now she would have to go back to worrying about Vince.

Deciding to go straight up to bed, she lugged her holdall up the stairs. At the top a strong smell of lavender wafted in from the little bedroom to her left. She went into the room and looked around. The door of the built-in cupboard at the far end of the room was ajar, but that did not surprise her, as it had a habit of swinging open because of what she assumed was a faulty catch. The smell of lavender persisted and Kate, shaking her head in puzzlement, shut the cupboard door and went out of the room.

291

Taking advantage of the fact that Duncan was staying with his father for the week, Elaine had come over to Tim's every evening during half-term and had supper waiting for him when he got back from London. She had done everything in her power to make him focus on her, wearing low-cut tops and diaphanous nightdresses, and arranging her hair in a tousled 'come to bed' style, but he had seemed distant and distracted. In her heart, Elaine suspected that he was thinking of Kate, and under her seductive demeanour, she hid a silent scream of rage against the girl who was wrecking her dreams. She tried to avoid mentioning Kate, and she certainly never meant to tell Tim that she had confronted her about her relationship with Tim, but her desire to deflect Tim's emotions away from Kate made her drop her guard momentarily.

When he came in on the Friday night, Elaine noticed a strained expression on Tim's face and asked him what was wrong.

Tim, taking off his coat, frowned and replied, "Well, it could be nothing, but as I was turning into the lane just now, I saw the figure of a man who seemed to have just emerged from the lane. He crossed the road immediately and disappeared and I didn't get a look at his face. I just hope it wasn't Dobbs. Not that I would recognise him if it was."

"Oh, I'm sure it was a perfectly innocent passer-by," Elaine said soothingly. "I shouldn't think it's anything to worry about."

"If Dobbs is hanging about near Kate's house, I think it *is* something to worry about."

It was then that Elaine's control slipped. Involuntarily, she snapped back, "Well, I don't know why the silly creature doesn't go back to London and live with her boyfriend."

Tim, going into the drawing room, stopped dead and swung round to face her.

"Do you mean Jake? How do you know he's her boyfriend?"

"She said so."

"When did she say so?"

Elaine, realising the trap she had put herself into, replied with deliberate casualness, "Oh, I saw her the other day, and she said something about the fact that she had Jake."

Tim stared at her. Elaine, refusing to meet his eyes, came up and kissed him.

"Never mind about all that. You go and wash and I'll fix you a gin and tonic." She turned away.

Tim, his mind seething with questions but not wanting to seem too insistent, went upstairs and stood at his bedroom window staring out into the darkness. Elaine was hiding something. It looked as though his instincts had been right and that there had been some sort of confrontation between Kate and Elaine. That was why Kate had suddenly decided to go up to Yorkshire and now Elaine was saying that Jake and Kate were in a relationship. Of course, Elaine might be lying but how could he know? Was she just extrapolating from the time when Jake had come up to Kate's studio? If Kate *was* with Jake, it seemed to be rather a long-distance relationship. She did not seem to see him very often. His anger towards Elaine grew. Knowing Kate, if Elaine had told her that Tim was her property, she would have immediately decided to distance herself.

When he went down again, he had difficulty being civil to Elaine. She noticed the barely concealed coolness in his manner and the hard shell she had built around her emotions, which had begun to crack when she confronted Kate, crumbled some more. At supper, when he pushed his plate away with the food half-eaten, saying he was not hungry, her composure nearly disappeared altogether.

"Oh, didn't you like it? I'm sorry, I thought you liked salmon."

Tim heard the quiver in her voice and, looking at her, was surprised to see tears shining in her eyes and an expression of vulnerability on her face he had not seen before. He immediately felt guilty. Smiling, he patted her hand across the table.

"I do like it, it's just that I'm a bit tired. It's been a busy day."

Elaine blinked away her tears and rose to remove his plate.

"Well, it's Friday, and our last evening alone, so let's enjoy it." She refilled his glass, and fearful that he would fall asleep again, hurriedly stacked the dishwasher and drew him into the den where she snuggled up beside him on the sofa. But in spite of her best efforts at engaging him in conversation, Tim still seemed preoccupied and uncommunicative.

Even in bed later she felt his attention was elsewhere and long after he had gone to sleep, Elaine lay awake, staring up at the darkened ceiling. Her inner rage, kept so tightly under control, rose to the surface in the stillness of the night. She could hear Tim's breathing beside her. He was *hers*. They were meant to be together. Hot tears welled in her eyes and trickled down the side of her face. He was falling for Kate. She knew it! She cursed herself for letting slip that she had talked to Kate. He would resent her for that. Oh! Why couldn't the wretched girl just disappear? Tim would soon forget her, she was sure. Her thoughts turned to what Tim had said earlier, about seeing a man emerging from the lane. What if it *was* Dobbs, and he was waiting for an opportunity to attack Kate again? In the depths of her despair, dark thoughts crowded into her mind.

*

When the children came noisily up the studio steps the following Monday night, Kate was delighted to see them. She waved out of the window to Lily, who was returning home from Woodcote, as Amy rushed up to her and gave her a hug, and Freddie, grinning, held out a small package to her.

"We bought you a present," he said, thrusting it into her hands, his eyes sparkling. Amy hopped about beside him, twisting her hands together in anticipation.

Kate took the package and, unfolding the tissue wrapping, found inside a little ceramic owl, modelled with intricate detail, glazed in tawny brown. She gave a gasp of delight.

"It's beautiful! I love it!"

Freddie's grin widened. "We got it at a church sale Gran took us to. I don't think it's new."

"Who wants new? It's lovely! Thank you."

Amy, anxious not to be left out, chimed in: "I paid for half and Freddie paid for half. Please could you call him Ollie?"

"Ollie it is! I'll put him on my mantelpiece with Old Shellover."

Amy looked mystified. "Who's Old Shellover?"

"The snail carving that Zachary gave to me. His name comes from a poem by Walter de la Mare. It's about two snails talking!" Kate quoted the poem to them.

"'Come!' said Old Shellover.
'What?' says Creep.
'The horny old Gardener's fast asleep;
The fat cock Thrush
To his nest has gone;
And the dew shines bright
In the rising Moon;
Old Sallie Worm from her hole doth peep:
Come!' said Old Shellover.
'Ay!' said Creep."

"Our gardener doesn't like snails either," Freddie said. "They eat his lettuces."

Kate was inordinately touched by the fact that the children had thought to bring her a present and also by the joy with which Amy had rushed up to hug her. The way the children had nestled into a special place in her heart was as precious as the sense of rightness she felt when she was with Tim. From her easel, as she looked across at the children sitting at the table, Amy engrossed in drawing a picture of two snails chatting and Freddie bent over some diagram he was drawing, her resolve to keep Tim at arm's length wavered. Freddie, glancing over at her, wondered at the sadness in her eyes. He came over to her to show her what he had been drawing.

"It's a plan of the games room!" he said, his eyes alight with enthusiasm. "Dad said we can get started on it now the spring is coming. They're going to start on mending the roof next week!"

Later, when Tim let himself and Binky in the side door of the garage and climbed the stairs, the children were hooting with laughter at

295

some drawings Kate had done of snails playing table tennis, a worm lifting weights and an owl on a treadmill.

"But snails and worms haven't got arms!" Amy was squealing.

"These ones do. They're in the arm-y!" Kate answered to another gale of laughter from Amy and a protest from Freddie.

"Then why aren't they in combat uniform?" Freddie demanded.

"They're off duty of course! They're in the animal gym." Kate looked up and saw Tim at the door. Her heart skipped a beat when their eyes met. Tim, as always when he saw Kate with his children, was struck by the way they seemed so totally at ease with each other.

Freddie flashed a grin at his father. "Dad, look at these drawings Kate did. They're so cool!"

Chuckling at the drawings, Tim looked up and met Kate's glance again. In spite of the smile in her eyes, there was a restraint there. She looked away and went to stick her brushes into white spirit before getting her coat. She picked up the ceramic owl.

"Have you seen what the children gave me? Isn't it lovely?"

"Yes, they showed me. That explains the owl on the treadmill. But what's with the snails and worms and things? I have to say, that would be a *very* slow game of table tennis!"

Chattering, they went down the stairs and out into the February night.

Over the following weeks life settled back into a routine. Often, after a quick sandwich at lunch time, Kate would go and fetch Binky and take him for a walk, usually along the footpath to the river, delighting in the celandines which starred the grass on either side of the path, heralding the imminent arrival of spring.

One afternoon, she decided to explore the common on the other side of the road. Once across the road and some way down the path, she let Binky off the lead and he went scampering away in search of interesting smells among the pine trees and silver birches. The common was criss-crossed with paths wandering off in different directions and Kate tried to remember the ones she had taken in order to find her way back. It was a beautiful afternoon, with real warmth in the sun. Kate stopped at the top of a rise and looked out over the vista of trees and gorse bushes yellow with blossom, fading into the blue distance. Something made her look behind her, and her heart lurched. She was sure she had seen a figure swiftly dodge behind the rough reddish trunk of a pine tree in the dappled shade of a coppice. For a long moment she stood frozen to the spot. Her eyes probed the shadows. She was convinced she could see something behind the tree. Panic began rising in her throat. Where was Binky? She took a grip of herself, shouted and whistled for the dog. To her relief, he came bounding up to her from further up the path.

Hurriedly, she clipped on his lead and began walking at a fast pace back along the way she had come. She could not help glancing behind her every so often, and on one or two occasions, she got a definite glimpse of a figure which seemed quickly to duck behind a gorse bush or a tree, and now and again Binky stopped in his tracks and turned, emitting a low growl deep in his throat. Once she saw another dog walker on a path some way off, and nearly called out to her, but she seemed quite elderly and Kate did not want to involve her.

Seriously frightened, but immensely glad to have Binky with her, Kate looked out for the landmarks she had taken care to notice on the way there, and relief flooded through her when she heard the sound of traffic, and glimpsed the main road ahead. By the time she got back to Woodcote and put Binky back in the house, she had calmed down, but felt drained by the nervous tension she had been under. She was convinced that it had been the presence of Binky which had kept her safe. But she decided that in future she would keep to the main road, limiting her walks to going to the village shop or in the other direction to the bridge where the road crossed the river.

Kate tried to put the frightening walk behind her. After all, it might not have been Vince. It might have been her imagination, a trick of the light. But why did Binky growl? She decided not to mention it to Tim, and gradually the incident faded as she once again immersed herself in her work.

After school and tea, the children would come up to the studio to stay with Kate until Tim got back, but after the clocks went forward, and the evenings were lighter, Kate insisted that there was no need for Tim to accompany her back home. In spite of Tim's protestations that it was no trouble, Kate was adamant that it was only a short distance and that she would be perfectly safe. Tim told her about the figure he had seen emerging from the lane in the dark, which caused a look of alarm to cross Kate's face, but she was sure that Vince would not try anything in broad daylight so close to Woodcote and the Babbidges' cottage.

Tim could see that Kate was not going to change her mind, so he agreed that she could walk back on her own, but he made a point of waiting outside his house every evening after she set off, till he was sure she had time to get back, in case she should scream for help.

The mild weather continued into March, and Kate was fascinated to see what would come up in the garden as spring arrived early. Daffodil and hyacinth shoots were pushing up through the earth, and leaves like tiny green flames were erupting from a bush by the gate. The branches of the poplars overhead took on a bobbly look as buds swelled along their lengths and delicate bronzy-green leaves began to emerge. Somehow, they wounded her with their fierce, fragile beauty, these harbingers of spring; the green spears seeming to pierce her through the heart.

From the studio window, Kate saw Elaine arriving with the children every evening when she brought them back from school. The children would get out of the car and be let into the house by Lily, while Elaine turned the car in the lane and drove off with a spray of gravel from beneath the tyres.

Later, when the children came up to the studio, they would sit and draw, or get on with some homework. Sometimes they spoke of their mother, and some of their remarks made Kate's heart ache for them.

On one occasion, Amy declared that she was going to draw the tallest tree in the world.

"That's a giant sequoia," Freddie said knowledgeably.

"Well, it's a giant sekwa then," Amy said. "It's going right up into the clouds, just like the Faraway Tree. Only this one goes up to heaven where Mummy is, not all sorts of other lands."

Freddie, glancing over at Kate, gave her a heart-breaking smile of amusement mingled with sadness. "I think it's more like Mummy's in another room, but the door's locked and we can't find the key," he said thoughtfully, causing Kate to shield her face behind the painting on her easel, till she was in command of her emotions again.

Freddie also kept her up-to-date on the progress on the games room. A pick-up truck, with *Hardy's Construction and Maintenance* painted on the side, was often parked outside Woodcote when Kate got to the studio in the mornings, and she could hear sounds of activity coming from the garden at the back.

Occasionally, Magda came up for a chat when she finished her cleaning stint at Woodcote, and Annie sometimes managed to come for some sittings for the triptych which Kate was still working on intermittently. Annie mentioned that she had seen Vince in the village the previous week.

"He was getting into that Reg's van. My heart nearly stopped, I tell you," she said, clasping her hands over her chest.

"Did he see you?"

"No, thank God! He had his back turned. I was afraid Becky would call out, but she didn't notice."

"Well, he wouldn't have breached the restraining order in full view of other people, hopefully."

"I know, but it gave me quite a shock!"

"I bet it did!" Kate did not mention that Tim had seen a man near Tuckers Lane recently, though the thought had been preying on her mind. Nor did she mention her walk on the common. She changed the subject.

"The triptych is going to be the centrepiece of my part of the exhibition. It would be good if you could come to the preview party on 2nd of June. It's a Saturday."

Annie's eyes lit up, but then she looked doubtful. "Ooh, I'd love to, but it's getting up there, what with the kids and catching trains and everything."

"Well, I was thinking… I'd love Magda to come. Maybe Mike could drive you all up there. I'll have a word with Magda when I see her next."

"That would be lovely! Are you sure? I mean, I'm not posh or anything. What would I wear? And the kids might get in the way."

"Oh, it's going to be quite informal. Just some drinks and people wandering around looking at the work."

"Well, if you think it would be alright, and Mike can take us, I'd love to go!"

"Good! It would be excellent to have the girl in the triptych there!"

"Oh, I'll be embarrassed! Please don't tell people it's me!"

Kate laughed. "Not if you don't want me to. But I'm sure you'll be fine once you get there."

After the mild spell, the weather turned cold again. The burgeoning spring growth, encouraged by the warm weather, slowed down, and night frosts threatened to scorch the newly opened buds. Kate couldn't help thinking it was a parallel of what was happening in her own life: it was as though her growing love for Tim had been blighted by the frost of Elaine's hostility.

Kate got a phone call from Grace, who said that Geoff had suggested that the four of them should come up and have a look at his gallery which was now up and running again after its expansion and refurbishment.

"You could stay at mine," Grace said. "Come for a few days. We could see some exhibitions, meet up with the old gang. Mummy said she'd love to have you. Please come."

"That sounds great! It *would* be good to come and have a look at the gallery, see how much space we each have."

"Good! Can you come next week?"

Kate thought for a moment. The children were due to break up for the Easter holidays at the end of the week, and she knew that they were

300

immediately going down to stay with Gwen for the week until after the Easter weekend. She imagined that Elaine would know about that and would want to do what she had done at half term, and try to spend the nights with Tim if she could arrange for Duncan to stay with his father. Kate felt that it would be better if she was out of the way, even though now that the clocks had gone forward, there was no need for Tim to walk her back in the evenings.

"Yes, that would suit me fine," she said in answer to Grace's question. "I could come up on Monday and stay till Thursday."

Grace gave a little whoop. "Cool! I'll tell the others. We could all meet at Geoff's on Tuesday."

When Grace rang off, Kate gazed unseeingly at the painting on the easel. She had now banished any possibility of seeing Tim alone, and though she felt it was for the best, she still felt a pang of regret. Anyway, Elaine was bound to be around in the evenings when Tim returned from London.

Tim had hoped to avoid telling Elaine that the children would be away. The thought of another week of Elaine's constant presence in the evenings filled him with impatience. He was hoping that he would be able to see something of Kate when the children were at his mother's, and was keen not to have to endure what he was beginning to think of as Elaine's suffocating ministrations. Any attraction that he had felt for Elaine in the beginning had begun to drain away the moment he had met Kate, and he rued the day he had let their relationship develop into a physical one, even though most of the overtures had come from Elaine. The aching loneliness that he had endured in the months after Claire had been killed had stretched into a year and beyond, making him vulnerable to Elaine's undeniable attractiveness and her obvious desire for him. One evening when Tim's children were away at Claire's parents' and Duncan with his father, she had homed in on him and his physical need temporarily blinded him to the fact that he was not in love Elaine and never would be.

After that night, she had assumed a possessive attitude regarding him, and took it for granted that they were in a relationship. He went to great lengths to shield the children from the situation, and he was troubled by feelings of being disloyal to Claire. He insisted that she did not tell Duncan about their relationship, and that she did not mention it to his own children. Elaine fulminated at this, but was too afraid of jeopardizing what she rightly sensed to be a rather fragile reciprocation on Tim's part.

Tim's hopes of keeping Elaine ignorant of the fact that he would be on his own during the first week of the holidays were dashed when Elaine suggested to Freddie that he could come over to play with Duncan, and Freddie had had to explain that they would be going to stay with their grandmother. Elaine immediately tried to arrange for Duncan to go to his father's for that week, but discovered that he and his wife Mel would be away on holiday. She also discovered that Mel was expecting a child. The two pieces of information caused Elaine to slam the phone down in frustration and impotent anger.

Selfish bastard, she thought furiously. He knows it's the Easter holiday. He could go away any time, but he has to go just when Duncan's on holiday. And now that simpering drip Mel is having his brat! She'll have even less time to have Duncan to stay when that's born!

She rang Tim.

"Tim darling, I'm *so* disappointed. Freddie told me that he and Amy will be away next week, and I was hoping we could have the nights together like at half term, but Giles says he and his woman will be away on holiday that week. The selfishness of the man, when he could have gone in term time! He says he'll have Duncan for the long Easter weekend. Will you be around?"

Tim breathed a silent 'thank you' to the heavens. He was off the hook! Elaine wouldn't be able to come round in the evenings if Duncan was there. His relief enabled him to put a note of regret into his voice. "Unfortunately not. I'm spending the Easter weekend at Lyme Regis with my mother and the kids. I'm taking the children down there this Saturday, then going back down on Good Friday morning and bringing them back on the Monday."

Elaine had been expecting that, but it only deepened her frustration. And looming large in her mind was the fact that Kate would be daubing

302

away at her paintings just yards away from Tim's house, and with the children away, who knew what might happen between them? Maybe she could at least arrange for Duncan to have a sleepover one night with one of his other friends. She mentioned the idea to Tim, then rang off and started making some phone calls.

*

Knowing that the children would not be coming for their art lesson that Saturday, Kate went to the studio and carried on with her own work. About mid-morning, she heard Binky barking, and there ensued a great deal of banging of car doors and calling out of voices as Tim and the children got ready to leave for Dorset. Before long, footsteps came running up the stairs and the children burst into the studio to say goodbye, closely followed by Tim.

"Why don't you take your sketchbooks with you?" Kate suggested. "Maybe you could do some drawing while you're down there."

"Oh yes, thanks for reminding me!" Freddie said, and he and Amy went to forage among their art materials for their books, while Tim came over to Kate, wondering how to broach a subject which had been on his mind ever since Elaine had said that she would not be able to come over every night.

"How's it going?" he asked, looking appraisingly at the painting Kate was working on – a monumental, lightning-blasted tree, whose stark branches reached jaggedly to the sky. The searing sunlight bleeding round the edges of the branches and the trunk, the thick impasto of the fissured bark, the deep blue shadows, made for an arresting image.

"That's stunning Kate! It's going to look great in your exhibition. When is it by the way?"

"Not till June. But I'm going up this week to stay with Grace, and we're all going to the gallery to see the space we have to work with. Then we can judge better how much more work we have to do to fill it."

Tim's heart sank. "Oh! How long are you going for.?"

"From Monday till Thursday. Thought I'd take in some exhibitions, see some friends while I'm there."

Tim's idea of asking Kate if she would go out to dinner with him one night that week went unspoken. Kate would be away, and no doubt one of the friends she spoke of would be Jake. He forced his voice to sound normal.

"Well, have a good time. It'll probably do you good to have a bit of a break from painting." He turned to the children. "Come on, you two. Time we got going, or Granny will wonder what's happened to us."

Kate watched from the window as they got into the car and drove off down the lane. She had got the impression that Tim was going to ask her something, then had abruptly changed his mind when she said she was going to London.

Tim arrived back from Gwen's in the pale sunshine of the following afternoon and, glancing towards Kate's cottage as he drove past, caught sight of her weeding the flower bed that bordered the path to the front door. He pulled up and, getting out, called a greeting as he walked to the gate.

Kate waved and stood up, brushing her knees. She pushed a strand of hair out of her eyes with the back of her hand and came towards the gate.

Tim surveyed the muddy spectacle she presented.

"Getting in touch with your inner Worzel Gummidge?" he grinned. "Not painting today?"

"No, I sometimes try to give myself a break on Sundays, and I thought I'd take advantage of the better weather after all the wind and rain we've had. I'm finding all sorts of little shoots and things among the weeds and fallen leaves. Hyacinths, daffodils, primroses." She glanced at the car. "Got the kids there alright?"

"Yes, fine. Freddie couldn't wait to get down to the beach in the afternoon, because they had a bit of a storm there on Friday and he was hoping there had been a cliff fall, which may have exposed some fossils."

"Did he find any?"

"One decent little ammonite, and various bits of mudstone with random markings on them. He's got loads of that sort of stuff already, but he can't bear not to collect it."

"I love it down there. We used to go quite a lot when we lived near Poole. Haven't been for ages."

Tim looked at her, and a delightful idea struck him. Without giving himself time to think, he said, "Well, why don't you come down with me next week when I go to pick up the kids? I'm spending the Easter weekend there. My mother would be delighted to see you. She's got a rambling house with plenty of room for you to stay. We'll be coming back on Bank Holiday Monday. You can spare two or three days from your painting, surely?"

Kate's eyes lit up. The thought of a couple of days in a part of the world she loved, in the company of people she loved, sounded wonderful. But then the thought of Elaine flashed into her mind and her face clouded.

"I'd love to…but..."

"But what?"

"I need to work. The exhibition's not that far off now," she replied, rather lamely.

"Look, a long weekend won't make much difference. Do you good to get away for a while."

Kate weakened. Apart from being with Tim, the prospect of seeing Gwen again and being by the sea with the children was very appealing. Also, she would get away for a while from the constant niggling worry of whether Vince would try to attack her again. She put aside her reservations about Elaine and grinned at Tim.

"Well, I must admit it sounds a lovely idea. But I don't want to impose on Gwen."

"You won't be imposing. I'll ring my mother. She'll be so pleased. I'll pick you up on Friday morning. I think we'd better leave quite early, to beat the Bank Holiday traffic - about eight?"

"That's great, I'll be ready."

Tim turned to go, saying casually over his shoulder: "Have a good time this week."

"Thanks. See you Friday."

305

Tim got back in the car and drove on down the lane, his heart considerably lighter than it had been since Kate had informed him that she was going to be in London the next week. The thought of spending the weekend with Kate even alleviated his exasperation at Elaine's determination that she should spend at least one night with him while the children were away.

*

The next morning, Kate took a bus to the station and caught the train to London, arriving at Grace's house in Richmond in the early afternoon. On the Tuesday, she and Grace met Mimi and Bea at Geoff's gallery, which was now up and running again, and although there was another exhibition currently on in the rooms, they were able to decide where each of them would put their own work. There were three large main rooms and Mimi, standing in the centre of the largest room, her hands on her narrow hips, asked if her soft sculptures could be distributed in the central space, since they were free-standing. Geoff agreed.

"Yes, that would free up space on the walls for Kate's paintings. Grace's tapestries could be in room 2 as it is more rectangular. Two of the pieces are quite long. And most of Bea's light sculptures would have to be against the walls."

Bea, wandering into one of the inner rooms, stuck her head back round the doorway.

"Can I have this room? I'll need it to be darkened, so the lack of windows will be good."

"Yes, that's the one I was thinking of for you," Geoff replied. "There are plenty of power points and we can curtain off the entrance."

It was decided that Kate and Mimi would share the biggest room, which was virtually square, with Mimi using the central floor space for her soft sculptures, and Kate's paintings on the walls. Grace's tapestries, the two largest of which were twelve-foot-long, would have the more rectangular room. Kate, standing in the centre of her and Mimi's room, mentally placed her paintings on the walls. She decided to put the triptych at the far end, so that it would be the first thing people would see as they came in.

Geoff, watching the four of them chattering about the exhibition, sensed the excitement which was starting to take hold of them, and felt pleased that he was in a position to help these young women get their work seen. He was a businessman first and foremost, however, and even though he was Grace's uncle, he would not be staging this exhibition if he did not think that all four of them had considerable talent and originality. He knew many dealers and gallerists who he would be asking to the preview, and had high hopes that many works would be sold. He was also pleased that their work was so different from one another's. It would make for a very interesting exhibition. He broke into their chatter.

"Well, if you're done here, come on - I'll buy you lunch."

Chapter XV

Good Friday dawned chilly but bright, and when Tim knocked on her door just before eight, Kate's heart leapt with anticipation of the weekend that stretched ahead of her. Tim, his own spirits soaring at the thought of being in Kate's company for the long weekend, smiled into her eyes as she opened the door to him. Taking her holdall from her, he stowed it in the boot of the car.

He had spent a mostly quiet week, coming home from work and cooking himself beans on toast or eggs for supper. But Elaine, having contrived to have Duncan go for a sleepover at a friend's house on the Wednesday had phoned him to say that she would come over and cook him supper. Knowing that he had the weekend to look forward to, Tim had felt a little sorry for Elaine, and did not try to put her off.

That evening, Elaine had not failed to notice that Tim had been more attentive to her than he had been of late. She dared to hope that her confrontation with Kate had had the desired effect, and that Kate had distanced herself from Tim. If she had known, as she sat sipping coffee in her elegant kitchen on Good Friday morning, that at that moment, Tim was bowling along the M3 with Kate at his side, every iota of her fragile peace of mind would have drained away in an instant.

The journey down with Tim was spent in easy conversation interspersed with companionable silence. Kate felt a deep sense of peace and rightness in Tim's company, as the countryside slipped past, with the new leaves on the hawthorn bushes and birches beside the road glowing an unearthly green in the sunlight and the gorse bushes almost incandescent with the intense yellow of their blossoms.

Dipping down into the pretty town of Lyme Regis, they glimpsed The Cobb stretching into the sea, with the waves, glittering in the sunlight, breaking up against it. Tim drove on through the town and up the hill on

308

the other side, and soon turned into the drive of a large Edwardian house with carved white gables, covered with Virginia creeper. No sooner had Tim drawn to a halt in front of the garage, when the front door opened and Freddie and Amy dashed out of the house, whooping and shouting, followed by Binky, who lolloped about among them in an ecstasy of joy. Amy flung herself at her father then turned to wrap her arms round Kate's waist, while Freddie, having hugged his father, shook Kate's hand in his quaintly formal way, grinning broadly. Gwen, her hair tied back in a messy ponytail, her glasses perched on top of her head, appeared at the door and hurried over to greet them.

"Kate, my dear! How splendid that you could come down," she said, kissing Kate on the cheek. "We've all been very excited, and have been planning all sorts of alarums and excursions."

"And expotitions!" Amy interjected.

"And picnics!" Freddie added. "And fossil hunts!"

Kate grinned. "Excellent! I can't wait!" She opened the rear door of the car and lifted out a bowl of narcissi bulbs just coming into bloom from the back seat, which she handed to Gwen. "Thank you for having me!"

"Oh, how lovely." Gwen sniffed them. "They smell gorgeous. Thank you."

Amy grabbed Kate's arm and began pulling her towards the house. "Come on Kate, I'll show you where your bedroom is. I put some flowers in a vase on the dressing table."

Kate allowed herself to be dragged into the house, closely followed by Gwen and Freddie, while Tim got the bags out of the car.

They went through an inner porch cluttered with wellington boots, coats, umbrellas and walking sticks and into a spacious hall. At the far end, the broad staircase had polished brass stair-rods on the slightly threadbare carpet, and the wooden tops of the newel posts on the banisters were carved into the shapes of large acorns. At the top, Amy rushed to open one of the bedroom doors, and led Kate into a big airy room with oriental rugs scattered about on the polished floor. A little vase of primroses stood on the dressing table. The back of the house faced the sea to the south, and though Kate's room was on the west side, her window jutted out in a square bay, and she could see the sea through the trees. She turned to Gwen, her face glowing.

"What a lovely room! In fact, what a lovely house! And such a beautiful position, with a view of the sea."

"Yes, it's a nice spot. The town gets rather crowded in the summer, but it's very peaceful off season. We've been here forever. It's too big for me really, but after Gerry died, I couldn't face moving."

"You wouldn't be allowed to move!" Tim said, coming into the room with Kate's holdall. "The kids would kick up an enormous fuss. They love it here. In fact, it was here that Freddie first got interested in fossils."

"That's because it's the Jurassic Coast," Freddie said. "I wish I could find an ichthyosaur like Mary Anning did in 1811. That would be so cool."

"Well, you might not have found an ichthyosaur, but you've found lots of other stuff," Gwen said. "Now, come on kids, leave Kate to get sorted out." She turned to Kate. "Come on down when you're ready and we'll have lunch. The bathroom is just next door to you."

Later, sitting and having lunch at the big table in the kitchen overlooking the back garden, Kate again had the feeling she had experienced at Christmas, of being incorporated into the heart of the family. Gwen seemed genuinely delighted to have her there, and the children, eager to show her all their favourite haunts, prattled excitedly about the things they intended to do over the weekend. Often she would catch Tim's gaze across the table, and the smile in his eyes was reciprocated in her own.

Gwen, while joining enthusiastically in the conversation, did not miss these exchanges, and a little seed of hope which had been sown on Christmas Day, began to put out green shoots, like the leaves bursting out on the lilacs outside the window.

In the afternoon, they tramped down the hill into the town and after strolling along The Cobb into the brisk north-westerly wind, Tim keeping a tight hold on Binky's lead, they walked along Monmouth beach, stopping frequently to investigate any interesting-looking stones. Amy's sharp eyes spotted a broken piece of ammonite, which she pounced on with glee, but the other fossils they saw were imbedded in large rocks. Coming back to the town, they had tea in a café then poked around in a fossil shop on the main street. They got back to the house wind-blown and dishevelled, the children's cheeks glowing pink from the fresh air. They all took it in turns to have baths and showers in the two bathrooms and then, with the children in their pyjamas and dressing gowns, they sat round the fire, which Tim had lit since it was a chilly evening, in the comfortable sitting room. Tim poured Gwen, Kate and himself gin and tonics and they sat chatting while the children watched television.

Kate picked up a framed photograph on the occasional table beside her chair.

"This must be your father, Tim," she said, "You look so much like him!"

Tim nodded. "Yes, that's Dad. Taken not long before he died, about five years ago, wasn't it Mother?"

"Yes, on his sixtieth birthday." Gwen made a face. "Kicked up such a fuss. Gerry hated having his picture taken."

Kate looked at the picture, noticing the hint of boyish mischief in his eyes. "He looks like fun."

"He was, always planning some nonsense or other," Tim said, adding with a raised eyebrow at his mother, "Mind you, my mother's not much better. They would ask people to dinner, then greet them in their dressing gowns, pretending they had forgotten, and embarrassing the hell out of them. Then they would fling off their dressing gowns, revealing their evening clothes and ply them with food and drink!"

Kate laughed delightedly. "A double act! Gwen and Gerry! A bit like the ice cream!"

"Or Tom and Jerry," Tim said. "Except that they never fought, as far as I know, unlike the cartoon." He looked at his mother. "We miss him," he said simply.

Kate caught a suspicion of tears in Gwen's eyes.

"Yes, we do," she said. "But I still feel he's here, keeping an eye on me. I talk to him all the time, like some batty old biddy. Well, I suppose I *am* a batty old biddy." She got up briskly. "Now, I'll just go and sort out some supper."

Kate got up too. "I'll come and help."

"Thank you - there's not much to do really. It's just homemade soup and garlic bread, and apple crumble. It's all ready, except for bunging the garlic bread in the oven."

After supper, during which they discussed plans for the following day, they played Monopoly until Gwen noticed that Amy was getting sleepy and bustled her off to bed. After Freddie had gone up a little later, Gwen, sipping her wine, asked Kate about her exhibition. As Kate described the work of her friends, and how the spaces were being allocated, Gwen's interest was evident.

"Oh, I must come and see it!" she exclaimed. She turned to Tim. "Are you going?"

"Oh yes, definitely! The kids will want to go too."

"Well, why not come to the preview party?" Kate said. "My father's coming down from Yorkshire with his wife. It should be fun."

It was arranged that Gwen would come up for the weekend of the preview. Then, stifling a yawn, Gwen finished her glass of wine and, declaring herself to be tired from all the fresh air, went up to bed. Kate and Tim were left by the fire, Kate curled up on the squashy sofa and Tim in one of the big armchairs. A silence fell between them, with both being content just to be in each other's company, then Kate, taking a sip of her wine, broke the silence.

"It must be lonely for your mother, without your dad."

"Yes, it was too cruel. They had been planning to do a lot of travelling when he retired and then out of the blue came the massive stroke and that was that. She doesn't wear her heart on her sleeve, but I know she still misses him desperately."

"Awful for you too, and then Claire..." her voice tailed off. Tim had his face turned away as he gazed into the fire. He turned to look at her.

"Yes, it was a hard few years. I do feel we are starting to come out

312

the other side, but there are still times when it knocks you for six. If it wasn't for the kids ... it was knowing we had to be there for them that kept Mother and me going, and Claire's parents too of course."

"I don't know how you've coped. I know Gwen and Claire's parents have done a huge amount, but wouldn't it have helped to have a live-in nanny?"

"Well, as you know we tried au pairs, who didn't work out. And then I heard that Lily Babbidge was prepared to step in as a sort of nanny-cum-housekeeper. I was so relieved, because the children knew her and were fond of her. She had done a lot of babysitting for us in the past, especially when Claire was away playing and I was at work. I didn't want to introduce too many new people into the children's lives when everything was so raw. Then Elaine came on the scene and insisted on doing the school run. It seemed the answer at the time." He stopped and looked back into the fire, the unspoken implication that it no longer seemed such a good idea hanging in the air.

Kate felt a small surge of hope that perhaps Tim was not as emotionally involved with Elaine as she had feared, then immediately thought again of Elaine's thinly veiled desperation when she had confronted her in the studio. What would it do to Elaine if Tim rejected her? Leaving Elaine's role aside, she said, "Mrs B. would probably feel very hurt if you got a full-time nanny, wouldn't she?"

"Well, I worry that she might. But I do sometimes think it's a bit too much for her. She's got Bill to worry about as well, even though he seems hale and hearty, and is a dab hand in the kitchen. He will often cook their own supper if Lily has been busy with the kids at our house."

"He's a dab hand at making up my canvases too," Kate said. "I feel awful, because he won't take any payment for the work. He says he enjoys doing it."

"I'm sure he does. Have you asked him and Lily to the preview?"

"Yes, and she said they'd love to, though they don't have the faintest idea how to get to the gallery."

"Well, they could come with us. There'll be space in the Discovery."

313

"That would be great! Magda's coming too, with Mike and Annie and the children."

"Quite a posse of groupies!" Tim laughed, adding: "Are there going to be any dealers or whatever you call them, who might be interested in buying?"

"Geoff, the gallery owner, says he's inviting everyone he knows who is in that line – gallerists, dealers, collectors of contemporary art."

"Well, I'm looking forward to seeing the show. Let's hope you all sell lots of stuff."

Later, when they too went up to bed, Tim paused with Kate at her bedroom door before going on to his own room.

"Good night, Kate. Nice to have you here," he said softly.

"Nice to be here. I've had a lovely day!"

He bent to kiss her cheek, his hand involuntarily going up to touch her hair. That touch, even more than the peck on the cheek, made Kate's heart lurch, and she turned away quickly before she lost control and did what she longed to do, which was to kiss him full on the mouth.

The same longing had swept over Tim, and he too turned away with a last murmured, "Night, Kate," and made his way to his own room, shutting the door behind him.

Kate, closing her own door, walked to the window and gazed out into the blackness of the night. The wind had got up and was buffeting the window, throwing rattles of rain against the panes. She imagined the sea flinging itself against the stones of The Cobb and surging up the beach, all the time remembering the touch of Tim's hand in her hair.

The storm blew itself out in the night and the day dawned fresh and breezy, with sun glittering on the sea in the distance. Everyone was up early, getting ready for their day out. They planned to show Kate the town museum and then drive to Charmouth beach to do some serious fossil hunting. Freddie had been delighted when he had heard the storm brewing the previous night and was excited about seeing if it had exposed any new fossils.

Kate and Gwen made a stack of ham sandwiches and a flask of tea.

"Better wrap up warm everyone," Gwen said, stuffing a packet of chocolate digestive biscuits into a rucksack. "There's a chilly wind blowing."

Since it was still early, they managed to find a place to park down by the Cobb, and leaving Binky in the car to snooze with the windows open a little, they walked along to the fossil museum. Freddie, who knew the place like the back of his hand, was eager to show Kate all his favourite exhibits, and found her gratifyingly fascinated by everything.

"Look at this huge ammonite, Kate," he said with a proprietorial air. "Coroniceras Sinemurian. It's two hundred and six million years old! And look at this ichthyosaur skeleton. It's supposed to have a baby in its tummy, but I can never quite make out which bit is the baby."

Kate agreed that it was difficult to see the baby, but together they decided which they thought were the baby's bones.

Before going back to the car, they stopped to buy fat, freshly baked Chelsea buns and then headed out of town towards Charmouth. They parked in the car park, which was rapidly filling up with Easter visitors, and everyone was given a rucksack to carry, even Amy, who carried the Chelsea buns in a bright pink rucksack with a picture of a cat on it.

As they set off along the beach, Tim called out to Freddie who had already gone on ahead. "Freddie! Remember to keep away from the cliffs. There may be cliff falls."

Freddie turned and waited for them to catch up. "I know Dad, but that's where fossils may have just fallen out!"

"No matter how good the fossil, it's not worth getting clonked on the head by a chunk of rock!"

Tim went with Freddie, keeping him at a safe distance from the cliff face, while Gwen, Amy and Kate walked along near the waterline. The roaring of the sea, still turbulent after the stormy night, the sun glinting on the blinding white foam and the wet stones, the crying of gulls and the gusting of the wind made it seem as if all the world was full of sound and light and motion. Kate took photo after photo, especially of the sunlight on the breaking waves.

They stopped for their picnic lunch in the shelter of a large rock.

Everyone was ravenously hungry and made short work of the food. Later, at the furthest limit of their walk, they stopped for tea and biscuits, then they headed back into the slanting rays of the late afternoon sun. Amy was exhausted by the time they got back to the car and promptly fell asleep as they started for home. Freddie was delighted with his one find – a near-perfect belemnite.

Tim had booked a table for dinner at a restaurant in Lyme, and after sprucing themselves up and with Amy refreshed after her nap, they walked back down the hill to a restaurant perched up on the hillside overlooking the bay. Sitting at a table by the window, they watched the moon rise over the sea, causing a silver pathway to stretch out to the horizon.

The next morning was Easter Day and Gwen had announced that she was going to church and whoever wanted to come was welcome. In the end they all went, and then Tim drove them into Devon where they had lunch in a little pub in the middle of Dartmoor. Afterwards, Tim stopped the car near one of the Tors, and they all scrambled to the top, from where they could see the hills stretching away on all sides, fading into the far distance.

By the time Sunday night came, Kate felt a pang of sadness that the weekend was coming to an end. Much as she loved her little cottage, and in many ways was keen to get back to her painting, the feeling of being safe and enfolded by Tim's family was very comforting. She would have to go back to the possibility of Vince lurking near her house, of not feeling safe on her own, inside the house or out. But above all, the knowledge that Tim was close, that she was where he was, was like balm to her spirit.

As they went up to bed on Sunday night, Tim gave her his customary peck on the cheek - and then a quick, soft kiss on the lips. He turned away quickly and headed for his room, leaving Kate's heart hammering in her chest.

Gwen was sad to see them go. "It'll be very quiet around here now," she said, and turning to Kate, added, "You must come again. It's been lovely having you."

Kate kissed her. "It's been lovely being here. Thank you so much.

I'll see you at the exhibition."

"Yes, I've just realised it must be the half term weekend, so I'll be up to look after the children anyway. It works out very well."

She stood waving as Tim turned the car and drove off, with Kate and the children waving back through the car windows.

*

It was inevitable that Elaine would discover that Kate had spent the weekend with Tim and the children at Gwen's house. Tim had casually said to the children that it would probably be better if they didn't mention it to Elaine or Duncan, in case they were upset that they had never been asked.

"Well, we don't want her down there!" Freddie said with conviction. "I wouldn't mind Duncan, but not *her.*"

"No need to be rude, Fred," Tim said reprovingly, though he felt exactly the same way. "Anyway, as I say, best not to mention it."

However, when the holidays were over, during which Claire's parents had come to look after the children, and the school run started again, Amy got into Elaine's car one morning clutching a seascape she had done with Kate and was taking to show her teacher. She showed it to Duncan who was sitting in the front seat.

"Look Duncan, I painted the fossil beach. Look here's a fossil lying on the stones."

Duncan, who was a kind-hearted boy, expressed admiration for the painting, adding, "Did you find any fossils?"

"Well, Freddie found one, and I found a bit of one. Kate didn't find any, nor did Daddy or Gran, but we found lots stuck in big rocks." Amy was oblivious to the fact that she had let the cat out of the bag, but Freddie froze.

Elaine, having turned the car round in the lane, heard the exchange and her head snapped round to stare at Amy.

"Kate? You mean the Kate that lives here?" She pointed to Kate's cottage as they drove past.

317

Amy still did not realise her mistake and prattled on. "Yes. She found some stones with holes in them though. She said they're called Hag Stones. They keep witches away." Freddie dug her in the ribs.

"Ow! What did you poke me for?" she said loudly, then saw Freddie's finger come up to his lips and realisation dawned on her. Her eyes widened and she bit her lip, subsiding into her seat.

But the damage was done. Elaine's hands tightened on the wheel.

"You mean Kate went down to your grandmother's? How long for?"

Amy had suddenly become mute, so Freddie had to answer.

"Oh, just for the weekend," he said casually. He thought quickly, then added, "Gran invited her because she thought she would like to paint the scenery."

"Did your father take her down?" Elaine's voice was tight and strained.

"Um, yes."

Elaine was silent. She wasn't going to demean herself by pumping Freddie for more information. Driving much too fast, she continued on to the school, her knuckles white on the steering wheel. Back at home after dropping the children off, she slammed the front door and going through to the kitchen, stood staring unseeingly out of the window at the rain-drenched garden, her mind a turmoil of raging thoughts.

So the little snake had disregarded the conversation Elaine had had with her. She had lied when she said she was involved with Jake and when she had implied that she had no interest in Tim. She had lied when she said she had not set her sights on Tim. Far from leaving him alone, she had taken the first opportunity to go and spend the Easter weekend at his mother's house, continuing to worm her way into the family, no doubt sucking up to Gwen, who had never asked Elaine to spend the weekend down there, after all she had done for Tim and the children. Kate had known them five minutes, and already she was spending weekends with them, teaching the children, using Tim's garage room, spending Christmas Day with them. When had *she* been asked to spend Christmas Day with them? She thought of the expensive scarf she had given Gwen for

318

Christmas. You'd have thought the old trout would have appreciated that, but it didn't seem much like it.

Her first instinct was to ring Tim and tell him to stuff the school run, that he could make other arrangements, and that he and his precious children could go to hell. She went out to the hall, but with her hand on the phone, she stopped. Her reflection stared back at her from the mirror above the telephone table. It shocked her. Her expression was ugly, her face distorted with rage. She let go of the phone and put both hands up to her face, breathing deeply and forcing herself to relax her expression. When she looked at herself again she was reassured. She was attractive, she knew it, and she knew how to make the best of herself. She had seen Tim look at her appreciatively. And what good would it do her to alienate him? He might lose out if she stopped doing the school run, but think of what she would lose. No, she wouldn't confront Tim about Kate spending the weekend in Lyme. She would pretend that it was of no consequence. She wouldn't give it importance by making a scene about it. She had too much to lose. It was not only that she loved him. She also wanted to marry him to feel financially secure. To her mind, Giles did not give her enough to live on, and she knew she was living beyond her means. She had planned it all. She and Tim would marry, and the kids could all go to boarding school when they were a bit older. Then in the holidays, they would often go and stay with the grandparents, so it would not be too onerous to be saddled with two more children, especially if they could keep on Mrs B. as a housekeeper.

But now, all this was in jeopardy, because Kate had come on the scene. A fresh wave of resentment washed over Elaine. Tim had changed. He seemed cold towards her, and even seemed to avoid her. She had not missed the exchange between Freddie and Amy in the back seat of the car. It had seemed as though they had been told not to mention that Kate had gone down to Lyme. That could only have come from Tim. He had wanted to keep it a secret. That must mean that he was falling for Kate. A bitter stab of jealousy pierced her solar plexus like an ice-cold knife. She was not a fool. She knew Kate was beautiful and considerably younger than herself. Why did she have to be so beautiful? Why couldn't it have

319

been a plain, middle-aged woman who had come to live in that cottage?

Elaine was still staring at herself in the mirror.

"If something happened to her face..." she said softly to her reflection.

*

"Elaine found out that Kate went to Gran's," Freddie said, as they went back into the house after Tim had picked them up from Kate in the studio that evening.

Tim's heart sank. "Oh? How?" he said, trying to keep his tone casual.

"Amy accidentally said she was there at the weekend."

Amy's lip trembled and tears brimmed over. "I didn't mean to!" she said miserably. "Sorry Daddy."

Tim put his arms round her. "It doesn't matter, sweetheart. Don't worry about it. Now tell me what you've been up to today at school."

Later, when Amy was in bed, Tim asked Freddie if Elaine had said anything when she had found out.

Freddie told him, adding, "She seemed rather cross!"

"Oh, she probably would like to go down there herself, that's why."

"But you won't ask her, will you Dad?" Freddie asked anxiously.

"No, Fred, I won't," Tim said with conviction.

*

In the weeks that followed, the reluctant spring finally gained the upper hand and Kate watched her little garden burgeon fully into life. Hyacinths, daffodils and polyanthus burst into bloom in the borders, and bluebells and primroses dotted the rough grass at the end of the back garden. Overhead, the bronzy-green of the new leaves on the poplars turned properly green and once again the sound of the wind playing among them filled the air.

As the date of the exhibition drew closer, Kate turned her mind to

320

how she was going to transport her paintings up to Geoff's gallery. Talking to Paul in one of their catch-up telephone calls, she was relieved when he immediately offered to come down and take her stuff up in his van.

"Paul, you're a saint! I thought I would have to hire a van and drive up myself."

"No problem, Kate. When will you want to bring the work up?"

"The Monday before the preview, which is on 2nd June. Geoff says the premises will be emptied of the previous exhibition the week before, then there will have to be some cleaning and re-adjustment of partitions and stuff like that. We can start setting up on the Monday. That only gives us five days to get it all ready, but we should be okay."

"Well, I'm fairly clear early on that week I think. I'll come down on the Monday to transport you and your paintings. I'm off to Bali on a shoot on the Saturday, which means I won't be able to come to the preview, unfortunately, but I should be able to help you set up."

"What would I do without you, Paul? Thank you! But only if you're not too busy getting ready for your trip."

"It should be fine. I'll be in touch nearer the time. Take care, my lovely."

"Bye Paul, and thanks again!"

Kate rang off and, not for the first time, thought how lucky she was to have a friend like Paul.

During the next few weeks, Kate spent long hours in the studio, arriving early and leaving as late as she dared, before the light failed altogether. Tim quietly kept an eye out to see when the light went off in the studio, and, if she had left it a bit late before going home, he would appear in the lane, leaving Binky on guard at the house if the children were in bed, for the few minutes it would take to walk Kate back. Occasionally, he would miss her coming out of the studio, and would walk quickly down to make sure she had got home safely.

One evening, seeing the light in the studio was still on until it was nearly dark outside, Tim kept a lookout and when Kate finally emerged, he

321

went out and insisted on walking her back. As they rounded the bend in the lane, Jake's blue van was just drawing up outside Kate's cottage. The headlights picked them out then died as Jake turned them off and switched off the engine. Tim's heart sank and he said abruptly, "I see your friend's here. You'll be fine now. I better get back to the kids. Night, Kate." And he was gone.

Jake waited by the car as Kate, hiding her annoyance, came up to him. He kissed her on the lips and then held her at arm's length, his hands on her shoulders.

"You're looking good, kid. No more attacks by psychos in the woods?" His tone was light-hearted, but his eyes were unsmiling as he searched her face.

"No, haven't seen hide nor hair of the man, thank goodness."

Jake jerked his head in the direction Tim had gone. "I see you've got a bodyguard." He looked quizzically at her. "Or maybe he's something more?"

Kate gave a short laugh. "He's a friend. Just looking out for me." She pulled away from him and started walking down the path, saying over her shoulder. "You'd better come on in. What brings you down here?"

"You of course! I bumped into your partners in crime at the pub, and they said your exhibition was coming up a week on Saturday. They asked me to the preview. I thought you might like some help taking your paintings up to the gallery."

Kate turned at the door and looked at him. It made a change for him to be thinking of how he could help her. It had always been the other way round when she had been with him.

"Actually, Paul's offered to come down and transport them next week, but it's very sweet of you to offer."

Jake felt annoyed with himself for not having offered sooner.

"You could have rung me and asked me to do it." He sounded quite put out, and Kate had to smile.

"I didn't like to bother anyone. I was going to hire a van."

Jake rolled his eyes. "Typical! You were going to do it all on your

322

own, when you've got people who are willing to help you." He said it in an exasperated tone, but he knew that her independent spirit was one of the things which endeared her to him.

Kate shut the front door and led the way into the room. "I'd have managed, but thanks for the offer anyway." She put a hand on his arm. "I'm glad you're coming to the preview party," she said, and she meant it. A part of her still needed his opinion and a certain amount of involvement in her life, albeit in a different way.

Jake's arms came around her and he drew her to him. Burying his face in her hair, he smelled her familiar scent of roses tinged with turpentine, which brought back memories of the time they had been together. Seeing her friends in the pub the previous day had stirred up those memories, and he had had a sudden need to see Kate again. Now, as he held her, feeling her fragility through the coat she still had on, his need for her intensified. His hands slid up and entangled in her hair. Tipping her face up towards him, he brought his mouth down onto hers, half drowning in the taste of her.

For several long moments, Kate responded to his kiss, his very maleness and strength, momentarily answering his need with the loneliness deep inside herself. But she knew, even as she kissed him, that he would never make her feel the way she knew she would feel if it had been Tim kissing her. Gently she drew away, leaving Jake thirsting for more.

Outside, the poplar leaves stirred in the breeze. A muffled oath escaped from the figure standing in the field, as Kate drew the curtains across the window.

*

Later that week Kate phoned Annie to arrange a last sitting for the triptych. When they broke for a coffee, Annie told Kate that she had seen the white van belonging to Vince's rat-faced friend driving through the village on a couple of occasions but had seen nothing of Vince.

"I was contacted again by the Victim Support people at the police station," Kate said. "They told me two indictments were being prepared by the Crown Prosecution Service of two counts of assault – the beating he gave you and the attack on me. But when the trials will come up I don't know."

Annie grimaced. "Yes, they told me that as well. I just wish they would put him away quickly, so that we can all sleep easy in our beds!"

"There's no guarantee that he'd get a custodial sentence even if he is convicted," Kate said grimly," which would leave us no better off than we were before."

"Honestly, I don't know how I put up with him all that time," Annie said, shaking her head in exasperation with herself.

"You were trapped, Annie. You felt you had nowhere to go."

"That's true. Once, when I was a child, we were taken to the zoo on an outing, and I saw this tiger. It was pacing up and down, up and down in a small cage. That's how I felt when I was with Vince."

"Well, you're free of him now, hopefully."

"Yes, but I still have to look over my shoulder in case he suddenly turns up. Even if he is banged up, he'll be out one day, and may come after me… and you too." Annie's eyes briefly took on their old haunted look, before she gave herself a little shake, and smiled. "Still, it's so much better now without him coming back drunk and lamming me. And the kids are so much happier. He was a rotten father to them. Darren's much less clingy now. Before, he never wanted to let me out of his sight, even when I left him with Magda. And Becky's a different little girl, laughing and singing all the time." Annie's face, which so closely reflected her emotions, took on an expression of calm and hope and a hint of joy, which touched Kate profoundly. She looked at the canvas she was working on – the third in the triptych, where Annie's face was emerging from the transparent barrier, and knew what she had to do to capture this expression in the painting. By the end of the sitting, she knew she had nailed it, and that the triptych was now finished. She lined the three paintings up against the wall, and Annie stood looking at them, her lips slightly parted, her hands clamped together. Then she turned to Kate.

"I've never seen them all together like that. Imagine! I'm in a work

324

of art! And it's so amazing – the expression on the face, and the figure coming through like that. You've shown my life, Kate. You've shown my life!" Her eyes brimmed, and she blinked the tears away, her lovely smile breaking through like a sunrise. "Thank you for making me into a work of art!"

Kate hugged her. "It's I who have to thank you! I'm putting the triptych in the prime position. You'll be the star of the show!"

Annie looked terrified. "Oh my God! I hope no one realises it's me when I come to the opening party! And, Kate, I don't know what to wear! I haven't got anything. I just live in jeans all the time. I can't come!"

Kate was about to tell her that jeans would be fine to wear, when they heard Magda's voice at the bottom of the studio stairs. Appearing at the studio door, she began, "I knew Annie was coming over this morning, so I thought I'd come up after cleaning at Tim's..." but she broke off as her eyes were drawn to the three sections of the triptych lined up at the far end of the room.

"Kate! That's stunning. Makes you stop in your tracks! Is it finished now?"

"Yes, I think it is, at last!"

Annie gave a little wail. "It's so brilliant, but what will people think if they recognise me, and I'm in my jeans, looking grotty. I haven't anything to wear to the opening!"

"It's not a posh preview. We want it to be friendly and informal," Kate said. "I'm wearing a dress I bought for last Christmas, but I'm sure there'll be other people in jeans."

Magda looked thoughtful. "Leave it with me," she said. "I think I have an idea."

Annie looked mystified, but Magda would say no more.

After she had left the studio, she walked along to the Babbidges' cottage to have a word with Lily.

*

When Tim arrived home that evening, to his surprise Lily Babbidge

325

was still there and the children were in the house with her instead of up in the studio with Kate.

"Hello Mrs B. You're here late," he said, giving a hug to Amy who had run downstairs to greet him.

"Hello Tim. Yes, I just wanted to have a little word." Lily, her hands clasped in front of her, composed herself, looking a little awkward.

"Tim, you know you were talking about what to do with Claire's clothes, and we were thinking of charity shops and things?"

Tim nodded. "Yes, I know. I should do something about it. Have you got any ideas?"

"Well Tim, I wouldn't ask this if you hadn't already talked about giving Claire's dresses away, but Magda came and saw me yesterday, and apparently Annie - you know, the ex-partner of that awful Vince - is worried about not having anything to wear for Kate's preview evening. We were wondering if there was a dress that Annie could borrow." Lily stopped, then added hastily. "She doesn't know anything about this. It was Magda's idea, because I had talked to her about you wondering what you should do with the clothes…"

Tim looked at her anxious face and held out his hand to stop her. "Mrs B, of course she can borrow a dress. She could have it, for that matter. Tell her to come and try some on and choose one to wear – and any other clothes she would like. As long as she doesn't think we regard her as a charity case. Is she the same sort of size as Claire?"

"I think she's not as tall as Claire, but Annie is about the same dress size I should think, and she should be able to fit into something."

"Well, do tell her to come and choose something, Mrs B. I think Claire, if she knew, would be delighted."

When Lily had gone, Amy, who had heard the whole exchange from where she was sitting on the bottom step of the stairs, said to her father: "I don't want you to give away *all* of Mummy's dresses, Daddy. I like to go and smell them. They still smell of Mummy. That scent she used to wear."

Tim sat down on the step next to her and put his arm around her shoulders. "We won't give them away yet, if you're not happy with it, sweetheart. But you don't mind if Annie has one, do you?"

"No, I don't mind, Daddy. She's the lady in Kate's pictures. Kate told me her name was Annie."

Later, Amy slipped into her parents' bedroom where Claire's wardrobe was, with all her dresses hanging where she had left them more than two years ago, when her life had been so tragically cut short. Amy opened the wardrobe door and stepping forward, stroked the dresses, feeling the different textures of silk, cotton, jersey. Then she buried her face in the fabrics, inhaling the faint perfume that still lingered there. Though it was becoming difficult to recall her mother's face in her mind's eye without looking at a photograph, the beloved smell of her still awoke strong memories and tugged at her heart. After a while, the little girl closed the wardrobe door and walked out of the room. Behind her the shadow of a bird flying past outside flickered across the shaft of evening sunlight falling on the wardrobe door.

Having been given the go ahead by Tim, Lily Babbidge contacted Magda, who in turn told Annie that she was welcome to try on Claire's dresses. Annie was at once plunged into a state of anxiety.

"Oh, Mags, I couldn't! I just couldn't! It wouldn't be right! The poor lady gets killed, and I go poking through her clothes like a... a... vulture or something! What would she think?"

Magda folded her arms across her chest and looked at her calmly. "I think, God rest her soul, she is beyond worrying about her clothes. Anyway, she was a lovely person. She would be delighted to know a dress of hers was being put to good use. Tim has been saying to Lily that he ought to do something about Claire's clothes. At least come and have a look."

After a great deal of persuasion, Annie agreed to go to Woodcote House. She insisted, however, that it would be at the weekend when Tim was there.

"I'm not going to go rummaging among his wife's things unless he's in the house. I would feel like a thief!" she said stubbornly.

327

Tim smiled when this was relayed to him via Lily. Asking for Annie's telephone number, he phoned her himself and insisted that it was absolutely fine with him if she came any time. Annie wavered.

"Well, if you're sure you don't mind. I suppose it *would* be easier if the kids were at school."

"There you are then. Why don't you come on a day when Magda comes here to clean, then she can help you choose. Maybe Mrs B. and Kate can also join the selection committee!"

When Magda heard an account of this conversation, she immediately contacted Lily and Kate, and the following week, they all gathered in the bedroom, feeling, in spite of Tim's reassurances, rather intrusive at being there. The selection was soon made however – a simple dress in cornflower blue with a softly flaring hemline. It was a little long, but Magda said she could easily take it up. Otherwise it fitted perfectly.

Annie refused to take it straight away and insisted that Lily should show it to Tim and ask if it would be alright if she took that particular one.

"It might be a favourite of his, you never know," she said, carefully putting it back on the hanger.

Kate had felt very uncomfortable looking through Claire's wardrobe in Tim's bedroom, but for Magda, who was used to cleaning in the bedroom, it was less of an issue.

When Tim came up to the studio that evening to collect the children Kate told him about Annie's selection of a dress.

"Yes, I know the one you mean. Tell Annie that's absolutely fine. I just hope she didn't think I regard her as a charity case."

"Not at all. She's very grateful. And she looks lovely in it."

"That's settled then." He turned to the children. "Right kiddos, off we go. You need to do your piano practice, Amy." Ushering the children out of the studio, he glanced outside.

"It's quite overcast this evening. It'll get dark early. Don't leave it too late."

"I won't," Kate said with a smile.

But Tim still kept a lookout when she finally started home later on, standing in the lane in the gathering dusk, watching Kate's figure disappearing round the bend. He waited for a while, listening, until he was sure she would have got home, then he went back into the house.

Chapter XVI

She was standing on a wide terrace. It was dusk. In front of her, a weathered, lichen-covered stone balustrade bordered the terrace. To her right, from the centre of the terrace, a wide flight of stone steps descended to a shadowy garden, which stretched away, across lawns and low-cut privet hedges enclosing flowerbeds laid out in a symmetrical design. Even in the dim twilight, she could see that the hedges and flower beds were overgrown and neglected. Beyond the formal garden a gleam of water from a lake reflected the last light in the sky, low down above the wooded horizon. Behind her, without turning her head, she knew was a large, grey, stone house with mullioned windows. She knew it was deserted, the windows dark, except those which reflected the faint gleam from the sky. She put out her hand and felt the rough stone of the balustrade. To her left, on a plinth which was an integral part of the balustrade, a large owl, made of the same grey stone, sat with its head turned towards her, its stone eyes staring into her own. As she stood looking at the sculpture, she heard a soft swoosh of wings, and a real, living owl flew down and perched on the balustrade next to the stone one. Slowly, it pivoted its head round to look at her, until it was in exactly the same position as its stony counterpart. This owl was a warm, tawny colour, with huge amber eyes. The contrast of colour between the real owl and the cold grey of the stone one and the grey-blue of the terrace and the garden beyond made it seem even more a vital breathing entity. It was so close, she could see every detail of the markings on its feathers. For long seconds it stared at her, unblinking, its eyes gleaming in the half-light. Then, gathering its body, it took off with an almost silent but powerful flap of its wings and flew up over her head and out of sight. She was left standing there on the wide deserted terrace, the stone owl still staring at her with its blank stone eyes, so different from the luminous gaze of the living owl. Gradually, the light died on the horizon.

330

Kate awoke with a jolt. She lay disorientated, the vividness of the dream, the intense detail of it, still filling her mind, as did the strange, indescribable feeling that had filled her as she stood on the terrace. It was a combination of a sense of wonder, of somehow having communicated with the living owl on some deep, unfathomable level, and the intense loneliness of that abandoned place. In the dream, she had been certain that no human being had come there for a long time, but the knowledge that the house behind her held many memories of the people who had lived there, now long, long gone, struck her forcibly. The utter silence, except for the soft *swoosh* of the owl's wings, the feeling of the rough stone against her hand, the implacable stare of the stone owl, were all so vivid in her mind, it was hard to believe she had not really been standing on that terrace.

She had no idea where such a strange dream had come from, and lay staring out at the dim rectangle of the bedroom window for a long time before drifting off into sleep again. The next morning, the dream was still as vivid as ever, and she felt a powerful urge to try to capture it in paint. Arriving early at the studio, she sorted through her canvases, but none were of a suitable size. She heard a car draw up and stop outside in the lane, and shortly after, the sound of children's voices. Glancing out she saw Freddie and Amy getting into Elaine's car, which then made a three-point turn and disappeared off down the lane. Lily Babbidge, who had come to the door to see them off, went back into the house and shut the door.

Kate, possessed with a desire to paint her dream, went down and across to the Crawfords' front door. Lily's face broke into a smile when she opened the door to her.

"Oh, hello dear! Anything the matter? Come in. I'm just clearing up the breakfast things and putting some washing on."

"I won't come in, Lily, I just wanted to ask if Bill would be able to knock me up a canvas today. There's a particular thing I want to paint, and I haven't got the right size. It needs to be quite big."

"I'm sure he can, dear. He's been at a bit of a loose end, and seems to spend half his time watching his seedlings grow! You pop over to the cottage and have a word with him."

"Thanks Lily. I've got all the wood and the canvas, and I could do it myself, but Bill would do it much faster and better!"

Bill was only too pleased to come up to the studio and make up a stretcher for her. While Kate made some preliminary sketches in watercolour for the painting, Bill worked away happily, whistling under his breath as he made up the frame and stretched the canvas over it. By lunchtime, the canvas was finished and primed. Kate tried again to make him accept some payment for the work, but he would have none of it. He went off for his lunch, still whistling to himself, his bag of tools in his hand. Kate, waiting for the primer to dry properly, walked back to her cottage and then nipped into the village in her car to get Bill some tobacco for his pipe as a thank you.

Over the next few weeks, as the exhibition date drew ever nearer, Kate worked frantically on the large dreamscape, hoping to get it finished in time. The details of the scene were still so clear in her mind that the composition of the painting was not a problem. It was the unearthly light, the sense of silence and loneliness that was harder to achieve. Gradually, however, she felt she was beginning to capture something of the atmosphere of the dream.

The children, coming up to wait for their father in the evenings, were fascinated by the evolution of the work, and the mysterious scenario that was emerging. They would stand in front of it, eager to spot new areas that Kate had painted that day. Freddie was particularly taken with the contrast between the two owls, and Amy gave a squeal when one day, the figure of a woman appeared, back turned towards the viewer, standing at the balustrade, her head turned to meet the gaze of the owls. Like the living owl, the figure stood out due to the fact that the colours were warm, rather than the cold blues of the landscape.

"Ooh! That looks like you, Kate." Amy exclaimed. "She's got the same hair."

"It's *supposed* to be her," Freddie said. "It's Kate's dream, and she's in the dream."

332

The painting was nearly finished, but there was something missing, and that was the fact that there was no sense that there was an old house behind the figure on the terrace. The only way to show that was to put a window frame in the foreground, through which the viewer of the painting surveyed the scene. Kate got some pictures of old mullioned windows from the internet, and, taking a deep breath, hoping it would not ruin the whole thing, began to superimpose the window in the foreground, which framed the scene outside. Immediately, the figure, the terrace, the owls, all got pushed further back into the picture plane. Kate made the frame very dark, silhouetted against the crepuscular light outside, as though the room in which the viewer was standing was wrapped in darkness.

Kate was glad she had added the window, but gazing at the painting one gloomy, rainy afternoon, she found herself picking up her brush and adding, on the right-hand side, a group of shadowy, etiolated figures, who stood at the window, looking out at the woman and the owls on the terrace. The figures were ephemeral and semi-transparent, so that the balustrade could be seen dimly through them. Gazing at the painting, she was reminded of the poem *The Listeners*, yet another by Walter de la Mare, one of her favourite poets. Who were they, these watchers in the deserted mansion? She didn't know, but she knew that the painting was now finished.

*

Kate had not seen Zachary for some weeks and needing to speak to him about the exhibition, she rang his recently acquired mobile. It rang several times before he picked up.

"Kate! I was going to come and see you. How's it going?"

"Fine. Been pretty busy."

"You ready for the exhibition?"

"More or less. Just doing some last-minute adjustments here and there. None of the paintings are framed. Can't afford it, but most of them look better without frames anyway. How about you? "

333

"Well, I've been branching out. Decided to try my hand at stone carving! Got myself some stone carving tools with the money Geoff gave me. I'm working on a figure of Pan!"

"Oh! I'd love to see it! Can I come over?"

"Sure. I'll meet you half-way. Just to be on the safe side."

Kate had not been through the wood to Zachary's cottage for some time and was struck at the transformation from the wintry starkness of the bare trees to the lushness of late spring. Sunlight dappled the path where Vince had attacked her, shafting through the canopy of vibrant new leaves. It was hard to believe it was the scene of her terrifying experience. She saw Zachary coming towards her along the path, through the flickering sun and shadow. He waved a hand in greeting, and reaching her, gave her a peck on the cheek. Together they walked to the barely discernible path which branched off to the cottage. The clearing was bathed in sunlight, a woodland glade surrounded by silver birches and hazels, with the occasional large oak. The new grass which had sprung up from the bleached remains of last year's growth grew lushly around Zachary's sculptures.

"We could be in the middle of nowhere, it's so peaceful," Kate said, drinking in the tranquillity. "It's the land that time forgot!"

Zachary laughed. "More like me forgetting time! Sometimes I can't remember which day of the week it is!"

"Well, you better remember that we are setting up the exhibition next week. I'm going to be spending the week in London, staying with Grace. Are you coming up to set up your work, or do you want us to do it for you? Geoff's been keeping some of your pieces back so that he can put them in the exhibition."

Zachary looked uncomfortable. "Well, you'll have to tell me how to get there. Remember, I'm a country bumpkin."

"Listen, you don't need to come up before the preview. We could always set out your stuff. Geoff says he's going to put it in the foyer, where people will see it as they come in, and maybe put the odd piece in the gallery itself."

"Well, that would be fine by me. I'm sure you would set the stuff out as well as I could, if you have time to do it."

"Okay, that's fine. But you have to bite the bullet and come up to the preview. Tim and his family, the Babbidges, Magda and Mike and Annie and the kids are all coming. We can work out who you can go with. I'll speak to Mags."

"Thanks Kate, but I'll probably go up by train. Just give me instructions."

As they came up to the cottage, Zachary led her to the lean-to at the side of the house, where he stored his wood, and which doubled as a workshop of sorts. On a work bench, sitting on an as yet roughly carved rock, was the sculpture of Pan. It was about two feet high, the curly head tilted to the side as it held a set of panpipes to its lips. One goat-like hoof was resting jauntily on the knee of the other shaggy leg. Unfinished as it was, it exuded a sense of life and movement, as if it could get up and dance away at any moment. Kate was enchanted.

"Zachary, you're a genius! It's wonderful! And to think you've never had any formal training. What kind of stone is it?"

"Purbeck stone. I like the golden colour."

"It would look fantastic in someone's garden."

"Yeah, I was picturing it in an outdoor setting. I'm really enjoying working in stone, though my first love will always be wood. Now come on in and have a cup of tea."

As Kate went into the cottage, her eyes were immediately drawn to the sculpture sitting in the middle of the table at the far end of the room. It was an owl, carved from walnut wood, about eighteen inches tall. She recognised it as the piece Zachary had been working on when she first met him back in the autumn, when she had stumbled across his cottage in the clearing.

"Oh!" her exclamation caused Zachary to turn and raise an eyebrow inquiringly. "It's in exactly the same position – its head turning to the side like that, to stare at you."

Zachary followed her gaze. "Oh, the owl. Yeah, I've only just finished it. She went missing over the winter, and I thought she had gone for good, but in the spring she came back, so I was able to carry on with the piece."

Kate went up to it and stroked the carved feathers, the grain of the wood suggesting the markings on the plumage. She turned to Zachary.

"Zachary, can you put this piece in the exhibition? I've just done a painting of a dream I had, and it would be great if this could be displayed beside the painting." She went on to describe her dream. Zachary was intrigued.

"Yes, I can put this in. How are you going to get it up there? It's quite heavy."

"No problem. My friend Paul is coming to transport my canvases for me, and we could take this as well, plus any more you want to send up."

"Okay, but I'll carry it to your studio for you when you leave here. I want to see the painting anyway."

Later, when Zachary saw the painting of Kate's dream, he drew in his breath sharply, and stood staring at it for some time before turning to Kate.

"That's a haunting piece of work, Kate. Very mysterious." He was still holding the owl carving, and now he set it down on the windowsill next to the canvas. It added a further dimension to the painting and seemed as though the two pieces had been created in tandem, the enigmatic stare of the wooden owl echoing the gaze of those in the painting. Kate and Zachary looked at each other in delight.

"It works so well!" Kate said. "It would be good if someone bought the two pieces together!"

Magda's voice called from the bottom of the studio steps. "You up there, Kate?"

"Yes, hi Magda, come on up!"

Magda appeared at the door, looking surprised to see Zachary. Kate took her across to look at the sculpture and the painting standing next to each other.

"Well, that's spooky all right!" she said, her hands on her hips. "Great minds think alike! Must be telepathy. Artistic telepathy! You going to display them like that in the exhibition?"

336

"Yes, definitely. And, talking about the exhibition, is Mike still driving you up there?"

"That's what I wanted to talk to you about. Mike's going to drive up, and we said we'd give Annie and the kids a lift. Be a bit of a squash, but still." She looked at Zachary. "Are you going?"

"Yes, I'll probably go up by train. Kate's going to tell me how to get there. I've only been to London once. Don't know my way around. I'd get completely lost if I drove up, and anyway, I don't know whether I trust the old van to get me there!"

Magda looked thoughtful. "Listen, why don't you and I go up on the train? I know London well. I was born there, and my brother still lives in Hackney. I often go up to visit. Then there'll be more room for Annie and the kids and pushchair and whatnot in Mike's car."

Zachary managed to look relieved and anxious at the same time.

"That would be great. But surely you would prefer to go by car?"

"I'm not fussed, honestly. Mike can drop us at the station and then go back and pick up Annie and drive up."

"Well, if you're sure. As long as you let me buy your ticket."

Magda gave a sigh of mock exasperation. "There's no need, but if it persuades you, then alright, you can buy my ticket!"

"That's settled then," Kate said, pleased with the solution. "And I think Tim said he could take Lily and Bill up."

"Yes, Tim's bringing them in the Discovery. They'll have Tim's mum with them as well, so it makes sense to go by car instead of on the train. That's why Mike decided to take the car, what with the kids and all."

That evening, when Tim came up to collect the children, Amy ran to him and dragged him by the hand to look at the wooden owl standing next to the painting.

"Look Daddy, there are three owls now. I'm calling them Stony, Woody and Realy!"

Tim, like the children, had been following the progress of the painting, and now he stood looking at the painting with Zachary's owl

337

standing next to it.

"It gives you a strange feeling, doesn't it?" he murmured thoughtfully, his arms folded and his head slightly tilted. He dragged his eyes away from the painting and gestured to the other canvases stacked against the wall.

"You say your friend Paul is coming to take your stuff up? Will he have room in his van? Some of these paintings are quite big." Privately, he wondered why Jake wasn't doing the transporting of the canvases but didn't voice his puzzlement.

"Yes, I measured the biggest, and Paul says it'll just about fit in!"

Before Tim took the children away, Kate told him where Geoff's gallery was, and which roads nearby would be the best places to look for a place to park.

"Anyway, I'll see you before I disappear on Monday for the week. The kids will still be able to have their lesson this Saturday. Obviously the following Saturday I can't do it, since it's preview day."

"You must be getting rather nervous and excited. You've been building up to this for a long time." Tim noticed slight shadows under Kate's eyes, and her face seemed a little thinner.

"You could say that!" Kate laughed. "I keep worrying that no-one will buy my work. I'm finding it hard to sleep, thinking about setting it all up, and what I'm going to put where."

Tim waved a hand at the stacked canvases. "You've got some brilliant stuff here, Kate. I'm sure it'll be a great success."

"I wish I could be so sure!" Kate replied with a wry smile.

*

Kate looked round at the chaos surrounding her, then at her three friends, as they stood in the middle of the first and largest room of Geoff's gallery. Kate's canvases were stacked against one wall, while against the opposite wall, Bea's large lightboxes and table sculptures stood with tangled wires trailing from them. Grace's textile wall hangings were at the far end of the room, rolled round large cardboard tubes and swathed

338

carefully in bubble-wrap. It was obvious that they had been professionally packaged, unlike Mimi's pieces, haphazardly bundled in plastic sheeting or stuffed into large cardboard boxes scattered about the room, with multi-coloured protuberances escaping out of the tops here and there.

"Well, here we are!" Mimi said, her hands on her hips. She was dressed in micro shorts and a crop top, her hair, which was now green with magenta streaks, pinned up with a variety of clips and combs, sticking out crazily around her head. She looked at Kate.

"If you and I are having this room, we can't really do anything until Bea and Grace get their stuff shifted."

Bea, dressed in her usual biker's garb, moved towards the lightboxes, muttering, "I'll need help moving this lot."

Two of Geoff's staff, a stocky middle-aged man and a youth of about eighteen, who had been helping to unload the work from the vans, came back into the room, followed by Geoff, who said briskly, "Right, let's get Bea's stuff shifted into room 3. They involve the most installation work. The electrician will be along in a minute. Then we'll get Grace's tapestries up." He turned to Kate and Mimi. "Meanwhile you two can decide where you want to put your pieces in here."

Paul appeared at the door with the last of Kate's paintings which he had unloaded from the van. He put it with the others and turned to Kate.

"Kate, I've got to move the van or I'll get clamped or something." He put a hand on her shoulder. It's such a shame I can't come to the preview, but I'll come and see the exhibition when I get back from Bali."

"I'll miss you not being here, but it can't be helped." Kate gave him a hug. "Thank you so much for lugging all my stuff up here."

Paul kissed her affectionately, then left, promising to come and give her a hand the following day.

She was immensely grateful to Paul. He had arrived at her studio just after nine that morning, and together they had manoeuvred the canvases down the narrow stairs leading from the studio, and stacked them in the van, separated by sheets of corrugated cardboard. The widest paintings had only just fitted in the aperture of the rear doors, but finally all were stacked snugly in and they had driven up to Geoff's gallery, arriving at almost the same time as Bea, who turned up in a big van driven by her biker boyfriend Pete.

The rest of the day was spent in a flurry of activity, mainly putting the various pieces in place ready for hanging and installing. Alan and Josh, the two assistants, started on the wall fittings on which to hang Kate's paintings and Grace's textile pieces. Bea was busy in the inner room with the electrician, while Grace wafted around fussing about where to hang what in the room assigned to her. Halfway through the afternoon, Grace's mother, a delicate blonde woman, arrived with a generous supply of sandwiches, doughnuts and flasks of coffee, which everyone fell on ravenously.

"You're a life-saver, Mrs Deller," Kate said gratefully, biting into a sandwich.

"Yes, well done Mummy," Grace agreed, sinking onto a low plinth intended for one of Mimi's sculptures.

"Well, I thought you poor darlings would need sustenance. I don't suppose you've had any lunch." She looked at Kate. "Your room's all ready for you, Kate. So glad you're staying. Grace has been in such a twitch lately about the exhibition. It'll be nice to have you there to give each other moral support." She swept her arm around, including Mimi and Bea in her gesture. "In fact, it's lovely that there are four of you to back each other up." She looked from Kate to her daughter. "What time do you think you'll be finished for the day? Will you be in for supper?"

"It'll just be Kate and me," Grace said, daintily licking doughnut sugar off her fingers and sipping her coffee. "Mimi and Bea are both doing other things. We'll probably get back about six."

"Well, I'll be off then. I've got the taxi waiting outside. See you later." She hurried off, her heels clicking on the polished wooden floor.

"What a lovely mum!" Mimi said, draining her coffee.

Bea, looking at Lara Deller's retreating back, felt a mixture of envy and bitterness. Envy for the way in which Grace's parents indulged their only child's every need, both because they worshipped the ground she walked on and because they had the means to do so, and bitterness that her own mother had walked out on her and her little brother when Bea had

340

been just twelve, leaving her father to cope on his own. Fiercely private, she never said anything about her circumstances to the others. How she had had to fight every inch of the way to get herself to art school, working in cafés at night to supplement her funds.

Grace for one had no inkling of the fact that without the leftover chips at the cafés Bea worked in, she would have gone to bed hungry more often than not, having spent any available cash on materials for her art. Kate and Mimi, however, while being far from well-off, had some idea that things were a lot harder for Bea than for themselves. They noticed that when they went to the pub, Bea would usually just drink tap water, and rarely ordered food if they were having something to eat, unless Pete was there to pay. It did not escape Kate that under her thick leathers, Bea was painfully thin, her big, strapped biker's boots failing to disguise her stick-like legs. Even the clothes she wore had been bought for her by her boyfriend. She saw Bea surreptitiously eyeing the last doughnut and thrust the box at her briskly.

"Come on Bea, do us a favour and finish this, so I can chuck out the box. We'd better get on."

She breathed a sigh of relief when Bea took the doughnut and disappeared back to her light boxes.

Over the next few days, the exhibition gradually took shape. Pieces were put up, mulled over, changed to another spot, returned to the original place, or moved to a completely different one, until everyone was satisfied. Kate had brought her paints with her and had spent a large part of the last few days making small changes in several of her paintings. Seeing them from the greater distance afforded them in the larger room called for certain alterations in emphasis. The *Annie* triptych was at the centre of the wall at the far end of the room, flanked by other paintings. The three large square works based on fossil forms hung on one long wall, along with two paintings of huge grey pebbles veined with white. The muted colours on that wall contrasted with the paintings on the opposite wall, with their more vibrant colours, such as *Quiet Shell*, *Poplars*, *Stricken Tree* and some semi-abstract works. On its own on the nearer end wall next to the door

341

was *A Dream of Owls,* with Zachary's owl sculpture on a plinth next to it. The rest of Zachary's pieces, which Geoff had kept in storage, Kate set up in the foyer, on the purpose-built display shelves. Mimi's crazy, painted fabric sculptures took up the centre of the floor in the same room as Kate's paintings, some on plinths and some on the ground. *Eye See You*, a big stuffed eye with huge wire eyelashes, each one of which ended in a mini eye, was placed next to *Angle Angel*, a fat angler fish with a great gaping mouth, the lure sprouting from its head taking the form of a halo. Next to that was *O Maggot,* a large red apple, pitted with several holes, from which worms with human faces were emerging. Nearby was *Footloose*, simply a large foot with blood vessels dangling out of the top and *A Meeting of Minds,* which consisted of six pink brains, was arranged in a circle on the floor. The most bizarre one, *Give Me a Hand*, was a hand with immensely long fingers which stretched across the floor, in among the other sculptures, winding around them like stretched rubber and ending in spatulate tips.

Kate, surveying the finished effect looked across at Mimi and said, grinning, "I always thought you were crazy, but now I know. You are completely bonkers! But they do look good!"

"They bloody well better. I nearly broke my neck getting them finished." Mimi, who had been doing running repairs all week, clutched her back in agony.

"I need a drink. Let's go to the pub."

"Let's see how Bea and Grace are getting on."

Kate went into Bea's gallery space and stopped at the entrance with a gasp. It was the first time she had seen all of Bea's light sculptures lit up at the same time and the effect was stunning. Some of the pieces were wall mounted, while others were free-standing. Some were constructed of wood and light-gathering Perspex, others used stained glass and metal, but all glowed with jewel colours. Fiery oranges and yellows, deep sea blues and greens, smouldering purples and reds. Here a free-standing piece like a great crystal glimmered purplish red; there, a wall-mounted piece of multi-layered glass glowed green and blue, its ethereal strands of colour seeming to move as you walked towards it. Another wall-mounted piece really did have a kinetic element, the lights gleaming through the frosted glass undulating and changing constantly, forming ephemeral abstract compositions that came into being and then were gone.

"Bea, these are fabulous," Kate said, awestruck. "If there's any justice in this world, you should sell the lot!"

"Let's hope so!" Bea said, taping down the last of the wires. "I owe a lot of money to a lot of people."

Grace was still busily adding more embellishments to one of her wall hangings. Her room too was an impressive sight. Most of one wall was taken up with a very large piece inspired by the seashore. Rounded fabric pebbles in the foreground interspersed with clumps of sea thrift and marram grass diminished in size as they led to the water's edge which curved away in foam-edged waves created with strands of tangled white yarn and muslin. Blue-green appliquéd strips of fabric cleverly evoked the restless waves, while a huge sun sent its rays across a sky scattered with wheeling gulls. The whole thing was a lyrical amalgamation of texture, colour and a feeling of movement. Elsewhere, a vertical tapestry of floral shapes was a gorgeous symphony of red, orange and purple, embellished with beads and intricate embroidery. Another purely abstract piece combined yarns in rich, earthy colours with fabrics Grace had dyed herself, using natural dyes. The combination of all the pieces together gave an opulent, exotic effect, redolent of a souk.

Geoff, coming into the gallery a little later, walked around the rooms, eyed anxiously by the four girls. His face broke into a grin.

"I'm glad my instincts were right, sticking my neck out for you! You girls have certainly come up with the goods! It's an excellent show. I've got some bigwigs coming along on Saturday, and I have to say I was a bit worried as to how it would all gel together. From what I can see, it should be a great success." He looked around him. "You just need to label everything. I've had all the labels done as per the info you gave me. And I've just picked up the catalogues too. Come and see, they're in the foyer."

Seeing the smart, printed catalogues and the official-looking labels somehow brought home to Kate the rather frightening prospect of the

343

preview in less than two days' time. What if the 'bigwigs' thought her work was rubbish? What if none of her paintings got sold? After all the months of work, albeit doing something she would rather do above anything else, the thought that no-one would want to buy her work was too depressing to contemplate.

The next day was spent putting up the labels for each piece, dealing with any last-minute adjustments and generally tidying up. Kate packed away her paints, telling herself that for better or worse, there was no more time to make any more changes.

"There's nothing more you can do now," Geoff told the four of them, as they hung around anxiously surveying their work. "Go and chill."

As they left, they saw that the foyer was set up ready for the drinks and canapés and the catalogues sat on a table by the door. On shelves at the far end, where Kate had set them out, were Zachary's carvings, making an impressive display.

Mimi looked at her friends and made a mock gesture of biting her nails.

"I don't know about you lot, but I'm petrified!" she said, her voice rising to a squeak.

"I think we all are!" Kate agreed. "Geoff's talk of bigwigs is exciting, but scary."

As they went out into the street Bea's boyfriend drew up beside them on his motorbike, and Bea, putting on her helmet, got on the pillion seat.

"See you at about five tomorrow," she called, as Pete drove off with a low roar of the engine.

"I'd better go too," Mimi said, looking at her watch. "I promised Mum I'd go over for supper tonight. I need to explain how to get here tomorrow."

Kate and Grace walked with her to the tube station, where they parted, Grace and Kate heading towards Richmond and Mimi to her parents' house in Surbiton. When Kate and Grace arrived at Grace's house, her mother was in the kitchen, preparing supper, and greeted them as though she hadn't seen them for weeks instead of hours. She refused any offers of help, instead pressing on them a glass of chilled white wine each.

"You girls go and relax. You've got a big day tomorrow. It's so exciting, isn't it? You've all been working so hard, you deserve it to be a success."

Grace gave her mother a hug. "I couldn't have done it without yours and Daddy's help. Believe me, I know how lucky I am!"

Her mother hugged her back. "Oh, I know we've helped you materially, but it was all your own talent and determination which created such beautiful work."

Kate knew the truth of this. Despite Grace's sweet and gentle nature and her privileged upbringing, she was utterly committed to her art and was as focused and hard-working as any of them.

Carrying their glasses, they went into Grace's airy, spacious studio, which looked much barer, now that all her tapestries were removed. It was immaculately tidy, with all her materials neatly stacked and labelled on shelves and in cubbyholes. A large table for spreading out her work took up the middle of the room and a loom stood in a corner, for once not bearing a work in progress. A large sink in another corner was flanked by buckets for dyes and an angled drawing table stood by the window, where the evening sun slanted in through the trees edging the lawn. Kate looked at her friend with affection. It would have been so easy for Grace to have lived an idle and directionless life, but she possessed that fire in the belly which any true artist needs. Kate was glad that the lines between what used to be regarded as Art as opposed to Craft were now becoming so blurred that one couldn't tell where one ended and the other began. To her mind, Grace's work was Art in the true sense of the word. Perching on a stool, Kate raised her glass.

"Well, here's to us all. Let's hope tomorrow goes well!"

Grace clinked Kate's glass with hers. "To us all!" she said. "Bring on the bigwigs!"

*

By five o'clock the next evening, Kate, Grace, Mimi and Bea were at the gallery, well in advance of the preview party, due to start at six. Kate wore the green jersey dress she had worn at Christmas, with green pendant earrings and her hair hanging loose. Mimi was in skinny zebra-striped leggings with vertiginous red stilettos, black mini dress and a short silver jacket. Her hair was done up in an assortment of silver butterfly-shaped clips and her nails were painted silver. Grace drifted around in a long floral dress in flimsy cotton, draped with her customary beads and dangly earrings, her blonde wavy hair falling to her shoulders. Bea looked just as she always looked, dressed from top to toe in black biker gear. Her boyfriend Pete had brought her, and they spent most of the time before the party in Bea's room, fiddling with wires. As six o'clock approached, Kate stood with Mimi just inside the entrance to their own gallery space, both clutching their champagne flutes, while Grace hovered at the door of her own room.

The first people to arrive, on the dot of six, were Grace's parents. Her father, a tall, avuncular man, greeted Geoff warmly, then, procuring a glass of champagne each for his wife and himself, strolled over to examine Zachary's pieces on the display shelves. What he really wanted to do was make a beeline to his daughter's work, but felt that good manners dictated that he showed interest in everything. As it happened, he was enchanted by Zachary's carvings, and determined then and there to buy one – an otter, twisting its body to look over its shoulder, with one paw raised.

Kate's father and Doreen were next to turn up. Kate was hugely pleased to see them, especially her father, who, when he saw Kate's paintings up around the gallery walls, beamed at her with such pride and delight on his face, that she felt a lump in her throat.

"If only your mother could have seen this," he said quietly to her, his eyes holding a gleam of tears.

Doreen, nervously sipping her champagne, and fiddling with her pashmina, stood gazing around her, her eyes wide.

"Kate love, I never knew you could paint like this! I think they're amazing!" She looked a little askance at Mimi's sculptures, however.

346

"Ooh, I'm not sure about these though," she said, gesturing with her glass. "They give me the heebiejeebies!"

Kate laughed. "I think that's the point!" she said. Suddenly, she spotted Zachary and Magda by the door. "Excuse me a moment. I must just say hello to someone."

Magda, being the sort of person who feels at home in any situation, looked completely relaxed, but Zachary, tightly gripping his glass of orange juice, looked very ill at ease. He kept running his finger around the inside of his collar, as though his tie was about to choke him. He wore a slightly shabby suede jacket and brown cords, and his hair was tied back in his customary ponytail. Had he but known it, he looked very much the "arty type," and perfectly in keeping with his surroundings.

The gallery began to fill up as more and more people drifted in. Kate saw Mike arrive with Annie and her children, and went to greet them, feeling relieved that Annie had not got cold feet at the last minute. She looked transformed in Claire's blue dress, though at first she seemed very nervous, clutching Becky's and Darren's hands tightly.

"I'm terrified Darren's going to go and start playing with those sculptures," she said. "I wish I could have left the kids with someone, but Mags is the only one I can trust, and she's here!" She looked over at the triptych. "It looks grand, Kate," she said. "Imagine, little old me being in something like that!"

"I'm the lucky one, having such an interesting sitter!" Kate said, adding, "You look lovely, Annie. That dress really suits you."

"That's what I told her," Mike said, handing a glass of champagne to Annie, who had to let go of Becky's hand to accept it. He turned to Kate. "Great show, by the way. Your paintings look fantastic. And I bet these crazy sculptures are Mimi's!"

"Of course, whose else could they be?" Kate laughed. She felt a hand go round her waist and turned to see Jake standing beside her. He bent to kiss her full on the mouth, just as Tim, accompanied by Freddie, Amy, Gwen and the Babbidges, came through the door.

The first thing Tim saw as the crowd momentarily parted, was Kate being kissed by Jake at the far end of the room. His ebullient mood

347

immediately vanished, to be replaced by an inner anguish which he struggled to hide.

Kate, who had been keeping one eye on the door, watching for when Tim arrived, caught sight of him as she pulled away from Jake's kiss. Jake still had his arm possessively round her waist. Exasperated that Tim had come in just at that moment and may have seen Jake kissing her, she moved away, saying she had to greet some people who had just come in.

Jake followed her gaze, and it was his turn to feel a darkening of his mood when he saw Tim, and noted the eagerness Kate displayed at going to meet him. What was *he* doing here? It had not occurred to Jake that Tim would come up to the party. He had planned to take Kate out for a celebratory dinner later, which hopefully would lead to her coming back to his flat for the night. He had also not reckoned on Kate's folks being here either. He determined that he would still try to engineer things so that Kate would spend the night with him.

Kate, meanwhile, had reached Tim's group standing at the entrance to her gallery space and was greeting everyone warmly.

"This is so exciting!" enthused Gwen, kissing her and waving her arm in an expansive gesture to take in the whole room. "Stunning paintings, Kate. I'm going to mosey around with my catalogue and enjoy them." She wandered off, fiddling with the catalogue while holding her glass in one hand.

Lily and Bill Babbidge stood appearing a little lost, with Bill looking as though he would rather be holding a pint of beer than the champagne flute. Lily, in her turn, eschewing champagne in favour of orange juice, would probably have preferred to be sipping a cup of tea. After affectionately kissing Kate hello, they pottered off to join Magda and Zachary, whom they had spotted on the other side of the room. Freddie and Amy, already familiar with Kate's paintings, were much taken with Mimi's sculptures and went off to examine them more closely. Kate was left alone with Tim, who, having given Kate a peck on the cheek, stood slightly aside while she greeted the others. He gave her a friendly grin.

"Congratulations, Kate. It's all come together beautifully. Your paintings look really impressive."

348

"Well, I don't know how I could have coped without your studio!" Kate said earnestly. "Imagine having to work on big canvases in the cottage, not to mention storing them. They would have had to languish in the shed, getting covered in spider's webs, even if I could have got them all in among the spades and mowers and stuff."

"I'm just glad the room has been put to such good use."

Kate sensed a slight reservation in Tim's manner, and wondered if it was because he had seen her with Jake. She spotted her father and Doreen not far away, gazing at *A Dream of Owls*.

"Come and meet my father and his wife," she said, putting a hand on his arm and drawing him towards them.

Soon afterwards, Geoff's contacts in the art world began to arrive, and Kate had little time to talk to anyone else as Geoff brought them to meet her and the other girls. Halfway through the evening, she was amazed to see David Straker himself enter the room. Geoff brought him over and introduced him to Kate and Mimi. He of course already knew Jake - who had barely left Kate's side all evening, and the group stood talking for a while before Straker drifted off to look around, accompanied by Geoff and Jake.

Mimi glanced at Kate, her eyebrows raised and her eyes stretched wide, and hissed, "Didn't know *he* was coming, did you? Jake seems to be very buddy-buddy with him. Has he still got Jake's stuff in his gallery?"

"Yes, I think so, though he does tend to sell on his pieces after a while. Jake's got a show coming up in New York in the autumn."

"Quite the blue-eyed boy of the moment, isn't he? Mind you, I think you're better off with your other blue-eyed boy!" Mimi's eyes rested on Tim standing in front of the Annie triptych, talking to Annie and Mike.

"He's not *mine,* Mimi! And if you dare say anything, I'll *kill* you!"

Mimi gave a sly laugh, the champagne eroding her already tenuous self-restraint.

"The lady doth protest too much, methinks!" She tapped the side of her nose and sashayed off to talk to a dealer who was showing an interest in her sculptures.

Kate, half-exasperated and half-amused, was about to go and join Tim's little group, when a well-known gallerist friend of Geoff's, Veronica Whitehorn, to whom she had been introduced earlier, came up to her and began asking about her paintings. She found herself walking around the room with her, talking about the individual works.

Seeing that Annie was still standing near the triptych, she took Veronica across, and introduced her to Annie. Though she still looked nervous, Annie managed to exchange a few words with her. At the end of their little tour of Kate's paintings, Veronica Whitehorn turned to her with a thoughtful smile.

"I'm intrigued by your work. Your paintings seem to be informed by a very emotional response to what goes on in your life. I'd like to represent you and give you a solo show eventually. Are you interested?"

Was she interested! Kate could hardly believe what she was hearing. It was one thing Geoff giving them a show partly because he was Grace's uncle, and quite another to have a London gallerist offering to represent her and give her a solo show purely on the strength of the work she had seen that evening. She knew she should act cool and composed, but she couldn't help her eager response.

"You bet!" she exclaimed enthusiastically, if a little inelegantly, her eyes shining with excitement. "That would be fantastic!"

Veronica Whitethorn smiled back. She took a business card from her bag and handed it to Kate, who read with shining eyes: *Veronica Whitethorn Gallery, Burlington Gardens, Mayfair.* Kate had visited the gallery on several occasions, never dreaming that she would one day exhibit there.

"Meanwhile," Veronica continued, "I'd like to buy the three fossil-type paintings. I have a client who I think would be very keen to acquire them. I'll go and have a word with Geoff. I'll be in touch with you via Geoff. Keep painting!" She wandered off and Kate was left shaking slightly with nervous excitement.

She had hardly caught her breath when she realised that Jake was approaching, accompanied by Straker. Jake gestured towards the triptych.

"Mr Straker wants to talk to you about your triptych, Kate," he said. "I told him there was quite a story behind it."

The expression on Straker's famously grumpy countenance barely changed as they walked towards the triptych and Kate explained that the work was inspired by someone who was trapped in an abusive relationship and who was struggling to break free. If Annie had still been standing nearby, she would have introduced her, but she had moved away. Straker stood looking at the paintings in silence. Then he turned to Kate.

"You may know that I have started a foundation for young artists so that they can get their work out there. You and your friends are in the right demographic for the enterprise, and I intend to buy some pieces from each of you. I'm interested in this piece and this other one..." he glanced at his catalogue, "*Quiet Shell*. Come and tell me about it."

As Straker moved across to the painting in question, Jake glanced at Kate, winked and gave her a thumbs up sign. Kate smiled back, her heart softening towards Jake. He was obviously fighting her corner, and while she knew Straker would not buy anything unless he liked it, she was still grateful to Jake for helping to engage his interest.

Tim, always conscious of Kate's whereabouts in the room, saw the exchange, and the possessive way Jake's arm came round Kate's waist as he steered her to stand beside the important looking individual in the cream linen jacket.

The gallery was thinning out. Most of the dealers and gallerists had left, as had many of Grace's parents' friends and acquaintances who had been asked along, partly because, as Mr and Mrs Deller were the first to admit, they had money, and may be tempted to buy. Allan Deller, being the owner of an advertising company, had access to many people in the media and the arts.

Kate was finally able to chat to her father and Doreen and the Surrey contingent, and to see how Mimi, Grace and Bea had fared. She herself, apart from the works she had sold to Veronica Whitethorn, had sold three of her pieces to another buyer, an Amsterdam-based dealer,

351

while Straker had bought the triptych and *Quiet Shell*. Both of her grey stone paintings had also gone, bought by the owner of a seaside hotel in the West Country, who, much to Grace's delight, had also bought Grace's large seascape tapestry. Grace had sold five pieces altogether, and Bea had done best of all, selling all but two of her works.

"That should get the creditors off my back!" Bea said, her face breaking into one of her rare smiles. "And there's still two weeks of the exhibition to go. It would be good to sell the lot."

Kate hugged her friend, delighted for her, and went back to hers and Mimi's room, to ask Mimi how she had done, knowing already that Straker had bought the tentacle hand. She found her talking to a late arrival, a flamboyant young woman who looked vaguely familiar, who was accompanied by a lanky, wild-haired young man in ripped jeans. It was some minutes before she realised it was Bella Madison, the pop singer. She seemed particularly taken with Mimi's "Eye see you" sculpture, and it was not long before she decided to buy it. Bella then continued round the room and came to rest in front of Kate's *Dream of Owls* painting.

"Oh!" she gasped. "I've got to have this! It's so strange and spooky! Does the owl carving go with it? Is the artist here? I must ask about it!"

Kate had been watching her, and went up and introduced herself, explaining about her dream, and the strange coincidence of Zachary's sculpture echoing the two painted owls. She called Zachary over and introduced him.

"Well, I must buy the carving too! They go so well together. I know exactly where I'm going to put them." Bella clapped her hands in delight, and continued round the exhibition, accompanied by her monosyllabic friend.

Grace's mother came up to Kate and, nodding in Bella's direction, said in a conspiratorial voice, "That was Bella Madison, wasn't it? We know her agent, and asked him along tonight. That's him over there," she pointed towards a portly little man who had gone up to talk to Bella. "He said he would try to get Bella to come tonight, as she's interested in art. Is she going to buy your owl picture?"

"Yes, she said she wanted it, and Zachary's sculpture too," Kate said, grinning at Zachary. "Maybe we should go into partnership!"

"Oh! She's going into Grace's room. I wonder if she'll buy anything of hers!" Lara Deller edged off, trying not to seem as though she was watching Bella like a hawk.

By the time she was ready to go, Bella had bought two of Grace's flower tapestries and a table-sculpture-cum-lamp from Bea, in addition to the pieces she had decided to buy from Kate, Mimi and Zachary. She wrote Geoff a cheque for thousands of pounds as though it were a mere bagatelle, and then, draining her glass of champagne, swept out of the gallery into her waiting car.

Soon, the only people left in the gallery, apart from the two waitresses, were Mimi's parents, whom Kate had met before, Grace's parents, Bea's father and brother and her boyfriend Pete, Kate's father and Doreen, Kate's Surrey friends, and Jake. Geoff broke open some more champagne, and they all gathered in the foyer to have a last drink before dispersing.

Geoff held up his glass. "Let's have a toast to our five exhibitors. Congratulations on a very successful evening. You've all done extremely well."

There was a chorus of approval and much clinking of glasses. Mike took the opportunity to engage Mimi in conversation. He had not been far from her side all evening.

Kate turned to Zachary, who was still on the orange juice. "How did you do, Zachary? I hope people realised your stuff was for sale out here."

"I sold nine pieces," Zachary said with satisfaction and slight incredulity. "One chap bought three!"

"Brill! Is that counting the owl?"

"Oh, no I forgot about the owl. That's ten then!"

"That's fantastic! But something makes me think you didn't really want to sell the owl!"

"You're right. I'll just have to make another one!"

353

Mike appeared at her side accompanied by Annie, saying he would take Annie back home, as the kids were starting to grizzle.

Annie gave Kate a hug. "I've had such a good time, Kate," she said. "I was so nervous, but everyone was so nice, I really enjoyed it in the end."

"It was great that you came. Thanks for bringing them," Kate said, looking gratefully at Mike.

"No problem. I enjoyed it too. I've never been to an art exhibition before. I think I'll start going to galleries now! Mimi says she'll educate me!"

"That's what I like to hear," Kate laughed, turning towards Magda and Zachary as they too came up to her.

"We'll be off now too, Kate," Magda said. "By the time we've taken the tube to Waterloo then caught the train to Woking, it'll be quite late."

"Well, why don't we all go back together? Dad and Doreen are coming back to my cottage tonight."

"Oh, okay. But are you ready to leave yet?"

"I think so. I'll just go and ask Geoff if there's anything else we have to do."

Jake had been listening to this exchange and before Kate could go and talk to Geoff, he grabbed her arm and drew her aside.

"Kate, I was hoping you could come and have dinner with me. Have a little celebration of our own. And I was hoping you would come and see my new installation tomorrow."

Kate looked at him, startled to see the hunger in his eyes.

"I... I can't Jake. I've got my father and his wife here. They're coming back to my house to stay the night. They've never seen the cottage."

Jake's hand tightened on her arm. A muscle in his jaw worked as he strove to hide his disappointment. He realised his plan had been foiled and dropped his hand. His elaborate spiel to Lucinda about why he couldn't bring her to the preview party and why he couldn't see her tonight had been unnecessary after all. He shrugged offhandedly.

354

"Oh well, maybe another time. Well done, kid," he said lightly. But then he took her face in his hands and kissed her hard on the mouth. Then he turned on his heel and went to get a refill for his glass before she could catch her breath.

Tim had been about to approach Kate to say that they would be going too, when he saw Jake take her aside and had witnessed the passionate way he had kissed her. He saw Kate stand very still for a moment, and mistaking her surprise for reciprocated feeling, suddenly felt he had to leave. He rounded up Gwen, the children and the Babbidges, and approached Kate.

"Kate, I think we'll be on our way. I think Lily and Bill are ready to go, and Amy's getting tired. It's been great! A marvellous show!"

Kate smiled at Amy's protestation that she was "not even tired at all" and turned to Lily and Bill.

"Thank you both for coming," she said. "And I'm not forgetting how indebted I am to you Bill, for making all those canvases for me."

Bill patted her hand. "It was a pleasure. Any time. I expect you'll be wanting some more made up soon. You only have to ask."

"Thank you, Bill," Kate said affectionately and then turned to say goodbye to Tim, reaching up to kiss him on the cheek. Again, she felt a slight constraint in his manner, and a sadness in his eyes belied his smile.

"Thank you so much for taking the trouble to come. I really appreciate it."

"We wouldn't have missed it for the world!" Gwen said. "And I would have bought one of your stone paintings, but someone pounced on them before I got my act together."

"I'll paint you another one as a present. It's lovely that you could come tonight."

"I'll probably see you before I go home," Gwen said, giving her a kiss on the cheek. "I'm here for the week of half-term. Bye for now." She herded Amy and Freddie to the door, followed by Tim, who gave Kate a wave as he turned away.

Jake, on the other side of the room, watched as Kate stood looking after Tim as he disappeared out of the door. He knocked back his drink and poured another. Then he got out his phone and called Lucinda.

"Change of plan, princess. I'm free tonight after all," he said. "I'll see you in half an hour."

Chapter XVII

Elaine was seething. When she brought Freddie and Amy back from school on the Friday at the start of half-term, Gwen, who had arrived earlier that day, came out of the house to meet them, with Binky bounding out in front. Elaine got out of the car to say hello, and to put to Gwen a plan she had for the next day.

"How about taking the children to Legoland for the day tomorrow?" she asked Gwen, while Binky greeted the children ecstatically, as though he had not seen them for a month.

"What is Legoland?" Gwen asked. "Oh, wait a minute, isn't it some sort of amusement park?"

"Yes, a theme park, with all sorts of rides and things. I thought it would be fun. The kids loved it last time we went, and Tim enjoyed it too. What do you think?"

"Well, I'm sure the kids would like it, but I'm afraid we wouldn't be back in time."

"In time for what?"

"We're all going to London to the preview of Kate's and her friends' art exhibition. It starts at six, so we would have to leave before five."

Elaine froze. That blasted girl again! It was always Kate this and Kate that. And now they were traipsing up to London to her exhibition, as though she were one of the family. They had only known her for less than a year, for God's sake!

She saw that Gwen was looking at her curiously and realised that her expression must have reflected her thoughts. She forced herself to give a tight smile.

"Oh, that's a pity. Duncan was looking forward to it." She turned to her son, who was sitting in the front seat of the car with the window down. "Weren't you darling?"

"Maybe we could go on Sunday instead?" Duncan said equably. "Doesn't make much difference."

"I'll put it to Tim when he gets back," Gwen said. "We can ring you if he's up for it."

Elaine had had to be content with that, and had driven off, her mind still churning with irritation and jealousy. Even when Tim phoned to agree to go on the Sunday if the weather was fine, it didn't do much to lighten her mood.

He could have sounded a bit more enthusiastic about it, she thought to herself. *He* did *enjoy it last time we went, before that little madam came on the scene.*

Her thoughts darkened still further the following evening, when she knew Tim would be driving to London, and would be spending the evening at Kate's exhibition, looking at Kate's paintings in Kate's company. She went to the kitchen and, taking a bottle of wine out of the fridge, poured herself a generous glass, even though it was only five o'clock.

When Sunday dawned with a lowering sky and torrential rain set in by nine o'clock, she knew that when the phone rang it would be Tim, calling off the outing.

"No point in getting drenched," he said. "Let's make it another day."

Elaine had no wish to trail around in the rain like a drowned rat, so she had to agree. She pointedly refused to ask Tim about the exhibition, and rang off, cursing the rain and Kate - and bloody art exhibitions.

Kate stood at the window of her little sitting room, watching the rain sheeting down on the poplars and the field beyond. She had just dropped her father and Doreen at the station, and had been sorry to see them go, having failed to persuade them to stay longer.

"I've got a student coming for a lesson tomorrow," her father had said. "And another one on Tuesday. Too much of a hassle to re-arrange them. But it was wonderful to be at the exhibition and to see your cottage at last."

358

In fact, it had been Doreen who had gone into ecstasies over Lavender Cottage, throwing up her hands in delight when their taxi from the station had dropped them off in the lane after getting back from the preview the previous night. It had not been quite dark, and a bright moon added its light as it peered down from above the poplars moving softly in the breeze. Once inside, Doreen had wandered round the cottage, exclaiming at the inglenook fireplace, the ceiling beams, the leaded windows, the crooked little staircase.

"Of course, it needs complete redecoration," Kate said, gesturing around her. "Now that the exhibition is over, I'm going to get down to it."

"I'll make you some new curtains," Doreen said, surveying the shabby green ones hanging limply at the window of the sitting room. "I'll measure up and send you down some samples of material to choose from. They can be a belated house-warming present from us."

Kate had thanked her gratefully, while keeping her fingers crossed that there would be something in the samples that she could live with.

Now, she was possessed by a sense of anti-climax. The exhibition, towards which she had been working with so much focus for so long, was over. Although it had been very successful, and to cap it all, she had been taken on by a London gallerist and offered a solo show, she had been keyed up about it for months and now that the buzz of the evening before had faded, she felt suddenly very alone. For a fleeting moment, she wished she were up in London with her friends, chatting about the exhibition and discussing each other's plans. She knew the feeling would pass, but at the moment she felt physically and emotionally drained. She also knew that something else was contributing to her mood, and that was the constraint she had felt in Tim's manner at the preview. He had not made much eye contact with her, and when he did, his eyes seemed sad, veiled. She wondered if it was because of Jake and his possessive attitude to her. But that would mean that he cared whether she was in a relationship with Jake and she was by no means certain that he did care. Then there was Elaine, whose visit warning her to back off from getting involved with Tim still lurked at the back of her mind. In fact, in retrospect, it seemed more of a threat than a warning, now that she had had more time to mull it over.

Kate gave herself a mental shake and decided that the way to lift herself out of her downbeat mood was to busy herself with redecorating the cottage. She had more time on her hands now so she decided to take a trip to the DIY store and stock up on paint, brushes and all the paraphernalia needed to set about repainting the rooms.

She started with the sitting room and by the middle of the week was well into the task when Zachary turned up at the door.

He grinned when he saw Kate. She was in old jeans and a paint-daubed shirt, with the sleeves rolled up. There was a streak of white paint down her cheek and more in her hair, which was pulled back into a messy ponytail. There was white paint all over her hands and forearms.

"Decided to go in for some body-art, have we?" Zachary commented when Kate had greeted him and asked him in.

Kate laughed. "I'm finally getting round to smartening up the place. I'm painting all the walls and ceilings white. I thought it would look best with the dark beams, and help the rooms look bigger. I'm just about to start on the ceiling."

"Good choice. You can't go wrong with white." He looked approvingly round the room, then turned back to Kate. "I just came to say a proper thank you for setting out all my stuff for the exhibition and well... for making it possible for me to exhibit in the first place. But now I'm here, why don't I say thank you in a more practical way and paint the ceiling for you? I can reach without standing on anything. We don't want you to break your neck, just when you're about to become a famous artist!"

Kate started to protest, but Zachary was already rolling up his sleeves. He picked up the paint roller and started on the ceiling, while Kate got out the gloss paint and set to work on the window frames. It was much nicer working with Zachary than on her own. They chatted about the exhibition or worked in companionable silence, and by the end of the afternoon Zachary had finished the ceiling and Kate had also finished painting the windows and the skirting board.

"Just the doors to do now, and this room will be done!" Kate said, handing Zachary a mug of tea and taking a sip of her own. "You don't know how grateful I am, Zachary. I was dreading doing the ceiling!"

"Are you painting the other rooms too?"

"Yes, the whole house needs doing."

"Well, I'll come back in the morning and do the other ceilings."

Once again Kate tried to protest, but Zachary insisted and disappeared into the kitchen to wash the roller out. He was back the next day and started straightaway on the walls of the staircase, parts of which Kate would have found difficult to reach. Halfway through the afternoon, Gwen knocked on the door, accompanied by the children and Binky.

"We wondered if you would like to come for a walk with us," Gwen said, "but you look as though you're in the middle of decorating!"

"Yes, Zachary's helping me with the ceilings and things. The house is in dire need of sprucing up. Come in and see the sitting room."

They all trooped in and admired the transforming effect that a coat of white paint had achieved, after which Gwen rounded up the children and the dog and made for the door.

"We'll leave you in peace, Kate. Hopefully I'll see you before I go back on Sunday."

As Kate walked out to the gate with them, Gwen turned to her, seemingly struck by a sudden thought.

"How about coming over for supper this evening? The weather's so warm, we were thinking of having a barbecue."

Freddie and Amy enthusiastically added their endorsements to the invitation.

"You can see how the new games room/gym is getting on," Freddie said eagerly. "It's almost finished now. We just have to buy some things like a table tennis table and a treadmill and stuff."

"I'd love to see it," Kate said with enthusiasm. She turned to Gwen. "Thank you, I'd love to come."

"Good. Come at about six. We could leave it till the weekend, but I don't think this weather will last. Ask Zachary, too."

Zachary left about five, saying he wouldn't come to the barbecue as he had promised to visit old Sam that evening. Kate nipped along to the village shop before it shut and bought some sausages and a bottle of wine to contribute to the barbecue. Then, after cleaning herself up as best she could, walked up the lane to Woodcote House. It was very warm for early June. The new leaves on the poplars lining the right-hand side of the lane quivered and danced in the evening sunlight and the grassy verges on either side were a riot of cow parsley, as though a wave had broken against the hedgerow in a mass of foam. As she approached Woodcote, she caught a whiff of barbecue smoke which mingled with the smell of the sun-warmed verdure all around her. She walked up the path to Woodcote's front door and rang the bell. When no-one answered, she guessed Gwen and the children must be out in the back garden and made her way round the side of the house. Billows of smoke were emanating from the barbecue over which Freddie was hovering proprietorially, while Gwen and Amy brought plates and cutlery out to the garden table.

Catching sight of Kate, Gwen waved and beckoned her over.

"Sorry, Kate. Did you ring the bell? We didn't hear. Come and have a glass of vino. Oh thanks! There was no need, but thanks," she said as she took the sausages and wine from Kate. "Better not put them where Binky can get at them. I know what Labradors are like!"

Chaos reigned as the smoke got in everyone's eyes, while Binky bounced around barking in excitement and Amy dropped the basket of burger buns on the floor of the terrace.

"Never mind, darling. We'll just dust them off. It's clean dirt!" Gwen said cheerfully, scooping them up and putting them back in the basket, giving them a cursory flick with a tea- towel as she did so.

"Oh Kate, could you go and pull up a couple of lettuces from the vegetable garden?" Gwen said, tearing open a packet of beef burgers. She gestured towards the bottom of the garden. "Beyond the rose pergola. And could you give them a wash? There's a salad bowl in a cupboard somewhere. Thanks."

"Will do!" Kate said, and walked down to the bottom of the garden, breathing in the scent of roses as she passed under an arch in the pergola. A kitchen garden lay beyond, where she spotted the two rows of bushy lettuces among the other neatly laid out vegetables.

362

She was rinsing the lettuce in the sink when she heard the front door bang, and a moment later Tim came into the kitchen.

"Hello! Didn't expect to see you here!" he said, his eyes widening with surprise and pleasure when he saw Kate.

"Hi Tim. Yes, Gwen and the kids decided to have a barbecue and asked me to come along. I hope you don't mind."

"Of course I don't mind. It's good to see you. Have you recovered from Saturday?" Tim seemed to be much more relaxed than he had been at the exhibition. He came to stand beside her at the sink and looked at her curiously.

"Are you back painting already? You've got white paint in your hair!"

Kate laughed. "Yes, but not pictures. I'm doing some decorating in the cottage. It really needed a lick of paint. Zachary's helping me, especially with the ceilings. I thought I'd better do it before I started on working towards my solo exhibition."

"That's nice of Zachary. I suppose it's his way of saying thank you. And it's terrific that you've been offered your own show. You must be thrilled."

"I am! Even though it means putting in massive amounts of work in the next few months."

When Tim went up to change out of his suit, Kate found the salad bowl and took the lettuce out to the garden.

When the smoke died down a bit and the charcoal glowed red, Freddie, spurning any adult help, put the sausages and burgers on the grill and before long they were sitting down to tasty, if somewhat blackened, hamburgers and hot dogs. Tim, sitting next to Kate put his hand up to her hair to finger the paint clogging some of the strands.

"How are you going to get this out? It looks really stuck on."

"Oh, it'll come off in hot water. It won't be the first time!" Kate answered unconcerned, biting into a sausage.

No-one heard the front doorbell, so when Elaine came round the side of the house with Duncan, she was unobserved as she surveyed the

363

scene. She had smelt the smoke as soon as she got out of the car, so she was expecting to see them having a barbecue, but her face paled as she saw that Kate was there too, sitting next to Tim, who had his hand up to Kate's hair. Something in his body language, something like tenderness, caused an almost physical pain in Elaine, like a knife twisting in her gut. So they were having a barbecue and had asked Kate, but had not bothered to ask her and Duncan. Duncan, who was Freddie's friend, and herself, who did the school run every day. She felt frozen to the spot, but Duncan, oblivious of his mother's reaction, called out a greeting to Freddie, who waved back and got up to meet him. The others turned round and saw Duncan and Elaine standing at the corner of the house, Elaine's face mask-like.

Tim got up and with his innate good manners, stepped forward and ushered her to the table.

"Hello Elaine, come and join us. Have a glass of wine. When I came back just now, I found a barbecue in full swing."

With a superhuman effort, Elaine pasted a smile on her face. At least it seemed that Tim had not asked Kate. It must have been Gwen. She felt a wave of resentment towards Gwen, who had invited Kate to stay with her in Lyme Regis, but had never asked her. But Gwen was now holding out plates for her and Duncan. Duncan was soon munching a burger and chatting to Freddie, but Elaine declined any food, sipping at her wine instead. She knew good manners dictated that she should ask Kate about her exhibition, but she could barely bring herself to acknowledge Kate's presence. She sat down on the other side of Tim and said with studied casualness, "I thought we'd come round when you were home, to see if we can pin you down to go to Legoland this Saturday. It's a pity Sunday was so foul."

Tim sighed inwardly. It was the last thing he wanted to do. But he had seen Elaine's stricken face when she had appeared round the side of the house and taken in the scene which had confronted her. He supposed he would have to bite the bullet and go to Legoland.

"Alright, we'll go on Saturday." He turned to the children. "That okay, team? Legoland on Saturday? You can get back to your art lessons the week after."

The children chorused their approval with the caveat from Amy that she wasn't going to go on anything "spooky or scary". Turning to Kate, Amy asked, "Can you come too, Kate?"

Tim was aware that Elaine stiffened and her hand tightened on her glass.

Kate smiled, but shook her head. "I can't, Amy. I'm in the middle of painting the house. I must get it finished."

Amy stuck out her bottom lip, but was somewhat placated when Kate added, "Some other time maybe."

The sun was setting, sending long, low rays across the garden and bathing the old house in a golden light. Freddie got up and insisted that Kate and Duncan should come and see the new games and exercise room. Kate willingly agreed and followed the children to the barn at the far end of the garden where it bordered the field, leaving Elaine sitting alone with Tim, while Gwen started to clear the table and take the plates and leftovers into the house.

Resisting the urge to make an acid remark about Kate always seeming to be around, Elaine said in a low voice to Tim, "It's ages since we had an evening together. Since your mother's here to babysit, why don't you come over for dinner tomorrow night?"

Tim looked at Elaine and saw the desperation in her eyes, no matter how hard she tried to appear casual and relaxed about the invitation. He noticed how her hand shook slightly as she raised her glass to her lips, and he did not have the heart to refuse her.

"Okay, thanks. About eight?"

Elaine let out the breath she hadn't realised she was holding. She smiled and lightly touched his cheek with the tips of her fingers.

"Eight would be perfect."

When Kate came back from the inspection of the barn, Elaine stood up. She called over to where the children were throwing a ball for Binky. "Come along, Duncan. We'd better go." She went over and gave Gwen a kiss on the cheek as she came out of the house, and in her victory she also felt able to say a casual goodbye to Kate. Then she turned to Tim and gave him a light kiss on the lips, and said, just loudly enough for Kate to hear, "See you tomorrow, Tim. Why don't you get a taxi, so that you can have a decent bit to drink with dinner."

Tim, noticing how Kate turned quickly away and picked up the salad bowl from the table, knew that Elaine was showing Kate that he was her property and that they had an assignation for the following night. He wished he hadn't agreed to it or to the day out on Saturday. But he had to go through with it now. When Elaine had gone, Kate helped to clear up and then, thanking Gwen and Tim, said she too ought to be going. It was getting dark by this time, so they all decided to form a guard of honour and see her home. The little exchange between Elaine and Tim seemed to have cast a shadow over Kate's spirits, but she put on a good act of appearing light-hearted as they tumbled out into the lane and walked to Kate's cottage singing "One Man went to Mow" at the tops of their voices.

At Elaine's the following night, Duncan had been packed off to his room and his PlayStation, while Tim and Elaine had dinner by candlelight in the dining room. Tim was concerned about how Duncan would interpret the intimate dinner Tim was having with his mother, but Elaine airily dismissed his reservations, saying that Duncan was not one to read anything into it. After dinner, Elaine drew Tim down to sit beside her on the sofa in the sitting room, while soft music played in the background. It was all so clichéd that Tim would have laughed inwardly if he had not felt so ill at ease. He had been annoyed at Elaine for making sure that Kate knew that he would be seeing Elaine tonight, and he really had not been in the mood to go out. Elaine tried to ply him with wine, but he had deliberately brought his car so that he would have an excuse not to drink much.

Irritated but undeterred, Elaine decided now was a good a time as any to broach the subject of Tuscany again.

"Tim, you know I mentioned to you about us all going to Tuscany in August?"

Tim groaned inwardly. He had hoped she had forgotten about Tuscany.

366

"Vaguely," he said noncommittally.

"Well, I was getting worried about leaving it too late to book a villa, so I've gone and booked one!"

Tim's head snapped round. "You've what?" He looked at her incredulously.

"You were taking so long to make up your mind. I've asked the Hunters, and they are definitely up for it. Oh please come, Tim. I don't think I can afford the whole of the other half of the cost myself."

Tim got up and started pacing the room. "I wish you hadn't done that!" he said in exasperation. "For one thing, I'm not sure I can get away. When have you booked it for?"

"The 3rd of August. For a week. I'm sorry Tim, I got the impression you wanted to go. I've already put down a deposit, which I'll lose if I renege." She got up and went up to him, pressing her body against his. "Don't be cross. Come and sit down. Look, I've got some pictures." She pulled him down to sit beside her on the sofa again. She opened her iPad which was sitting on the coffee table in front of her, already open at a website about holidays in Tuscany and scrolled down, stopping at a photograph of the terrace of a beautiful villa with a swimming pool in the background.

"Doesn't it look gorgeous? We'd have such a wonderful time... all that sun and lovely food and wine, and the kids would love the pool."

"Elaine, of course it's very nice, but you shouldn't have assumed we would be joining you. Work is hectic at the moment. I can't give you a yes or no just yet, but don't worry, I'll make up my share of the cost, whether we come or not."

Elaine felt like screaming out, "You've *got* to come! It's not just the money. It'll be so humiliating to tell the Hunters you won't be joining us! And I *need* you there!" But with an immense effort, she smiled and said, "At least think about it Tim, darling. You need a relaxing holiday. We're having a chef and everything!" Shutting the iPad, she snuggled up to him and undid the next two buttons of his open-necked shirt, sliding her hands under the material to stroke his chest.

She started to kiss him and for a while he humoured her, but when she became more insistent, undoing the buttons of her own blouse and guiding his hand to her breast, he pulled back.

"Elaine, Duncan may walk in at any moment. And anyway, I really must be going. I've got an early breakfast meeting tomorrow. Got to be up at five." He gently extricated himself from her arms and stood up. Elaine looked up at him as he did up his buttons again, her hair dishevelled and her blouse gaping open, showing her bra. Her face was a mixture of emotions. There was anger and humiliation but also a vulnerability which made Tim feel guilty at his rejection of her. She had had too much to drink and it loosened her tongue.

"It's *her* isn't it?" she spat out. "Your bloody little artist friend. You've fallen for her, haven't you? Why did you have to go to her precious exhibition? What's it to you, unless you're in love with her? Then I find her at a barbecue at your house. I notice *I* was not asked! And tonight! You would never have pushed me off before! Have you slept with her?"

"No, of course not!" Even as he said it, he wished he had. "She has a boyfriend. There's nothing going on between us." In his irritation he nearly added, "And even if there were, it's none of your business" but he couldn't utter such harsh words to her. After all, in a way, it *was* her business. He *was* in a relationship of sorts with Elaine, even though emotionally it was almost completely one-sided. Instead he said, a little more mildly, "Look Elaine, please don't get into a state. It just doesn't feel right, with Duncan upstairs." He took her hands and pulled her up from the sofa, and gently did up her buttons. He kissed her on the lips. "Thank you for dinner. And I'll see you on Saturday for this trip to Legoland." He went out to the hall, slipped on his jacket and let himself out of the front door.

Elaine remained standing in the middle of the room, gazing blankly into space, slow tears rolling down her cheeks.

*

By the Friday, all the walls and the ceilings in Kate's cottage had been painted except for in the kitchen, which needed to be emptied of all the paraphernalia before painting could begin.

"I can manage this by myself," Kate said to Zachary as they inspected the kitchen. "It's so small, and there's not much ceiling to paint. It's mainly the woodwork of the cupboards and shelves to be glossed."

"Well, if you're sure. I'm very happy to come and do the ceiling when you've cleared the stuff out."

"No, there's really no need, thanks Zachary. I must finish the painting of the woodwork upstairs first, and I'll tackle this as and when. You've been a huge help. It would have taken me a lot longer on my own. Thank you so much!"

When Zachary had gone, Kate stood and looked appreciatively at the newly painted sitting room. The dingy yellowing walls had been transformed by the coat of white paint, causing the old beams to stand out in contrast. True to her word, Doreen had sent her a swatch of samples of various curtain materials. Kate flicked through them and decided on a plain terracotta colour which tied in with the pinkish colours of the old bricks around the fireplace. She was just about to go upstairs to resume her painting of the woodwork when she saw the empty nail where the framed Valentine card had hung. Going to the bureau where she had put it while the decorating was going on, she took it out and hung it back on the wall. She stood looking at it for a few moments, remembering the tragedy which lay behind it. Then she went up to the second bedroom where she resumed the painting of the woodwork around the window. She had already noticed that the window frame was rotten and cracking and the panes seemed a little loose. Eventually she would have to get it replaced. Finishing the window, she moved on to painting the door of the cupboard set into the wall.

The house was very quiet, with only the faint sound of the wind in the chimney which went up through the middle of the house. Kate had the cupboard door open and was about to start painting the shelf inside, when a waft of lavender scented air which seemed to come from the back of the cupboard drifted past her. The scent hung in the air for several minutes before fading away. She looked curiously into the cupboard to see if there

369

were any cracks through which air could be escaping from the chimney but could see no obvious ones. Gradually, she became aware of a prickling in the back of her neck and turned quickly, glancing round. A shaft of afternoon sunlight coming in through the window lit up a myriad dust motes which danced like fireflies. She had pulled her desk out away from the window and it stood in the middle of the floor. A stack of old canvases leaned against the wall and the mannequin Kate had used for the triptych stood in the corner near the window, draped in the old sheet Kate had been using to cover the furniture when she and Zachary were painting the walls and ceilings. Kate had dried the wig she had used for the painting and, for want of a better place to keep it, had put it on the head of the mannequin. Often when she came into the room, Kate would for a split-second think there was someone standing there. She put her feeling that there was someone in the room down to the mannequin in the corner and went on with her painting. But before she went to bed that night she went back into the room to see if there was any scent of lavender. She flicked on the switch, but there was a loud pop as the bulb blew.

That was the fourth bulb that had gone since she arrived at the cottage. Realising there must be a faulty connection, Kate made a mental note to have it looked at. A dark rectangle in the corner showed where Kate had left the cupboard door open because of the wet paint. There was no scent of lavender, only the smell of gloss paint. She went out of the room and closed the door.

Tim was still furious with Elaine for going ahead and booking the Tuscan villa and then resorting to emotional blackmail to get him to agree to the proposition. He conceded that the villa looked beautiful, and if it hadn't involved virtually acting as Elaine's significant other he would probably have liked the idea. But he knew that Elaine would use the holiday to enmesh herself more closely with him and the children. For one thing, his innate decency made him reluctant to give Elaine false hopes that she would one day marry him, because he was under no illusion that that was her end game. He also knew with certainty that he would never marry Elaine. He did not love her and never would. He had never done the running as far as Elaine was concerned. It had been she who had proposed that she did the school run and at the time, in his grief and confusion, it had seemed like the answer to at least one of his problems. It had been she who had proposed dinner dates and she who had instigated intimate little suppers at his house when the children were away. And it was always she who had initiated any lovemaking. Yes, he had gone along with it quite willingly, especially at the beginning. She had been very sweet and sympathetic and his body had ached for Claire and what they had had together. Elaine had provided some sort of relief in his loneliness; but now he was seeing another side of her. It was Elaine who was the needy one now. Her attitude to Kate bordered on the downright rude and, while Tim knew it was driven by jealousy and her love for him, it only served to alienate him further.

Trying to be honest with himself, he attempted to analyse whether his attitude to Elaine was coloured by how he felt about Kate. Did he hold out any hopes that Kate felt the same about him? There were times when their eyes met or the precious few occasions when he had kissed her lightly on the lips that he was sure there was a mutual hunger for each other. But he had also seen her with Jake, and they seemed somehow so *together.* The way Jake's arm would go possessively round her waist, the way he had cupped her face in his hands and kissed her at the gallery, the fact that he stayed the night at her house, all pointed to something more than friendship. Also, he was much more her age, extremely good looking and also an artist. How could he, Tim, expect Kate to be interested in him, a widower fifteen years older than she was, with two children?

He was not to know that the familiar body language he had noticed between Kate and Jake was the legacy of the mutual passion they had once shared and of two years of living together. He was not to know that for Kate at least, that passion was spent, and that now her feelings for Tim transcended anything she had ever felt for Jake.

The trip to Legoland was not a success from Elaine's point of view. The children and even Gwen had a whale of a time, but Elaine felt that Tim seemed distant and uncommunicative. She supposed it was because

371

she had booked the Tuscan villa off her own bat. But for God's sake, if she'd waited until he had made up his mind, all the villas would have gone. Men were so hopeless about that sort of thing. They needed a woman to organise things like holidays. Several times during the day, she tried to engage him in conversation, but he was monosyllabic and took every opportunity to accompany the boys on the various rides, which seemed to her mind an excuse to avoid her company. Gwen and Amy enthusiastically tried out the gentler rides and Elaine was left for the most part to stand around waiting for them. She was hot and thirsty, and thought longingly of the cold bottle of Sauvignon Blanc in her fridge.

*

Having painted all the woodwork in the rest of the cottage, apart from the doors which were stained black to match the beams, Kate tackled the kitchen. All the shelves and cupboards had to be emptied, and their contents cluttered up the sitting room, on the table and the floor. Even after finishing the shelves, she had to wait till the gloss was completely dry before replacing everything. Hardly able to move in the sitting room, Kate decided it was time to get back to work in the studio. She had been going there in the evenings to wait for the children to come home from school and had started working through some ideas. Now she needed to go and see Bill to ask him if he could make up some canvases for her. Though she now had some money in the bank or would have when the exhibition finished and Geoff transferred the money, less his commission, from the paintings she had sold, she knew she could afford to buy some ready-made canvases from the art shop or online. These would do for some of her pieces, but for the larger works, she needed canvases which were made to her specifications. She also wanted to experiment with irregular-shaped pieces, incorporating collage elements, for which it would be easier to work on board.

Leaving the clutter of the sitting room, she went to the studio and spent some time on the computer ordering some readymade canvases and some two-by-one lengths of timber for stretchers. She also ordered

372

another large roll of canvas, and some sheets of MDF, feeling a new sense of liberation in the fact that she now had the funds to order materials without worrying too much about the cost.

She started working through some ideas on paper, but in spite of a feeling of anticipation at starting on another phase of her work and though her mind was churning with ideas, there seemed to be an ache somewhere in her chest, which she knew derived from the knowledge that Tim was still seeing Elaine, going round to her house for dinner - and probably a lot more. The children had been enthusiastic when she had asked them how the day at Legoland had gone, but she was none the wiser as to how Tim had enjoyed it, apart from the information that he had gone on lots of rides.

That evening, when the children arrived back from school, Kate looked out of the window to see the red Volvo disappearing down the lane. What were Tim's feelings towards Elaine? How involved was he?

When the children came up to her after their supper, Amy asked, "Shall I get my mermaid sculpture out ready for our lesson tomorrow?"

"Yes, that's a good idea, and the papier mâché materials, then you can get started straightaway in the morning."

Freddie was looking critically at his painting of an eagle's head propped on the easel Tim had given him for his birthday in April. Kate had found out about his birthday just in time to rush out and buy him a couple of canvases. Now she stood looking at the painting with Freddie. The draughtsmanship was excellent and he was quickly getting used to the medium of oil paint, applying it with increasing confidence and a good use of tone.

"It's really coming on, Freddie," Kate said truthfully. She looked at the photograph from which Freddie was working. "You've caught the fierceness of the eye so well, and the curve of the beak, and the light on the feathers here."

"I've decided I'm going to be a wildlife artist as well as an entomologist," Freddie announced with conviction. "I'll do painting in the morning and entomology in the afternoon. And I'm going to go on expeditions to discover new species in rain forests and swamps and things.

373

I can do drawings of insects and paint them with watercolours."

Not to be outdone, Amy interposed, "And *I'm* going to be a pianist like Mummy *and* I'm going to go exploring to find mermaids."

Kate remembered the first evening when she had come down to see the cottage for the first time and had seen Amy playing the piano through the drawing room window.

"When do you do your piano practice, Amy?" she asked.

"When Daddy comes back and we go back home," Amy said, turning the somewhat lumpy mermaid round to look at it from all angles. "I used to do it after Mrs B. gave us supper, but now we come up here."

"It must get a bit late to be practising by then."

"Yes, sometimes I'm too tired."

Kate was thoughtful and later when Tim came home, she broached the subject of Amy's practising with him.

"Tim, Amy says that she can't do her piano practice till you come home, which is a bit late isn't it? If you like, I can come and wait with them in the house while she does her practice until you get back, or if she's done enough, we can come up here afterwards to wait for you."

Tim looked at her gratefully. "Well, it has been a bit of a problem actually. She's often quite tired by the time I get back and sometimes the practice doesn't get done. Her teacher says she's got real ability, but she needs to keep up the practice. She tries to do extra at the weekends, but it's not always possible."

"Okay then, when I see them arriving back home, I'll pop over, and after Mrs B. has given them their supper, Amy can do her practice."

"That'll be great! But won't it be interrupting your work too much?"

Kate assured him that it was no problem and the suggestion was agreed on. It was only later that the thought struck Kate that there was one person who would find the new arrangement galling. Elaine would probably see it as a new ruse of Kate's to insinuate her way into Tim's affections. Kate bit her lip apprehensively.

Well, there was nothing she could do about it now. Maybe Elaine would not find out.

But Elaine did find out. Amy's chatter in the car about a new piece of music she had been given to learn and how she was going to practise it that evening when Kate came over, ensured that. The information, not particularly significant in itself, served to push Elaine nearer to the chasm of despair that seemed to be opening up in front of her. Her mind imagined a series of scenarios in which Kate spent more and more time in Tim's company. Once the children were in bed, did Kate stay on for a glass of wine with Tim? And what else might that lead to? Or perhaps Tim went round to her house when the children were asleep? After all she was only just down the lane. He could easily slip out for an hour or so, leaving Binky on guard. If she had been thinking rationally, she would have known he would never dream of leaving the children alone for more than a few moments.

He had still not said whether he was coming to Tuscany. The conviction grew in her mind that he was reluctant to come because he would rather be near Kate than go to Italy.

Elaine's cheeks burned when she thought of the humiliation she had felt when her seduction technique had not worked the night Tim had last come to dinner, brushing her off with the spurious excuse that Duncan might come in. She thought of the times they had made love and her body ached for him. He had seemed passionate then, she thought, not realising that it was sheer, desperate loneliness which had given Tim's lovemaking the semblance of desire for her.

It was only when Kate had come along that he had started cooling towards her, and Amy's revelation that afternoon that Kate was going to spend every evening in Tim's house was the last straw. Sitting alone, staring unseeingly at the television screen, with her glass of wine at her elbow, her imagination went into overdrive. Were they together? Was Kate still at Tim's? Was he even now walking her back home in the dark? She glanced at the clock on the mantelpiece. Getting on for a quarter past ten. She got up and went up the stairs to Duncan's bedroom. Softly she opened the door and looked in. Duncan was soundly asleep, his head nearly buried in the duvet. She shut the door and, going downstairs,

375

pushed her feet into some boots and picked up her cream coloured jacket. Then she hesitated. Replacing it on the coat hook in the porch, she chose a dark blue hooded raincoat and put it on. Grabbing the car keys, she went out to the garage and drove the car out. It was starting to drizzle slightly as she eased the car out onto the road. It took only a couple of minutes to reach the other end of the village, where she parked at the end of Tuckers Lane. It was getting on for midsummer, and there would normally have been some residual light in the sky even at this hour, but the heavy rain clouds were cutting out the last of the evening light. She got out of the car and closed the door quietly. She made her way down Tuckers Lane, walking on the grass verge to muffle her footsteps.

As she rounded the bend in the lane, two dim rectangles of light glowed from the curtained windows of Kate's sitting room, a small one at the front of the house and a larger one at the side. Silently, Elaine opened the garden gate and walked carefully down the uneven path. She stood at the front door listening for voices. Hearing nothing, she crept round the side of the cottage to stand outside the window, her ears pressed to the pane. Nothing. Why did the curtains have to be drawn? Suddenly, she saw the outline of a figure approaching the window and dodged back to flatten herself against the wall of the house. Kate opened the curtain a little and peered out into the darkness, cupping her hands round her eyes to see past her reflection. Then she closed the curtain again.

Elaine let out her breath and noiselessly made her way back to the front of the house. She froze as a light went on in the room to the left of the front door, which Elaine realised was the kitchen, but then it dimmed as Kate drew the curtains on that window too. Cutting across the little lawn to avoid walking on the path, Elaine slipped out of the gate. It was very dark and Elaine, no longer driven on by the adrenaline that had made her oblivious to the fact that she was a lone woman out in the dark, started to feel nervous. But she had to know that Tim was in his own house and not with Kate. She pulled her hood more tightly over her head and started down the lane towards Woodcote, still walking on the grass verge, trampling down the cow parsley and soaking her boots. The front of the house was in darkness, so she went round to the side, keeping well back as

376

she passed the kitchen window. The light was on but the kitchen was empty, so she continued round to the back, keeping clear of the light which spilled out through the windows of the family room.

Tim was sitting on the sofa, reading the paper. The television was on, with a weather girl gesturing at a map of the British Isles. Elaine had built up such an irrational and vivid mind picture of Tim being with Kate that the relief of seeing that Tim was at home on his own made her choke out a little sob. Immediately, she clapped her hand over her mouth, but Tim did not look up. She drew a shaky breath and for another long moment stood gazing at him, before turning away and going back round the side of the house and out into the lane, shutting the gate quietly behind her. The walk back to her car seemed much longer somehow. The hawthorn hedge was a line of deeper blackness on the right-hand side. Once she was past Kate's cottage, she stepped off the verge and into the lane, heedless of the sound of her footsteps on the track or the unseen puddles she stepped into and hurried back to the car.

As she walked on round the corner, a figure detached itself from the cover of the hawthorn hedge and stood looking at her dimly seen, retreating back. A match flared and the smell of cigarette smoke drifted out on the damp air.

*

Kate's orders of wood and canvas arrived within a few days and she and Bill worked together to make up a good stack of canvases. They worked companionably, Bill making the frames and stretching the canvas over them and Kate priming them ready for painting. Bill also brought along his electric jigsaw which Kate used to cut her MDF sheets into the curving, irregular shapes she needed for a particular series of paintings she wanted to work on. Lily would come up for a chat sometimes, always bringing with her a plate of rock buns or cakes straight out of the oven. In the evenings, Kate looked out for the children coming back from school in the red Volvo and after Elaine had driven away, Kate would lock up the studio and go down to the house. Having got the children's supper ready,

377

Lily was able to go home, leaving them in Kate's charge. Walking to the door with Lily one evening, Kate stopped her.

"Lily, you must tell me what I can buy Bill apart from tobacco for his pipe. I want to say thank you for all the work he's done for me."

Lily, taking off her apron and tucking it into her large black handbag, gave her a mock-severe look.

"Kate, I told you, he loves doing it. Believe me, you are actually doing *him* a favour. Otherwise he mopes around the house getting under my feet. In fact he was quite glum when all your canvases were finished and there was nothing left for him to do. I know you don't usually get your paintings framed, but he was wondering if you would like him to do some framing for you once the paintings were finished."

Kate's eyes lit up. "Well, there certainly will be some which would benefit. *A Dream of Owls* would have been better framed." She thought for a moment. "I can buy the mouldings online and if Bill really does want to do it, that would be fantastic!"

"Good! Thank goodness for that! Bill will be delighted!" Lily patted Kate on the arm and let herself out of the door. "Bye for now. And make sure Amy eats her cabbage. She's quite likely to try to palm it off onto Binky!"

Once the children had had their supper, Freddie usually went into the family room to finish any homework he had not done at school, while Amy went into the drawing room to do her piano practice. Once she had cleared up the supper things, Kate often went and listened to Amy practising. She was surprised at how disciplined the little girl was. First, she spent fifteen minutes on scales, playing them over and over until she was fluent, then she would move on to her pieces. The child obviously inherited her mother's talent and seemed to lose herself in the music. Kate loved listening to her. Sometimes Tim phoned saying he would be a bit late, in which case, if Amy had practised enough, Kate would take the children up to the studio to wait for him while she got on with her work, or if he was going to be very late, Kate would get the children to bed. Tim was always very apologetic if he was late, but Kate was pleased that there was something she could do to reciprocate for the use of the studio. The

378

long summer days meant that it was usually broad daylight when she made her way home and by now the memory of the attack was not as vivid, so she had no qualms about making the short walk home on her own.

Just occasionally, when she was on her own in the cottage at night, she got the feeling that there was someone outside. Was it Vince? Or was it perhaps a deer walking softly past the window?

Chapter XVIII

By the time the exhibition closed after three weeks, Kate had sold all but one of her paintings, Mimi was left with two of her sculptures and Grace and Bea had both sold all of their pieces. Zachary had also done well, having sold fourteen of his carvings. When Geoff phoned Kate on the Friday following the close of the exhibition, he pronounced it an unqualified success.

"I've transferred the proceeds from the paintings you sold, less my commission, to your bank account," Geoff informed her. "But you'll need to come up sometime soon to take your remaining painting away, and you could pick up Zachary's money too. I wish the dear chap had a bank account; it makes paying him rather unwieldy.

Kate laughed. "Yes, he's a bit of a throwback. He can't be doing with the trappings of modern life. It would be progress to drag him into the twentieth century, let alone the twenty-first! At least he has a mobile phone now." She paused and said more seriously, "I'll come up to pick up the painting and Zachary's money. I think I'll drive up. I don't think I'd feel happy walking around with all that cash on me. Also, it would be easier as I have to bring the painting back. Which one is it?"

"One of the smaller ones. A shadowy figure of a woman standing by a river. A bit spooky."

"Oh, yes. Actually, I'm rather glad it didn't sell. It's sort of connected to my cottage."

"Hmmm... as I say, rather spooky. Anyway, when do you think you can come up? How about Monday?"

"Yes, that's fine with me."

"Good. Could you ask Mimi to come and get her pieces too? Bea's sold all hers, but she might want to come over. I thought we could have a little chat about how it all went. I was just about to phone them, but if you're going to... I've already told Grace. Hopefully you could all come

380

on Monday."

"I'll phone them. See you Monday."

"Bye Kate. And well done!"

"Thanks for all you've done for us, Geoff. Bye."

Kate rang off and immediately keyed in Mimi's number. When Mimi answered, Kate could hear loud chatter and music in the background.

"Is that you Kate?" Mimi bellowed into the phone. "You'll have to speak up, there's a huge racket going on in here. I'm in the Slug. Folk night. Bea's here and," she lowered her voice slightly, "she's actually eating something and drinking a glass of cider!"

"Wonders will never cease! Listen Mimi, I'm coming up on Monday to collect a painting that didn't sell. He wants you, Bea and Grace to come over too. Can you make it?"

"I can. I'll just check with Bea. Hang on." There was a pause during which the confused chatter and music continued to emanate from the phone, then Mimi came back on the line.

"Yes, she can make it. What time?"

"Late morning. About eleven?"

"Okay. But, hang on. Why don't you stay for a few days? You could doss down at mine. There are some good exhibitions on. And don't you want to go and see Jake's new installation? Apparently you named it!"

Kate thought for a moment. "Well, I could maybe stay for a couple of days. I'll have to check if Mrs B. can look after the children in the evening."

"What children? Oh, you mean your dishy stockbroker's kids!"

"He's not a stockbroker and he's not mine! But yes, those kids."

"Well, see if you can get away. It'll be cool. We didn't have time to do stuff when you were up the other week."

Kate rang off and also called Grace to arrange to meet at Geoff's gallery on the Monday.

The next morning, before going to the studio, Kate called in at the Babbidges' cottage to ask Lily if she would be able to revert for a few days

381

to her previous arrangement of staying with the children until Tim got home.

"Oh yes, dear," Lily said without hesitation. "You go and have a nice time with your friends. Stay as long as you like."

"It'll only be for three days at the most, and I'll have to let Tim know what I'm doing, but thanks Mrs B, it's very good of you."

"Not at all. Now sit you down and have a cuppa. I'm just about to make one for Bill."

Later, in the studio, Kate surveyed the stack of pristine new canvases leaning against the wall with satisfaction and a strong sense of anticipation. She was looking forward to getting started on her painting again. At the same time, she felt that a few days with her friends, combined with visits to various exhibitions, would help her recharge her batteries and kick-start what promised to be a new direction in her work.

That evening, when Kate mentioned to Tim that she would be away for a few days, he was at pains to assure her that there was no problem. Inwardly however, his first thought was that she would probably be seeing Jake. She might even be staying with him. The thought caused him no small degree of anguish, especially late that night when the kids were in bed and he was sitting at his desk in the study, attempting to do some work. Was Kate going to be staying with Jake or with one of her girlfriends? He told himself to be realistic. She was bound to be staying with Jake. He had seen their closeness at the exhibition, as well as Jake's possessiveness and their intimate body language. And yet... and yet... There seemed to be long periods when they did not see each other. What *was* the truth of their relationship? The ringing of the phone at his elbow startled him out of his reverie. It was Elaine.

"Tim, darling, sorry to call so late. You weren't in bed, were you?"

"Hello Elaine. No, I'm in my study. Got some work to do."

"Well, I won't keep you. I just wanted to know what you've decided about Tuscany. We have to book the flights and it would be good to be able to travel together."

Tim's heart sank. He knew he would have to decide soon, one way or the other. He had put the issue to the back of his mind, not wanting to think about it, but he knew it was not being fair to Elaine. True, she had gone ahead and booked it without properly consulting him, and in a way it was her problem if he decided not to go. But he realised how devastated she would be if he said he wasn't going. Quite apart from keeping her on side as regards doing the school run, he was very aware of the hurt he would inflict on Elaine's hungry and lonely heart. But if he agreed to go, wouldn't it give her the message that their relationship had developed to a more involved status? There was also the question of his work. He hadn't yet decided if he could spare the time. And if he could, did he want to spend it doing something he really did not want to do?

"Look, Elaine, can you give me a couple more days? I'll definitely let you know by Monday evening. I have to talk to some people, sort out whether I can get away."

There was a short silence at the other end of the line. Then Elaine replied, her voice tight with the effort she was putting into sounding casual, "Fine. But I really need to know no later than that, Tim."

"I'll definitely let you know in a couple of days."

"Alright. Talk to you soon. Goodnight Tim."

"Goodnight Elaine."

Elaine crashed the phone's handset down on the cradle and stood staring at it. He was going to back out of it! He was going to make some excuse about work, saying he was too busy. But it wouldn't be because of that. It was because he was in love with Kate. If it had been Kate asking him, he would have gone like a shot. Look at the way he had taken her down to Gwen's that time, when she herself had never been invited. Damn and blast her to hell! She ranged round the room and into the hall. Catching sight of the car keys on the tray on the hall table, she snatched them up and slammed out of the house. At least Duncan was at his father's that weekend. His father! There was another man who had let her down. Left her for a simpering, devious, little airhead.

She got into the car and sent the gravel in the drive flying as she screeched out into the main road, narrowly avoiding a passing car. When

383

she got to Tuckers Lane, she barely slowed till she came to a slithering stop in the middle of the lane outside Kate's cottage.

Round the side of the house, the figure which was leaning against the wall walked to the corner and peered cautiously round at Elaine as she stormed down the path to the front door.

Kate had heard the sound of the car coming up the lane and the clunk of the car door slamming, followed soon after by the loud rapping of the door knocker. She went to the door and called through it.

"Who is it?"

"It's me, Elaine. I need to talk to you."

Kate groaned inwardly. Elaine sounded very agitated. Was she going to make another scene? What had set her off this time? She opened the door.

Elaine pushed past her and stepped down into the room. Kate, shutting the door, walked past her to stand by the window, her hands clutching the back of a chair. Elaine turned to face her. She was obviously making a supreme effort to appear calm, but there was a deranged look in her eyes, and she restlessly twisted the car keys clutched in her hand. She said, without preamble, "I thought we'd agreed that you were going to back off from Tim."

"I don't know what you mean." Kate stared at Elaine, wondering what particular incident had caused her agitation.

"Oh, don't play the innocent with me. You know exactly what I mean." Elaine's voice rose as she walked to the window and faced Kate from the other side of the table. "Inviting him to exhibitions, taking on more babysitting to wriggle your way into his affections. And now he's probably going to say they can't come to Tuscany in August. He'll say it's because of work, but it'll just be an excuse!"

"Tuscany? What's that to do with me? I don't know anything about him going to Tuscany!"

"That's the point. He probably won't come. And I've booked the villa, thinking he'd agreed to it. I can't afford to pay his share as well and there's a penalty if I back out altogether. Also, the Hunters are coming

384

and they think Tim will be there. Amy would be company for their daughter and Freddie for Duncan."

"But what has all this to do with me?" In spite of herself, and in the face of Elaine's distress, Kate couldn't help a secret surge of hope at the implication that Tim may not go on this holiday to Tuscany.

"Oh, you know perfectly well! But don't kid yourself that Tim is in love with you. He's only trying to keep you sweet so that you go on looking after the kids."

"Elaine, I offered to look after the kids because I feel indebted to Tim for letting me use the studio. That's the only reason."

Elaine stared at the girl standing white-faced before her. For a moment she almost believed what Kate had said. Could it be true that Kate was innocent of any machinations regarding Tim? Well, it was irrelevant anyway. The fact was that she was convinced that Tim had fallen for her, whether she had encouraged him or not. The mere sight of Kate, who despite the fact that she was dressed in her shapeless painting clothes, her face devoid of make-up and her hair dragged back into a scruffy ponytail, still managed to look ravishing, filled her with despair. And no matter what she said, Kate must have some sort of inkling that Tim was attracted to her. A woman knew these things. And a woman also knew when a man stopped finding her attractive, she thought with a fresh surge of anguish. In spite of her best efforts to appear in control, she felt the tears well up and spill down her cheeks. Angrily she brushed them away, leaving smudges of black eyeliner under her eyes, and dragged a hand through her hair.

"Don't take him away from me," she suddenly said bleakly, her voice breaking on a sob. She felt her pride fall away from her like a carapace, leaving her vulnerable, lonely inner self exposed to the gaze of this young woman.

Kate looked at her in astonishment. The controlled, immaculately groomed and attractive woman was gone, and in her place stood a dishevelled, wild eyed creature, her face streaked with make-up, her mouth set in a rictus of pain. She was at a loss as to what to say to her. Though she disliked Elaine, her heart went out to her. And to feel that she herself was the cause of this woman's anguish was in turn a source of distress to herself. She cast around for some comforting words to say.

"But you said yourself that Tim was only interested in me for babysitting purposes. In that case, you have nothing to worry about."

Elaine was silent for a moment. She turned to the window and opening the curtains roughly, stood staring out into the darkness.

The figure which had been standing with his ear pressed to the pane, jumped back and flattened himself against the wall.

Elaine turned back to look at Kate. "Oh, I don't know! All I know is he changed towards me as soon as you arrived on the scene. And you've just gone on and on, getting more and more involved in his life and the kids' lives. Admit it! You've fallen for him, haven't you? *Haven't you?*" Elaine's voice rose to a shriek. She came round the table and gripped Kate by the upper arms and shook her. Kate, taken by surprise at the suddenness of the movement, at first seemed powerless when confronted with the surprising strength of the older woman, her head snapping back and forth with the ferocity of the shaking. Then, adrenaline kicked in and she tore herself free of Elaine's grasp. Her heart pounding, she walked to the front door and wrenched it open.

"Please leave, Elaine," she said levelly. "Your relationship with Tim is nothing to do with me. You'll have to work things out between the two of you."

Elaine stared at her for a few more seconds, then she flung her head back and ran her hands through her hair again. She marched to the door and without another word, went out into the night, her footsteps fading as she went down the brick path and out into the lane.

Kate shut the door and stood leaning against it, shaking with shock, her mind in turmoil. What had set off such distress in Elaine? What was all that about Tuscany? It was the first she had heard of it, but it seemed as though Tim was not too keen on the idea. Elaine was obviously frantic that he should go and was probably pinning all her hopes on the holiday cementing their relationship. She gave a shuddering sigh and sat down heavily on the sofa, her head in her hands. The thought that she was the cause of such unhappiness to someone else was anathema to her, but how could she back out of her commitments to the children without explaining why? No, she couldn't do that. She thought of the agony in Elaine's face, of the crumbling of her pride. The words "Don't take him away from me!" echoed in her mind.

She knew what she must do.

Meanwhile, Elaine, getting back into the car, began to reverse down the lane. She did not dare to go down to where she could turn outside Tim's house, in case he saw her. The lane was dark and the reversing light was not much help. She forced herself to go slowly, twisting round in the seat to look over her shoulder. She was approaching the end of the lane when there was a rap on the driver's window. She let out a startled cry as a face loomed into view on the other side of the glass. Instinctively, her foot pressed down on the accelerator, and the car jerked backwards, the near-side wheel slipping over the lip of the ditch, then the car stalled. In panic, she slammed it into neutral, flicked on the door locks and fumbled with the ignition. The face reappeared and the man's mouth came up against the glass.

"Wait, I'm not going to hurt yer. Open the window, woman. You'll be interested in what I have to say."

Elaine shot him another terrified glance and frantically turned on the ignition again. The car roared into life, but the rear offside wheel was over the edge of the ditch and the other rear wheel spun on the slippery grass and mud of the verge. The front tyres churned up the unmetalled surface of the lane ineffectually. She heard his voice again, muffled by the glass between them.

"I'll push yer out. Just listen, can't you?"

She stopped revving the engine and turned to look at the man stooping to peer into the car. She couldn't see him very clearly in the darkness, but what she did see did nothing to allay her fears. The face was fleshy and unshaven, in contrast to his shaven head, and the moist lips pushed up against the glass made her shudder.

Who was he? What the hell was he talking about? What did he want? She desperately revved the engine again, but the car seemed to slip

387

further backwards. Seriously frightened now, she looked round wildly. The main road was still at least twenty yards away and she had come out without even her mobile phone. She heard his voice again.

"Just open the window a tad."

She had no alternative. She gave a short jab to the window button and the glass slid down enough for a crack to open up. The man put his mouth to it.

"Yer got problems with 'er down the lane? I can help yer there."

Elaine's mind whirled. What did he know about that? Who *was* he?

She answered him, her voice shrill. "What do you mean?"

"I mean I can fix it that 'er lover boy would never want to look at 'er again."

Elaine stared at the wet mouth so close on the other side of the window, the teeth bared in a grin. Overriding her horror at the implication in his words, however, was the phrase "lover boy". He obviously meant Tim. He must somehow know that he and Kate were lovers. If so, how? It didn't matter. She had been right. There *was* something going on between them. The agony of what seemed to be a confirmation of her fears tore through her, almost overriding her fear of the bulky figure beside the car. Her hands gripped the steering wheel convulsively. The man spoke again.

"I can see to it that 'er pretty face has a little makeover. That'll stop 'im sniffing round 'er for good an' all. And I've got me own reasons."

Elaine heard herself answering, "What would you do?"

"Maybe acid – or a nice sharp blade." The man's hand went to his pocket and drew out a large penknife which he opened up, touching the blade lightly with his thumb while Elaine stared at it in fascinated horror.

"'Course it'll cost yer. Five hundred quid - cheap at the price." Vince snapped the knife shut and stuffed it back in his pocket.

"Think about it. Here, I'll give yer me phone number." He rummaged round in his pocket and dragged out a crumpled betting slip and a stub of a pencil. He scribbled a number on the paper and pushed it through the gap in the window. It fell down into the side pocket in the door.

"Now we'd better get yer out of 'ere 'adn't we? Wouldn't do to 'ave lover boy find yer stuck 'ere in the morning, would it? Put 'er in first an' I'll get be'ind and push."

Numbly, Elaine did as he ordered. The man got down into the ditch and Elaine revved the engine till she felt the tyres bite as the car began to move forward. As soon as she felt herself on firm ground again, she wrenched the wheel round and, going as fast as she dared, continued reversing till she reached the end of the lane and recklessly backed the car out into the road. Taking a long, shuddering breath of relief, she forced herself to slow down as she drove through the village, and it was only when she was back at home gulping at a large brandy did the shaking in her hands start to subside.

*

When the children came clattering up the stairs for their lesson the next morning, Kate did her best to appear normal. Freddie, who was working on a wire and plaster sculpture of a praying mantis, was soon absorbed in his work, and Amy prattled away while making a family of owls out of clay.

"This is the father, this is the mother and these are the two children owls," she announced when she had finished, surveying the owl family lined up in front of her.

"Most owls do have mummies," she added solemnly, tweaking the beak of the mother owl gently.

Freddie glanced at her. "So do humans," he said quietly.

The little girl's mouth suddenly turned down at the corners and her eyes filled with tears. "I wish we still had a mummy," she said, a catch in her voice.

Kate came over and put an arm round her shoulders, bending down to her level. "She's watching over you, I know it," she said softly, stroking the hair out of the child's eyes. "She's very close, it's just that you can't see her."

389

Amy instinctively looked around her, then her eyes came to rest on Kate's face.

"I wish you could be our visible mummy," she said. Her clayey hands came up and she wrapped her arms round Kate's neck, burying her face on her shoulder. Kate held her tightly for a long moment, stroking her hair, then gently drew away.

"Come on, let's put these chaps on the shelf to dry. I hope the beaks don't break off."

Amy got up and bustled around helping to clear up, and by the time Tim came up to collect her and Freddie, she was back to her usual, cheerful self. Kate did notice though, that Freddie remained quieter than normal.

Kate had not expected to see Tim that morning, since the children usually made their own way back to the house at the end of the lesson, but today he came up to fetch them.

"Kate, I was wondering if you could do us a huge favour," he said, the inflection in his voice making it into a question.

"Of course," Kate said, glancing up from wiping the table down.

"Well, it's a bit of a cheek asking you, but Amy needs some summer clothes. There's a possibility that we'll be going to Italy in August, and anyway she's grown out of most of the clothes she was wearing last year. I can just about manage getting clothes for Freddie, who also needs some things, but I'm a bit clueless with girls' stuff. It would be good to have you there to help her try things on, since I can't go into the ladies' changing rooms."

Kate hesitated a microsecond. It was not that she didn't want to do it. She did, very much. But the last time she had resolved to make some distance between herself and Tim, he had asked her down to Lyme Regis and now, just when she had every intention of renewing that resolve in response to Elaine's impassioned pleas, here was Tim asking her to act like a surrogate mother, by helping to buy Amy's clothes. But of course, she couldn't refuse to do it.

"I'd love to!" she said. "It'll be fun!"

"Great! We'll go and have some lunch in Guildford first. Set us up for the afternoon." He looked at Freddie who was liberally daubed with plaster and at Amy's clayey hands.

"I'll just get these two artistic geniuses to clean themselves up first."

Kate laughed. "I'm not much better! I'll pop back home and change."

"Great. Pick you up in ten minutes."

As they disappeared down the stairs, Kate heard a barrage of questions coming from the children about Italy, since his remark to Kate was the first they had heard of it.

Kate for her part felt her heart sink, but thought that at least Elaine would be placated if he did decide to go.

The shopping expedition was a success on the whole. They had lunch upstairs in an old restaurant looking down into the high street and Kate would have enjoyed it more if she hadn't been worrying about the situation with Elaine. After lunch, Kate had taken charge of finding some summer clothes and new underwear for Amy, all the while trying to persuade her to buy the occasional garment which wasn't pink, while Tim and Freddie had taken much less time in choosing new jeans, shorts and T-shirts for Freddie.

Later, stopping to drop off Kate at her gate on their return, Tim turned to Kate gratefully.

"Bye, Kate, and thank you so much for your help today."

"I really enjoyed it – and thanks for a nice lunch."

"Have a good time in London." He hesitated, then voiced with enforced casualness, the question which had been hovering at the back of his mind. "Where will you stay?"

It was the moment she had been dreading.

"Oh, I'm staying at Jake's," she said lightly. "Though I'll be spending most of the time going to exhibitions with Mimi and the others."

She saw the change in Tim's face, and she wished she could snatch back the lie. For a second he looked into her eyes, then he dropped his gaze, and with a forced smile on his face, said again, "Well, have a good time. See you next week."

391

"Yes, I'll be back on Thursday morning, so I'll be here for the kids in the evening."

"Okay, Kate. Bye, and thanks again."

"Bye Tim." She turned round to the children in the back. "Bye, you two. See you on Thursday."

She got out of the car and Tim moved off, with Amy waving through the window. As she stood and watched it disappear round the bend, Kate felt a wave of desolation sweep over her. She turned and walked down the garden path and let herself into the house, the tears blurring her vision.

In the back seat of the car, Freddie had immediately noticed the slight slump of his father's shoulders and the alteration in his expression, even though he could only see his father's profile, and instinctively knew it was to do with what Kate had said about staying with Jake. Right from the start, when Kate had first come into their lives, he had noticed that his father was happier when she was there. He had also noticed that, as at the art exhibition, when that man Jake was around, his father seemed ill at ease. Jake was a threat to his father's happiness, he was sure of it.

That evening, Tim sat at the garden table on the terrace at the back of the house, looking down the garden to the fields beyond, which were bathed in the slanting rays of the setting sun. The ice in his gin and tonic clinked as he took a long sip. So she *was* staying with Jake! And there he was thinking that Kate had feelings for himself. He realised that his procrastination about going to Italy with Elaine had been bound up with the hope that Kate cared for him. How wrong he had been! What he had hoped was an attraction to him had merely been Kate's innate friendliness shining through in her eyes. He smiled self-mockingly to himself.

Well, you've got your answer now, he thought. She would hardly be staying with Jake if she wasn't involved in a relationship with him. She would surely stay with Mimi or one of the other girls. He felt the chance of happiness slip inexorably away from him - the chance which he had thought would never come again after Claire died, but which had been beckoning to him ever since he had met Kate, in spite of all his misgivings about whether she could ever care for him. It was time he stopped deluding himself. Kate only thought of him as a friend and was very appreciative of the loan of the studio. That was all. He drained his glass. He knew what he would say to Elaine on Monday.

Kate was glad she had the distraction of her few days in London. When Tim had driven off down the lane, she had felt sick at heart, a feeling which persisted when she and Mimi met the others at Geoff's gallery. The thought of Tim's face when she had told him she was staying at Jake's remained at the back of her mind even when visiting the various exhibitions Mimi had lined up for them to see, but it would have been worse if she had been on her own.

As it was, Mimi shot her a thoughtful, questioning glance now and again. For all her extrovert zaniness, Mimi had a great deal of empathy when it came to other people's feelings and it seemed something was not right with Kate. She longed to ask her what was wrong but, unusually for her, she kept her own counsel, doing all she could to take Kate's mind off whatever was troubling her.

They went to Straker's gallery and saw Jake's *Quality of mercy* installation which Kate and her friends felt was quite simply breathtaking. The room was filled with 'falling' globes of clear Perspex, all at different heights, suspended from the ceiling by thin, transparent strands. Some of the 'raindrops' had been made to look as though they had hit the ground and had thrown up coronets of splashes around the central globule of Perspex. Others had seemingly disappeared into puddles on the ground. Coloured lights embedded in the ceiling glowed down onto the globes, suffusing them in ever changing sequences of colour, while cascades of musical notes sounded softly all around. At one end of the room were giant silvery beanbags in which you could sit and absorb the peacefulness and the spectacle.

That evening in the pub, Kate caught sight of Jake at the same time that he spotted her across the room. He was with a willowy girl with long blonde hair, but he made his way across to her immediately.

393

"Kate! I didn't know you were in town. Why didn't you tell me?" He bent down and kissed her on the lips. Over his shoulder, she could see his blonde companion, whom she guessed must be Lucinda, looking in their direction.

"I only came up this morning. We went to see your *Quality of Mercy* installation. It's stunning, Jake!"

"Glad you like it. I wish you'd told me. I would have come with you."

"Well, we didn't have any definite plans. We all went first to Geoff's gallery for a de-briefing, then decided to go on to Straker's."

Looking across again at Lucinda standing rather forlornly sipping a glass of wine, Kate caught her eye and instinctively beckoned her over to join them. Jake glanced casually at the girl as she came up to them and made a perfunctory introduction.

"Oh! This is Lucinda. Lucy, this is Kate."

Kate extended her hand with a smile and Lucinda shook it, smiling back a little uncertainly. She had a beautiful face and her expression was, Kate thought, rather sweet. She was not at all how Kate had imagined her, which had been as a confident and slightly supercilious denizen of the upper reaches of society. She felt herself warming to her, and quickly tried to allay any worries Lucinda might have had about whether there was anything between herself and Jake.

"We all met at art school," she said lightly, indicating her friends and pointing them out as she introduced them. "This is Mimi, Grace and Bea. We keep an eye on Jake's career, which seems to be going great guns!"

"You're not doing so badly yourself!" Jake said, putting his arm around Kate's shoulders, seemingly oblivious to the discomfiture on Lucinda's face, which she sought valiantly to hide.

She's completely besotted with him, Kate thought to herself, willing him to remove his arm. It was at that moment she caught sight of Paul, whom she had texted earlier to ask him to meet them at the pub. Gratefully, she disengaged herself from Jake's arm and waved to Paul to come and join them.

For the rest of the evening, Kate tried to keep a distance between Jake and herself, but it wasn't easy. Jake would grab her attention at every opportunity, virtually ignoring Lucinda, in spite of Kate's efforts to include her in the conversation. On more than one occasion, Kate noticed tears pooling in Lucinda's big, blue eyes, which she hastily blinked away. Later, when they were all going their separate ways, Kate made a point of having a quiet word with her.

"It was lovely to meet you." She rolled her eyes in Jake's direction, and added, "Good luck with his moods! He's not the easiest guy to get along with. The mad genius syndrome!" Kate squeezed her hand warmly, hoping her words would give the message to Lucinda that Jake was Lucinda's concern, if not her property, and that she, Kate was not involved in any way.

Lucinda smiled back, and seemed about to say something, when Jake, turning back to her after mock-strangling Mimi over some remark she had made, said casually, "Come on Lucy, let's go." As Lucinda turned away, Jake said quietly to Kate, "Stay the night with me."

"I can't, Jake. I'm staying with Mimi. Anyway, it's not fair on Lucinda."

Jake shrugged and conceded defeat. "Well, come to my studio before you go back. See what I've been doing. I'll ring you."

He was gone before Kate could answer him.

Over the next few days, Kate felt herself being reconnected with the lifeblood of the art world. Together with Mimi, Grace and occasionally Bea - who said she was too busy to do much gallivanting- she went to various exhibitions, not only at the major galleries, but also several of the smaller ones dotted around the capital.

Jake phoned her three times before she agreed to go along to his gallery on the day before she was due to go home. He looked decidedly put out when he saw Kate had brought Mimi with her, which made Mimi turn away to hide a sly grin. It was however interesting to see the various projects Jake was working on simultaneously. Straker was putting on a solo exhibition for him the following year and there was talk of taking it to

395

New York later on. It was all very exciting, but if there was a fleeting moment when Kate may have thought it would be a heady feeling to be caught up with it all if she was part of Jake's life, it was quickly replaced by the knowledge that his rising star would quickly obscure her own creativity. Jake might be Lucinda's lodestar. He was not hers.

*

Tim picked up the telephone and dialled Elaine's number.

"Hello Tim," Elaine said, before he could speak. "What's the verdict?" Her voice was tight with control.

"Hello, Elaine. Well, I've been able to sort things out at the office and I think I can get away. How long did you say it was for?"

Relief flooded through Elaine. He was going to come after all! In spite of her efforts, her voice quivered a little as she replied.

"Just a week. Saturday 9th to 16th. I'm so glad you're coming. I'm hoping we'll be able to go to Siena for the Palio horse race on the Friday. The Hunters have got friends who live in an apartment overlooking the Piazza del Campo, and they've invited us to watch the race from their balcony. So exciting! The boys will love it. Shall I book the 'plane tickets?"

"Yes, could you? I'll reimburse you immediately." He hesitated. "By the way, how many bedrooms has the villa got?"

Elaine had been bracing herself for this and had her answer ready.

"It sleeps eight to ten. We can sort out the sleeping arrangements when we get there."

"As long as you realise, Elaine, that we won't be sharing a room. I think it would upset Freddie."

Elaine gritted her teeth. She would have to work on that one. In the meantime, the main thing was that he was coming. She answered lightly.

"Of course, Tim. Whatever you think best." Anxious to avoid any more interrogation about bedrooms, Elaine ended the call.

Tim, replacing the receiver, put his head in his hands. Elaine's vagueness about the sleeping arrangements hinted at a hidden agenda. Oh

God! What had he done?

It was through Amy that Kate discovered that they would definitely be going to Italy.

"Guess what, Kate, we're going on a plane in the summer holidays!" she said when she and Freddie came up to the studio for their Saturday lesson. "It's…" she screwed up her face, "somewhere to do with elephants."

"Elephants?" Kate echoed, images of safaris coming into her head.

"Yes, elephants with tusks," Amy said with confidence.

Freddie rolled his eyes. "Tuscany," he said with exaggerated patience. "It's in Italy. It's got nothing to do with elephants!"

Amy looked deflated. "Oh!" she said glumly, then brightened. "Maddie's coming too and there's a swimming pool."

Kate, her mind shying away from the fact that Tim was going to be holidaying in Tuscany with Elaine, said, "Who's Maddie?"

"She's my friend from school. She's coming with her mummy and daddy."

Kate looked at Freddie, who did not look particularly pleased with the prospect of the holiday in Italy.

"I expect Duncan will be going," she said, "so you'll have a friend there as well."

"It would be okay if it was just Duncan," he said in a low voice.

Kate's heart constricted. He really seemed to dislike Elaine. Whether it was simply because of her character or because he sensed that she had designs on his father, she didn't know. Probably a bit of both, she thought, and couldn't help wondering how Freddie would feel if she herself became romantically involved with Tim. Perhaps he would resent any woman who tried to take the place of his mother.

At the end of the lesson, the children thumped back down the stairs, and Kate watched them disappear round the side of Woodcote to the back door. It was only then that she allowed her mind to consider the implications of Tim going on holiday *en famille* with Elaine. It seemed like an almost inevitable precursor to an ever-closer relationship between the two families, and between Tim and Elaine. Would they share a room? If they did, what would the children, particularly Freddie, think? Had Tim decided to go to Tuscany because of what she had said about staying with Jake? Had she but known it, the same thought which had resounded in Tim's mind, also resounded in hers. What had she done?

Over the next few weeks, Kate's encounters with Tim were friendly and light-hearted. Any observer would have been hard put to discern the heartache behind their inconsequential exchanges. Only once or twice when their eyes met and held, did they catch a glimpse in the other's eyes of anything deeper between them. Glimpses which each dismissed as wishful thinking.

Kate, meanwhile, immersed herself in her work. Her unhappiness seemed to trigger off a frenzy of creativity, often making her feel as though she couldn't get her ideas down fast enough. The paintings which emerged were enigmatic, inchoate, intrinsically bound up with juxtapositions of light and shadow. Half-open apertures led from shadow into areas which suggested landscapes suffused with light. The shadows themselves seemed to be peopled by amorphous, ambiguous forms drowned in darkness.

Working through the long summer days, Kate was filled with a bittersweet anguish. On the one hand, she felt so fortunate to be able to spend her days doing what she loved in the light, airy studio, with the poplars sending their unique music through the open windows, their leaves glittering in the sunlight. But all the while, the anguish of giving up Tim was heightened by his proximity and the closeness of her relationship with his children.

June segued into July, and the children began begging Kate to come along to their end of term events at school. Amy turned to Kate in the middle of practising a piece on the piano one evening.

"I'm playing this at the concert at the end of term," she said, then as a thought struck her, she added emphatically, "Oh Kate, can you come? I'm playing this and I'm in the choir as well. Oh *please* come to it!"

Before Kate could answer, Freddie wandered in, holding a dog-eared sheaf of papers stapled together. Kate recognised it as the script for *Bugsy Malone* in which Freddie was playing Dandy Dan. He had been asking her to hear his lines for the last couple of weeks and was now almost word-perfect. Hearing Amy pleading with Kate to come to her concert emboldened him to ask Kate straight out the question he had been wanting to put to her, but had felt reticent about doing.

"If you go to Amy's concert, maybe you could come to see *Bugsy* as well," he said shyly. "I think it'll be quite good."

Kate's heart lurched with the by now familiar feeling of affection mingled with dismay that assailed her when she was put in the position of doing something with Tim's family that would make it seem to Elaine as though she was trying to enmesh herself even more into their lives. Elaine was bound to see her at the musical since Duncan was also in it, playing one of Dandy Dan's henchmen. If she went on a different night, she would still find out one way or another. But Amy's pleading eyes and Freddie's diffident invitation were impossible to refuse. She looked from Freddie to Amy and smiled.

"I'd love to come to both," she said. "I wouldn't miss them for the world!"

And so it was that a week later, she found herself sitting with Freddie between her and Tim, watching Amy settle at the piano stool on the stage to play her solo at her school concert. She was surprised at how nervous she felt for the little girl, almost as though she were her own child. She willed her not to take it too fast, and knowing from listening to her practise that there was a difficult part in the middle, she bit her lip in anxiety till it was safely negotiated. Tim, glancing across at her, noticed her tense focus on Amy as she played and felt a new wave of tenderness towards this young woman who seemed to care so much about his children.

The piece came to an end and the audience broke into applause as Amy slipped off the stool, picked up her music and took a little bow. Kate felt inordinately proud of her. Not only had she been note perfect, but the sensitivity with which she had played and her mature use of dynamics had made the piece into a real performance. She turned to look at Tim, who answered her smile of delight with one of his own.

Two rows back, Chloe Hunter watched the exchange curiously. She turned to her husband sitting beside her.

"If Tim Crawford is supposed to be Elaine's property," she murmured in his ear, "who's the ravishing redhead he's sitting with over there?"

Two days later, it was the turn of Freddie's production. Kate, getting out of Tim's car in the school car park, braced herself for the almost inevitable event of coming face-to-face with Elaine. She had not been worried about that happening at Amy's concert, since Elaine did not have a child in the juniors, but she felt sure Elaine would be here on this second and final night of *Bugsy*. She had wanted to come to the previous evening's performance, but Freddie had insisted that they should come to the final one as it would be much better.

"We're going to make much more mess with the splurge guns and custard pies," he said with relish. "You've got to come on Friday!"

As they entered the school's little theatre, she immediately spotted Elaine, who had arrived some time earlier. She was standing a few rows from the front, scanning the faces of the other parents, obviously looking for Tim. Her smile on seeing him froze on her face when she saw Kate. She recovered enough to beckon Tim over and put on a credible show of friendliness for Tim's benefit.

"Oh! Hello! I didn't realise *you* were coming," she said to Kate. "I've saved these three seats. There isn't one for you, I'm afraid!"

"It's okay," Kate said quickly, "there are plenty of seats at the back. I'll sit there."

"Oh! I want to sit next to Kate!" Amy said, jutting out her bottom lip. "I'm going to go with Kate!"

Tim gave Elaine a helpless shrug. "I better go to the back with them. Then Amy can stand on a chair. I don't think she'll see much even from here. But thanks for saving the seats." As Tim started ushering Amy towards the back, Kate caught the murderous look Elaine was directing at her and heard her hiss, "Still at it are you? You devious little cow! Well, you aren't going to snuggle up to him while I'm around!" She snatched up her bag from a chair and followed Tim and Amy to the seats at the back. Kate followed more slowly and, by the time she reached the others, Elaine was ensconced on the right side of Tim with Amy on his left. Kate sat down next to Amy and began looking at the programme with her, pointing out Freddie's name next to Dandy Dan in the cast list. She tried to ignore the low murmuring of Elaine's voice as she monopolised Tim's attention. Mercifully for Tim, the lights soon went down and everyone's attention was focused on the play. Amy, standing on her chair, was entranced, her eyes wide with excitement, giving little squeals whenever Freddie came on stage.

Afterwards, while they were waiting in the hall for Freddie to emerge from backstage, Kate stood somewhat awkwardly to the side with Amy, while Elaine tried to keep Tim's attention. But Tim drew Kate into the conversation, turning it to what tremendous fun the production had been and how brilliantly Freddie and Duncan had performed. When the two boys finally emerged, having changed back into their uniforms, but still covered in their stage make-up, Amy went into a fit of giggles at Freddie's heavy black eyebrows and 'unshaven' chin. Then the two boys went off to the dining room for the post-production refreshments for the cast while the others waited in the hall. Elaine drew Tim aside to talk to him about the holiday, while Kate and Amy played noughts and crosses on the back of the programme.

Later in the car park, once the boys had re-appeared, Elaine watched, seething, as Kate got into the front passenger seat of Tim's car. As Tim reversed out of the parking space and drove off with *her*, she thought of how Tim had opted to go and sit with Kate at the back to watch the play, even though she, Elaine, had saved him a seat. It was just one more thorn driven into her heart, making her take one more step along the dark road her mind had been travelling lately.

401

Chapter XIX

When Kate came into the kitchen from the back garden to make a cup of coffee, she caught sight of a car drawing up outside her gate. A car door banged and to her surprise, she saw Jake come round the side of the car and wave to the driver, who then reversed back down the lane. What was he doing here and why hadn't he brought his van? She gave a sigh of exasperation. This would put paid to her gardening for the day. She had decided to have a blitz on the garden over the weekend since June had been warm and wet, followed by a sunny July, and the weeds had completely taken over. She had spent the whole of the Saturday tackling the front garden. She had now started on the back, and was feeling as though she was making some progress. She had not had the children for their usual lesson that weekend because Tim had taken them down to Lyme on the Saturday morning to stay with Gwen for the week before going to Italy and planned to leave Binky there while they were away. Claire's parents had come to stay for the first two weeks of the summer holidays, so Kate had not seen much of the children, but they had told her what they would be doing.

Kate had been out since early morning in the back garden among the neglected flowerbeds, trying to rid them of the couch grass which had become established among the roots of the straggly roses. She took a gulp of her coffee and went to open the front door. Jake, leaning against the doorjamb, felt a stab of desire as he took in her appearance. Her hair was tied up with an old piece of string, and she was dressed in a crop top and tiny, ragged denim shorts. She had caught the sun, and her skin had a golden sheen to it.

"Jake! I wasn't expecting you! Where's the van?"

"She's in dock. Argument with a lorry. When I heard a mate was coming almost past your door, I thought I'd come down and see you. Why have you got mud on your face? Are you going in for landscape art?"

"Well, I suppose you could call gardening landscape art!" Kate responded. "We landowners have to look after our estates, you know! Mind you," she added ruefully, "I've left it too long. It's a jungle out there! Look, I've more or less done the front. Come and see what I've done so far at the back."

She led him through the house and out of the back door into the afternoon sunshine where, in spite of her efforts of the day, the riotous greenery of the weeds still dominated the back garden.

"The trouble is, I really *like* the weeds!" Kate said. Gazing around, she murmured softly,

"What would the world be, once bereft
Of wet and of wilderness? Let them be left!
Oh let them be left, wildness and wet;
Long live the weeds and the wilderness yet!"

"Who wrote that?" Jake asked, tucking a strand of her hair behind her ear.

"Gerard Manley Hopkins. And I completely agree. Look at the ground elder flowers. They're beautiful, and these grasses are so graceful." She sighed. "But I suppose it'll just become impenetrable after a while if I don't clear it. And these roses deserve a chance."

"And I suppose this is meant to be the lawn!" Jake said, flinging himself down on a pocket handkerchief of long grass and pulling off his T-shirt. He stretched out luxuriously, closing his eyes and breathing deeply. Kate looked down at his beautiful face, the blond stubble on his chin glinting in the sunshine, his lean torso rising and falling with his breathing. Slowly, Jake opened his eyes, and looked up at her. He sat up and reached out for her hand. Gently, but brooking no resistance, he drew Kate down onto the grass beside him. He pulled off the piece of string, which was tying her hair back, and her hair tumbled around her shoulders. Burying his face in it, he murmured, "Oh Kate, baby." His lips were on her throat, his hands cupped her breast. The scent of his body was still familiar to her. It mingled with the heady earthiness of the sun-warmed grass. A bee droned by.

As Jake drew her over on top of him and his lips found hers, the long

403

lonely months when her body had ached for Tim, the trauma of Vince's attack, the emotional lacerations she had had from Elaine, all combined to awaken a need in her to be held.

He in his turn, felt her body respond as her mouth came down on his and he was lost in her remembered taste.

*

Driving back from Lyme Regis, Tim tried to concentrate on the road ahead. He had seriously begun to regret having agreed to go to Tuscany. Elaine's attitude to Kate, though outwardly civil, at least in his hearing, was far from warm. He supposed he could understand that she should resent Kate, but it was obvious that her attitude made Kate very uncomfortable. Though he had almost convinced himself that Kate had no feelings for him, it must still be unpleasant for her to be on the receiving end of Elaine's thinly disguised hostility. Something in Elaine's eyes when they were saying goodnight on the evening of Freddie's play had made him uneasy. It was a look he could only describe as slightly deranged.

He cursed himself for his knee-jerk reaction of agreeing to go to Italy when he had discovered that Kate still seemed to be involved with Jake and had (as he thought) been going to stay with him in London. Even if he had no future with Kate, that was still no reason to get too involved with Elaine. Well, it was too late to pull out of the holiday now. The kids were excited about going and it would be silly to waste the money. He was under no illusions that Elaine was expecting to sleep with him at the villa. He would have to face that one when the situation arose.

As he turned into Tuckers Lane and drove past Kate's cottage bathed in the hot afternoon sunshine, he had an intense longing to see her on her own to discover if there was still the connection between them that he had felt before, but which she had seemed to be shielding from him for some time. Somehow he had to try to find out before he went to Italy. Would she be at home or in the studio? He drove on past, the engine virtually silent in the quiet afternoon, and after taking his overnight bag

404

into the house, he went round to the studio door. It was locked, so she was probably at home, since her car had been parked outside the cottage. He began walking down the lane, the shadows of the long lush weeds on the verge falling across the uneven ground and the sunshine warm on his shoulders. As a pretext for going to see her, he would ask Kate if she could feed Socrates while they were in Italy. There was no sign of life at the cottage as he walked up the garden path and there was no answer when he knocked. Looking around at the front garden, he saw that she had been busy weeding and, deciding she was probably at the back, he walked round the side of the house and stopped dead.

Kate was lying in the long grass, half on top of Jake, whose blond head contrasted with the auburn of Kate's hair falling in wild profusion around her shoulders and trailing into the grass. Jake was kissing her passionately and Kate was kissing him back, her arms around him, her legs entwined with his.

The agony which assailed Tim at that moment was visceral. He stood transfixed, unable to tear his eyes away as Jake pulled Kate on top of him, sliding his hands under her sun top. They both had their eyes closed, seemingly lost in each other, oblivious to his presence. With a supreme effort of will, Tim tore his eyes away and stepped back round the side of the house. For a moment he leant against the wall while a wave of despair washed over him. Then he slowly turned and made his way back to the front of the house and out into the lane. The sunshine of the glorious day seemed to mock him as he reached his house and, walking round to the back, flung himself down on a chair at the garden table, his head in his hands. Well, he had the irrefutable evidence of what the situation was between Jake and Kate. The vision of their entwined bodies was seared into his mind's eye. The sight had been so shattering in its unexpectedness. Where was the fellow's van? At least if he had seen it parked outside, he would have been more prepared. Over and over again, he replayed the scene obsessively in his mind. Kate's hands entwined in Jake's hair, his hands sliding under her flimsy top, her body on his. How often he had imagined Kate being in his arms like that!

Well, it wouldn't happen now. He had his answer loud and clear.

405

How could he ever have thought that Kate had feelings for him, when she had that Greek god sculptor who seemed besotted with her? He gave a small, bitter laugh.

"You're an idiot!" he muttered to himself. "A deluded idiot."

The only saving grace was that he had not made a total fool of himself by telling Kate about his feelings for her. It would have put her in a very awkward position. The only thing to do was to continue with the status quo. He would have to put any thoughts of Kate becoming more than a friend right out of his mind. He gave a small derisive laugh. "Pigs might fly," he said bleakly to the sunlit garden.

*

When Jake pulled off her top in one practised movement and buried his face in her small, firm breasts, Kate at first continued to drink in his maleness, the caress of his hands on her breasts, the desire that was rising ever more insistently in him awakening an all too human response in herself. Jake rolled her over till she was lying with her face upturned to the sun. It shone through her eyelids with a rosy light. Jake's lips came down on hers again. She opened her eyes. High above her, against the blue of the sky, the poplar leaves danced and glittered in the sunshine. Their song washed over her. The song of the trees which stretched from her cottage up to Woodcote House, connecting her with the man she had seen through a window on the day she had first come down here to see the cottage. She remembered, as though it were yesterday, the strange sensation she had felt when she had seen him walk into the drawing room as she stood outside in the lane on that windy, autumn evening.

Her hands fell away from Jake and her body became very still. Jake immediately noticed the change in her. He lifted his face from hers and looked deep into her amber eyes. What he saw there stilled his own body, raging as it was with his need for her. Slowly, Kate's hands came up on either side of his face. She raised her head and kissed him lightly. But her lips that had responded so readily to his a short while ago, were now cool and passionless.

406

"I'm so sorry, Jake. I can't do this. I shouldn't have... led you on. And it's not fair to Lucinda. It's just... I've been so lonely... and..." Her voice trailed off.

"And what, Kate? And what?"

"It doesn't matter." She pushed him gently away and sat up, pulling her sun-top back on.

Jake also sat up, leaning his forearms on his bent knees. He looked at her, his face grim.

"Who is he? Your rich neighbour with the big house down the lane? I saw the way you looked at him at the preview."

Kate returned his gaze, then her eyes dropped to the feathery grass-head she had picked.

"Yes," she said quietly. "But nothing has happened between us. Nor will it. He's got a woman. They're going off to Italy on holiday next week. His... his wife was killed nearly three years ago. I've been helping to look after his children and giving them art lessons."

"But how can you fall for a pinstripe suit? Kate, you're an artist. You should be with me. We should be together. It was great when we were together."

"Have you forgotten, Jake? Have you forgotten the nights you didn't come home? The girls who draped themselves all over you at parties? And what encouragement did you give me with *my* work? It was all about you, always. I went along with it for a while, but when this house was left to me, I suddenly saw a way of being my own person."

Looking at Kate sitting there so close to him, with the sunlight striking fiery highlights in her hair, Jake finally knew that he had lost her. He had lost her because of his own arrogance and self-centredness. He had treated her work as though it was of scant importance. He had hurt her with his playing around. How could he have behaved so badly, when this beautiful creature had, at one time, been deeply in love with him?

"You loved me once," he said softly, touching her bare, grubby foot beside him on the grass.

"Yes I did, Jake. But that was in another life. I can't go back."

"What will I do without you?"

407

"You'll be fine. More than fine. You're leaving me far behind, Jake. New York beckons. The art world is sitting up and taking notice of your work. And you've got Lucinda. She's a beautiful, sweet girl, and totally besotted with you. She'll be very good for you, Jake. Soon, I'll just be part of the flotsam left in your wake."

Jake shook his head. "You'll never be flotsam. Promise me you'll stay part of my life. Not lose touch."

"Of course. I'll always follow your career avidly. And I do love you, Jake. It's just that I'm not *in* love with you anymore."

He smiled wryly. "And the stupid thing is, it was only once you went away that I realised how much I need you."

"You don't need me, Jake. All you really need is your work. Now come on, I'll make us a sandwich. I'm starving!"

In the week that followed, Kate, from her vantage point in the studio, would see Tim arriving back from work, parking the car and vanishing into the house. She kept hoping he would come up for a chat, but he never even glanced up at the studio windows. On the Tuesday, she saw Elaine's car draw up not long after Tim arrived home. It was still there when Kate shut up the studio to go home.

Longing to have some contact with Tim, when he arrived back on the Thursday evening Kate leaned out of the open studio window and called down to him.

"Hi Tim! I was wondering, do you want me to feed Socrates next week while you're in Italy?"

Tim, briefcase in one hand and his jacket over the other arm, looked up at her. She was puzzled by his expression. It seemed to consist of pleasure at seeing her mixed with a bleak constraint.

"Hello, Kate. No, it's all sorted. Mrs B. is here and she'll be coming in to do this and that, so she'll see to Socrates. Thanks anyway."

"Okay. If you're sure. When are you collecting the kids?"

"Going down this evening. Back tomorrow and catching the plane early Saturday."

"Have you packed?"

"Mrs B's been laying out clothes on the guest bed for the kids, and my mother will have got the stuff they've been using down there washed and ready. Shouldn't be much hassle."

"Well, if I don't see you, have a lovely time."

He gave a curious little grimace, answering somewhat enigmatically, "Thanks. I'm sure the kids will anyway."

Kate resisted the impulse to comment that he didn't seem too keen and said instead: "Well, bye then."

"Bye, Kate."

When he had disappeared into the house, Kate thought about his remark. He had certainly not sounded enthusiastic about the holiday. Surely if he and Elaine were together he would be happy about spending time with her? She sighed, not knowing what to think, and went back to her painting.

*

The afternoon was still and quiet, the only sound drifting in through the open studio windows that of the slight breeze in the poplars on the other side of the lane, laced with birdsong. Shafts of sunlight caught the dust motes drifting in the air currents and the sound of her brush strokes on the canvas sounded very loud to Kate as she scumbled a layer of blue-grey paint over a darker area.

When she had walked up to the studio that morning, Tim had been loading cases into the car and Lily Babbidge had been trying to keep an excited Amy still while she re-plaited her hair neatly. Freddie was already in the car, with a rucksack on his knees, stuffed with electronic paraphernalia, including his iPad, phone and earphones.

Kate stopped and offered her help.

"I think we're almost there, thanks Kate," Tim said, looking hassled, but giving her a quick grin. "Whatever isn't packed we'll have to do without. We should have left by now. I hope the M25 isn't clogged up. I have checked in online, but we should try to get to the airport by ten thirty."

Amy gave a small shriek. "Oh! I nearly forgot Pooky!" Pulling away as Lily finished her hair, she dashed back into the house and emerged with a battered teddy bear, which she stuffed into her pink rucksack before getting into the car alongside Freddie.

"Well, I think that's everything," Tim said, turning to Kate and Lily standing by the car. "Will you lock up, Lily?"

"Yes, don't you worry about all that. And I'll be in every day to check on things."

"Thanks. We'll be back late next Saturday." He gave Lily a peck on the cheek and, as he turned to do the same to Kate, instead of brushing cheeks, and seemingly involuntarily on both sides, their lips came into contact instead. Kate felt Tim's hand tighten on her shoulder momentarily, and her heart lurched with the bittersweet jolt the contact caused in her. Tim pulled away and got into his car, his face averted.

The car door clunked shut and the Discovery's engine growled into life. As it pulled away, the children waved from the back seat and Lily and Kate waved back as it disappeared round the curve of the lane.

Lily had not failed to notice the little exchange between Tim and Kate, and sighed as she watched Kate make her way to the studio.

"I wish those two could stop tiptoeing around each other and just get together," she muttered to herself, as she went back inside to clear up the breakfast things.

Ensconced in front of the easel, Kate could not focus on her work. The brief kiss she had shared with Tim had unsettled her to a disproportionate degree, and she found herself gazing out of the window at the glittering mass of poplar leaves against the sky as the wind played among them, sounding like the sea on shingle. The connotations with the sea drew her thoughts towards Scarborough and her father. She made a sudden decision to go up to Yorkshire to see him and Doreen. Washing her brushes and covering the blobs of paint on her palette in the vain hope that they wouldn't dry out too much, she locked the studio, called in on Lily to say she would be away for a few days, then went home and slung some clothes into a holdall. After phoning her father to say she was on her

410

way, she set off. By evening, she was drinking a glass of wine on the little patio in the back garden of her father's house.

Nearly a thousand miles away, Tim was also sipping a glass of chilled wine but, in contrast to the slightly chilly northern evening Kate was experiencing, the terrace he was sitting on was bathed in the warmth of a Tuscan evening, the low rays of the sun streaming through the leaves of the vine clambering over the pergola. Below the group of adults sitting on the terrace, and beyond the balustrade edging it, the children were already splashing about in the pool, their shouts echoing out over the garden. Far beyond the garden and surrounding vineyards, the blue Tuscan hills lay stretched out lazily in the hazy sunshine. Dotted here and there were hilltop villas like their own, surrounded by the dark spires of cypress trees. It was a truly idyllic spot and Tim found himself relaxing in spite of himself. Elaine, who had seated herself next to him on the sofa, was looking very glamorous. Her hair was freshly coloured and styled, and she wore a caramel and turquoise patterned dress which showed a generous amount of cleavage. She wore strappy stilettos on her manicured feet and oversized sunglasses shaded her eyes. She had already downed a glass of prosecco and was on her second.

Across from them sat Chloe and Phil Hunter, an easy-going couple whom Tim had got on well with in the past. Chloe, an attractive brunette in white Capri trousers and blue blouse, was dressed much more casually than Elaine, and Phil lounged back in his chair in linen shorts and a somewhat crumpled open necked shirt.

On arrival at the villa, the bedrooms had soon been allocated, with the Hunters settling on one with a double bed and Amy and Maddie sharing a room with twin beds next to them. The boys were delighted to be given a room in a little turret and Tim had claimed a single bedroom for himself. Though put out, Elaine had managed to grab the bedroom with a double bed next door to his, confident that she would eventually be able to persuade Tim to share her bed, in spite of the fact that the children would probably find out. Surely the combination of the glorious weather, the beautiful surroundings and the delicious wine and food would put him in the right frame of mind?

411

Phil was talking about the proposed trip to Siena on the Friday to see the Palio, the famous horse race that takes place there every July and August.

"As I mentioned to Elaine, our friends Luca and Paola have an apartment overlooking the Piazza del Campo, where the race is run. They've invited us over to watch it with them. We'll have a fantastic view of the action up above the crowds." He glanced from Tim to Elaine. "Are you up for it?"

"Absolutely!" Elaine said, looking at Tim, her eyes shining. "You want to go don't you?" she asked him entreatingly.

"Sounds like fun, yes, definitely." Tim said. "I presume we can take the kids?"

"Oh yes," Chloe interposed. "They adore children, and have two of their own. Freddie and Duncan will absolutely love it. The girls may be a bit upset if any of the horses fall, which they may well do – it's absolutely frantic. But they don't have to watch."

"That's settled then. I'll ring Luca this evening." Phil took a swig of his wine. "Now, what are we going to do tomorrow?"

*

The following Friday saw them gathered in the elegant apartment of Luca and Paola Fabiani, glasses of fragrant Tuscan wine in their hands, looking out over the sun-drenched Piazza del Campo, where a huge milling crowd packed the central area of the temporary racetrack which ran round the Campo. The outside edges of the track were also packed with people, all in a high state of excitement, waving the banners of their own contrade or city district, whose representative jockeys and horses would be competing in the race. Men were spraying water on the track to dampen the hard-packed sand and sweeping it evenly with brooms. The tall tower of the town hall, the Palazzo Pubblico, loomed up against the dazzling blue sky and people were clustered on balconies and at the windows of the buildings surrounding the Campo.

Tim stepped out onto the Fabianis' balcony to join the children,

412

including the Fabianis' two sons, who were avidly taking in the scene, and watched the jockeys beginning to manoeuvre their horses into position at the starting rope, each trying to get to the inside of the track. Paola, effortlessly chic in a cream-coloured dress which hugged her figure and contrasted with her beautiful olive skin and glossy raven-black hair, came out to stand beside him.

"So Tim, how do you like Siena?" Her voice was warm and friendly as she gestured with her wine glass over the scene below and the city in general.

"Wonderful! What an atmosphere!"

"Yes, it is exciting, Il Palio, but I prefer when the crowds have gone." She glanced at Freddie and Amy. "You have lovely children!" She paused and said enquiringly, "Elaine, she is not their mother?"

"No, my wife died nearly three years ago. A car accident."

Paola's brown eyes filled with sympathy. "Oh! I am so sorry. Forgive me."

Tim smiled. "Nothing to forgive. You weren't to know."

Inside, though she was engaged in conversation with Luca, an expansive bear of a man, Elaine was very aware of Tim and Paola standing close together out on the sunlit balcony, and did not miss the sympathetic hand which Paola placed on Tim's arm at one stage. What were they talking about? Paola was much too attractive for her liking, and the frustrating week she had spent at their holiday villa had put Elaine more on edge than ever.

She had with difficulty restrained herself from going to Tim's room on the first night but the following one, after a wonderful dinner in a restaurant in San Gimignano, when everyone had turned in for the night, she had showered, slipped on a silky nightdress and knocked softly on Tim's bedroom door. Hearing no answer, she opened the door and went in. Tim was already asleep, his hair tousled and still damp from the shower. She stood looking at him for a moment, her habitual, slightly brittle expression softened with longing. Then, sliding the delicate shoulder straps of her nightdress off her shoulders, exposing her breasts, she sat down on the edge of the bed and bent over to kiss him on the

413

mouth. At first, still half-asleep, he had responded to her kiss, but when he came fully awake, his eyes snapped open and he pulled away. He took in her semi-naked state and grasped her shoulders to hold her away from him.

"Elaine, I don't think…"

She shushed him, her fingers on his lips. "Tim, please. We're on holiday. What harm is there? It's not as though we haven't made love before." She took his head in both hands and pulled his face against her breasts, burying her hands in his hair.

Tim felt himself wavering. Her perfume invaded his senses. The wine he had drunk, the softness of her breasts against his face, all began to erode his resolve to keep a distance between himself and Elaine. Maybe she was right. What harm was there? Kate seemed a million miles away, both physically and emotionally. The image of Kate entwined in Jake's arms flashed into his mind. He felt her receding out of his reach.

Then the bedroom door opened, and Tim heard Freddie's voice.

"Dad, when are we…" Freddie stopped abruptly as he took in the scene. Tim jerked his head away from Elaine's clasp and instinctively pushed her away from him, turning to look at Freddie who stood transfixed in the doorway in his pyjamas, his face ashen.

Elaine hurriedly pulled up the straps of her nightdress and stood up.

"Freddie…" Tim began, but Freddie had already turned and disappeared down the darkened upper hallway. Tim flung back the sheet and stood up, reaching for his trousers lying on the back of a chair.

"Elaine, please go back to your room. I must go and talk to Freddie," he said, his voice harsh with distress.

Elaine, her face a mask of disappointment and annoyance, turned on her heel and went out of the door. In her room, she sat on the bed, her hands clenched, a storm of frustration raging in her head and heart.

Tim went up quickly to Freddie's room in the little turret and softly opened the door. Freddie's bed was empty and the only occupant was Duncan, fast asleep in the other bed. Tim shut the door and checked the bathroom before padding downstairs. He finally found Freddie out on the terrace, sitting on one of the sun loungers, his knees drawn up under his chin, gazing out over the moonlit garden. When Tim approached, putting

414

his hand on Freddie's bony shoulder, Freddie shrugged it off and turned away from his father, brushing his hand angrily across his eyes.

"Freddie…" Tim stopped, not knowing how to handle the situation. He tried again.

"Freddie, I didn't ask her into my room. I was asleep."

"No, you weren't. You were kissing her… her…" Freddie's voice came to a choking halt. He turned to glare at his father, his eyes glinting with tears in the crepuscular light.

"You're going to marry her, aren't you?" he said in a fierce whisper.

"No, I'm not Freddie."

"I don't believe you. Duncan said one day we might be brothers if you and his mum got married."

"Freddie, I'm not going to marry her."

"Then why were you hugging her? And she had no top on. I don't believe you! I don't believe you! Why can't you marry Kate instead?"

Tim was taken aback at the suddenness of the question.

"Freddie, how can I just decide to marry Kate?"

"I thought you liked her."

"I do, very much. But she's got a boyfriend. She wouldn't want to marry me."

"Would you marry her if she didn't have a boyfriend?"

Tim looked out over the moonlit garden. He found himself saying softly, "I would marry her tomorrow… if you and Amy didn't mind. But there's no question of it. You need to love someone to marry them and Kate doesn't love me."

"Do you love her?"

Tim turned to look at his son.

"Yes, I do," he said simply.

"Then why don't you tell her?" Freddie's voice was harsh. "You'd just rather hug Elaine without her top on. Kissing her boobs. Yuk!"

He leapt up and headed for the French doors. "Leave me alone," he hissed over his shoulder, and rushed inside and up to his room.

Tim stood leaning against the balustrade for a long time, his heart aching for his son, his mind full of rage against Elaine and against himself for succumbing, even momentarily, to her seduction. He felt terrible for blighting Freddie's holiday, which he had been enjoying hugely and was at a loss as to how to put Freddie's mind at rest that he was *not* going to marry Elaine.

As it happened, although Freddie couldn't get the image of his father in the arms of Elaine out of his mind, his fierce love for him ensured their relationship got back to a more normal footing over the next few days. He studiously ignored Elaine however, and Tim tried to keep a bit of a distance from her himself.

Meanwhile Elaine, seething inside with resentment and disappointment, with a supreme effort of will maintained a cool exterior, though she in turn barely acknowledged Freddie's existence. Why did the wretched child have to come barging in like that, in the middle of the night? He'd ruined the whole holiday. Tim seemed impossibly distant from her. She despaired of ever achieving her heart's desire of marrying him. And always she was aware of the existence of Kate, who she felt was waiting in the wings to pounce on Tim. And now, here was the alluring Paola cosying up to him at the Palio.

As soon as she could extricate herself from her conversation with Luca, Elaine followed Tim out onto the balcony and stood close to him, slipping her hand possessively through his arm. She felt Tim tense at her touch but, determined to show Paola that she and Tim were an item, Elaine did not take her hand away. But the race was about to begin, and under the pretext of moving closer to the edge of the balcony, Tim managed to dislodge her grip.

The horses and riders were still milling about in a rather confused bunch, then suddenly they were off, careering madly round the track to a huge roar from the crowd. A roar which intensified when the first rider was unseated and fell heavily, while the riderless horse continued to gallop round the track. At the next bend, another horse careened into the side barrier and fell, horse and rider narrowly avoiding being trampled by the rest of the field. By the time the three circuits had been run, taking only about 90 seconds, four horses were riderless and one jockey had had to be

416

stretchered off. To tumultuous cheering, the victorious horse and rider were mobbed by the ecstatic members of the winning Contrade. Banners waved, horns blew, the track was overrun by cheering crowds.

Elaine barely registered the excitement. All she could think about was how Tim had moved away from her at the first opportunity.

Sitting toward the back of the room, immaculately manicured hands clasping a silver-topped cane, Giulia, Luca's elderly mother, sat observing the little drama playing itself out on the sunlit balcony, her sharp, grey eyes missing nothing. She had watched Elaine's glance flicking constantly to the group on the balcony while she was talking to Luca, and how she had gone out to join Tim at the first opportunity. She had noticed Tim's lack of response to Elaine's touch and the fact that, as soon as he could, he had edged away from Elaine, forcing her to relinquish her grip on his arm. When Luca urged his mother to come out to watch the race, she declined. She had seen the race many, many times, and preferred to watch the people on the balcony instead. When the race was over, and everyone started drifting inside, her laser glance took in the brittle smile on Elaine's face and didn't miss the look of hostility Freddie directed at Elaine as she brushed past him.

After lunch, which Luca and Paola provided for them, when Tim came over to say goodbye to Giulia, or Nonni as she was affectionately known by the family, she clasped his proffered hand with both her own. As he bent to kiss her on the cheek, she whispered into his ear, "That woman, Elaine. She is… *predatore*. Be careful. Your son, he knows it."

She pulled away and Tim briefly locked eyes with her, blue staring into grey. A strong understanding passed between them and he gave an almost imperceptible nod, before straightening up and continuing with his goodbyes.

*

The footsteps echoing up the stairway which stopped at the open doorway of the studio caused Kate to peer round her easel.

417

"Oh! Hi Freddie! How was Italy? Did you have a good time?" Kate greeted him brightly, but something in Freddie's demeanour caused her to stop and look at him enquiringly. "Did you not enjoy it?"

Freddie came slowly into the room and went to stand by the window, staring out down the lane with his back to her.

"Yes, it was a great place. There was a swimming pool and stuff. And we went to Florence and saw Michelangelo's sculpture of David. Awesome. But..."

The "but" lingered in the air and Kate put down her brush and went over to Freddie, who continued to stare out of the window.

"But what, Freddie?"

Suddenly he turned to her and she was taken sharply aback by the anguish on his face. Beneath his tan his face was pallid and hot tears stood in his eyes.

"I saw Dad and Elaine... they were... she...she... had no top on, and he was hugging her and kissing her... boobs." A flush stained his cheeks. "I went into his room in the night..." He stopped, and the tears brimmed over and spilled unheeded down his cheeks. Kate put out a hand to touch his shoulder, torn with a mixture of compassion for Freddie's distress and an almost physical pain at the mental picture Freddie had conjured up of Tim and Elaine together.

Freddie angrily shook off her hand and blurted out, "He's probably going to marry Elaine, even though he would rather marry you, because you've got a boyfriend and you don't love him. If you didn't have a boyfriend, he could marry *you*."

Kate stared at him. "But... why do you think he would rather marry me?"

Freddie hesitated. What would his father say if he knew he'd told Kate about their conversation? He turned back to the window, and said in a low voice, "I just know. And *I* want you to marry him. I hate Elaine. She's like the Grand High Witch in that Roald Dahl book. It's like she's got a mask to cover up what she's really like. But I can see what she's like under her mask."

Kate felt at a loss. What could she say to ease Freddie's troubled

418

young soul? That she herself would give anything to be with Tim? That she would march up to Tim and tell him that? That she was *not* with Jake and never would be again? She had a sudden vision of a wide river with Tim and the children on the far, shadowy shore, and herself on the opposite bank, unable to reach them. She could at least tell Freddie that she did not have a boyfriend. If Tim knew that...

She began, "Freddie, I..." but through the open window she saw Tim emerging from his front door. He looked up and saw Kate and Freddie standing at the open window. He waved and called out, "Hi Kate, how are you doing?"

Kate waved back. "Fine, thanks. Good holiday?"

"Yes, thanks. It's a beautiful part of the world. But now we're all off again. I have to go to Seattle tomorrow for a couple of weeks, so I'm taking the kids to Claire's parents today." He beckoned to Freddie. "Come on, Freddie. Mrs B's unpacked and washed all your clothes. Come and help her pack again."

Freddie glanced at Kate. "At least he'll be away from *her* for a while," he muttered, before turning and disappearing out of the door and down the stairs, rubbing his face with the back of his hand as he went.

Kate saw him running out to join his father in the lane and stood and watched as they went back into the house.

*

Tim was standing staring out of the window of his study when Lily came bustling into the room.

"The kids are all packed and ready, Tim. I haven't ironed everything, but never mind. Maybe their gran could do it." She stopped and tilted her head, noticing Tim's pensive face. "Penny for them?"

Tim turned to look at her. "I've been thinking, Lily. I think I'm going to have to employ an au pair. Mainly to do the school run and things like that."

Lily looked at him quizzically.

"Have you fallen out with Elaine?" she said, then added quickly,

419

"None of my business, of course."

"It is your business, Lily. You've been our lifesaver for two and a half years. You're family. And yes, things have changed somewhat. Let's say I would rather put some distance between Elaine and us from now on. I don't want to be dependent on her. And an au pair could take some of the pressure off you. I've often felt that we are asking too much of you, especially as you've got Bill to look after as well. What I don't want is for you to feel pushed out in any way. And your payment would remain the same."

"Lord love you, Tim, don't you worry about me! What is important is what's best for the children and you. I know you were put off having an au pair because the two you had didn't work out, but it might be third time lucky. And I must admit I've been feeling my age a bit. I'll be seventy this year, and Bill's going on seventy-five. If you can get someone good, I'll be happy to step back and help out when needed. Of course, there's no question of my pay staying the same. What nonsense!"

Tim was about to protest, but Lily held up a hand.

"Now Tim, no arguments. I wouldn't dream of it. You just let me know when you've found someone, and I'll help to settle her in."

Tim walked over to Lily and put his arm around her shoulders affectionately.

"You're a gem, Lily. I'll get in touch with the agency and see who they've got on their books." He walked back over to the window. "The thing that's worrying me is how I'm going to tell Elaine!"

*

It was a stiflingly hot, late August afternoon. Kate had opened all the windows of the studio in the vain hope of catching any stray breeze. Even the leaves of the poplars, which quivered in the slightest movement of air, hung motionless, and the only sound Kate could hear outside was the occasional distant cawing of a crow.

The painting she was working on was not going well. The oppressive heat was enervating, and her head ached. She walked to the

420

window and looked up and down the deserted lane. Tim's house stood wrapped in silence, dreaming in the sun. The family was still away: Tim in the States and the children and Binky with Claire's parents, but they were all due back in a couple of days.

When she returned from Yorkshire, Kate had gone to visit Annie and Magda, and had arranged for Magda to sit for her. Magda's strong, high-cheekboned face and dark colouring cried out to be painted, and the first sitting had gone well. The painting stood against the wall, awaiting the next sitting, and meanwhile Kate continued to struggle with another painting she had on the go, which had given her problems right from the start. She needed to get away from it for a while, walk off her headache. She glanced down the lane again. It was hard to believe that Vince would be prowling about on the off-chance that she would venture out for a walk.

Sticking her brushes into the jar of white spirit, she shut the windows, went down the stairs and locked the outer door. She headed to the end of the lane, passing the Babbidges' cottage, which also showed no signs of life, and was soon walking down the shady little path which ran through the woods where Zachary's cottage lay hidden. The sunlight, sifting through the trees, dappled the ground with coins of light and, as she passed the place where Vince had attacked her, the peaceful afternoon belied the remembered terror of the incident.

The wood petered out, and the path emerged into the sunlight again at the corner of the large cornfield at the top of the hill where she had come sledging with Tim and the children the previous winter. Now, it looked very different. The field had been reaped and large round bales of straw lay scattered about. Kate sat down on a fallen tree trunk at the edge of the wood, the same one where they had all sat drinking tea on that snowy, winter day, and let the peacefulness of the late August afternoon seep into her. Beside her, the tall, umbelliferous plants had mostly finished flowering and sported handsome seedheads. The grass edging the field was dry and brittle and, though the leaves on the trees still clustered thick and shady behind her, here and there tinges of yellow and brown were beginning to appear.

As she sat there, Kate felt an overwhelming sense that the year was on the cusp of turning from high summer to the start of autumn. It was as though a huge, invisible wave was poised above the land, pausing for a breathless moment at its zenith, before tipping over into the new season, the calm, high, glassy arc of summer about to crumble into the foam of autumn's falling leaves and the decline of the year.

Slowly, she stood up and, almost in a dream, began to make her way back along the path, deciding to call in on Zachary, whom she hadn't seen for a while. Reaching the clearing that bordered his house, she was surprised to see Magda coming towards her, a basket over her arm. When Magda saw her, she gave a slightly embarrassed smile.

"Hello Kate. You going to see Zachary too? I've just taken him a pie. That man, I think he lives on porridge oats made with water!"

"I think you're right! He's as thin as a rake. Yes, I thought I'd call in on him. I've just been for a walk – my painting's not going too well. I'm looking forward to getting back to your portrait."

"Well, I'll see you next week for the next sitting. Bye Kate."

"Bye Magda."

Kate watched her go, with the pleasing thought that it would be wonderful if Magda and Zachary got together. Magda's slight embarrassment could mean that there was something brewing there. She hoped so.

*

The slight click told Elaine that Tim had put the phone down, but she continued to stare at the handset she was holding as though it were a scorpion. Then she put it slowly back on its cradle and walked unsteadily to a chair and sat down, bolt upright, her hands on her knees, clenched into fists.

So he was dumping her. Well, that was what it amounted to. All that nonsense about how he was worried about Mrs B's workload, and not wanting to take advantage of Elaine's kindness in doing the school run indefinitely, so he had decided to get an au pair. Strange that he should suddenly become conscience-stricken after that terrible holiday in Italy.

422

Holiday! Christ! It had been a disaster from start to finish. Or at least from the second night, when that bloody child Freddie had barged in on them in the bedroom. That had put paid to any chance of sleeping with Tim. Why he paid any attention to the tantrums of a child, she couldn't understand. He would have to accept that his father needed to move on, find love again. She, Elaine, could provide that love, and for a time it had seemed that things would work out for them. That was until Kate had appeared on the scene. She could, in retrospect, pinpoint the moment when she had felt Tim changing towards herself to the day when Kate had turned up at Tim's door, soaking wet and dishevelled, simpering her thanks for him giving her some logs or something. Next thing she knew, Kate was spending Christmas Day there. She would never forget the way Tim had looked at Kate in that green dress, with her glorious hair tumbling around her beautiful, young face.

And, much as it pained her to admit it, Kate *was* beautiful. She knew that she herself was an attractive woman, but she knew that much of her attractiveness was due to a high level of maintenance. Hairdressers and colourists, make-up, beautiful clothes and constant dieting. Kate had youth and natural beauty on her side. That lovely face – she longed to rake her nails across it, ruin its perfection.

As she sat there, her fists still clenched, the nails in question digging into her palms, with her anguished heart seeming to be hurtling around in her breast like some frantic creature, a dark memory crept into her mind. The memory of a brutish face peering at her through the window of the car. Of a voice coming from the fleshy lips pressed to the tiny gap at the top of the window, hissing something about giving Kate's face a "makeover". Something about "acid, or a nice sharp blade". Gradually, her pounding heart slowed. Instead of wild anguish, a cold hatred settled inside her like a stone. She remembered something else the man had said through the window. "Lover boy will never look at her again."

If Kate lost her looks, Tim would surely come back to her. She must try to get hold of this man, even though he frightened her. But her fear of him was nothing compared to the thought of losing Tim. How to find the man? Then she remembered the piece of paper he had pushed through the window of the car. She got up and went out to the car, parked in the drive. Opening the driver's door, she fumbled in the door pocket, and among some old tickets from car parks, she found the scruffy betting slip on which was scrawled a mobile number. She walked back into the house. With Duncan away at his father's, she could talk freely. With a shaking hand, she picked up the phone.

Chapter XX

By the start of term, Erika - a twenty-three-year old German au pair - was installed at Woodcote, and had immediately settled in, as though she had been there for months. Friendly and cheerful, with short blonde hair and an infectious giggle, she was proving to be energetic, efficient - and an excellent cook. She spoke good English and the children took to her immediately. Tim would often come back from work to the sound of gales of laughter, because of her tendency to turn everything into a game. She also got on well with Lily, which was an added blessing.

When he told the children of his intention of getting an au pair, who would be doing the school run instead of Elaine, Freddie had punched the air joyfully, and Tim was aware of a palpable relaxation in his general demeanour in the days that followed. He bought a small car for Erika to drive, and in no time she had adapted to driving on the left side of the road. Soon she was not only doing the school run, but the weekly grocery shop and any other errands that needed to be done. Gwen, who had come up to look after the children till Erika arrived, stayed for a few extra days to show her where the school and the shops were. She was greatly relieved that there would be a live-in childminder, and that she seemed to be so reliable and capable. When she brought Erika up to the studio to meet Kate, the girl pounced on the paintings stacked against the wall, examining them with great interest.

"I also like to paint," she said. "I am trying to improve the technique. Maybe you could give me advice?" She looked at Kate inquiringly, and Kate, responding to her enthusiasm, suggested that when the children came for their lesson on a Saturday, Erika could do some art too.

Kate realised that her role in looking after the children until Tim got in from work would now not be necessary and though it saddened her a little, she was intrigued that Tim had decided to dispense with Elaine's services taking the children to and from school. Perhaps the incident that Freddie had told her about had caused a rift in their relationship. The thought brought a surge of hope into her heart.

Elaine, seeing Erika at the school collecting Freddie and Amy at picking-up time, felt as though a knife were twisting in her gut. Since Tim's phone call "sacking" her, as Elaine thought of it, she had seen nothing of Tim, and began to realise that he was unlikely to get in touch to suggest seeing each other. The only way she would ever see him would be if she instigated it. She considered going round to Woodcote to talk to him face-to-face – to ask him if their relationship was over. But she ruled that out, not wanting to have a confrontation when the children were there. Even when the children were away at their grandparents, the au pair would probably be there at the house and they wouldn't be able to be alone.

The only chance she would get to see Tim at all would be if Duncan went to play with Freddie, and she could hardly have a confrontation with Tim in those circumstances. But at least if she could just see him, she might be able to get some idea of how he felt towards her.

It seemed as though her wish would be granted when Duncan told her that Freddie had asked him to come round to Woodcote to play table tennis in the games room on a Friday evening after school. Freddie and Duncan had hatched the plan between them, and the au pair had subsequently phoned to confirm that it was okay with Elaine. When she went to get Freddie and Amy from school, Erika had picked up Duncan as well, and Elaine had gone over to Woodcote later to collect him in a state of nervous tension at the thought of seeing Tim. In fact he had not got back from London yet, and it was only when she was driving back down the lane with Duncan that she saw his car coming towards her, its headlights shining through the dusk. It was a narrow squeeze getting past one another in the lane, and as they drew abreast, Tim had lowered his window and she had done the same. Her heart was thumping in her chest as though it was about to burst, but Tim seemed calm and unemotional when he spoke.

"Hello Elaine. How are you?"

426

Elaine stared at him. Was that all he could say? She hadn't heard a peep from him since the phone call telling her he was dispensing with her school run services, and all he could say was, "How are you?"

"How am I? How do you think I am?" she hissed under her breath, aware that Duncan was in the back, albeit with his earphones on, engrossed in his phone.

Tim stared back at her, taking in the hot, unshed tears glittering in her eyes, the ugly twist to her mouth, the vice-like grip of her hands on the steering wheel. What could he say to her? This wasn't the time or the place for a confrontation. The disastrous episode with Freddie in Italy and Elaine's attitude to Freddie had angered him so much and was still too fresh in his mind to allow him to feel sorry for her. He began to speak.

"Elaine..."

But Elaine cut in, "You can stuff your little pleasantries. I'm not some casual acquaintance."

She jabbed at the button to wind up the window and slammed her foot down on the accelerator. The car sped off in a shower of dirt, startling Duncan and leaving Tim sitting at the wheel of his car, his mouth set in a grim line.

When she got home, Elaine poured herself a large glass of wine with hands that still shook from the effects of her encounter with Tim. He had been so cold, so distant, but she now began bitterly to regret losing her temper with him. Had she burned her boats completely? Everything was ruined, and it was all the fault of that devious little artist. Well if she, Elaine, couldn't have Tim, then neither would Kate.

In spite of her anguish, ever present in her mind was the mingled fearfulness and anticipation caused by the thought of what she had set in motion.

*

The heatwave had continued unabated into the second week of September. On a Friday afternoon, not long after the start of term, Kate saw Erika arriving back from the school with the children. She called out

427

and waved from the open windows of the studio, and as she did so, she noticed a change in the air. The sky looked whitish, bleached. The poplar leaves had begun to stir in a slight breeze, causing a faint susurration. Far away, on the edge of hearing, she thought she heard a grumble of thunder.

Walking back to her cottage later on, she saw that the sky was becoming overcast. On the western horizon, dark clouds were beginning to gather. It was still sticky and hot even at eight in the evening. When she let herself into the house, the air in the small sitting room felt close and airless. Making herself a sandwich, she went out to the back garden to sit on the rickety bench to eat it. The clouds were piling up overhead, roiling slowly in fantastical formations of purple, grey and sulphurous yellow. It started to grow very dark as they blotted out the sky, save for one last, baleful ray from the setting sun, which shafted out under the cloud bank, touching the land with a sort of dark light. Then that too turned to ashes and vanished. She went back inside and looking out of the kitchen window to the west, saw lightning flickering in the clouds, and heard again the intermittent rumble of thunder. It looked as though there was going to be an apocalyptic thunderstorm. She watched from the kitchen window as it grew darker still, then she went up to the second bedroom to get a better view, leaving the light off and pushing her desk away from the window, so that she could stand up close to the little panes of glass. The wind had got up and was buffeting the window, whistling through the cracks in the rotting wood of the window frame. She made a mental note to find out how much it would cost to get the frame replaced. As she stood there, a jagged flash of lightning split the sky, almost immediately followed by a deafening crash of thunder, and the storm was upon her, right overhead. It was followed shortly after by another flash, and another as all hell broke loose. Then the rain started, lashing down in sheets, driving against the window like hails of bullets. Interspersed with the cacophony of noise were momentary lulls when the wind dropped a little before renewed onslaughts. It was in one of these lulls that Kate heard what sounded like a door banging. Had she not locked the back door? Had it blown open in the wind? She went to the door and was about to go downstairs, where she had left the light on, when a shadow passed across the light. She froze to

428

the spot, just as another flash of lightning seemed to crackle through the house itself. Terror flooded through her. Had she imagined that shadow? But as she stood there at the top of the narrow flight of stairs, she saw a bulky figure come round the bottom of the steps, silhouetted by the light behind.

Galvanized into action, Kate dashed back into the room, and slamming the door, fumbled with the key and turned it in the lock just as a heavy thud sounded on the other side. She dragged her desk over to the door and pushed it hard up against it, then looked wildly around in the intermittent light of the lightning flashes for something else to barricade herself in with. She flung open the door of the cupboard set into the wall. The heavy tin trunk containing her great aunt's wedding dress was still there in the space below the lower shelf. Dragging it out she pulled it over to the door and pushed it under the desk and against the door. She rushed to the window and flung it open. Leaning out into the teeth of the wind and rain, she screamed at the top of her voice.

"Help! help! Tim, Help!" Over and over again, while all the time the thumps on the door went on as the intruder kicked and launched himself at it.

Even as she stood there screaming, Kate knew there was little chance of anyone hearing her with all the noise of the thunderstorm. But she kept on, because at the back of her mind she remembered Tim telling her that if she needed anything, to give him a shout, and her jokey reply that being so close, he probably *would* hear her if she shouted. Not in a violent storm though, with thunder, lashing rain and howling wind.

Behind her, she could hear the sound of the door starting to splinter. She looked down into the darkness below the window. Jumping out didn't seem an option. She looked around again for anything more she could drag across quickly to use as a barricade. The mannequin that she had used in the triptych of Annie stood in the corner near the window, still with the wig on its head and draped in a shawl, and some portfolios and canvases and suitcases stood against the wall. Only the chest of drawers might be heavy enough to keep Vince out. She was convinced that it was Vince on the other side of the door. But before she could begin to drag the chest of drawers over to the door, she heard another heavy kick and again the splintering of wood. She backed away, coming up against the open cupboard from where she had dragged the trunk. Shaking violently, she crouched down and wriggled herself into the space where the trunk had been and tried to pull the door shut on herself. It wouldn't close properly. She pushed herself hard, further against the wooden back of the cupboard, until she felt the slats give way and clatter into an empty space behind. Frantically wriggling, she pushed herself into the hole, slipping down a small step in the floor as she did so. The slats she had dislodged lay under her. In the intermittent flashes of lightning, she gathered them up and pushed them as best she could back into the space they had occupied. The cupboard door had swung open again, and peering through a gap in the slats, she could see into the darkened room beyond, her hand brushing against what seemed like a pile of straw on the ground, and something that felt like rags. A faint smell of lavender came to her, mingled with an unidentifiable musty smell. But she didn't have time to wonder, because at that moment, the lock to the bedroom splintered away, the barricade at the door was pushed aside and the menacing figure of the intruder loomed in the doorway.

*

Freddie had always loved thunderstorms. He stood at the window of his bedroom in his pyjamas, staring out into the night, counting the seconds between each flash of lightning and its accompanying crash of thunder. Wanting to experience it more at first hand, he opened his window and holding on to the catch as the wind tugged at it, let the rain spatter his face. He was just about to close it again, when the wind dropped momentarily, and in the brief lull, he heard a faint scream, then another. It seemed to be coming from Kate's cottage, which, because of the bend in the lane, was almost directly opposite his window, across the corner of the field bordering Woodcote. Again he heard a scream, then a ferocious gust of wind and rain drowned out any other sound. He slammed the window shut and ran out of the room, hurtling down the stairs to the

430

family room where Tim sat reading the paper.

"Dad! Dad! I think I heard Kate screaming! From her house. I was watching the storm!" Freddie's voice was a hoarse yell.

"What!" Tim leapt up, dropping the paper, and rushed over to Freddie to grip him by the shoulders. "What did you hear?"

"It sounded like someone calling for help and it was coming from her house!"

Tim stared for a frozen second at Freddie's white face, then brushed past him and raced to the front door, pausing only to grab a torch and ram on a pair of old shoes in the porch. Then he was out of the front door, slamming it behind him. Both Amy and Erika appeared at the top of the stairs, looking wide-eyed at Freddie, who had run to the door after his father and who now stood in an agony of anxiety in the hall.

*

Vince's meaty hand felt for the light switch and flicked it on, but immediately there was a flash and a loud pop as the bulb blew. Momentarily dazzled by the flash, Vince's eyes darted round the room. At first he could see nothing, then a brilliant bolt of lightning lit up the room, and picked out what looked like the figure of a woman standing in the corner. With a grunt of triumph, Vince pushed the chest out of the way and lurched into the room,

From her hiding place, Kate saw the gleam of the knife blade in his hand, and she stifled the scream that rose in her throat. Then suddenly, out of nowhere, a fierce anger flared within Kate. For weeks and months she had lived in fear of Vince coming after her again. Her independence and freedom had been severely curtailed. How dare this low-life think he could terrorise women like herself and Annie? Well, she had had enough of it. She was sick of worrying if he was lurking behind every tree. Now that he was here before her, in her house, her fear inexplicably left her completely. She pushed aside the slats she had hurriedly propped into place and scrambled out of the cupboard. Vince had not heard her through the noise of the storm. He was lunging towards the dim figure of the mannequin in

431

the corner of the room, slashing at its face.

"Get out of my house!" screamed Kate, her voice cutting through the cacophony outside.

Vince swung round and in the intermittent flashes of lightning, he saw Kate, standing ashen faced, but with her chin lifted in defiance, on the other side of the room. He moved towards her, waving the knife mockingly in front of him.

"So there you are, you little bitch!" he snarled. "It's payback time. It's your fucking fault I got chucked out of me house and was had up by the pigs. Giving Annie ideas. Painting her picture for Gawd's sake."

Kate felt for the broom she knew was leaning against the wall behind her, and her fingers grasped it tightly.

"Yes, it *is* payback time," Kate shouted, "for you!" She dodged to the side, swinging the broom with all the force of her pent-up anger, at Vince's head. It connected with a crack, sending him staggering towards the window. He stumbled against Amelia's trunk in the middle of the room and Kate swung the broom at him again as he fought to regain his balance. This time she missed her target, but the end of the broom caught the mannequin which toppled forward onto Vince, causing him to fall against the window. The sound of splintering wood and shattering glass mingled with Vince's harsh scream as the rotten window frame gave way and his heavy body fell out through the jagged aperture and disappeared from sight.

Shaking violently, Kate ran to the window, her shoes crunching on broken glass, and peered out into the garden below, the rain driving into her face.

It was hard to see anything, but she thought she could make out a figure lying on the ground below the window. At that moment she saw the light of a torch bobbing down the lane towards the cottage, and she faintly heard Tim's voice calling her name. The torchlight turned into the garden and Kate made out the figure of Tim running down the path.

"Tim!" she screamed out of the window, pointing at the ground. "Be careful, he's got a knife!"

Tim, hearing her scream, looked up at the window, and made out

432

the pale oval of Kate's face looking down. He looked wildly around and saw the figure lying face up in the lavender bushes under the window. He shone his torch onto the upturned face, mostly obscured by a sodden, black balaclava, momentarily startled to see the eyes were open, slick with rain, staring sightlessly up into the streaming sky. The head was at an unnatural angle, and his right leg was twisted under him. One out-flung hand still clutched a vicious-looking knife.

Without moving the body, Tim felt for the jugular vein in Vince's throat, but as far as he could tell, there was no pulse. He looked up at Kate.

"I think he's dead. Broken neck. Is it Vince?"

"Yes, I think so. Oh my God!" Kate's voice shook with the shuddering of her body.

"Can you open the door, Kate? We need to call the police."

"Yes, yes, sorry." Kate's face disappeared from the window and shortly after, the front door opened and Kate stood there, her hair wringing wet, her eyes huge with horror and distress. She looked at Tim then fearfully stepped outside and stared at Vince, lying not far from the front door.

"Are you sure he's dead? Tim, he has a knife."

"Pretty sure." Tim turned Kate's face towards him, away from the grisly sight, pushing the soaking strands of hair out of her eyes. Drenched to the skin himself, he gathered her into his arms and held her, feeling the uncontrollable shaking of her body. He felt Kate's arms come around him as she clutched him desperately. For a long moment they stood there, the rain streaming down on them, as reaction set in, and Kate began sobbing. Long, shuddering sobs which racked her already shaking body. Tim, his own senses reeling from the drama of the situation, and Kate's close proximity, gathered his wits, and with his arm still around her turned her towards the door.

"Come on, Kate, let's get you inside. You need to dry off. And we must call the police."

Once inside, Tim shut the door and for a moment they stood looking at each other, dripping on the doormat. Kate looked so vulnerable and

433

fragile, her hair, darkened by the rain, plastered to her head, and her thin cotton top clinging to her body, that his heart lurched not only with the fear of what could have happened to her, but also with desire.

Kate could not help noticing Tim's quickly averted gaze as he took in the way her breasts were defined by the wet material. To cover her confusion, she gave a shaky laugh.

"What a couple of drowned rats! I'll go and get towels."

When Kate came back downstairs, Tim was already on his mobile to the police.

"Yes, I think he's dead... No, I haven't moved him...Yes, yes, okay. See you shortly." He rang off and took the towel Kate handed to him. Rubbing his wet hair vigorously, he then draped it over his shoulders.

"I don't suppose you have any brandy? You need it!"

Kate, also towelling her hair, shook her head. "No, 'fraid not. I'll make some tea."

Tim pushed her gently down onto the sofa.

"You stay here, I'll make it. The police should be here very soon."

Indeed, before the kettle had boiled, there was a rap on the door. Kate got to her feet, suddenly feeling lightheaded, while Tim went to answer the door. Two police officers, a man and a woman stood at the door. She just had time to recognise the face of the policewoman who had come to Tim's house on the first occasion she was attacked by Vince, before the world went black and she crumpled to the floor.

When she came to, she was lying on the sofa, with the policewoman, Linda Miller, sitting beside her holding a glass of water. It took a moment or two for Kate to take in the situation, and when she did, her eyes momentarily widened in fear, then focused on the policewoman's face.

"Is... is he dead?" Her voice came out in a croak.

"Yes, don't worry, he's dead. He can't hurt you now." The policewoman lifted Kate's head, and proffered the glass of water. Kate took a sip and slowly pulled herself into a sitting position. Suddenly, she felt as though a heavy weight had rolled off her shoulders. Vince was dead! Somehow she knew without doubt that the intruder had been Vince. She didn't have to worry any more that he was lurking out there somewhere, looking for an opportunity to attack her again.

"Thank God. Thank God." She looked up at Tim, hovering anxiously nearby, and gave him a weak smile as she shakily took the mug of tea he handed to her. She said to the policewoman, "What's happening now?"

Linda Miller nodded towards the open front door, through which Kate could see the flashing blue lights of the police cars and ambulance.

"We're waiting for the forensic team to get here. Until then, we need you to stay in one place to avoid contaminating the scene. We need to establish where the intruder got in, footprints, fingerprints etc... The medics are here, attending to the body."

Tim picked up the towel which had fallen from Kate's shoulders, and wrapped it back around her.

"Can't she go and get some dry clothes on? She's drenched."

Kate looked at him and said wryly, "You're even more soaked than I am."

Linda Miller said regretfully, "You need to talk to the investigating officer first, and wait until after the Crime Scene investigators have made a sweep of the place. They'll be here soon."

Not long after, a man completely encased in overalls, overshoes, mask and hood appeared at the front door and said something to the police officer standing by the door. Kate sipped the hot tea and tried to breathe steadily and calmly among the confusion around her, grateful for Tim's presence on the sofa beside her.

The next two hours were a blur of police coming and going, making out the scene attendance log, barking into their radios and the forensic people in protective clothing taking photos and fingerprints, tramping up and down the stairs. Outside, a tent was erected over the body to await the attendance of a pathologist the next day. Identification found on the body, confirmed that the dead man was indeed Vince Dobbs.

In the midst of it all, Kate and Tim gave their statements to the

435

investigating officer. When Kate described how she had fallen into a space behind the cupboard, the officer dispatched one of the forensic team to check it out. A little later, he was back, holding what looked like a bundle of rags wrapped in a protective polythene sheet. As he stood there, something about his demeanour made them all look towards him.

"I found this in the space behind the cupboard. Probably a priest's hole. It's the remains of a baby. Very small. It was lying on a bed of dried lavender. Looks as though it's been there for a very long time."

"*What?*" Kate's voice was shrill with shock. "*A baby?*" Her mind whirled. All the time she had lived at the cottage, there had been the tiny body of a baby hidden in the dark behind the cupboard. A memory nagged at the back of her mind. Suddenly she gasped, "Oh my God! I think I know whose baby it is." She twisted round and pointed to the little framed Valentine card on the wall near the front door.

"Can I get that picture? I need to show you something."

Linda Miller looked at her curiously then, gesturing to Kate to stay seated, said "I'll get it," and walked over to take it off the wall. "What's this got to do with a dead baby?" she asked, handing it to Kate.

"Wait till you read this," Kate said, carefully removing the back of the frame and slipping the card out from behind the glass. Opening the card, she showed the newspaper cuttings about the deaths of the young girl Susan Gatling and that of Edwin Locksley to the two police officers.

The investigating officer looked up from reading the cuttings.

"This cutting mentions that the drowned girl had recently given birth. You think the dead baby belonged to this Susan Gatling?"

Kate nodded. "I'm sure of it."

Tim put out his hand. "May I?" Taking the card and cuttings, he too examined them.

"It does seem likely that it's Susan Gatling's baby. How tragic."

The forensic officer turned to Kate. "We'll have to take the baby's remains for forensic examination, but when we release the body, you may want to give it a little funeral."

Kate nodded. She felt sure the vicar of the village church would bury the pitiful little body in the churchyard. If only they could find where

436

its mother was buried, so that the baby could be buried with her. Why did she hide the baby in the house, instead of burying it in the garden or a field? Perhaps she couldn't bear to put it in the cold ground. Perhaps she was afraid someone would see her. She couldn't believe Susan would have killed the baby. Maybe it was a stillbirth. Questions coursed through her mind, crowding out all else, so that the policewoman had to repeat what she had just said to her.

"We just need to ask you a few questions about how Dobbs came to fall out of the window," Linda Miller said. "Can you tell us what happened?"

Kate, trying to think clearly, described how she had suddenly felt she had to come out and confront Vince, before he found her cowering in the priest's hole. How she hit him with the broom, and how the mannequin had toppled over onto him, causing him to crash against the window.

"The woodwork was very rotten and the window was open anyway. The whole thing gave way with his weight," she ended, leaning back on the sofa.

Miller nodded. "The mannequin has a deep slash to its face and was lying on the floor, which ties in with your account."

When she had finished taking Kate's statement, she turned to Tim, who described how he had come into the garden seconds after Vince had fallen.

Miller closed her notebook.

"We've done what we can inside for now. I suggest that you don't sleep here tonight. Is there anywhere else you can go?"

"You must come to Woodcote," Tim said at once to Kate. He turned to Miller. "Can she go upstairs now, and get some things?"

"Yes, I'll come with you." The policewoman turned to Kate and helped her up, then followed her up the stairs to Kate's bedroom. As she passed the door opposite her room, Kate gave an involuntary shudder as she looked through at the disorder within. The mannequin lay amongst the splintered glass from the window over which a plastic sheet had now been fixed.

Kate hurriedly changed into some dry clothes and flung some wash

437

things into a bag. She caught sight of herself in the bathroom mirror and grimaced at the bedraggled image she saw there.

Back downstairs, the investigating officer informed her that Vince had come in via the back door after breaking one of the little panes of glass set into the upper half of the door.

"He would have found it more difficult if you had not left the key in the lock, but he would probably have got in anyway," he said. "A few hefty kicks would have splintered the lock or the hinges."

Kate shivered. "But he could have done that any time over the past few months. Why wait till now?"

"Who knows?" The investigating officer shrugged. "Maybe he thought he could get away with it under cover of the noise of the storm. Now I suggest that you both go back to Mr. Crawford's house. There'll be a police officer posted here all night. We'll come along in the morning, let you know when they've taken the body away."

Tim put his arm around Kate's shoulders and led her to the door. He turned to the police officers.

"Thanks. Goodnight then. See you in the morning."

Outside, Kate realised the storm had passed. She could see ragged scraps of cloud scudding across a gibbous moon. Glancing at the tent which had been erected under the window, she was glad Vince's body was hidden from view.

Out in the lane, she and Tim picked their way round the faintly gleaming puddles. Tim kept his arm around her shoulders and in the circle of his arm Kate experienced a feeling of complete safety and peace. She could have walked for miles through the night like this, but all too soon they were at Woodcote's gate. Kate looked over at the Babbidges' cottage, half expecting to see Lily at the window wondering what had been going on, but though a light showed at the kitchen window, all was still. She realised that the bend in the lane must have shielded the Babbidges' cottage from all the commotion. Later she discovered from Lily that she and Bill had been watching television in their sitting room at the back of the house and hadn't heard a thing.

Having left the house without his key, Tim tapped the knocker of the

438

front door quietly in case the children were asleep. He needn't have worried, because when Erika opened the door, he saw his two anxious children peering at him worriedly from behind the au pair, who also looked thoroughly overwrought.

Tim ushered Kate in through the door and grinned reassuringly at the children.

"It's all fine, kiddos," he said in a steady voice. "Everything's under control. Nothing to be worried about now. Kate's staying here tonight. And I think you guys ought to get to bed. It's past midnight."

"But Dad!" Freddie protested. "What happened?"

Tim held up his hand in a stop gesture.

"We'll tell you all about it in the morning. Bed now."

Kate smiled at the children as brightly as she could.

"Goodnight Freddie. Goodnight Amy. See you in the morning. Everything's fine, really."

Reluctantly the children went upstairs, and Tim, seeing Erika hovering uncertainly in the hall, asked her to take Kate into the family room while he went to get some brandy. Erika put her arm round Kate and solicitously propelled her to the den at the back of the house, fussing around with cushions till Tim came back with the brandy and three glasses. He poured a generous measure into each glass and indicated that Erika sit down with them.

"You'd better hear what's happened," he said to her, sitting down on the sofa beside Kate.

He took a sip of brandy and outlined the background of Vince's grudge against Kate, his first attack, and what had just happened. Erika listened in horrified fascination, taking tremulous sips of brandy and leaning over from time to time to pat Kate's hand sympathetically. Kate, nestled in the corner of the sofa, felt a continuing sense of relief and solace, albeit laced with flashbacks of the sheer terror she had felt when Vince had come crashing through the door of the upstairs room.

"Now, I think we all ought to get some sleep," Tim said, taking Kate's empty glass.

Kate stood up and followed Tim up the stairs to the same room she

439

had slept in after Vince's first attack. This time she saw no figure at the window, but sank into a dreamless sleep, aided by the brandy, and did not wake till nine the following morning.

*

Elaine stood at the window of her drawing room, looking out across the back garden where the gardener was mowing the lawn. Her outward calm belied the turmoil of her mind and the visceral churning in her gut which made her feel physically sick. Only the slight shaking of the newspaper she held in her hand betrayed her agitation. Mrs Logan, her cleaning lady, had thrust it into her hand when she had arrived shortly before.

"You don't take the local paper, do you, Mrs Grainger?" she said, bursting to impart the news which had set the whole village abuzz.

"No, why? What's happened?"

"Oh, quite a hoo-ha! The young woman who lives in old Miss Hopkirk's cottage in Tuckers Lane was attacked on Saturday night, by that awful Vince who used to live on our estate. But he fell out of the window and was killed! Here, it's on page two." She opened the paper and pointed out the article. "You know the family that lives further down the lane, don't you? Have you met the girl from the cottage?"

Elaine took the paper. The blood had drained from her face and her heart was hammering in her chest.

"What? Oh, yes, I've met her once or twice." Elaine hesitated, then added with studied casualness, "Why was she attacked?"

"Who knows? It doesn't say in the paper. Wouldn't put anything past that Vince. He used to beat up poor Annie, his partner, something awful. Then he got a restraining order and had to leave the estate and not go anywhere near her."

Elaine went into the drawing room with the paper. The article was quite short, detailing the bare facts of what had happened. Elaine scanned it quickly. When she read the sentence "Kate Atkins escaped unhurt" she felt a curious mixture of despair and relief. It had been over a week since

440

the phone conversation with the man she had encountered in the lane that dark night, and she had spent the interim period in an agony of dread and indecision as to whether to call the whole thing off. It was hard to reconcile what she had set in motion with her perception of herself as a person. But whenever her conscience reared its head, the vision of Kate's lovely face would flash before her, and what she saw as a rejection of herself by Tim compounded her torment. She felt she was losing her grip on reality.

It had seemed, when she keyed in the mobile number the man had scribbled down, as though someone else was making the call, and she was some sort of spectator. When he had answered the phone with a barked, "Yeah?" she had almost ended the call there and then, but after a hesitation, when the voice had repeated, "Yeah? Who's that?" she heard herself saying,

"It's about what you talked about the other night. When my car…about the girl from the cottage…"

A momentary pause, then, in a lower voice he said, "Oh! Yeah. You want her cut? Or acid?"

"I… I don't care. Just as long as…" Her voice tailed off.

"As long as there are some…*changes* made to 'er pretty little face, eh?" He gave a snort of laughter. "Consider it done. 'Course I'll have to choose me time. Can't afford to get caught. I'm in enough trouble with the fucking Bill already, mostly thanks to our little bitch artist. Painting Annie's picture, giving 'er ideas she's better than she is."

"I don't know what you're talking about. All I want you to do is… What you said…Make some alterations."

"What about me payment?"

"I'll give you two fifty in advance and two fifty… afterwards."

"Alright. I'll come and pick up the money from yer. Where do yer live?"

The thought of the man knowing where she lived filled Elaine with terror.

"No! I'll meet you somewhere." She thought quickly. "There's a little road leading into the woods before you get to Tuckers Lane, on the

441

village side."

"I know it. I'll see yer there. When?"

"Tomorrow evening. About eight." Elaine put the phone down before she could change her mind.

For the rest of the day and late into the night, Elaine agonised about what she had started. It was almost made worse by the fact that she could still put a stop to it, and she was racked with doubts and indecision. In the end, the despair she was feeling about the disintegration of her relationship with Tim stayed her hand and, at eight the following evening with the money sealed in an envelope on the car seat beside her, Elaine backed her car a little way down the narrow road which led into the woods, wanting to be facing out in case she needed to get away quickly. She worried that it was quite close to the lane where Kate and Tim lived, but she had been unable to think of another spot which they would both know but which was shielded from observers. Besides, she couldn't think that anyone would be around in the woods at that time in the evening.

The shadows were beginning to close in, with the dusk creeping through the quiet wood as she picked up the envelope and got out of the car, leaving the engine running. Her heart was hammering in her chest as she scanned the lane in both directions, looking for the man. She still did not know his name nor did she want to. She hoped that after he had collected his second payment, she would never set eyes on him again.

Then she saw him, sauntering down the lane from the direction of the main road, a cigarette hanging out of the corner of his mouth. He had the collar of his donkey jacket turned up, half covering his face, and a scruffy beanie hat was pulled down low almost to his eyes. He came up and stood uncomfortably close to her. She took a step back so that she was half protected by the open door of the car. He circled round until he was also standing by the open car door. He grinned, showing discoloured teeth.

"We 'aven't been properly introduced. The name's Vince."

Ignoring this piece of information, and declining to tell Vince her own name, she thrust the envelope towards him. He whipped it out of her hand, tore it open and checked its contents before pushing it into the

442

pocket of his jacket. Elaine got back into the car, but Vince was still standing with his hand on the top of the door, the other hand in the pocket of his jeans. He turned his head and spat the cigarette out of his mouth onto the road, and stood looking down at her as she put the car in gear. Her dress had ridden up when she had got into the car and looking up at him, she noticed his gaze lingering on her legs. Hastily pulling down her skirt, she started to let the clutch out, but he reached in and turned off the ignition. The engine died and the quiet of the woods flooded in around her.

"Hang on a fuckin' minute, woman," Vince said, an undercurrent of menace in his voice. "How am I going to contact yer when I've done the necessary? To get the rest of the dosh? I dunno where yer live. Yer could just go back on the deal and I'd never get me money."

Elaine felt a stab of panic. The menace in his voice and the way he was looking at her made her mouth dry with fear. Why had she started this? She forced herself to speak calmly.

"You'll just have to trust me. I'll give you my mobile number so that you can let me know when you've done it. I can meet you here to give you the other two fifty."

"Okay, but if yer don't, I'll inform the police anonymously that a woman had set up the attack. They'll hunt you down."

Elaine looked into his hooded eyes, and knew that he meant it. Suddenly, she lost her nerve.

"Look, let's forget the whole thing. You keep that money, but let's leave it at that."

Vince gave a snort. "Oh no yer don't. Yer in deep, lady. And I want the rest of the dosh. Yer not backing out now."

Elaine's knuckles were white as she gripped the steering wheel.

"Oh, alright, alright. Call me when you've done it."

"I don't know yer number. There was no caller ID when you phoned me."

Elaine scrabbled in her bag and pulled out a diary, tore out a page and scribbled her number down. Thrusting it into Vince's meaty hand, she turned the key in the ignition again and began to move off. This time he

443

stepped away from the door and let her go, slamming the car door shut. In the rear-view mirror, she saw him begin to follow her down to the main road. He was almost up to her when a break in the traffic allowed her to pull out. She breathed a shuddering sigh of relief as she drove away.

Zachary stepped out from the woods on to the potholed tarmac of the track which led to his cottage. He had been sitting on a stump a little way into the trees, quietly watching a squirrel foraging for hazelnuts and burying them in the leaf litter, keenly observing its bright eyes, the shape of its head, the way it flicked its tail, the tiny claws gripping the nuts.

As he sat there, he heard the sound of a car engine and shortly after, the murmur of voices. Hoping the squirrel would not be spooked, Zachary remained motionless, but the sound of the car door being slammed caused the squirrel to scurry away up the trunk of an oak, and Zachary stood up, stretching to loosen up after sitting motionless for so long. Dressed as he was in dun-coloured clothes, the better to observe the woodland creatures without being seen by them, he remained invisible in the gathering dusk as he emerged into the lane. He saw the rear of a red car disappearing round the corner into the main road and the vague shape of the bulky figure which was following it. Zachary watched as the figure turned into the road and went off in the opposite direction from the car. Something about the figure looked familiar, and he realised with a jolt that it reminded him of the man he had seen disappearing down the path after Kate had been attacked. He smelt cigarette smoke, and looking down, saw the butt of a cigarette lying on the road, a wisp of smoke still curling from the tip.

And now, as Elaine folded the newspaper with trembling hands, the relief that the man who could incriminate her could not now do so, was invaded by the insistent thought that nothing had changed. Kate still had her beauty, and she, Elaine, was still without Tim.

444

Chapter XXI

When Kate woke in Tim's guest room on the Saturday morning after the traumatic events of the evening before, the sense of a load having lifted off her shoulders persisted. Although the grisly sight of Vince's lifeless body lying in the rain kept flashing into her mind, she focused on the lucky escape she had had. The set of circumstances which led to Vince falling to his death seemed somewhat unreal - the light bulb blowing, the trunk on the floor which tripped Vince up, the mannequin falling on him, the rotten window frame - everything seemed to have conspired in her favour.

But the one thing which troubled her almost more than Vince, now that his menace was removed, was the tiny skeleton that the police had found in the hidden alcove. Was it Susan Gatling's baby? The thought that it had lain there all those years, forgotten and unmarked, saddened her and made her determined to confirm with the police that she could arrange for a burial as soon as the forensic tests were completed.

Downstairs, she found two police officers in Tim's kitchen, who informed her that Vince's body was due to be removed shortly, and that she would be free to return to her cottage very soon. She asked about the baby, and was told that she could go ahead and arrange for a funeral to take place after the baby's remains had been released.

Tim walked back to the cottage with Kate, where they saw that there were still a couple of police cars and a van parked in the lane. Soon, however, the officers and the investigating team said their goodbyes and drove away, taking Vince's body with them in a body bag. Kate stood in the garden, surveying the trampled mess which had been the lawn and flower bed under the window. She could not repress a shudder when she thought of the twisted body which had lain there in the stormy darkness the night before. She looked up at the broken window across which the police had taped a piece of plastic sheeting.

"I'll have to get someone to come and fix that," Kate said ruefully.

445

"Bet it costs a fortune. It looks as though the entire window will have to be replaced."

Tim nodded. "Yes, the whole frame must have been pretty rotten. But you could probably get most of it done on the house insurance. I know an excellent chap who replaced some of the windows at Woodcote not so long ago. I'll give him a ring, but you'll have to wait till the insurance people approve the repairs."

Kate flashed him a grateful smile. "Thanks Tim. I'll find out about the insurance. I know I've got some sort of cover." She walked towards the open front door. "Better see what state the house is in!"

"Doesn't look too bad, apart from all the muddy footprints," Tim remarked, following her into the house. He walked through the kitchen to the back door and examined the smashed panel of glass through which Vince had broken in.

"This'll have to be fixed too. Don't worry, Clive will sort you out. I'll go and give him a ring in a minute." Tim looked at Kate. "Are you going to be okay? Are you sure you don't want to stay with us for a few days?

"No, I'm fine, really. After all, my main source of worry is now gone. I'm going to do a bit of clearing up. I'll let you know when I've been to see the vicar about burying the baby. Maybe we could have a little ceremony with the children?"

"I think that would be lovely. Just let us know when." Tim hesitated. He longed to know if Jake would be coming down to support her after her ordeal. He had begun to dare to hope that her relationship with Jake was not a particularly close one. He certainly did not seem to be on the scene much. Even so, he could not get the sight of him and Kate together in the garden on that hot summer's day out of his mind. That had looked like a pretty close relationship! In the end, Tim said nothing about Jake. He just bent and gave Kate a peck on the cheek and went to the door.

"I'll go and ring Clive about the window. Let me know if you need anything."

Kate went to the door and watched him disappear down the lane.

446

Then she went back in and started cleaning up the cottage.

*

On the following Monday, when the local paper came out, Magda read the report about Vince's attack, and rushed next door to show it to Annie. Annie's smile faltered when she opened the door and saw the expression on Magda's face.

"What is it? What's happened?" she said, following Magda who went into the kitchen and spread the paper out on the kitchen table. She pointed at the article.

"Read that," she said grimly.

Annie skimmed it, then sat heavily down on a kitchen chair.

"Oh my God! He's dead. He's dead!" She looked at Magda, her eyes wide with shock. Then she closed her eyes and put her hands over her face.

Magda watched her anxiously. Surely she didn't still have feelings for Vince? Then Annie dropped her hands. Her eyes were shining, and a smile of relief spread across her face.

"Thank God! I'm free of him! Forever!" Then her eyes darkened. "Oh, but poor Kate! I hope she's alright." She looked back at the article. "It says she was unharmed, but it must have been so frightening! I must go and see her. I've got time before I have to pick up Becky from nursery." She scooped Darren out of his highchair, took him to the sink and washed his face.

"I'll come with you. I'm going to clean at Tim's house anyway," Magda said. "I'll just get my things."

At Kate's cottage, they found two men working on the broken window frame, one on a ladder leaning against the outside of the house. Tim had lost no time in getting Barkers Household Maintenance to make out an estimate for the repairs, and the insurance company had sent an assessor out very quickly to view the damage and agree to the work being carried out. Tim had prevailed on Barkers to start the work immediately.

Annie hugged Kate, then scanned her face for signs of damage.

447

"He really didn't hurt you then?" she said anxiously.

"No, he had a knife, but he fell out of the window before he could use it." Kate looked curiously at Magda and Annie.

"How did you know about it?"

Magda pulled the newspaper from her bag and handed it to Kate.

"Local paper. Here, read it. But it's quite short. Tell us exactly what happened."

Kate told them the sequence of events, ending with the discovery of the remains of the tiny baby, which caused tears to spring to Annie's eyes and Magda's hand to fly to her mouth as she gasped,

"But… whose baby was it? What was it doing there? The paper doesn't mention it at all."

Kate told them about Susan Gatling and her theory that it must have been her baby.

"I don't know why, but I'm sure it was a little girl. I'm hoping to get the vicar to give her a decent burial in the churchyard when the police release her. I want to have a little service. Maybe you could come?"

"Of course we will." Magda said, immediately echoed by Annie. She added, "I'll make a little wrap for her. Poor little mite."

"But at least you're safe," Annie said, looking at Kate. "We're rid of Vince, both of us."

"Yes," Kate agreed, smiling at her. "We're rid of him."

*

Kate let herself in through the lych gate and walked up the path between the gravestones to the front door of the church. When she found the church empty, she walked round to the rectory next door and rang the bell. A pleasant looking, plumpish woman opened the door and, at Kate's request to see Reverend Blackwell, said regretfully, "Sorry dear, my husband's out visiting parishioners at the moment. He'll be back about half-past twelve, if you'd like to pop back then."

Kate agreed to do so, resolving to visit Lydia Campbell while she was waiting. When she knocked on Mrs Campbell's door, it was opened

448

by a brisk little woman in a bright pink nylon overall, clutching a tea towel. She beamed when Kate asked to see Lydia.

"Ooh, Mrs C will be so pleased! She loves having visitors, but most of her friends have passed away now."

Kate followed her into the drawing room, feeling guilty that she had not been to visit the old lady for a while.

Lydia's face broke into a welcoming smile when she saw Kate.

"My dear! How lovely to see you," she said, taking off her reading glasses. "I've just been reading about the attack on you." She indicated the paper on her lap. "How perfectly dreadful! Are you really unharmed? Come and sit down and tell me all about it. Betty dear," she said to the woman who had let Kate in, "could you be an angel and get us some coffee?"

"Just going to suggest the same thing, Mrs C. Won't be a mo." Betty bustled off, and Kate sat down in a chair facing Lydia, who nodded in the direction of the door through which Betty had disappeared.

"Betty comes every day to get my lunch. She's a dear." She leaned forward in her chair. "Now, do you know why this horrible man attacked you?"

"Well, I'd better start at the beginning," Kate said, and explained about Vince's predilection for knocking Annie about, his anger at her sitting for Kate, the first attack back in February, and finally the dreadful events of the previous Friday night. Lydia listened, fixing Kate with a gaze of fascinated horror.

"You poor child! What a terrible experience! And all those months worrying that he might be lurking behind every tree." She leaned back in her chair and picked up the cup of coffee that Betty had brought in halfway through Kate's narration.

She continued, "But he's out of the picture now. You can relax."

"There's something else," Kate said, and told her about the tiny body that had been found in the cottage, and how she believed it to be the baby that Susan Gatling had given birth to before she drowned in the river. Lydia's eyes were wide with shock.

"You mean, all those years Amelia lived in the cottage, this baby

449

was lying hidden behind the cupboard?" She stopped, then said slowly, "Do you remember I told you that she had once seen the figure of a young woman walk into a cupboard in one of the bedrooms and vanish?

Kate nodded and said, more of a statement than a question, "Susan Gatling."

Lydia nodded in her turn.

"I'm sure of it. Not only did she see a figure, but she always said she felt there was something strange about that room. She said she sometimes got the scent of lavender, and sometimes she heard a sobbing sound, though she thought it must be the wind in the chimney."

"It was the same with me. Although I didn't see anything, I often felt a presence. And my friend Bea was very disturbed by something about the room when she came to visit."

"Perhaps Susan couldn't rest while her baby was lying there. An unquiet spirit," Lydia said softly, almost to herself.

"I'm going to ask the vicar to perform a little burial ceremony when the forensic people have finished with the body," Kate said. "I'm not sure what the procedure is. I hope we don't have to get undertakers involved. I just feel we ought to lay the little thing in a proper resting place."

"Will you let me know when you are going to bury it? I would like to be there, for Amelia's sake," Lydia said, her eyes shining with unshed tears. She blinked them away impatiently. "The church is very close. I'm sure I can manage it."

"Of course. I'll let you know, and come and fetch you on the day." Kate stood up. "I'd better go. I'll call in and see the vicar now." She bent to kiss the old lady on the cheek. Lydia took her hand, giving it a little squeeze.

"Thank you for coming my dear. Good of you to visit an old woman."

"I'll see you soon, Mrs Campbell. Goodbye for now."

Lydia watched Kate as she went out of the room, then turned and gazed at the bright rose hips on the bush outside the window, trying to imagine what Amelia's thoughts would have been if she had known about the baby.

"Not *again!*" Mimi's voice on the other end of the line was horrified. "For God's sake, girl! Here I am living in the big, bad city, and never had a single spot of bother from nasty men, and there you are in the so-called peaceful countryside, being attacked every five minutes by knife-wielding, homicidal maniacs!"

Kate grinned at Mimi's characteristic use of hyperbole.

"Twice is not exactly every five minutes! Anyway he's dead now. So that should be that."

Kate went on to tell Mimi about the discovery of the baby, to which Mimi listened with gasps of astonishment.

"Good grief! What will you come up with next? A treasure trove under the floorboards?"

"I wish! Anyway, I spoke to the vicar of the church in the village, and he's going to perform a little burial ceremony when the police release the baby."

"We'll come!" Mimi said instantly. "I'll tell the others. Let me know when it's going to be."

"Of course I will. I wish we could find Susan Gatling's grave, so that we can bury the baby with her."

"It may not be her baby at all," Mimi said. "But you're right, it does seem likely."

"I'm sure it's Susan's baby. As sure as I've ever been of anything."

"Well, anyway, ring me when you know when the burial's going to be. Bye for now. I must tell the others about all this." Mimi rang off, and Kate went into the kitchen to make more tea for the men repairing the window. As she waited for the kettle to boil, she saw the grizzled, lanky figure of Zachary turning into the gate, and went to open the door before he had time to knock.

"Hi Zachary! I've just put the kettle on. Come in and have some tea."

Zachary put a hand on her shoulder.

451

"Are you okay? Magda's just been to see me and told me what happened. Brought a pie she made. She thinks I'm going to starve. Don't know how she thinks I've managed all these years!" He spoke flippantly, but Kate detected an affectionate tone in his voice, and a slight shyness. Not for the first time she wondered if something was developing romantically between Magda and Zachary.

Kate took the tea up to the workmen, then she and Zachary went out into the warm September sunshine of the back garden with their mugs of tea, and sat on the bench.

"Magda told me what happened to you the other night," Zachary said, looking at her gravely. "By God, you had a lucky escape - again!" He inclined his head towards the house. "Is that the window he fell out of, the one they're repairing?"

"Yes. Thank God it was in such a rotten state!"

"And it was the same person who attacked you before? That thug Vince?"

"Yes, it was him."

Zachary took a sip of his tea, then said slowly, "There's something I think I ought to tell you, and maybe the police too."

Kate looked at him curiously. "What is it? Is it something to do with Vince?"

"Well, it may be nothing, but the other evening, about ten days ago, I was watching a squirrel in the woods near my house, when I heard voices and a little while later I saw a red car going off down the little track that leads from my house to the main road, and a man walking along behind it. It was getting dark, but he reminded me of the figure I saw running off after Vince attacked you that first time."

Kate stared at him, her mug halfway to her lips. "A red car? Did you see the number plate?" Her voice shook with the effort she was making to stay calm.

"No, it was too dark. The driver only turned on the lights as the car went out into the main road."

"Did you see what make of car it was?"

"It looked like a Volvo, but I can't be sure. I'm not that good at

452

cars."

Kate realised she had been holding her breath. She lowered her mug and exhaled slowly. She said quietly, "Elaine has a red Volvo." She looked quickly at Zachary. "Do you think she..." Her voice tailed off. The thought was too preposterous.

Zachary voiced her thoughts. "You think she may have hired a hitman? Magda said that Elaine and Tim had a relationship, but Lily told her that it seems to have cooled. Maybe Elaine sees you as a threat."

"Yes, she does. She's laid into me about it on two occasions. She was distraught and seemed a bit crazy. Then Tim gets himself an au pair so that he doesn't need her to do the school run any more. She must have felt rejected by him as well as threatened by my presence. But I can't believe she would actually get someone to *kill* me. Anyway, how would she have known how to get hold of Vince?"

"I don't know, but it does look rather suspicious. If it was her car I saw, and if it was Vince she met in the lane..."

"Too many ifs. There's nothing we can do. We can't accuse someone on such flimsy evidence. And anyway..." Kate thought of Elaine's distress the last time she had talked to her. She also thought of Duncan. How would the poor kid feel if his mother was arrested on suspicion of being party to a crime? Anyway, Vince was dead. He couldn't hurt her now.

She looked up at the poplars. Their leaves were starting to turn now, and their green-gold shimmered against the blue of the sky as the breeze streamed through them. She thought of Elaine, and couldn't help putting herself in her position. If she *had* collaborated with Vince, she must have been in a desperate state of mind. But surely not so desperate as to get someone to kill her?

"Maybe," she said thoughtfully, turning back to Zachary, "maybe she didn't want me killed, just disfigured or something. I saw the way he was holding the knife. He was slashing at the mannequin's face, not stabbing."

Zachary snorted. "Oh, that's okay then! Just as long as she didn't want you killed, just cut up a bit!"

453

"We don't know whether she was involved at all! It may just have been Vince acting on his own, just like the first time."

"Well, it looks pretty suspicious to me."

"But what good would it do to get Elaine convicted as a party to the attack? She has a son. What would that do to Duncan?"

Zachary rolled his eyes and shook his head in mock despair.

"Kate, you are impossible! Aren't you afraid she'll try it again? She may even do it herself. Chuck acid in your face or something." He looked at her quizzically. "Have you got no idea of how beautiful you are?"

It was Kate's turn to roll her eyes. "No more so than Elaine. She's very attractive."

Zachary sighed. "You're hopeless, Kate." He drained his cup and stood up. "Well, I thought I'd better tell you about what I saw. If you don't want me to report it to the police, I won't, but I think you're making a big mistake."

Kate reached out and patted his arm.

"Thank you, Zachary. I *will* think about it. But I can't help just being grateful that Vince is gone. I don't like Elaine, but I don't want to cause more misery to her than I already have."

"Through no fault of your own, my girl. Remember that."

Kate said softly "How do we prevent the 'Turbid ebb and flow of human misery,' as Matthew Arnold put it? I can't help seeing her on a desolate beach, facing the 'drear and naked shingles of the world' all alone, when once she thought she would marry Tim."

Zachary looked at her and she had to look away. She knew she would never report what he had seen to the police.

*

Dusk was falling as Elaine turned her car down the potholed little road, just as it had been on the evening she had driven down it to meet Vince. She drove a short distance down the track and stopped the car. She guessed that the woods that hemmed in the track on either side were the

454

same woods which butted up against Woodcote. If she cut through the woods, she would probably come to Tuckers Lane eventually. She had not seen Tim since the acrimonious encounter in the lane, and the hollow, empty feeling inside her threatened to consume her. She desperately needed at least to catch a glimpse of him. Was Kate with him? Did she go round and have cosy evenings with the family? She had to go and see, but she did not want to park in Tuckers Lane where Tim or Kate might see her car. Though she shuddered in distaste at the connotations of the wooded track where the fateful meeting with Vince had taken place, her need to try to catch a glimpse of Tim overrode everything else.

She walked soft-footed down the track, her eyes on the ground to prevent her stumbling in the potholes. She was upon Zachary's cottage before she realised there was even a house there. The track petered out at the cottage, behind which a clearing let in the last of the evening light. The cottage was in darkness and looked as though it may be deserted. Elaine decided to risk following the indistinct path which cut across the clearing. To her astonishment, she saw the shadowy forms of animals dotted about among the dry grasses, the biggest of which was of a roe deer, its head raised as though testing the air. Further on, a badger nosed the ground beside the path. When she realised they were wooden sculptures, her puzzlement deepened. What was this place? It now looked as though someone must live in the tiny, hidden cottage crouching in the shadows under the oaks, and it wasn't deserted after all.

At the other side of the clearing the path joined a wider one. She guessed that if she turned left it would lead in the direction she wanted. She carefully noted that the entrance to the smaller path was marked by a huge oak tree, thrusting a snaking root right across the bigger path; this would tell her where to turn off on her return. It wasn't long before the wider footpath came out at the end of Tuckers Lane. Elaine stood for a moment, looking down the lane. To her left, the light from the Babbidges' kitchen window glowed in the dusk and further down on the right, she saw the lights from Woodcote glimmering through the trees.

Elaine stepped out into the lane. Keeping to the verge, where the seed heads of cow parsley brushed against her legs, she made her way down to Tim's house, almost invisible in her dark jeans and jacket, her hair covered with a dark blue headscarf. To her horror, she saw that the lights were on above the garage. Kate must still be working in her studio. What if she saw her creeping about in the dark outside Tim's house? But Elaine's need to see Tim prevented her turning back. Keeping close to the wall of the garage, she cut through the gap between the garage and the house and quietly slipped through the gate that led to the back garden. The window which she knew to be that of Tim's study was in darkness, but she nevertheless gave it a wide berth and crept towards the large windows of the family room, the lights of which blazed out across the terrace and lawn. She walked out on to the lawn into the darkness beyond the rectangles of light on the grass and looked into the windows. The whole family seemed to be there, as well as the au pair, who was ironing in one corner. Freddie was at the computer and Amy sat with her blonde head bent over something she was doing at the table. Tim stood behind Freddie, pointing at something on the computer screen. They were both laughing. To her relief, there was no sign of Kate. Elaine watched as Tim walked towards the window and picked up the paper which was lying on the arm of the sofa, and she got a good view of his face; the face of the man she had become besotted with and whom she had hoped to marry.

Physical, visceral pain almost doubled her up as she stood gazing at Tim, heedless of the dew seeping into her flimsy shoes from the damp grass. She longed to rush up to the window and hammer on the glass, to get him to look at her, acknowledge her existence, anything rather than the chasm of silence that had opened up between them. Involuntarily, she took a step forward, into the full light blazing out from the big picture windows. The movement must have caught the periphery of Tim's vision and he turned to look out of the window.

In spite of the reflections in the glass of the room behind him, Tim saw the figure of Elaine standing outside, transfixed, like a rabbit in the headlights. With a sharp intake of breath, Tim strode to the French doors and wrenched them open. The kids looked up startled, and he said as casually as he could over his shoulder, "Stay here, kids. Elaine's out there.

456

I think she wants a word." He stepped quickly out on to the terrace and closed the door. Elaine, suddenly galvanised into action, turned quickly away, but Tim strode over to her and grabbed her upper arm firmly. Without a word, he marched her down to the far end of the lawn, beyond where the light from the house spilled onto the grass. There, he swung her round to face him, grasping both her arms above the elbow. He could just make out her face in the gloom.

"Elaine, what are you doing creeping around the house in the dark? If you have anything to say to me, why don't you come to the front door or phone me?"

Elaine looked up at him, her eyes darting about his shadowy face like those of a trapped animal. Suddenly she lunged forward, trying to throw her arms around him, but he held her away from him. She gave a choking sob.

"But Tim, how could I? You dumped me! That's what it amounts to. You phone me up and casually tell me you don't want me to do the school run anymore. Then weeks go by and you don't get in touch. After all I've done for you, after all we had together, you just cut me out of your life. Just because Freddie barges in on us in Italy without bothering to knock, then goes off in a huff and ruins the whole holiday."

Tim's mouth hardened into a grim line. "So it's all Freddie's fault, is it? Nothing to do with the fact that you come uninvited into my room and proceed to take off half your clothes, so that my son - who by the way is perfectly entitled to come into my bedroom whenever he wants - is confronted with a very upsetting sight." He released her arms and stepped back from her, but that enabled Elaine to fling herself at him, wrapping her arms round his neck.

"Don't forget, you responded! Don't pretend you didn't. If Freddie hadn't come in…"

Tim realised the truth of her words, even though it had not been him who had instigated the clinch Freddie had found them in.

"I know. All I can say is that I'm only human, and I was half asleep."

"So if you had been properly awake, you wouldn't have touched me

457

with a barge-pole!" Elaine choked out, then stumbled on. "It... it's not just Freddie, it's that scheming little artist of yours, entwining herself around your family, while pretending to me that she's with someone else."

Tim reached round and gripped her wrists, prising her arms away from his neck and holding them in front of him at arm's length.

"You've confronted her about it?"

Elaine looked wildly around her. "Tim, you're hurting me. Yes, if you must know, I talked to her a couple of times, asked her if you and she..." she tailed off, her voice dissolving into sobs.

Tim gazed at her, appalled. "Elaine, what were you thinking?"

"What am I supposed to think?" Elaine's voice was harsh with despair. "As soon as she arrived on the scene, you changed towards me. You've fallen for her, haven't you? You're in love with her! So you just cast me off without any explanation. Have you slept with her? *Have you?"*

Tim looked at her, still grasping her wrists. In spite of his anger, he couldn't help feeling desperately sorry for her. Perhaps he *had* treated her badly. He should have let her down more gently. Taken her to dinner and explained that their relationship wasn't going anywhere as far as he was concerned. But he had been so dismayed at the debacle in Italy and Elaine's subsequent hostility towards Freddie, that he had wanted nothing more to do with her. Now, looking at her distraught face, he got some inkling of the anguish she must have been going through during the last few weeks. In a gentler tone, he said, "Elaine, I'm sorry you've been unhappy."

"*Unhappy!"* She gave a bitter laugh. "Yes, I suppose you could say that, after how you've treated me. You took me to your bed, made use of me, then when a nubile young girl comes along - who's much too young for you by the way - you decide you can just dispense with my services."

"Elaine, it wasn't like that at all and you know it. I never gave you any cause to think our relationship, if you can call it that, was going anywhere."

"If you can call it that! What would you call it then? A nice chat over a cup of tea? And what sort of *relationship* have you got with your artist?"

"Nothing has happened between Kate and me."

"I don't believe you! You're lying! Let me go!" She wrenched at her hands and Tim released her, causing her to stagger back. Regaining her balance, she took one last look at him, a look filled with bitterness mixed with longing, then turned and ran back up the lawn.

Tim stood looking after her but made no attempt to follow. His mind churning, he made his way slowly up the lawn and sat heavily down on one of the chairs on the terrace. How much of Elaine's state of mind had been his fault? It seemed that he had seriously miscalculated just how fixated Elaine had been on him: he should have realised that one phone call was not the way to "dispense with her services," as Elaine so starkly put it. There had been a serious crisis at work while he had been in Italy and, in the stress of sorting it out when he got back, he had not treated Elaine with enough consideration. He blamed himself for his insensitivity, but then he remembered how she had admitted to having confronted Kate about her relationship with him, and how Kate had kept silent about the confrontations. His heart hardened again towards Elaine, and not for the first time, he regretted ever having become involved with her.

Elaine reached the gate at the side of the house and as she let herself through, she saw the lights in the studio above the garage go out. She ducked behind the back of the garage, straining her ears. The last thing she wanted was for Kate to see her prowling around Tim's house in the dark. It was not long before she heard the side door of the garage open as Kate came out, locking it behind her. Peering round the corner of the wall, Elaine saw Kate's retreating figure disappearing into the darkness of the lane.

After a few minutes, Elaine stepped out from her hiding place and made her way out into the lane herself, turning left towards where the lane merged into the path through the woods. It was now very dark and though there was a moon, it was hidden by a big bank of cloud, so it was difficult to see her way in the enclosing darkness of the trees. If it had not been for the fact that the root from the big oak tree she had noted earlier nearly sent

459

her sprawling, she would have missed the smaller path altogether. As it was, she could barely make it out and it was hard to see her way along towards the clearing. As she reached it, the clouds drifted away from the moon, which cast its pale light across the long dry grass, picking out the half-hidden forms of the sculptures. The place seemed otherworldly, with the moonlight shining on the animals, the enclosing trees and the dim light coming from the window of the cottage across the clearing. So someone was at home now.

Elaine shivered, partly at the strangeness of the place and partly in trepidation that whoever lived in the cottage would see her cutting across the clearing. She did not dare try to find another way, fearing she would get lost. There was nothing for it but to keep going. She stepped out of the shadows and started across the open space.

And Zachary, standing outside his back door, watched her coming.

Earlier, when Zachary, returning home in his van, turned into the track which led to his cottage, he saw Elaine's car parked rather haphazardly, half blocking his way. He immediately knew it was the same car he had seen driving out of the lane some weeks before. What was it doing here again? Vince was dead. Elaine (if it was indeed her car) could not be here to meet him. Had she come to harm Kate?

Zachary parked his van and went round to the front of the cottage. His instincts were to rush over to warn Kate. But then he might miss Elaine when she returned to her car and he was determined to confront her. She might be just spying on Tim and she might well come back past the cottage to get to her car. As he stood there undecided, the ghostly form of the tawny owl he had raised from a chick flew down and perched on the arm of a bench and began preening her chest feathers.

As Elaine approached the cottage, her shoes and the hems of her jeans becoming ever more soaked in the dewy grass, she nearly jumped out of her skin as a dim shape launched itself from the shadows and flew away over her head, and almost simultaneously, a soft, deep voice said, "Hello Elaine."

She stopped dead, her heart hammering in her chest, and made out the tall figure of a man standing outside the cottage door. From a dry throat, her voice came out in a hoarse whisper.

"How do you know my name? Who are you?"

"My name is Zachary. A friend of Kate's. I guessed you must be Elaine. That's your red Volvo in the lane, isn't it?" He paused, then said quietly, "That's the second time I've seen it parked here."

Elaine stood frozen to the spot. What was he implying? Did he know something about her involvement with Vince? She drew herself up. She must keep calm.

"So what? It's not a private road is it?"

"No, but I know who you met there."

This time her self-control nearly left her and she felt her knees begin to buckle. She sat down suddenly on the stump Zachary used to chop firewood.

"You saw me?"

"Yes. Well, I saw your car."

"Does Kate know?"

"Yes, she does. I thought she ought to know that you had been meeting the man who subsequently tried to kill her."

Elaine blurted out the words before she could stop herself: "He wasn't going to kill her! Just..." She stopped, realising she had incriminated herself.

"Just what? Just cut her up a bit? Just destroy her looks? Just ruin her life?"

Zachary took a step towards her. Elaine looked up at him. Somehow she knew he would not hurt her physically. There was no sense of menace like she had felt in the company of Vince. He could destroy her though. He could go to the police. In fact, why had he not done so already? Why had Kate not done so?

She voiced her thoughts. "I suppose you'll go to the police."

"Kate refuses to do so. She said that since Vince is dead, he can't hurt her anymore. And she was worried about your son if you got arrested."

At this, Elaine's self-control crumbled completely. The fact that Kate had strong suspicions that she, Elaine, had been involved in the

461

attack, but refused to do anything about it because she was worried about Duncan, made a chink in the hatred she had in her heart for Kate. More than anything else in the world, more even than what she felt for Tim, and though she found it hard to be overtly affectionate towards Duncan, the fierce love she had for her son was the main reason for her very existence. The devastation she felt over the disintegration of her relationship with Tim was not as powerful as the despair she would feel if her son was taken away from her because of what she had done. The tears gathered in her eyes. She stared at the ground, her eyes unfocused.

"They would take Duncan away from me and give him to his father. Then what would be the point of anything, especially now I've lost Tim." She looked up at Zachary. "Tim is in love with Kate, you see. I know he is. I don't know if they are lovers, but as soon as she arrived on the scene, he changed." Elaine's shoulders slumped hopelessly.

She looked up at Zachary again.

"Are you sure Kate won't go to the police? How can I be sure?"

Zachary returned her gaze, pity vying with the anger and distaste he felt for Elaine.

"Not unless there's another attack. You say you can't be sure she would never go to the police, but how can *she* be sure you won't throw acid in her face or something? What are you doing here anyway?" His voice grew more urgent. "Have you harmed Kate?"

Elaine recoiled. She stood up and backed away. "No! I just went to see if...if I could see Tim. See if they were together." She stopped and took a step forward, wringing her hands. "Look, you've got to believe me. I'm not going to try to harm Kate. I know now, it's hopeless with Tim, with or without Kate. I wish I had never talked to...Vince, or whatever his name is. Horrible, horrible man."

Zachary said curiously, "How did you meet him anyway? I wouldn't have thought he's part of your social circle."

Elaine shuddered. "Ugh! No, my car got stuck in Tuckers Lane and he pushed me out. It was dark. I had been to...to see Kate."

"So he'd been hanging about outside her house! Just what she was afraid of since he attacked her last winter."

462

"Oh God! So it was the same man! I wondered why he said he had his own reasons for attacking her." In spite of herself, Elaine's curiosity was piqued. "What *did* he have against her?"

"Kate thinks it's because his ex-partner Annie sat for Kate as a model for her paintings. Annie thinks so too. He gave her a hell of a beating when he found out, which led to her going to a refuge and getting a restraining order against him. He was a very nasty piece of work." Zachary looked at Elaine with a mixture of incredulity and disgust. "And you decided he was just the person to enable you to go off into the sunset with Tim! You should be locked up. Kate's too kind-hearted. Ridiculously so."

Elaine looked at Zachary's shadowy face, lit palely by the moonlight, unable to read his expression.

"*You* won't go to the police, will you? Please! I'll move away. Change Duncan's school. Or maybe he could board. That way he won't lose his friends, especially Freddie. I won't hurt Kate, even though I wish she had never come here. They'd know it was me anyway."

Zachary looked at her and knew she was telling the truth. Despite his words, in his heart he agreed with Kate that nothing would be achieved by telling the police - except more misery for this broken woman and her blameless son.

"No, I won't go to the police. What you do with your life doesn't concern me, as long as you don't harm Kate. But yes, it would be better if you moved away. Now I think you'd better go." He turned away and walked to the door of the cottage, went inside and closed the door.

Elaine stood looking after him. Around her the woods were silent and still. The moonlight bathed the clearing in its baleful light. Then the tears came, coursing down her cheeks, blurring her eyes and a fierce tightness gripped her throat. A bleak future without Tim stretched before her. Would he have married her if Kate had not come along? She forced herself to be brutally honest. Looking back, she knew it had always been she who had initiated any intimacy with Tim, she who had suggested going out for romantic dinners, she who went round to his house when the children were away to cook for him, often staying the night. He had never

463

stayed over at her house. She now acknowledged to herself that the relationship had always been somewhat one-sided. Was she so unlovable? What more could she have done?

But at least she would still have Duncan. At least she wouldn't be prosecuted as an accomplice to a crime. She had to be thankful for that. Slowly, she began to make her way back to the track which led to her car. But then a thought struck her. Would Kate tell Tim about her suspicions that she had had something to do with Vince's attack? Though she knew it was over between herself and Tim, she did not want him to know what she had done. Reaching her car at last after groping her way down the dark track, stumbling into water-filled potholes, she got in and sat there, her hands gripping the steering wheel, her feet soaked and muddy. She must go to see Kate. She had to get her assurance that she would not tell Tim about her connection with Vince.

She put the car in gear and, unable to turn in the narrow lane, reversed slowly and erratically back to the main road. A couple of minutes later, she drew up outside Kate's cottage. A light glowed out from the kitchen window as she walked down the path and knocked on the front door. After a pause, the light came on in the porch, and the door opened. As soon as Kate saw Elaine's pallid, ravaged face, she made to slam the door shut again, but Elaine wedged her foot in the gap, wincing as it closed on her foot.

"Wait! I need to talk to you. I'm not going to hurt you. I've just been talking to your friend, the one who lives in the woods. He... he knows what I...what I tried to do."

Cautiously, Kate opened the door wider, but did not ask her to come in. "You mean Zachary? Are you talking about Vince breaking in here? You admit you had something to do with it?" Kate looked at Elaine, aghast. "You actually wanted me killed?"

"No! Not killed! I just wanted him to... to ruin your looks."

Kate gave a short, mirthless laugh. "Oh, that's alright then. You just wanted him to lacerate my face. Possibly blind me. And who knows, he may have intended to kill me anyway, in case I guessed who he was, in spite of the balaclava on his head."

Elaine put her hand out to steady herself against the door jamb. "I know. It was a terrible thing to do. I... I can't have been in my right mind. Tim...he..." Her voice choked on a sob. "He dumped me. Ever since Tuscany, when Freddie..."

"When Freddie saw you together," Kate finished for her.

"You know about that? Tim told you?" The thought of Tim and Kate having an intimate discussion about her tormented Elaine's mind.

"No, Freddie told me. He was very upset."

"I knew the wretched boy had poisoned Tim's mind against me."

"The 'wretched boy' as you call him is a vulnerable child who has lost his mother and must have felt very bewildered by what he saw."

"Well, it wasn't even because of Tuscany. It's you. Ever since you arrived, Tim became colder and colder towards me. I thought if you weren't beautiful any more, he would come back to me." She looked at Kate, hopelessness in her eyes. "I realise how wrong I was. I know now, he never really loved me, even before you came. But I loved him. I still love him. But I know I've lost him. I'm not a fool." She looked down the lane towards Tim's house, then turned back to Kate and said urgently, "Will you tell Tim about me having connections with Vince?"

Kate looked at her in silence, taking in the wretched expression on Elaine's face, the streaks of mascara, her bedraggled appearance - so unlike the immaculately groomed image she normally presented. Elaine took her silence for indecision.

"Please don't. Please don't ever tell him!"

"I won't tell him."

Elaine looked at her and realised she never would. But one thought still tore at her like a rat gnawing on her insides.

"Are you and Tim lovers?"

"No, we're not."

"I was sure you were. That's what was tearing me up. But I know you will be. I know he's in love with you."

"How can you know that, if even I don't know it?"

"Of course you know it! Well I wish you joy!" Elaine said bitterly. "But I know I must be thankful that you're not going to go to the police. If

465

I lost Duncan too…" Her voice trailed off. She turned away from the door, then paused and looked back over her shoulder. "I'm moving away. Duncan will become a boarder so he doesn't have to move schools, but I'll move to Dorking or somewhere. Well, goodbye," she said curtly, and walked out into the night, leaving Kate standing at the door, gripping white-knuckled at the door frame.

She saw the headlights of Elaine's car come on and heard the engine start. The car moved off down the lane towards Tim's house. Was she going to see him or just going to the end to turn? Kate waited at the door, and a minute or two later, saw the car lights come bouncing back along the track and disappear out of sight. Kate closed the door on the chilly October air. She hoped that would be the last she would see of Elaine.

*

Tim settled himself by the window in the First Class carriage of the 6.15pm out of Waterloo and opened the *Evening Standard*. Skimming through the first few pages, an article in the arts section caught his eye. It was headed *London Sculptor Wins International Competition*. The article went on to say that Jake Ward, a relatively unknown young sculptor based in London, had won a competition to create a work to be installed outside a new design museum in Berlin. Below was a photograph of Jake with a maquette of the winning piece. Next to him stood a girl with long blonde hair, who was smiling up at him. The caption underneath the photo read "Ward with his girlfriend, The Honourable Lucinda Moreton at his studio in East London".

Tim re-read the article, then gazed unseeing out of the window. His girlfriend. What did that make Kate? Was their relationship over? How did she feel about it? But often the papers got things wrong. What was the truth of the situation? How could he find out without asking Kate directly and perhaps making a fool of himself and embarrassing her?

*

466

It was a bright October day of scudding, fair-weather clouds when they gathered in the oldest part of the churchyard for the burial ceremony for the tiny child that had been found in Kate's cottage. Kate had gone to fetch Lydia Campbell, who stood beside her, leaning on her arm, well wrapped up against the chilly wind. Magda stood near Zachary, with Annie and her children standing next to her. Tim, Freddie, Amy and Erika stood in a little group near Mimi, Grace and Bea. Mimi was dressed in her usual style, somewhat inappropriately for a funeral ceremony, in shorts and thick leggings, with a puffa jacket clutched round her. Grace stood like a Brontë heroine, her long hair, tasselled shawl and flowing skirt blowing in the wind, and Bea, an enigmatic expression on her face, stood a little apart, clad as usual entirely in black. Lily and Bill Babbidge stood near Tim and the children, and even Magda's son Mike was there, standing beside Mimi.

A tiny wicker coffin, which Tim had bought on the internet, stood near a freshly dug hole close to some old gravestones which stood at crazy angles among the long dry grasses. Bright leaves from a huge beech tree nearby blew around them as the vicar conducted the poignant little ceremony, giving the child the name Mary, which had been Kate's choice. At the committal, Tim and Zachary stepped forward to stand beside the small coffin. Kate felt a lump rise to her throat and couldn't stop the tears filling her eyes and spilling down her face. She could see that the other women present, especially Bea, were similarly affected. Lydia clutched Kate's arm a little tighter. When the vicar had finished speaking, Freddie and Amy, together with Annie's children, Becky and Darren, were ushered forward by Tim and Annie. Each clutched a cuddly toy, which they placed carefully on the coffin. Then Tim and Zachary lowered the little casket down into the hole and refilled it, and Zachary placed a beautiful wooden cross, which he had made, at its head. Kate then stepped forward and laid a bunch of dried lavender from the garden on the grave, together with a small wooden plaque on which she had written two verses of a simple poem by Hannah Kahn. Magda then added a posy of Michaelmas daisies from her garden.

In spite of her sadness, Kate felt a comforting sense of closure,

467

knowing that the baby was laid to rest in the peaceful graveyard. She thanked the vicar and shook his hand, then turned to the little group gathered round the grave.

"Please come back to the cottage for a glass of wine, everyone. If we can't all fit in, we can go in the garden!"

The vicar had other duties elsewhere, but everyone else piled into various cars and made their way to Kate's cottage.

Lydia was delighted to come to Lavender Cottage again, where she had been a frequent visitor when Amelia had been alive. Kate installed her in an armchair by the fire and gave her a cup of tea, which she chose over wine, while Kate urged the others to help themselves to the wine. She poured soft drinks for the children and handed round some nibbles.

Looking round affectionately at the people gathered in the little sitting room, she felt a strong connection to every one of them. A year ago, apart from her three college friends, she had not met any of them, and yet now they seemed woven into the fabric of her life. She glanced at Tim, disconcerted to meet his eyes. She quickly averted her gaze, in case he guessed how much *he* had become a part of the fabric of her life.

Zachary, talking to Magda by the window, glanced at Kate and said quietly, "I was thinking the other day, that even though we've both lived in this village for years, we may never have met each other if Kate hadn't introduced us."

Magda grinned at him. "Well, maybe you'd prefer to have your old peaceful life back, instead of me coming round organising you and forcing you to eat proper meals!"

"Yes, it's terrible to have to eat all them delicious pies and things," Zachary said, rolling his eyes in mock despair. "It's hard, but I'll have to put up with it, if it means having you in my life."

"I like having you in my life too," Magda said, touching his hand. She looked across at Mike and Mimi who were sitting near Lydia, making her laugh until her shoulders shook, and the cup and saucer rattled in her hands. "And it was through Kate that Mike met Mimi. He seems very keen on her. Been up to see her several times since the exhibition."

468

Magda sipped her wine, and added thoughtfully as her gaze fell on Annie chatting to Grace: "When you think about it, it was Kate wanting to paint Annie that brought the terrible situation Annie was in to a head. I know Vince beat her up, but it caused her to finally make the break with him. And now she's free."

"It's as though…" Zachary paused, his eyes taking on a faraway look, then said thoughtfully, "…as though Kate is like a pebble dropped into a pond. Her coming here caused ripples to spread out to touch the people around her. Look at how she arranged an outlet for my carvings."

"I suppose we all cause ripples because of our actions. For that matter, it was old Mrs Hopkins who dropped the first pebble when she left the cottage to Kate."

"Mind if I go up to that bedroom for a minute?" Bea said to Kate, as Kate offered her some crisps. "I want to check something out."

Kate looked at her curiously. "Of course I don't mind. I'll show you where they found the baby."

Bea followed Kate up the stairs. When she went into the bedroom she stopped in the middle of the room and looked towards the cupboard in the wall. Kate went over and opened the door.

"This is where they found Mary, behind this panel."

Bea stood very still, her eyes closed. Then she opened them and said, "She's gone. The woman."

"The woman?"

"The one I sensed before. She's not here anymore."

"Susan Gatling," Kate said softly. "Tied to the spot where her baby lay, but now released."

As they stood there, the strong breeze gusted down the chimney, but this time, it sounded like nothing more than the wind.

Downstairs, Tim had seen Mimi and Grace go out of the back door so that Mimi could have a cigarette, and felt that it was his chance to ask them about the true state of Kate's relationship with Jake. How he would do so without giving away his own feelings for Kate, which they would be sure to pass on to Kate herself, he didn't know, but he had reached a point where he simply had to put an end to his uncertainty. He refilled his glass and followed the two young women outside. Grace had wandered off to the bottom of the garden, where the poplars formed the border between the garden and the field beyond, but Mimi was sitting on the garden bench, a glass of wine in one hand and a cigarette in the other. She looked up at Tim as he came to stand by the bench.

"Hi!" she said. "Want a ciggie?"

"No thanks, I don't smoke. I just wanted to ask you..." He paused, then tried again. "About Kate's relationship with Jake... are they... together? It's difficult to know."

Mimi took a puff of her cigarette. She tried to keep her tone casual, but there was a wicked glint in her eye as she replied.

"Jake? Oh no! That finished ages ago. Not through his choice, I'm sure. Bit of a blow to his vanity, that she should be in love with someone else!"

"Someone else?"

"Oh, come on! As if you have no idea who that someone else could possibly be!" Mimi looked at him and rolled her eyes. "It's you, you daft man!"

Tim's heart lurched. "Has she said so to you?"

"No, she didn't have to. It's pretty obvious... to anyone but you, apparently."

"You may be wrong."

"Well, there's only one way to find out! Go for it man! You're obviously besotted with Kate yourself."

Tim gave her a lopsided grin. "I hope it's not so obvious to Kate. What if you're wrong about her feelings for me? I'd end up embarrassing her horribly. Why would she prefer me to Jake anyway?"

Mimi sighed in exasperation. "It's a chance you'll have to take. Nothing ventured and all that."

She got up and crushed out her cigarette underfoot then picked it up to dispose of it in the bin.

"Well, we have to be getting back." She gave Tim a playful push, and repeated: "Go for it! But don't you dare tell her I told you she's keen on you. She'll kill me."

She turned to Grace, who was coming back down the garden.

"Come on, we'd better be getting back. I've got to go to my mum's tonight. It's my brother's birthday – family supper."

Grace and Mimi drifted off back into the house and Tim stood a little longer in the garden, trying to compose himself after the conversation with Mimi. Was she right about Kate's feelings for him? Well, at least he knew for sure that she and Jake were not in a relationship any more. He drained his glass then he too went back inside.

Gradually, people started taking their leave, until only Lydia and Tim's family were left.

"We'd better be off too," Tim said, unable to meet Kate's eyes, afraid that he would betray his feelings. He looked at Lydia. "Can I give you a lift home?"

Before Lydia could answer, Kate said quickly, "It's okay, Tim, I'll take her back."

Lydia smiled at Tim and stood up, helped by Kate.

"Thanks all the same. It was nice to meet you. As Kate probably told you, her great aunt Amelia had a strong connection with the house you live in. She was engaged to the son of the people who owned it during the war. Such a tragedy he was killed. Just one heartbreak among countless others."

Tim took her hand and kissed her lightly on the cheek. "Lovely to meet you too. Thanks to Kate I've met several people from the village I didn't know before." He turned to the children and Erika. "Come on gang, let's go. Binky will be wondering where everyone is."

Kate saw them to the door, and Tim lowered his head to drop a kiss on Kate's cheek.

"Bye Kate. It was a lovely little ceremony. I hope poor Susan rests in peace now."

"I think she will. Thank you for getting the little coffin." Kate looked up at him and their eyes met. Something blazed in his eyes briefly,

471

something that sent her heart thudding. Then he turned and walked away down the path. Lydia, standing by the fire, saw the little exchange, and realised her instincts had been right. Kate was in love with Tim. So history *was* repeating itself yet again. First Susan Gatling, then Amelia, and now Kate had fallen in love with someone who lived at Woodcote. Somehow she felt that this time there would be a happier ending.

*

Kate washed the last of the glasses and left them to drain beside the sink. Outside the kitchen window, the western sky glowed a burnished gold behind the hawthorns on the other side of the lane. Opening the back door, she went out into the garden. She walked slowly down the leaf-strewn grass until she came to the end of the garden and looked across the field where a couple of horses grazed in the golden October evening.

*

Tim stood by the fireplace in his sitting room. He picked up the photograph of Claire and gazed at it.

"It's not that I love you any the less," he whispered. "It's just that I love Kate too. Give me your blessing." The slight smile on Claire's lips was reflected in her eyes, and a feeling of solace washed over Tim like a warm wave. He put the photo carefully back on the mantelpiece and walked unhurriedly out of the room. Sticking his head round the door of the family room, he said casually to the children, "Just popping down to get the glasses Kate borrowed for this afternoon."

"Okay," Freddie said, engrossed in the computer, and Erika and Amy gave him a wave, busy with cleaning out Socrates' cage. In the hall, Tim pulled on a jacket and let himself out of the door, telling Binky, who looked at him hopefully in case there was a walk in the offing, to stay.

It was one of those autumn evenings when the raking light of the low sun touches everything with gold. It delineated every twig and leaf in the hedgerow and cast long, deep shadows across the lane.

472

At Kate's front door, he knocked, and when there was no answer, he made his way round the side of the house. Inevitably, he thought of the summer's afternoon when he had done the same thing, and found Kate in a passionate embrace with Jake.

This time, he couldn't see her at first. The back door stood open, but when he stuck his head inside and called, there was no answer. Then he saw her, standing at the far end of the garden, her hair aflame in the evening sunlight.

"Kate!"

She turned, slowly, unsurprised, as though she had been expecting him. He walked slowly up to her.

"I came to pick up the gl…"

The words died on his lips when he saw the expression on her face. She seemed half in a dream. In her eyes, hot sparks of longing and desire found an answering flame in his own. She reached out her hand and laid it against his cheek. Covering her hand with his own, he put his other hand around her waist and drew her to him. Their eyes locked, and for a long, long moment, they hung there, on some ineffable threshold of fulfilment. And then his lips came down on hers. Softly at first, then harder and more insistent, until a white heat engulfed them, melding them into one entity.

After what seemed an eternity, Kate became aware of the susurration of the poplars overhead, the song they had sung to her since the day she had moved into the cottage, which was, she realised with wonderment, exactly a year ago to the day. She opened her eyes and, still with Tim's mouth on hers, saw the tall crowns of the poplars towering above her, their leaves a mass of dancing, dazzling gold.

In the churchyard, the shadows were gathering under the beeches, whose upper branches arched overhead, forming a tracery against the fading sky. Below, where the leaf-litter had been cleared away, the bare earth was heaped into a small mound on which a bunch of lavender and another of Michaelmas daisies lay. The wind had dropped and the churchyard was wrapped in silence. The grey, lichen covered gravestones seemed to crowd round the tiny grave as though in sympathy with what seemed to be a dim figure which stood at its foot. A figure which slowly faded until it had dispersed into the surrounding shadows. A slight breeze stirred the flowers on the grave, then all was still again. As the twilight deepened, if anyone had been there to read the small wooden plaque which lay next to the flowers, they would have just been able to make out the poet's words written on it:

And the day will come
When you must go,
With the falling leaves
And the winter near-

You will not return
This I know –
But I will remember
That you were here

*

Lightning Source UK Ltd.
Milton Keynes UK
UKHW011439200420
361988UK00007BA/666